End Game

by Ginger Booth

ISBN: 1517162882
ISBN-13: 978-1517162887

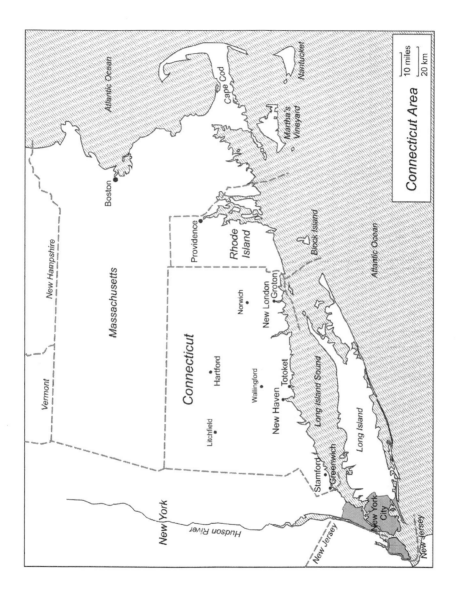

Connecticut Area

Chapter 1

Interesting fact: UNC Inc., headquartered in Stamford Connecticut and New York City, built its ark in mid-Tennessee.

My first shot at an ark berth arrived as one of life's little pop quizzes.

On a typical Tuesday I expected the usual afternoon meeting down in Stamford. Normally I'd take a long walk to the train station, make one transfer en route, and I'm there at corporate headquarters. I had navy chinos and blazer and professional-enough looking tops expressly for Tuesdays at HQ.

I'd been doing this once-weekly commute for a few years. One of the interns had begun to imitate my 'signature style,' right down to the bright horizontal stripes under a navy blazer. Maybe it was creeping me out. Well, no—it was definitely creeping me out. If she copied one more of my mannerisms, she and I were going to have a little talk of the brush-off variety. Asking my professional help as a mentor is one thing. Mimicking my clothes is just weird.

At any rate, that Tuesday I ditched my navy corporate camouflage gear, and wore my favorite steampunk outfit to Stamford. There are so few occasions to wear it, you know? And maybe Shelley the Intern and I could skip that little creepy talk.

One thing leads to another. It's a couple miles to the train station. I have gorgeous mid-calf lace-up boots with lace gaiters

1

to go with my steampunk ensemble. They wouldn't fit in my backpack the way my sneakers do. And the striped rose sateen skirt would just look foolish with sneakers. And I'd been meaning to try out the robot taxi service just unleashed in my area.

I own a car, mind you. I just hate driving.

The adorable robot vehicle showed up right on time, as promised on my mobile phone. To bolster their advertising, the robocar was painted as a cheerful pumpkin. A couple neighbors were out walking their dogs, and did a gratifying double-take. They enthusiastically waved me off in my Cinderella's carriage. I waved back. No doubt the feather in my little rose felt hat waved too.

My phone rang. The caller was the car I was sitting in. It called to ask me to open its special tracking app. I reviewed its proposed detour to pick up someone in East Haven on the way in to the New Haven train station.

Add 5 minutes to trip and save $0.50? Accept or Decline.

Accept.

Connect to a train at New Haven station?

Yes.

Are you going to New York City?

No, same train, but destination Stamford.

Apparently the car had nothing further to discuss just then. The app display returned to live tracking on the route map into East Haven. We stopped at a million dollar beachfront property. A very fine-looking man in perfectly fitted business suit—Adam—climbed in to join me in the robo-pumpkin.

As the car drove off, introductions were interrupted by Adam having to answer his own phone. I recognized the ever-widening goofy grin from my own face wearing it moments before.

"Holy—!" he finally began.

I lifted a 'wait' finger as my own phone buzzed for

attention.

Add 15 minutes to trip and save $25.50?

I frowned at this. A garden-variety yellow taxi could get me to the train station for $15, and the app had promised me $10. My pumpkin app hadn't let me down before. Then I saw that the proposed destination was all the way to Stamford, not just the New Haven train station.

Accept!

My ride partner was grinning like he'd just been waiting for me to see the punchline. "Stamford?" I asked, matching his grin.

Adam shrugged. "Greenwich actually. But we'll be together a while, it seems. Adam Lacey."

"Dee Baker," I replied, accepting his handshake. "This ride is just too entertaining. Do you work in Greenwich?"

"Well, meetings sometimes. You?"

"Meetings every Tuesday afternoon. I don't usually enjoy the commute so much!"

Other riders came and went. We collected a couple with skis—the pumpkin car featured a roof rack—and rendezvoused with a pumpkin limo. Apparently a half dozen skiers were taking a robo-ride up to Vermont.

"I should do that before the borders close," Adam commented.

Sad thought. I murmured, "Mm. I'd like to see Montreal again."

Adam smiled warmly. Maybe he felt guilty for disturbing my obvious delight with the transportation, which we had to ourselves again. "Don't ski, Dee? Though I like your idea better. I love those little sorbets they serve between courses at the French restaurants in Montreal."

"Oh, I love those!" I agreed, his downer promptly forgiven.

We passed the big sign to the Trumbull ark without comment. At that point, it was still considered vulgar to ask if

End Game

-o-

I don't want to remember my interview with the corporate psychologist. I was shaking when I escaped conference room 101E, or whatever it was. The meeting I was supposed to be in, the one I'd travelled to Stamford for, was still going on and would be for another hour or so. I took the elevator back upstairs on automatic. But then I turned the other way at our floor, and got my belated coffee in some other cubicle farm's break room.

I'd just have some coffee and calm down, I thought, then rejoin the meeting. I chose an empty stretch of high-rise glass to look out of. This patch of hallway was organized as a social area. There were orange upholstered seats and one of those plants that might as well be plastic, and some corporate art on a fragment of wall. No doubt someone somewhere selected the corporate art and orange upholstery for some carefully considered reason. I contemplated the pale watercolor print of an anonymous looking little brown songbird. The label advised that the portrait was of a boat-tailed grackle. This little nook was a mirror image of my usual side of the elevators. Ours featured mustard yellow and blue upholstery and a watercolor of beach toys abandoned to the rising tide. None of it meant anything.

Maybe that was the point. The décor was to distract you from the zombie rut of life in a cubicle farm. But I only visited cubicle land for a few hours on Tuesdays. My real life was out in the woods and shoreline, full of real birds. When I was out for a walk, I picked up lost beach toys and put them in the trash before they washed into the Sound.

Someone must have narked on me. Dan left the meeting and joined me at the window by the boat-tailed grackle. "That bad, huh?" he asked gently. Dan was a good guy. More heart than brains, but a good manager.

"Not the best day to wear steampunk to the office," I agreed, and stared out the window. The corporate psychologist had dwelt at length on my costume during my misbegotten interview, and not in a good way. The shrink was very impressed with herself for concocting a theory about my using steampunk as a way to avoid 'authentic' interaction with others. The conversation went downhill from there. I hate shrinks.

A squall of sudden rain had come and gone while I stood there. Indian summer was starting to break up into the cold clammy bleakness of late autumn. In Vermont there was already enough snow to ski.

"Why steampunk?" Dan asked.

"We need to talk about Shelley, Dan. She keeps copying what I wear. It's creeping me out. Maybe you should get one of the guys to supervise her instead."

"Oh. I tried that. She came on to Mangal. He was polite—you know Mangal—and told her he was happily married with children. But she told him she didn't mind if he was married. I'm thinking, not the guys."

I laughed, too hard, but it was good to laugh about something. I wiped tears from my eyes. "OK. So I'll talk to Shelley. Maybe I could get her a copy of *How to Win Friends and Influence People*. Giftwrap it nicely with a little bow. And *then* tell her if she ever wears my clothes again, she's fired. Because she's creeping people out."

Dan smiled. "You see, that's why I want to give her to you. A girl who's that clueless how to act—she needs a woman's guidance. She does know how to program, doesn't she?"

"Yeah, she's competent enough at the work. I'll deal with it."

"It's not just you, you know," Dan offered, after a pause. "They're not even going to interview most of the programmers. They've got these ideas, about who will fit in, in the company ark."

End Game

"Who will fit period, Dan," I said. "Less than half a percent of the population."

"It's not that way! Personnel says they're building room for 12,000 in our ark. Not everybody, but... It makes sense, what they're trying to do with the psychological interviews. Everybody needs to get along well in tight quarters. I thought, because of your gardening, you'd have the best shot of any of my people. And you're great with people."

I nodded slowly. "I think we already know which half of one percent will be in the arks, Dan. That wasn't really in any doubt. Was it?"

"Look, I'll talk to the shrink, get you another appointment. Promise me, you won't go looking for another job for the ark benefit."

That's how it was supposed to work. Everyone was scurrying after 'good jobs' back then, that offered an ark berth as an employment benefit. Of course 'everyone' couldn't get that kind of 'good job.' Probably less than a quarter of people had any benefits at all from their jobs, not even a living wage.

"Thank you, Dan," I murmured, in polite reflex, if not faith.

The storm clouds broke into a cloud pattern that looked weirdly like parasitic wasp egg sacs, in yellow, dangling from a giant grey tomato hornworm in the sky. I didn't mention it. Dan of corporate HQ didn't know what hornworms or egg sacs looked like. He probably wouldn't even realize that it was a bizarre cloud formation.

"Interesting times," I murmured. I kicked the glass window lightly and turned back toward our proper cubicle farm. "Anything else for me before I head home?"

I took Metro North back to New Haven. The commuter train was papered with advertisements for the most 'aspirational' arks. In the fabulously wealthy suburbs of New York City, there in the Gold Coast southwest corner of Connecticut, plenty of people didn't worry whether they could get into an ark, but rather which was the most prestigious one. As we got further from Stamford, the Wall Street business suits thinned out. Students, inner-city blacks, and tired women dominated the train. In my steampunk costume finery, I should have struck up more conversations than ever on the train. But I stared out the window.

The robo-pumpkin car was awfully cool, though.

Chapter 2

Interesting fact: The Calm Act was introduced by the U.S. President in closed session, debated, and passed with a 78% majority in the House, and 63% in the Senate. Few sections of the Calm Act were ever made public.

I met Zack just a few days after Adam, just after Halloween. An Alberta Clipper storm front hit while I was out for a lunchtime walk. I'd only been out twenty minutes. I was headed home when it hit.

It was so lovely when I went out. Most trees were bare, but the last of the maples shone orange and scarlet, fluttering jewels gleaming in the early November sun. The Clipper hit out of a brilliant blue sky at about 75 miles per hour, a roiling black bank of hail and lightning and sheets of rain out of the west. When branches started to crack and fall, running for home seemed like a bad idea. I pelted up onto Zack's covered porch for shelter.

I knocked on the door for politeness' sake. Actually I tried the doorbell first, but the power was out. One of the lightning flashes might have been a transformer. We didn't meet strangers at the door with a shotgun in that sort of situation yet. A neighbor taking shelter from a freak storm was a friendly occasion. Freak storms weren't so common then.

"Hi, I'm Dee," I babbled in a rush, when his door opened. "I live over there on Blatchely." I pointed. "I hope you don't mind if I hide on your porch for a few minutes." I smiled, then cringed, as lightning and a huge *boom!* of thunder arrived simultaneously.

11

"Come in!" Zack cried.

He didn't need to ask twice. I leapt into his house. We struggled to get the storm door closed, as the wind wanted to take it. But finally I was in, with the storm noise slightly muffled in the living room gloom. Soaked to the skin, I dripped on his hempen door mat.

"Maybe I should just, um, drip here. Thank you so much for letting me in. It's kind of scary out there. Was that in the weather forecast?"

"I don't think so. Let me get you a towel. Cup of tea?"

"Both sound *great.*"

"I'm Zack Harkonnen, by the way. You were—sorry, the wind was kinda..."

"Dee Baker. I live over on Blatchely. I wasn't gonna make it home."

"Yeah, no. You're welcome to wait out the storm. I'll get you some sweats, too."

Zack looked like a Harkonnen. Something Scandinavian, anyway—blond and muscular, over 6' tall, with a weathered angular face, maybe a few years older than me. His living room looked like a political party headquarters, leaflets and posters everywhere, over beautiful woodwork. Plenty of plants loomed as anonymous organic black humps in the midday storm dark.

I would never have met Adam Lacey in the course of my normal life. He was out of my league. I'd never have met Zack, either, except maybe to wave at him working in the yard as I walked past. Though all three of us lived within a few miles of each other. It was a pretty area, the shoreline east of New Haven, and gave a carefully staged impression of small town New England. But the towns weren't actually small, in population. They were right smack in the I-95 corridor, the megalopolis of 90 million souls that stretched from Maine to Washington D.C., embracing a quarter of the population of the U.S. At some level, we lived in a nicer neighborhood of the same city as Baltimore and the Bronx, only less friendly.

Yet charmingly, storms bring out the best in us. Everyone pops out of their emotional clam shells as instant friends, to pitch in, help clear downed branches, drain drowned basements, and cope with the power outages, in the wake of a storm. You'd think a hurricane was a ticker tape parade. It's just who we are.

Freshly toweled off, with all 5'4" of me draped in sweats sized for a tall man, I settled down with him at the kitchen table. A picture window offered a great view of tossing trees, and the electric exhilaration of a thunderstorm.

"I love watching storms," I said. "Thank you so much for letting me in. And the tea. This is good! I haven't had sassafras in years." The tea was deep orange and fruity, not quite similar to an unsweetened root beer flavor. The table offered sugar and honey, but we both drank it straight.

Zack smiled at me in pleasant surprise. "You know sassafras?"

"Mm. Used to make it out of sassafras saplings when I was a kid. Did you buy it?"

"Nope. Used saplings. Who does that, anymore?"

"Us two?" I grinned. "I don't know who else. They sold sassafras shavings at an antique store down by the reservoir when I was a kid. The store's not there anymore. I've never seen it for sale anywhere else."

"Huh! I've never seen it for sale." We contemplated the hail for a few moments and savored our tea. Some of those hailstones were worthy of Oklahoma, not New England. Then. "Do we have tornado sirens here?" he wondered.

I shrugged. "With the power out?" We both shrugged. I was glad to contemplate this with an attractive stranger over a good cup of tea, rather than alone.

"So do you know wild mushrooms too, Dee Baker?"

"No. My mother took me on a hike once with an expert,

when I was kid, up on Sleeping Giant, to learn edible mushrooms." Sleeping Giant is a large ridge in the area, running alongside I-91, one of many north-south ridges left when the glaciers receded 10,000 years ago. We were sitting and talking on another such ridge. "But we took the mushrooms over to a friend of hers, and the friend was afraid to eat them. Maybe I learned to be afraid of them instead of how to tell which to eat." I laughed. "More of a plant person."

"That's a shame. There should be good mushrooms up on Sleeping Giant in a couple days, after this."

I nodded. I vaguely remembered something like that from my long-ago mushroom lesson. "So what do you do for a living, Zack? When you're not rescuing damsels in distress. If you don't mind my asking." Thinking of the debris in the living room, I hoped he wouldn't say 'political organizer.' I couldn't escape just yet.

"I have an organic landscaping business," he said.

"Wow," I nodded, impressed. He had quite a nice house for that line of work. I honored the organic part. I'd had condos before my current house, and never felt good about the way they tossed chemicals around. Landscaping seemed to fit him.

"You?" he prompted.

"Web developer, for one of the Fortune 100 media companies down in Stamford. I telecommute."

He frowned slightly. Maybe programming didn't fit me as well as landscaping fit him. Maybe he knew exactly which Fortune 100 company I meant and didn't approve.

"I love to garden, though," I added, possibly to redeem myself with my host. "I've got flowers and vegetables spilling out of the house and down the driveway in season. Plenty indoors this time of year, too. Not so good with the lawn and shrubbery."

He chuckled. "Yeah, I know that house on Blatcheley. The azaleas and lilacs look good."

14

Eep. He knows where I live. Only fair. I knew where he lived, after all.

We chatted for an hour until the storm blew off to the east and deep blue skies returned. The temperature fell to near-freezing, though, and all my clothes were sopping wet. Zack drove me home, dodging a downed tree and a large bough with downed power line along the way. I was still wearing his sweats, so I invited him in to try my own fresh lemon balm tea while I changed out of his clothes. Lemon balm isn't nearly as good as sassafras.

It would have been surly, after all that, not to accept his invitation to teach me edible mushrooms again on Sleeping Giant on Sunday. Maybe his Nordic blue-eyed good looks had something to do with it, too. But much as we seemed to have in common, and rare as those things were, I still felt he was judging me about something. At any rate, I accepted. You can never have too many friends, right?

How would I know? I worked home alone. Outside of Mangal and Dan in Stamford, I didn't have a lot of friends. And I wasn't sure that my boss Dan counted as a friend.

The news said the Clipper front killed nearly a hundred people in the Midwest. It blew across from the Canadian Rockies, a couple thousand miles. I don't think I'd ever heard of an Alberta Clipper before. But the meteorologist on TV seemed to say they were a normal weather pattern, nothing new.

-o-

Dan asked me to come into Stamford early that Tuesday, to meet with him and Mangal before the usual telecommuter's meeting. I wondered if I could have run into Adam again if I took the robo-car at the normal time instead. But I decided that road led to madness. Adam had my phone number and email address on my card. He could reach me. And I fully expected to

15

never see him again. Adam was consigned to the daydreams-only file.

Of course, I'd just spent an hour daydreaming all the way down from New Haven.

"So what's up, Dan?" I asked, to get the real agenda rolling. Dan and Mangal and I all had our coffee. We'd each shared at least one personal anecdote, standing around in the blue and mustard break room, suspended between the plate glass panorama and the cubicle maze. Enough with the bonding.

"Right…" said Dan. He glanced furtively right and left along the hallway by the windows. Mangal and I looked, too. Dan gazed out over the cubicles. Someone joking with a neighbor popped his head up, caught Dan's eye, and popped back down. The neighbor popped up, and down. They looked like cartoon prairie dogs. "We'd better use my office," Dan murmured. Mangal and I shared a look behind his back as he headed off. Good—only our eyes were laughing.

Once we were settled, Dan solemnly leaned toward us, elbows on his desk. "We have some new assignments. This… isn't our usual." He leafed through some notes, and handed each of us an actual physical manila folder, with paper pages in it.

We programmers tend to favor electronic files. The last time I'd handled a manila folder was employee orientation at UNC, straight out of college. The media, news, cable, sports, and infotainment behemoth wasn't even called UNC yet back then. Intrigued, Mangal and I both immediately flipped our folders open to page one.

"Wait!" cried Dan, hand out in warning.

Mangal and I obediently closed our manila folders. I noted that mine said 'Mangal' on the tab, and glanced over. Mangal flipped up his tab labelled 'Dee' with a finger so I could see it. I decided to follow his lead and not swap them just now. I'd never seen Dan this flustered.

Our job in this infotainment conglomerate, was to build little explore-more interactives for the assorted news channel websites, build custom web pages that didn't quite work on the standard templates, create new standard templates, code up interactive video overlays, and things like that. I don't belittle the work—it was creative, technically leading-edge, and on tight deadlines due to the daily and weekly cycles of news broadcasts. The websites frequently won awards, and the brass seemed confident ours were the best news-program-support sites in the business. It was also a lot of fun.

But by its nature—national broadcast and cable media—it wasn't secretive. Until today.

"You two know that you're my most trusted section leaders," Dan confided in us. "And you've got the most tech-savvy teams. I want to pull you off the news merry-go-round for a couple new ongoing features.

"Marketing says the focus groups say we're losing viewer confidence in a couple key areas. And support says viewer queries and complaints are going through the roof. I bet you can guess what areas."

"Weather," I suggested.

"Closing borders," said Mangal.

Dan nodded gravely.

"Tracking politician's votes..." hazarded Mangal.

That got a knee-jerk reaction. "No! That's not our job!" denied Dan. "We... don't go there. We're still the infotainment division, not... *political* news. But you can see, these are... a lot more *controversial* issues than we usually deal with. They require media self-censorship. There's a lot of sensitive information here, and... Well. Our usual sixty-forty rule applies."

"Censorship," I echoed faintly.

"Sixty-forty rule," Mangal echoed in disbelief.

The UNC news editorial guideline was that 60% of our presentations had to be feel-good, positive, pro-American, and

40% negative, critical, or 'concerning.' Balancing an entire news broadcast seemed to be accomplished by substituting dog stories for hard news. But these were single subjects. Adding gratuitous puppies into a model of an Alberta Clipper weather system wasn't going to work. An upbeat treatment of barricading the borders was also hard to imagine. The heartwarming home life of a border attack dog?

And of course self-censorship implied lying to the public in our role as journalists. Well, UNC's role as journalists, anyway. I was employed as a programmer and graphics designer, not a journalist, as I was sure Dan would remind me if I got difficult about this.

Dan nodded somberly, "It's a real design challenge. But the projections show these'll be top features. You'll get a lot of eyeballs on your work. And I know you're up to it. Anyway, in those folders you've got background research from investigative reporters... Well, you'll have to suppress most of that. And privileged logins to the real info, and the rules about what can't be said. Federal security and UNC policy."

I opened my folder again, or rather Mangal's. I glanced at a few pages, then closed it slowly. My mind moved like molasses. Some experiences seem to draw me in, like a beautiful sunset, or diving into clear water. Other experiences, like this one, seem to kick me out, as though I held that bedamned folder with mile-long waldos. I swallowed.

Mangal rose abruptly and said the exact opposite of anything I expected. "Thanks, Dan. We'll get right on it. You can count on us!"

I rose in slow motion as Mangal enthusiastically pumped Dan's hand across the desk.

No. We did not ordinarily shake hands with Dan. We never shook hands with Dan. Mangal never laid hands on me, either, but now he put his arm around me, and grinned, confiding, "This is going to be great." And dragged me out of Dan's office.

I should point out that Mangal and I started within a couple months of each other at UNC. We'd been best friends ever since. Not romantically—he had an arranged marriage set up before he came to the U.S. Though the actual bride and wedding were delayed a couple years. The point is, I trusted him, at least ten times more than I trusted our boss Dan. I trusted Mangal enough to follow his lead, smile wanly at Dan, and be dragged out before I could say anything.

"*What the hell?*" I hissed at him once we were out of Dan's earshot.

"You are not going to quit over this, or make a scene, or argue," he whispered back, with a pleasant smile for anyone who might look our way. "We need to talk about this sub rosa. *Wuthering Heights,* 8 p.m."

I gazed at him like he'd grown three heads. Slowly I replied, "*Gulliver's Travels,* 7:52 p.m."

"Great!" said Mangal. He flicked my folder playfully. "Better put that away before you lose it." I started to hand it over to him, to swap back to my own assigned folder, but he waved that off. "Later. Ah, the gang's all here for the weekly meeting."

He avoided me the rest of the afternoon. We really weren't going to talk about it until 7:52 p.m. Encoded and decoded with two public domain manuscripts from Project Gutenberg as code keys, no less, plus the 3-digit combos 800 and 752. I thoughtfully used the office copier on the contents of his folder as a keepsake. I saw him in the copy room soon after me doing the same.

After the big group meeting, everyone under Dan, I got together with my own team. I didn't tell them anything beyond 'big new feature project coming up.' We plotted out how to wrap up our current projects.

Shelley wore a beige and fuzzy lavender ensemble, I was

happy to see. We'd had our little chat by video when she was assigned to my team. Today's outfit complemented her straight blond hair, but looked a decade too old for her. I gave her lots of positive reinforcement anyway, on the grounds that it wasn't my navy blue. Dan was smart—and I didn't often accuse him of that—to make me responsible for her. She was so desperately anxious to please, to be acknowledged. Now that she was my problem, I'd make a hero of her if I could. I sat and code-read her latest work with her, found two clever bits to praise her on, taught her two new tricks, and made sure she knew what to do for the next few days. "Thanks for the good work, Shelley. Keep it up!"

The rest of the guys didn't need petting. We wrapped it up and headed home.

-o-

"*Wuthering Heights,* eh?" I ribbed Mangal, once we got the extremely secure voice-over-Internet connection up, at 7:52 p.m., on the nose. "Do Brits actually read things like that in school?" A true international, Mangal was a Jain, born to Indian parents in South Africa, graduated from Edinburgh, and held E.U. citizenship. 'Brit' was an oversimplification.

"Of course. Haven't you read it?"

"No. Ick." I'd graduated from UVM in Vermont, where I successfully dodged all literature courses. "Back to the topic— *what the hell?*" I demanded.

We really weren't in the habit of stealing secrets and having evil hacker conversations. We *weren't.* We'd had too much time on our hands under a certain supervisor years before, and set this up on a lark. The political climate was really ugly then, and government spying a commonplace. So we had secure conversations sometimes. Because we could. Anyone monitoring our Internet traffic would see video files going back and forth between graphic developers. Even if anyone realized it was encoded audio, there was zero chance of them decoding it. But it was really quite innocent, *I* thought.

"You were about *this close* to quitting over this assignment," Mangal accused.

"…True. It's unethical."

"Because it's censored? It will be censored. You can't stop that and neither can I."

"It *shouldn't* be censored."

"…Have you looked at this stuff yet? It's censored under the Calm Act, and the Calm Act certainly applies."

"You know what I think of the Calm Act," I said. But I had to concede the point. Congress had voted itself the right to control all public information to 'preserve public order' in the face of the weather crisis. UNC, along with all the other major U.S. 'news' media, had agreed to the censorship.

Mangal was the voice of reason. "We can do whatever we can do, tell the public everything we can, and not lose our jobs, *or* our spots in the ark."

"…What price is too high?"

"I don't know," allowed Mangal. "But this isn't it. Look, Dee—at least we have access, and finally really know what's going on. I want that. I want to keep that. You?"

I was silent. He made sense. But I felt dirty, knowing things every American ought to have the right to know, and yet censoring it. And if I told people… Some hotheads at UNC had vanished. Questions were not encouraged.

Mangal was relentless. "The background researcher gave us access to way more than she should have, in those files. We have access to all the stories that got squelched. Dee—we have access to raw satellite feeds, Al Jazeera coverage of what's really going on in the Middle East since the embargo—"

"And the folders, Mangal? Why the game with swapping folders?"

"So we both have access to everything. Neither of us has to

pick and choose what to risk telling each other. We don't have to tell each other anything. We just share our access. So that we can cover for each other's sections, whenever."

"Oh, that'll hold up in a court of law."

"What court of law. Dee, the background researcher who put together these packets was Deanna Jo. Have you seen Deanna Jo lately? I haven't."

"Christ."

"She passed us this. And that may have been the last thing she managed to do."

"Mangal, I am not this person."

"The kind of person who goes along with what the company orders? No, Dee. You just look like you are."

"Screw you!"

"Cheerful, dressed in fun fashions, trying out the latest robo-cars, dabbling in her garden. You're the last person anyone would suspect of being subversive."

"That's because I'm not subversive. I'm honest to a fault. Love me love my steampunk."

"...I absolve you," Mangal eventually replied.

Dammit, Mangal had my number. I screwed my eyes up to stop the tearing up. "You absolve me of lying to the American people? While the government clamps down the borders, so that them that has, keeps? Takes away their freedom to travel? Refuses to tell them that the weather *will* kill them, that this is the end?"

"Yes," he replied quietly. "I absolve you."

"Are you going to absolve me of going into an ark while billions die, too?"

"I absolve you, and everyone else who seeks to survive." His voice changed over to ribbing. "That is, assuming you ever make it into an ark. I'd lay long odds against it."

I laughed. And I wiped off the tears. "Well, yeah, there's that. I can always salve my conscience by dying."

"And hey," he joked, "that option remains open."

"True."

"Deal? No hopeless stands on principle? We learn all we can for ourselves, and tell the American people only what we're allowed to."

It's not like we had a choice. We did websites, not live broadcasts. We couldn't leak unapproved truth by accident. Too many people had to approve the work before it went live on the Internet. By then there were no live broadcasts anymore on the big networks, either. Close, but UNC used a five minute delay. They only said it was 'live.'

I added, "And privately, we're very careful what we share, beyond us."

"Very. It won't do anybody any good for us to get caught. Like Deanna Jo."

"Agreed. Hey, Mangal, are you still in touch across the pond?" Meaning the Atlantic.

"Yes." His extended family and friends were scattered across Europe, Africa, and India. The censorship was extreme, to go along with the U.S. embargo of the Eastern Hemisphere. "I assume you're still in touch across the Pacific."

"Sure." I'd taken a year abroad in Tokyo. It was an international program. Aside from a few Japanese friends, I kept in touch with an Australian, a couple Chinese, and one Thai. "Don't share *Wuthering Heights* with them, OK? Or *Gulliver's Travels*. There are plenty more books on Project Gutenberg."

"Agreed. Dee…"

"Yeah?"

"There have to be millions doing what we're doing."

"Yeah." I drummed my fingers on my desk. "Let's not try to hook up with them, shall we?"

"Good plan."

That's how I joined a resistance movement, without any ties

to the Resistance. A cell of two, with no connections to other cells, is hard to crack.

Chapter 3

Interesting fact: When the U.S. abandoned operations in the Eastern Hemisphere as per the Calm Act, it had 2.6 million active and reserve military personnel. There were no subsequent reductions in force. The Defense budget grew.

It was a balmy day for mushroom hunting, the day Zack and I climbed Sleeping Giant, 70 degrees and muggy in mid November in Connecticut. Of course, that November followed the hottest summer on record. There were 20 hottest summers on record out of the last 23 years, before the media quit reporting the statistic.

We set out early with Zack driving, naturally. Mushrooms are a wily prey, he cautioned me. You have to catch them before someone else does. I kept Zack burbling happily about his past hunting prowess and mushroom misadventures. We gradually warmed to each other enough to compare notes on wild berry patches near home. There aren't many berries in any one suburban patch, and this risked sharing a limited resource. I was impressed. He knew some I'd missed. I knew some he'd missed, too, but I think he came out ahead.

The trick with berry patches is to spot them out of season, and know where to come back when the season is right. Apparently it's much the same with mushrooms.

"I think this is a con, Harkonnen," I announced about an hour into our hike. I don't know why some people inspire being called by their last names. They just do. "When do we reach these mythical mushrooms?"

"Patience, Baker," he replied in kind. "My best spot is just a few minutes further. Or do you need a break?" He said this as a challenge.

Zack did landscaping for a living, tossing bags of mulch and soil amendments around like feather pillows. I sat at a computer all day. Of course I needed a break. I growled at his back as he pressed along the rocky muddy uphill trail through brown trees.

The trail dipped into a local low clearing, and he stopped. I huffed up beside him and gazed around. A short stretch of fieldstone wall suggested someone had worked a farm up here once upon a century. You see that everywhere in the woods of Connecticut, though this spot seemed inconvenient. The break in the tree cover was large enough to see the top of the ridge, still well above us.

"A lot of new trees down," Zack murmured, pointing to a tangle ahead of us. A root ball nearly as tall as me stuck up from the ground. I stepped into the clearing and to the side to see better. Massive evergreens had fallen away from the clearing, knocking down other trees like bowling pins beyond them.

"I spy fungus," I said, in an attempt to be cheerful.

Zack shot me a look, and refused to rise to the false cheer. "Those mushrooms are too old," he said quietly. "I wonder if it was the heat, or a microburst."

"Or the drought," I added. "Cumulative effect of all three, is my guess."

I was as moved by the fall of these strong and noble old trees as he was. I simply chose to push back against despair and resignation.

But in this clearing, halfway up the ridge, there was only the one other person, not eight billion. And he cared about the trees, just like I did. I gave in to a bit of grief, and bowed to the downed trees. As I rose, I stretched my arms up to the muggy blue sky and breathed deep. Then I let my arms fall. *Thank you, great trees. Your lives and loss are appreciated.*

As I broke out of that brief ceremony, I caught Zack

looking at me, surprised and touched. He nodded silent acknowledgement.

I nodded back curtly, resenting the intimacy. "Mushrooms, Harkonnen," I prodded.

He nodded, with a slow smile at me growing. I shook an empty mushroom bag at him, and he laughed.

Mushrooms grew well amidst the wreckage of the downed trees. We soon had three bags full enough, of varieties called Chicken-of-the-woods, giant puffball, and oyster mushrooms. Zack nicked the puffballs with a knife to double-check they were a safe species. He kept each variety in a separate bag, so that any accidental poison specimens didn't contaminate other good ones. One of the rules of this hunt was that they needed to be eaten separately, too. You weren't supposed to eat two varieties of wild mushroom at the same meal, and you had to keep an uncooked sample saved, in case you had to call poison control. I knew there was something about this wild mushroom hunting business that turned me off.

Zack caught my distrustful glance at the bags. "You don't learn this in one trip, Dee. My grandmother taught me for years. I know what I'm doing. We have enough for now. This is all we can eat while they're still good."

Along the hike back, I said, "Zack, you should teach someone else. It's important. And I don't think I'm the right apprentice."

He nodded. "You should teach someone the berries."

"And *share?*" I quipped in mock horror.

He chuckled. "I guess it worked better having your own kids and grandkids to teach, so you had a vested interest in them. You ever think of having any?"

I shot him a look and he shrugged. I relented. "I would have liked a kid if I'd started fifteen years ago. I had other things to do at the time."

"Really? You would have brought a kid into the world, for

27

this?"

"If the kid could reach coping age by now, sure. Why not? Eight billion people agree, this is the greatest show on Earth. Not many volunteers to leave early."

"More all the time."

"Well, yeah. That's part of the drama. But even if I didn't supply my own fifteen year old, plenty of other people did. I wouldn't mind fostering one."

I refused to catch his eye after saying that. First dates—and this felt increasingly like a first date, with someone way too intense—should be quick and light. Dinner and a movie and drinks, four hour limit. By the time we got back to my house, it had been five hours, with no external diversions. And there were three bags of mushrooms to imply three separate meals of followup to top it off.

"I think you'd like the giant puffballs best," Zack said, as he turned off the engine on his pickup truck. I wondered if he felt the same way, about too much togetherness all at once. And if so, wasn't that kind of a good thing, that we were on the same wavelength. "I have some things I ought to do this afternoon," he continued. "Can I make you a puffball omelet tomorrow night for supper?"

"Yeah. That sounds really good. Shall I come over about six o'clock?"

"Sounds great. See you then." He let me get out of the truck and into my house by myself before he drove off.

I peeled off my jeans and T-shirt and burr-ridden socks, took a hot shower, and reveled in the solitude of my empty house. Why should it feel better to be alone, than with someone I had so much in common with? I didn't want to think about that. So I didn't.

-o-

End Game

I drove to Zack's Monday night, though it was only a ten minute walk. Before sunset, the cloudless sky had the strangest tinge of green, with large bluer spots. I'd never seen that before. But I'd spent my workday studying suppressed weather chaos information to specify our new web feature. That was enough to give anyone weather paranoia.

I brought a side dish for supper. "Homegrown," I explained, as I presented the home-fries to my host at the door. "My own potatoes, onions, peppers, herbs."

Zack seemed honestly delighted. "Smells *great*, Dee! Thank you. Come in, come in! Are these heirlooms?"

"F1 hybrid Carmen peppers. The potatoes and onions are Red Norland and 'yellow'. I don't know the pedigree." Political correctness was not an aspect of organic gardening I admired. If he wanted to pick out his peppers, he could feel free.

He smiled wryly. "I'm sure they're delicious. Is that... steampunk?" He admired the outfit openly with his eyes but didn't comment further. Some woman had trained this man well. "Come into the kitchen. I'll start the omelet."

Yes, it was steampunk. There are so few occasions to wear it, you know? Rather than the usual overdressed or oversexed lady's ensemble, this outfit was more of an impish girl mechanic look, form-hugging brown canvas bib overalls, rolled up at the knee, over a delicate white short-sleeved blouse. Low-slung leather belt with dangly bits and chunky jewelry suggested tools and clockwork. I only had the one pair of lace-up mid-calf boots, but replaced the lace gaiters with thick bright striped socks, mismatched and clumped low.

Zack in turn had dressed up slightly. He wore a fresh crisp blue-green gingham checked button-down shirt, tucked neatly into well-fitted bleach-blue jeans, with ragg socks. He had rubber clogs by the back door for stepping in and out of the house.

Also by the back door was a basket of eggs, with small

feathers sticking to them. "You have your own chickens?" I asked, delighted.

"Eight," he agreed. "A few goats, too. Couple turkeys."

"Can I see?"

"Ah, the birds are tucked in for the night," he said, peering out a window over the sink. "We could find the goats. But your potatoes would get cold."

"Maybe later," I agreed, settling at the table.

"Onions, goat cheese, and mushrooms on the omelet?" he offered.

"You even make your own goat cheese?"

"I supply the milk. A friend makes the cheese. She's pretty good at it."

She? Well, my best friend Mangal was a guy. "Sounds delicious. The omelet idea," I added, when he looked a little flustered.

"Right," he said, and got to chopping onions.

I would have offered to help, but there didn't seem any need. The dining room table was set, with bread and candles and wine laid out. The table had been cleared of political paper piles by dumping them here on the kitchen table. I took a seat and leafed through a few reluctantly. One demanded a Constitutional amendment to guarantee Americans the freedom to travel and communicate across state borders. Another demanded local self-determination setting up borders and siting peacekeeping forces. Several demanded public transparency on the Calm Act, as the people's right to know. Zack's personal position was murky from the range of opinion expressed.

"Are you politically active, Dee?" Zack asked, guardedly.

"Not really compatible with my job," I deflected this.

"Ah. I guess you know more about what's going on than the rest of us, working for the news media."

"Maybe not," I said. I'd been thinking that not telling anyone the secrets I knew, wasn't really Boolean, on or off, but more like a continuum. Experimentally, I flipped over one of the more numerous handouts and wrote on the back, "If I knew more, I couldn't tell you." I tapped the page with the pen, and gazed at Zack.

He stepped over from the stove and read it. He nodded thoughtfully and returned to sautéing onions. I rolled up the page, lit it in the gas burner, and used it as a taper to light the candles on the dining table. When the paper burned past all of my writing, I doused it in the sink and threw it away.

I was already thinking that this was a really bad idea. I'd risked what, for what? Even if Zack was in a protest group, he wasn't necessarily a real member. If I were the government keeping a lid on public protest, I'd plant ringers in protest groups to keep an eye on them and seed confusion and ineffectiveness.

Not that Zack struck me as a fake. In fact he seemed to have a lot more integrity and inner consistency than most. But that's what you'd want in a good agent. And whether he were ringer or ringleader, his house could be under surveillance. And would I hold it against him if he were a ringer, dedicated to public order, rather than a hopeless idealist? My few dabblings in local politics inspired me to run away, because people got into such petty squabbles. This whole convoluted line of thought hurt my head. *I'm not cut out for this, dammit, Mangal.*

"OK, no more politics," Zack said, laughing softly at my expression. My face is an open book.

"Yeah, no. Sorry." I laughed at myself with him.

"Omelet's ready. Come out to the dining room," he invited. He carried the frying pan to the table, cut the omelet in half, and slid the halves onto charming plates. The stoneware was a collection of deep autumn colors, orange and gold, olive and brown and red. Zack set a beautiful rustic table. "Pour the wine?" he invited. He took the pan back to the kitchen and turned the work lights down to a small glow over the sink.

Once we were settled, I rose a glass to toast. "To a master mushroom hunter. May you find worthy apprentices to your lore."

He nodded acceptance with a smile, and added, "To a fine local feast."

I could drink to that. The omelet was good. I would have preferred a milder cheese, but he didn't overdo it. The giant puffballs had a slightly wild flavor, but I was grateful that the texture was pretty similar to the supermarket white button mushrooms. After a few hesitant bites, I dug in happily. "This is great, Zack. You're a good cook!"

"Mm. Your potatoes are excellent. What did you call these?"

I shrugged. "Home fries. Oh, the potato? Red Norland. They're pretty easy to find, but I could give you seed potatoes if you'd like. Or, do you garden?" I hadn't seen a garden.

"Community garden in town. I have a plot. I'll take you up on those seed potatoes."

"Do the neighbors give you trouble about the livestock? Mine used to complain a lot about excessive farming."

Zack tilted his head toward the neighbor on the left. "One used to. Especially the turkeys. But he shut up after a while. He quit paying the mortgage and taxes and didn't want to make any waves, I guess. They vanished a few months ago. I keep the lawn mowed. Found the spare key, keep the heat on so the pipes don't burst. Like that."

I nodded. There were a couple abandoned houses like that near me. I wondered if the house to my right might not go that way soon. "I have my eye on an ex-neighbor's swimming pool."

"Do it," he said. "I can help you winterize it, if you want."

"They did that, actually. Before they left."

"Sweet."

"I wonder where they go." Another downer conversation. I rallied with, "So are your grandparents still around, Zack?

Parents?"

"No. My grandparents raised me, but they passed on years ago. My sister's around. And the gang from the community gardens." He indicated political piles with his head. "One of the turkeys is for our Thanksgiving spread."

"Oh, nice! How long do you grow a turkey before...?"

"Catch a baby in the spring, kill it in the fall. That's what the neighbor was worked up about. He didn't think it was safe, capturing a wild turkey and eating it." He bobbed his head so-so. "I was a little worried about that myself the first time. But hey, there are all these turkeys wandering about, so, I took one. It worked out, so I do a couple every year now, one each for Thanksgiving and Christmas."

I laughed. "That's great! Yeah, I'd wondered whether anyone ever did anything about all those wild turkeys."

He winked. "Now you know. You? Family?"

"I'm from here, obviously. My parents left a year ago, decided to move to Alabama before the borders closed. My sister and her kids are down there. My brother is in New Mexico. That's it. Friends from work. And online."

Zack nodded, then frowned slightly. "Have you had trouble reaching people interstate?"

I'd gotten the 'circuits are overloaded' message several times. But I also had an Internet line through UNC. "I... don't personally have that problem, no."

"Oh." Message received, clearly. "It must be hard, having your family on the other side of borders that have closed already."

"A few more months with my sister and her kids," I grinned, "and I wouldn't put it past my parents to join a gran caravan."

He snorted his wine. It was never on the news. But people claimed there were these wandering Winnebago packs of ornery armed senior citizens, barreling their way through the first border crossings. It could be urban legend for all I knew. They were still building the new borders in the Northeast at that point.

"Assertive, are they, your folks?"

"Could say that," I agreed. "My sister, too. It's a pity she doesn't use it more on her kids."

"Not the kind of fosterlings you were thinking of, then."

"Nope. They're safely behind the Mason-Dixon line border."

"You approve of these borders, then?" He grimaced.

I pouted at him through my wineglass. I thought we'd reached an agreement, no politics. He shrugged non-apology. I relented and answered. "I... understand the reasoning. Whether I approve or not, we've got more to gain than lose here in Connecticut."

"Gain?" he echoed in surprise.

"How many people are in greater New York, forty million? Ten million around Boston? And only three million in Connecticut."

He drank his wine in silence for a moment. "Is that what the borders are for," he eventually murmured.

I was trying to figure out whether I'd said anything untoward. I didn't think so. I thought the point of the borders was obvious. Divide and conquer. Keep local disasters local by blocking climate refugees from spilling over to create disaster domino effects. The first border, and the one most bristling with arms and trap zones, was the one facing Mexico. Desperate people still tried it, in both directions. Mangal's files told me that the death toll was higher by orders of magnitude than reported in the news. But I hadn't spilled any secrets.

From there, the conversation wandered onto safer topics. I learned more about him. He had a political science degree from UConn. He went ROTC to pay for it, and served his time in the Army. When he left, he had enough money to come home and start the landscaping business. He came alive talking about that. I would have thought November was pretty dead for landscaping, but he said not. His crew levelled lots and reclaimed industrial brownfields and abandoned parking lots. That work could continue until the ground froze, which wasn't until New Year's, if ever. The last couple years the ground never froze.

He started to slump into the couch cushions by 9:30. Landscapers wake up a lot earlier than programmers. I apologized for keeping him up with a laugh, and grabbed my washed potato dish. He scribbled something quickly on a business card, and met me by the door with it. I'd served him my card with the lemon balm tea the other day.

"My contact info," he said. "So... Do you have plans for Thanksgiving?"

"Yes, thanks, I'm eating with my friend Mangal's family in Broomfield. Well, more than family. More like a whole Jain community. It's colorful."

"Jain... Indian, vegetarian?"

"Extremely. Some Jains even wear masks so they don't accidentally hurt a fly. Not Mangal. More of an ethnic Jain, maybe."

"Ouch! Well, I could save you some turkey."

"You're eating with your sister?"

"Yeah, and the whole community garden crew. Many turkeys." He grinned.

In both senses of the word. I grinned back. "Well, I'll see you soon. If not Thanksgiving weekend, maybe another time. Oh!" I flipped the card to see what he'd written on the back.

If I were a plant, would I be sassafras?

Well, that was a worthy Zen koan, I thought. Especially since the identifying characteristic of sassafras was its three leaf shapes on a single tree—oval, mitten, and double-mitten. I nodded at the card, and stood on tiptoe to whisper in Zack's ear, "Sunflower." I stepped back and mouthed and mimed, *"Because you're tall."*

He laughed out loud obligingly. I like a man who laughs at my jokes. "So," he said. "Should I kiss you good night?"

"Please do."

He did. Quite well at that. He traced my face with a finger first, then cupped the back of my head. The other arm pressed me into full body contact from thigh to chest. He pushed my face up halfway to press my lips into his, first kiss dry and firm, second kiss mouth open. Then he stopped right there with a wry challenging smile, and let me go.

I climbed into my car on cloud nine. It's a shame I didn't stay there.

My phone had buzzed while I was at Zack's. I let it go to voicemail, of course. There's nothing more rude than playing with your phone during a date. But now I checked the transcribed message. Adam said to check my robo-ride app. I did, and the app invited me to share a robo-car with Adam Lacey to Stamford the next day, at the same time we'd shared it before.

I'd told him every Tuesday, and he remembered. Fancy that.

I didn't think about it. A great flash of lightning took me by surprise, followed by a giant *boom!* after only a second. No growly thunder, just *boom*. My thumb hit *Accept* on Adam's invite while I was flinching.

I shrugged and put the phone away. I probably would have accepted the offer anyway.

Zack stepped out on his porch to invite me back in, but I said I'd be fine in the car. I waved and drove away.

The rest of a thunderstorm never made an appearance, but I think another *boom* woke me in the night.

Chapter 4

Interesting fact: Ball lightning was a rare phenomenon until the 21st century. They weren't sure what caused it. But the New Dust Bowl kicked megatons of dust into the atmosphere. The particles rubbed against each other, and the static discharge took many forms, including ball lightning and St. Elmo's Fire. It wreaked havoc on electronics.

"Mm, this is delicious!" I assured Adam. He'd texted me in the morning not to eat before our robo-ride. "Thank you so much for sharing!"

"My pleasure. I forgot to cancel my service last week while I was away," he explained. "They kept delivering meals, and my housekeeper kept accepting them. I think she ate the best ones, though. There was supposed to be filet mignon."

My eyes widened. But Adam seemed only slightly vexed at the theft. Filet mignon, if you could find it, cost upwards of $100 a pound by then. We split two other single-person gourmet meals. They couldn't have been much cheaper—a delicate veal wienerschnitzl with spaetzle and green beans, and a carbonara with wild Alaskan salmon. He brought along a bottle of imported Riesling. But we agreed wine wouldn't help with the afternoon's business, and drank mineral water instead. It was quite a lunch, served from a deluxe wicker picnic basket, complete with wine goblet rack.

The robo-car didn't interrupt us once. Apparently Adam had instructed the pumpkin that we were an express to Stamford.

"Dessert?"

"No," I declined. "Thank you, Adam. I couldn't eat another bite." Following Adam's lead, I wrapped and tucked away the used dishes in the hamper. "Mm. Even without the wine, I'm going to sleep through the meeting."

"And is this a bad thing?"

I laughed. "No, perfect, actually. I'll have to rally later in the afternoon, but the first meeting is a snooze. You?"

He shrugged. "It's a work session, with the civil engineers. That's never boring." The picnic basket now fully re-packed, he leaned back and fixed me with a smile. "I just wanted to apologize for taking so long to get back to you. I wanted to, but work's been crazy, I was out of town..." He shrugged again. "Anyway. I meant to call you."

"Apology more than accepted. Sorry for being underdressed."

He laughed. "I was hoping for steampunk again. But it's not as though I could wear mine this afternoon."

"Yes. My steampunk wasn't too well received at work that day."

He lifted an eyebrow, and I waved it off as no matter. I didn't want to tell an arkitect that I flunked my ark-intake exam.

"Wait—you have steampunk?" I asked.

"You inspired me. It looked like fun. I saw a steampunk shop while I was walking around San Francisco on Saturday. And I thought, why not? Now I know someone I could wear it with!"

My smile ached. "How is San Francisco?"

"Beautiful. As always. I don't imagine I'll see it again. So, I had to stay a couple extra days to bid the left coast farewell," he quipped.

He had damned high clearance to have seen it this time. Even a UNC reporter couldn't cross from East coast to West coast anymore, let alone a programmer like me. Only a trickle of military air traffic remained. For surface travel, five north-south borders were already closed to civilians between here and there.

"How was the water situation?"

"About 5 dollars a gallon, or 2 dollars for a glass with dinner. I stayed at a 5-star hotel. They shut off the water to the tub and shower, and metered the tap water. There was a little sign on the toilet that requested you 'flush sparingly.' I imagine it's getting very difficult. San Francisco's not so bad. They get fogs, and dew. Down in Silicon Valley, I didn't see a plant left alive."

"And the people?"

"I had a driver. He seemed to take a lot of detours. The people I was meeting with... They were doing alright."

He sat up and leaned toward me. "I didn't intend for this to be a downer. What I *did* intend, is to ask if you still want to see Montreal again?"

It never rains, it pours. There's something about a little romance that makes you look happy, that inspires attention from other guys. This always seems to happen to me. No guys for a long stretch, then two or three at once.

"Ah, I think the Quebec border closes December first."

"And we have a long weekend before that."

"You want to take me to Montreal Thanksgiving weekend?"

"Say yes. Why not?"

No one's ever accused me of being suave. "Why... me?"

He met my eye intently. He had gorgeous grey eyes. "I like your spirit," he said slowly. "Your delight in the pumpkin carriage, the steampunk, the... *joie de vivre*. You don't look... haunted. I saw San Francisco. The shell is still beautiful, but... haunted. It grieved me. Then I saw the steampunk shop, and my day lit up. I just pictured you in Montreal. Still appreciating it. Laughing, delighting in another steampunk shop, catching snowflakes on your tongue, savoring the sorbet."

Wow, wow, wow. That was quite a compliment. My face was

burning. I stammered, "I… yes. Yes, I'd like to see Montreal one last time. This just seems, um, fast."

He opened an empty hand, and let it fall. "But time is running out. Including time on this ride. We're almost at your stop. Don't say no. We can do separate rooms, if you'd like. Actually, that kinda fits the Victorian clothes, makes it more romantic. Think about it. I'll call you later."

"…Alright. Later then. Here's my stop."

I managed to get out of the car without tripping or smashing my computer. I stood there on the curb at UNC and watched as the robo-pumpkin pulled away. He waved from the back window. I waved back in stunned slow motion. *Wow, wow, wow…*

-o-

Mangal disapproved. I didn't need his crap after the afternoon I'd had at HQ.

Dan's inspirational pre-holiday speech to our department was restful. I didn't catch a word he said, and didn't need to. A higher ranking suit from some business-oriented department presented 'business intelligence'. He illustrated his emphatic points with many (to him) emotional graphs of trending ROI (return on investment) and other TLA (three letter acronyms). It was corporate policy to bore salaried employees with this quarterly, on the theory that we'd be inspired to ascend ever greater heights of ROI and other alphabetic Mounts Everest. It was all gibberish to us programmers. There would not be a quiz. None of us were listening.

I spent half the time remembering last night, just about the nicest date I'd ever had, and Zack's good-bye kiss. I spent the other half remembering Adam's lunch, and his grey eyes as he delivered about the most nicest compliment I'd ever received. Were Zack's eyes grey, or blue… yes, blue. Later, days later, I might have considered practical comparisons and contrasts between the two men. But just then, not in the slightest. Eyes. Deluxe meals. Lips. The romance of Montreal. Picturing Zack catch a baby turkey.

This reverie was shattered when one of my guys suddenly rose in the middle of an especially melodramatic TLA graph (who knows what the speaker was on about). Connor caromed up the aisle, pulling himself on other people's seats or shoulders as though climbing a ladder, then slammed out the doors.

More decorously, with head-bowed apology to the speaker, and everyone whose feet I had to clamber over on the way, I followed Connor out. He came to rest in the conversation nook out by the windows. He sat on a blue-upholstered couch, hands on his thighs. He stared blankly at the print of beach toys. I stood a couple feet off his line of sight for a few minutes, but he didn't acknowledge my presence.

I fetched our computers and put them on the coffee table in front of the couch before sitting next to him. You saw this mental state more and more those days. People would just zone out. *It's the end of the world, and I can't care any more,* or something like that. I couldn't bear going into New York City any more. The streets were full of this dull stare. It was contagious.

I hadn't received any work from him the past week, and I should have. I checked his computer right in front of him. He didn't appear to have done any work the past week.

"Connor... Why'd you come here today? To work?"

"...It's Tuesday. I come here on Tuesday." He delivered this like one of the earnest but intellectually ungifted who corralled shopping carts in a supermarket parking lot. One of my brightest guys, a back end server wizard, turned zombie.

"OK. Good, Connor." Sort of. I mean, at least he knew it was Tuesday. We telecommuters came to Stamford on Tuesday. "But we need to work, too. You know?"

"...What's the point?"

"Money is good. Money is useful. We get paid for working.

So look, Connor, I need you to build some data gateways. The weather API I assigned to you. Remember?" API stood for Application Programmer Interface. We had our own set of holy TLA's, we programmers.

Slowly, I coaxed his fingers back to work. The fingers came back before the conscious brain. At first, I had to dictate every movement, every file opened, every line of code. Then I could dictate the first half of a line, and he finished it, before drifting back to a stop. After about 45 minutes, he was actually programming again, slowly but correctly. I sat back and watched him code for a few minutes.

"Dee," Dan interrupted gently. "Could I see you in my office?"

"Sure, Dan. Connor's doing OK now. Right, Connor?" I squeezed Connor's shoulder gently as I rose to leave. He kept coding.

Once we were behind Dan's closed door, he asked gently, "How much work has he delivered this week? Just the facts, Dee. Don't cover for him."

"He deserves me covering for him, Dan. He's *earned* me covering for him. He was fine last week. He may be fine again after the long weekend."

Dan smiled at me gently, compassionately.

"OK, none. He hasn't delivered any work this week. But he's doing it now. Come on, Dan. The world is ending and most of us are gonna die. There are days it gets to all of us. Don't tell me you haven't gone zombie now and then."

Dan fidgeted with a pen on his spotless paper blotter, on his habitually clear desk. "For a minute now and then. Sure."

"I know we say 'it's contagious', going zombie. But that's just something we *say*. It doesn't mean anything."

"It does mean something, Dee. We say it because going zombie *is* contagious." He held up his hand to stop my torrent of defense. "It got out. That the psychologist was interviewing people for the ark. And then the interviews stopped. And not everyone got interviewed. A lot of people lost hope. I've had to lay off three people this week. It *is* contagious, Dee. I'm going to lay off Connor. You don't have to do it. I'll do it.

"But look, Dee, you need to tell the rest of your team, that the interviews will resume. OK? After the holidays. Give them hope. When people lose hope, they give up. They go zombie."

I stared at him until he dropped his eyes and started to fidget with his pen again. "Like you're telling me now, Dan?"

"No. No! *You* are on my short list. I'm going to get you an ark berth, Dee. If it's humanly possible."

"And your boss? Marley's telling you that you've got an ark berth, too, right?"

"Dee." Dan held his hands up in surrender. "I gave you that folder. You know as well as I do. Everyone's being lied to. Bad as it looks, the truth is worse. But I'm doing all I can. I want you in that ark with me. I want Mangal and his family, too. If my boss is lying to me... You know, I don't even want to know."

"...Right. I'm sorry."

"You have nothing to be sorry for." He rose from his chair. "Look, let's just go wish everybody a happy Thanksgiving and call this day a bust, OK?"

"Yeah," I whispered, rising too. "Dan—"

"Yeah?"

"Have a really good Thanksgiving, OK? There's still plenty to be thankful for. Like, I've got you for a boss."

He laughed softly. "Yeah. Thanks. You too, Dee."

We practiced our happy-ho-ho party faces on each other at the door. Then we sallied forth to glad-hand and lie whitely to our close coworkers and friends. Shelley was the only member of the team I didn't have to lie to about Connor. Because she didn't ask.

So I really wasn't in the mood for Mangal's disapproval of

43

my going to Montreal with Adam. "Mangal, I realize this is shocking. But I may not be a virgin at my wedding." Pure sarcasm on my part—I usually told Mangal about my relationships, if not in much detail. He was my best friend.

He snorted. "OK, so I opted out of your whole whacked-out Western dating scene. You're perfectly normal in your own culture. Granted. But you liked Zack. I just think you're sabotaging yourself. You like Zack, you've just started this thing with Zack. So just give Zack a chance. Montreal with this other guy—that's too crazy, too fast. I think he's weird. And he's rich. So I don't trust him."

"Well, I don't think he's *that* rich."

"He's not in our class. Although it's OK for a woman to marry rich."

"Why do I even talk to you? You're medieval."

"I'm an intelligent outsider, a rational observer of your bizarre American dating rituals. I can be objective."

"If you don't realize you're sexist, you're not very objective."

"If you don't think America is sexist, you're not very rational."

"Touché. Anyway, yes, it's OK to *date* someone who makes more money. Nobody's talking about marriage. Just a weekend jaunt. Though the power differential is kinda... scary."

Mangal frowned. "What power?"

"He just got back from San Francisco."

"Good Lord. What does this Adam do?"

"He's an arkitect. Like, an ark-builder."

Mangal stared at me wide-eyed. Then he said, "Do it."

I missed the 180-degree turn. "He did say we could take separate rooms."

"Yes. Go with him to Montreal. Definitely."

"Wait. What?"

"He might get you an ark berth with him. Can Zack give

you that?"

"No. But maybe I could give it to him. In the UNC ark."

Mangal looked down and played with his coffee cup.

I narrowed my eyes at him. "Why are you so sure I won't make it into the UNC ark?"

"I'm not. Dee, truly, I'm not. But we're web developers. And you say this guy is an arkitect, who *flew to San Francisco* last week? He will be on an ark. Us?" He shrugged.

I had to concede the point.

Chapter 5

Interesting fact: Shortages of consumer goods and electronics preceded the ocean blockades. Epidemics devastated manufacturing production in China and southeast Asia. Japan and South Korea were the first countries to barricade themselves in to control contagion, unsuccessfully in Korea's case.

Wednesday was a workday, made awkward by having already wished my team a happy Thanksgiving the day before. That and pretending Connor was still among us. We needed his weather API, but I decided to wait until after the holiday to assign it to one of the other guys.

What I intended to do over the long weekend, before Adam invited me to Montreal, was spend some serious time digging through Mangal's secret background material on the borders. But my assignment was weather, and I was getting paid for today. I compromised and studied weather until lunch, then the Canadian border situation in the afternoon.

On weather events, the main difference between the truth and what Americans were being told at that time, was the severity. For instance, the Texas triple hurricane was reported in the news as one Category 3 and two Category 2 storms, with a combined death toll of 47. The storms were actually a Category 5 and two Category 4. The immediate death toll was in the thousands confirmed, with over 10,000 missing and unaccounted for. Between the Gulf coast refineries, offshore wells, and tankers caught off guard, the oil spills were catastrophic. Some tankers were caught in the Houston ship channel and spilled. Torrential rains overflowed the bayous and ship channel, and crude oil washed into the streets of Houston.

And then the water supply was fouled, for the fourth largest city in the U.S. The National Guard brought in bottled water—and barricaded the freeways to keep Houstonians from fleeing to the drought-besieged inland cities. Austin-San Antonio, Dallas-Fort Worth, and New Orleans were spared a tidal wave of refugees. But the secondary death toll started to rise from drinking contaminated water, sewage overflows, and shortages of antibiotics in the cholera and typhus outbreaks that followed. Even there, it wasn't clear whether the antibiotics ran out, or the disease strains were resistant, or both. Bureaucracy and statistics broke down in the chaos. But estimates placed the overall death toll closer to 30,000 than 47.

The economic toll was ongoing. Houston was left with only local resources to apply to cleaning up the oil spills. The wells and refineries were still shut down, and the Gulf Coast fisheries would remain contaminated for years. People ate the seafood anyway, because there wasn't much choice. Texas was in the Dust Bowl zone, and agricultural output sputtered as the aquifers emptied.

The technology for lying to the public was simple. Nationally, the event was reported but understated. Locally, the event was still understated, though not as much, and with a priority on maintaining public calm and order. When bottled water ran out—or rather, the authorities decided they couldn't afford to send any more—Houston was assured that the tap water was safe to drink again, even though it wasn't. Internet, phones, and travel were strictly curtailed by the Calm Act. People inciting disorder were dealt with promptly and effectively. They vanished. To be fair, those measures had strong popular support in Texas.

I couldn't help remembering what Zack said. "Is that what the borders are for." They controlled refugees, yes. They prevented information and resource flows, too. They substantially shut down transportation, one of the major contributors to greenhouse gases. And they controlled disease spread.

The Texas triple hurricane was only one example. The new Dust Bowl was worse, stretching from Texas to North Dakota, Oregon to San Diego. The stack of states from Texas up to North Dakota had its own closed borders to west and east, plus a border closing off Oklahoma and the Texas panhandle from the rest of Texas to the south. Between the drought and the GMO blight, conditions in there were worse than the mid 20th century Dust Bowl, and the people were left nowhere to run. The news did mention that, lightly and soft-pedalled. The photos shown on the news, though, were taken from the front range of the Rockies in Colorado, where things weren't nearly as bad.

Florida was sinking and tortured by hurricanes. The southeast baked under murderous heat waves. Freaky storms were everywhere, playing havoc with agriculture even where there was enough water. Storms like the Alberta Clipper weren't new. But they used to end in the Great Lakes, not blow straight out to the Atlantic coast. Phenomena like ball lightning and the northern lights visible in Connecticut, used to be rare.

Before breaking for lunch, I summarized this and more regarding the weather, and sent it in encoded form to my friends across the Pacific. I wasn't sure what good it would do them. But it's hard to learn such things and keep it bottled up inside. I was also pretty sure that at least my friend Down Under was still free to speak.

After lunch, I studied the Canadian border, since I was headed there. This border was more of an enigma, or at least a work in progress. Mexico and the Caribbean countries weren't given a choice. The U.S. shut them out unilaterally. But the Canadian border was more collaborative in nature. Canada considered itself somewhat underpopulated and was willing to take some climate refugees. Yet it was not willing to be overwhelmed with refugees, and was very cautious about disease spread. It's a very *long* border, and its closing was proceeding piecemeal. For reasons that remained murky, Washington D.C. was pushing the close of the Quebec and New Brunswick borders above New York state and New England. The local states and provinces involved were dragging their heels.

There had to be a reason that border was closing on December 1. But I couldn't find it.

-o-

A glance at the clock roused me from my studies to check on the gang. Everyone else had called it quits, but Shelley was still earnestly working at 4 p.m. I called her on the phone to thank her for her dedication and hard work, and told her to knock off for the weekend. She was reluctant because I was still working. Poor kid. I assured her I was done for now, and cheerfully chatted about my holiday plans and pre-cooking tonight for Thanksgiving. She was headed up to stay with her mother near Hartford for a few days. Apparently her family was just the two of them.

I intended the conversation be light and cheerful and short. After a few minutes it dawned on me that the girl was near tears and panicked at the idea of going back to her Mom's. "Hey, Shelley, what's going on? Not that it's any of my business." It really wasn't. And I didn't want to care. "But you seem upset."

"She doesn't want me to l-live down here in Stamford. It's too expensive, and I could telecommute from home—her home. And my internship's almost up anyway, so she wants me to move home now."

"And you don't want to do that."

"No. She's… It's… This semester is the first time I've lived away from her. It's like I can finally fight my way to the surface and *breathe*. I can't go back!"

"Wow. Well, first, you can keep working for UNC if you want. You're a valued member of my team. You don't have to leave in December or January to go back to school if you don't want to yet."

"Really? Oh, thank you, thank you, Dee!"

"You're welcome. Does that... Is that enough for now? I mean, you'll be physically safe going to your Mom's for just Thanksgiving dinner, right?"

"I don't have to stay all weekend." She said this wonderingly, as though it were divine revelation.

"Well, if I were that uncomfortable, I wouldn't. You're a strong, independent grown woman now." They stressed the Pygmalion Effect in supervisor school. I took the lesson to heart. "It's an adjustment with parents, that their little girl is growing up. You know, be kind to your Mom, but do what's right for yourself."

I winced my way through several more excessively intimate minutes until she seemed prepared to face her weekend, then signed off with her, and work, to go cook some yams.

Cooking yams isn't much of a challenge.

I called Zack to let him know I was going away for the weekend with a friend to Montreal. He wished me a good time, and said he'd freeze some leftover turkey for me. He was sweet. I got off the phone quickly, though, before I said anything awkward.

I called Adam to confirm our plans. He'd called the night before when I agreed to the trip, and then he was going to make reservations. The plan was an early start Friday, and the afternoon and Friday night in Burlington, recharging his Tesla, then on to Montreal for Saturday night. This sounded problematic for getting back on Sunday, but he assured me we could top up the charge during a leisurely lunch on the way back.

Boiling yams is no challenge. But I wanted brown sugar on my candied yams the next day. It was bad enough that I had to use margarine instead of butter, because Mangal's Jain 'extended family'—his preschool children were the couple's only blood relatives in the group—were eco-vegan. And yeah, I didn't have any brown sugar left.

Thanksgiving Eve always was a scary time to go to the supermarket. The ever-decreasing selection of fresh vegetables in the produce aisle was disguised by artful displays of what was available—lots of pumpkins and other squash, cabbages, onions, and potatoes, mountains of apples and bagged cranberries, and plenty of hydroponic salad greens. Remembering what I'd read about Houston earlier, I gave thanks yet again that I lived in New England, where water was plentiful and food grew well. The selection would get tedious between Christmas and Easter, but for now shoppers were content enough in the produce aisle.

As I wandered toward the baking ingredients, signs of stress grew. The long lines at the cashiers. The armed guards by the cashiers. Meat was scarce, and everybody wanted some for Thanksgiving. Prices were astronomical, especially for turkeys. I skirted a belligerent shopper in line who declaimed loudly that this had to stop, with his particular opinion of how to fix 'this.' He was a heavy guy with a nearly full cart, well over a thousand dollars of stuff. The woman ahead of him stared down defeated at her small basket of canned goods.

There was a crash just before I got to the juice aisle. Several armed guards pushed past me as they rushed toward the loud voices. A trickle of pomegranate or cranberry juice flowed out the end of the aisle like blood. I paused and glanced cautiously up the aisle before crossing on. *Aha. Beer aisle.* The guards wrestled a middle-class white man to the ground while his wife made the children look away.

I took a deep breath, and skedaddled past the double-wide

holiday specials aisle. I was nearly run over by a woman triumphantly bearing two dented cans of pumpkin pie filling, high in the air. The dents were probably fresh, and safe from botulism. I spied a number of other cans lying on the floor. The aisle was packed with people.

The next aisle was mine. Holiday baking. Hoarder central.

Everyone was struck by the hoarder bug sooner or later. Fortunately not everyone hoarded the same thing, nor usually at the same time, except before snowstorms, hurricanes, and holidays. My particular weaknesses were survivalist seed tins, canning jars with lids, toilet paper, and batteries. I had two spare batteries for my computer, plus a giant house battery that could run the natural gas furnace and the refrigerators during power outages, and charge the other batteries.

More people preferred to hoard sugar and flour. White flour puffed into the air like a cloud. The aisle was packed with humanity at its most neurotic. Sadly the sugar shelves were halfway up that crazed aisle. An older man dodged out hugging a 50-pound bag of sugar. I asked him if there was any brown sugar left. But he couldn't or wouldn't respond. He took position in a checkout line with nothing but his giant sugar bag. People thronged him begging to split the sugar after checkout. He shook his head spasmodically and refused to talk to any of them. When one of the other customers threatened to hit him with a frozen chicken, the cashier guard had enough. The sugar buyer was whisked to the front of the line.

I stole another glance into the aisle. It just wasn't worth it. Beet sugar with a dab of molasses would have to do instead of brown sugar.

I drove home in the muggy dark. Too late to do much good against climate change, the U.S. had finally turned off the colossal waste of streetlights in suburbs. Outdoor Christmas lights were also forbidden, so we got to celebrate Thanksgiving without the eager Christmas jump-starters. The night creatures like raccoons and possums seemed to be thriving. Or at least I saw them more often, in headlights or a flashlight. I've always admired their attitude—the brilliant and devious can-do cheer of a raccoon, and the way possums survived getting hit by cars over and over again. They just shuffled off into the woods to heal up and fight another day. Resilient critters.

Some of my neighbors felt differently about streetlights and the night critters. The couple with the nice swimming pool had been at perpetual war with Connecticut wildlife, both the furry and leafy varieties. But the raccoons had won, and the house stood dark and empty.

There were lights on in the house on the other side. An older single mom and her teenaged son lived there. I often chatted with them while I was out gardening. But the gardens were bedded down for winter now. Muggy heat wasn't enough to grow crops. There just wasn't enough sun in late November. I still had cabbages and potatoes out in the ground, but that was more of a storage convenience. I could harvest them through Christmas.

Maybe she had some brown sugar. If not, at least I could wish them a neighborly happy Thanksgiving.

I tried the doorbell, but wasn't sure if I'd heard it ring. I did hear footsteps. After another minute, I tried knocking on the door, and stood where someone peeking out the window could see me. More furtive footsteps inside, and a rustling at the curtain.

I smiled and waved. "Hi, Alex. It's me, Dee from next door."

The teenager opened the door a crack. "Um, hi." Alex was a handsome kid, with a compact muscular build, short straight black hair, and warm Hispanic features. Furtiveness didn't display the best in him tonight.

"Hi, happy Thanksgiving!" I said.

"Um, yeah."

End Game

"Hey, Alex, is your Mom home?"

"Um, no. She's, um, away."

I blinked. Away. For Thanksgiving? Leaving a 14-year-old behind. That wasn't who I thought his mother Anne was. Not at all.

"Oh. Sorry to miss her. I was wondering if I might borrow a cup of brown sugar. Do you have any?"

"Um, I dunno."

"May I come in?"

"No! Um, I'll look. Wait a minute."

I contemplated Anne the absentee mom while I waited on the dark front stoop. Not a divorcée, Anne had Alex solo from the start. She worked from home as I did, some kind of data analyst, fairly successful to afford a nice home and to raise a kid single-handedly. She didn't go overboard with the holidays, but spent quality time with Alex, shooting hoops or tending the lawn together. They seemed a nice family. Watching her with Alex, I'd even considered what it would be like to have a child by myself.

Alex returned to thrust a partly-used bag of brown sugar out at me.

The door started closing the moment I took the bag. "Thanks. Hey, Alex? Do you have plans for Thanksgiving?"

"Um, yeah."

I suspected this meant he had a date with virtual friends for online gaming.

"Well, if you need anything, while your Mom's away? Feel free to come over. Ah, I'll be away mostly this weekend. But I'll be back."

"OK." The door shut.

"Happy Thanksgiving, Alex," I said softly, hand on the door in benediction.

It never would have occurred to me, then, not to tell the teenager next door I'd be away a few days. In summer I hired him to water the garden while I was away.

Back in my house, the pathos of the day expressed itself with more hoarding. I hit the Internet to find what I could stock up on in Burlington and Montreal. Hoarding doesn't really succeed at soothing anxiety, but shopping is kinda fun.

Chapter 6

Interesting fact: The GMO blight virtually annihilated North American GMO corn and soy crops. Once the disease was identified, farmers were ordered to burn standing crops. This was too little too late to prevent the disease spreading throughout the continent. Limited production the following two years was largely confined to producing non-GMO seed. This turned into a brush war in several Minnesota counties when organic farmers were ordered to turn their soybean seed over to Montagro, the extremely powerful multinational inventor of the GMO crops. The U.S. military was dispatched in aid of Montagro, but on arrival, the commanding officer elected to back down. Somehow Canadian border forces mixed in on the organic farmers' side. Local news wasn't allowed to cover the story until fed up townsfolk took over the broadcast stations. Five Montagro executives were burned alive in the subsequent Montagro Bonfire that razed almost every Montagro facility in the state. The U.S. military commander eventually received an honorable discharge after serving some time in prison.

"Cabbages," Adam said blankly, as I tucked my crate of produce into his opulent leather-upholstered back seat. "I was planning to feed you on this trip."

I grinned. "Trade goods. I was hoping to do a spot of shopping in Burlington. The guy wanted some of my home-grown. There are dried tomatoes and canned peppers under the cabbage."

"You're a gardener!" He gazed at the winter bones of my

57

sleeping garden in surprise. "Is that what all that is. That's industrious. Is there also luggage?"

"Oh, yeah! Be right back!"

By 7 a.m., we were on the interstate, and the sun was barely up from the horizon, on a typical clammy November day. I was relieved that we were both the sort to keep to the schedule instead of complicating an 'early start' with last-minute errands. The latest-model Tesla sedan didn't require much driving, but Adam enjoyed himself doing it.

I was afraid the 6 hour drive up to Burlington would drag, but for one thing, we made it in 4 hours. The roads were near empty. The quiet and smoothness of the Tesla's ride obscured how fast he drove. But mostly, we found plenty to talk about to pass the time.

Thanksgiving, of course, was covered in detail. Adam's family 'compound'—his word—was down in Greenwich, one of the diamonds in Connecticut's Gold Coast. His stepmother laid on a full traditional Thanksgiving spread for about 15. She and her daughter, Adam's half-sister, were gourmet cooks. Adam and his older brother and father concentrated on traditional football, both on TV and tossing a ball outside with nephews and nieces and cousins. Other than Thanksgiving Day, none of the three men had any interest whatsoever in football. Besides the unfamiliar sheer wealth involved, it sounded all-American from a bygone era.

My dinner had been an eco-vegan feast for about a dozen of Mangal's Jain community of assorted ages. Aside from my candied yams and a disappointing vegan pumpkin pie, the traditional food was Indian, and unbearably spicy. You know it's hot when a dish of white potatoes is deep red and no tomatoes were involved. I had fun romping on the floor with Mangal's preschoolers, aged 2 and 4. And I enjoyed relaxing and talking with the older Jain neighbors. In my family, you could cut the judgmentalism with a knife. Jains were pacifists in every way, and sought not to judge or hold an opinion too strongly. I don't know that I could live that way, but it's ever so pleasant to visit and be included.

The familiar New England landscape rolled by outside the Tesla. From the highway I saw trees and rolling hills, gradually shifting into higher hills and mountains, from deciduous to evergreen trees, crop fields all sleeping. From that remove you don't see frightened people and their thwarted works. Unlike the West, our landscape still sustained us. It was easy to put Wednesday's research behind me with the miles.

"So what are you shopping for?" Adam inquired, as we hit the outskirts of greater Burlington.

"Cheddar, of course. We need more cow dairies in Connecticut. Goat cheese just isn't the same."

Adam laughed. "Agreed."

I continued itemizing. "The textile mills are back up and running in Winooski, so I wanted a nice bolt of cloth."

Adam looked puzzled. "Your ark will supply things like that."

"Eventually, probably," I agreed. "Actually, I have no idea what the UNC ark will provide. They haven't really told us about that."

"Oh."

Sometimes an 'oh' speaks volumes. In response to my continued gaze, he went on, "It's just... getting a bit late. For that. I'm sorry. I... shouldn't talk about it. What else are you buying?"

"A Tesla battery."

He laughed out loud. "Why?" He'd seen my old boxy gasoline car in the driveway.

"Power storage. To run the refrigerator and furnace and recharge my computer when the power is out. Or, store renewable power."

"OK. But why a Tesla battery?"

"Because I already have one. This is my second, and I don't want to re-do all the wiring for a different kind of battery. So I wanted one more of the same." I glanced at him sideways to see if he'd make fun of me for it.

He just nodded, a bit poignantly I felt. "Makes sense. You know... I'll need to board my ark kinda early. For shake-down. When I go, you can have my spare battery. For the car."

"I never knew Tesla cars came with spare batteries."

"They don't." He smiled crookedly. "Everybody hoards something."

"A fellow battery-hoarder! And what else do you hoard, Adam Lacey?"

"Oh, look! There's our B&B!"

The B&B was still all the way up the block. "That's not fair. You got three out of me—cool fabric, cheddar cheese, and batteries."

"Yes, but we need to *recharge* the battery."

"Ah, yes, that. Let's do that thing." Part of the battery hoarding complex was the compulsion to check, and double-check, that all the batteries were charged.

-o-

While the car got a quick charge, we wandered down to the shops on the Lake Champlain waterfront to find some lunch. As always, Burlington seemed a happy little bastion of not-the-U.S. Ahead of its time, Burlington was 100% renewable powered, well fed by local agriculture, and never allowed the big box chain stores in. The city looked much the same as when I was a student there. The people didn't.

"Cheese tasting," I said, coming to a stop in front of a charmingly rustic restaurant and cheese shop.

"Lady's choice," agreed Adam. He opened the door for me with a broad flourish and bow.

We interrupted a vehement but quiet argument between the

thirty-something year old staff, possibly a married couple. There were no other customers. Customers seemed in short supply at most of the restaurants we passed.

The woman rallied with a brilliant welcoming smile and indicated our choice of any seats in the house, that being a choice of about five wooden tables and a wooden counter with high stools. My eye was drawn to the cheese array behind the counter, so Adam steered us that way.

Apparently the man was in charge of the counter. "Can I interest you in lunch? Our lunch special today is a half pound of cheese in eight one-ounce samples, with seasonal fruit and bread and butter, and a craft beer. Or, a quarter pound of cheese," he offered to me, "for the lighter appetite."

I nodded emphatically, "A quarter pound is enough for me. Maybe we could pick different cheeses and share, Adam?" He nodded that it was a good plan. "I'd like local cow cheeses, please. Do you have four different local cow cheeses?"

"Absolutely. And you sir?"

Adam looked amused. "What is there besides cow?"

"Oh, cow, sheep, goat, water buffalo. I think that's it."

"One of each, then. Local. Different from hers, if possible."

Actual cheeses were determined to complement our choices of six craft beers. Adam chose a pint inspired by the dark and chewy Trappist Chimay ale. I picked a half pint of a light hoppy lager. They matched perfectly with the selected cheeses. His cheeses were too strongly flavored for my beer, and mine too light for his, but we did each sample all of them. The star of the meal for me was the fresh local butter for the rich bread. The woman cored and sliced late apples for us. The apples cleared the palette between cheeses much like a Montreal sorbet.

The proprietors receded regularly to be non-intrusive, but returned to provide a steady patter of knowledgeable local cheese lore whenever we asked.

The tab was astronomical. But Adam cheerfully added a

25% gratuity and a pound each of our respective favorite cheeses. His was a pungent washed-rind cheese with a gooey center, reminiscent of Brie. Mine was called Morning Wind, with a flavor similar to gruyere.

Adam pointed to a small foot locker behind the counter after we settled up. I raised an eyebrow in inquiry. He raised a 'wait' finger until we were back on the street.

He took me by the arm to snuggle up to walk, as the day had cooled, still above freezing but damp. A sharp wind rose off Lake Champlain. The Adirondack mountains across the water in New York state lay hidden behind grey.

"That was an ark locker," Adam murmured. "Military."

I blinked. The locker was about the size of the Army duffel bags once seen with servicemen on airplanes. "That's all you get to bring with you into an ark?"

"Military, yes. If it were up to me, everyone would get the same allowance. But most people, yes, that's about it."

"Military," I echoed. "So the UNC ark is supposed to be 12,000 people. How much of that would be 'military?' "

"UNC, 12,000? That seems... Well, I'm not on the UNC project. Probably one third defense staff, though. Inside the ark. More outside."

I digested this in silence for a block or so. I was pretty sure he thought the UNC ark would hold nowhere near 12,000 people. Teasing about the steampunk incident aside, Mangal used to believe we'd be on the UNC ark. Until after we received those secret folders. Now he didn't anymore.

The military angle I'd never even considered. But now that I thought about it, I realized with a sinking feeling that of course the arks would need protection. Why would the people outside the ark allow the privileged few to survive while they died quietly?

Big-time protection. And barriers to keep the ark outsiders away from the ark.

End Game

Satellite images. I bet Mangal had studied the raw satellite images. I made a mental note to do that, as soon as possible. And study the borders by satellite, too.

Say 10,000 instead of 12,000, for the whole ark complex, inside and this new military *outside* I'd never considered before. Over half military. There might only be room for 4,000 people in the UNC ark. With maybe an average of four people per family.

My guess was that my boss Dan didn't tell us about the footlocker sized belongings limit because *Dan* didn't stand a chance of getting into that ark. And Dan didn't know it.

"I shouldn't have said that," Adam apologized. "That beer was stronger than I thought. I'm sorry, Dee."

"No, God forbid anyone tell the truth these days. Thank you. I'd want to know." I stopped and met his eye. "*I* would want to know."

He swallowed. "Did you come with me on this trip to... No, never mind." He started walking again, pulling me along.

I pulled him back to a stop and looked him in the eye again. "I wanted to visit Burlington and Montreal again. I went to school here. And the two of us had fun together on a magic pumpkin ride. It's the end of the world. Why the fuck not?" A passing elderly couple shot me a look. "Pardon my French," I tossed at them sunnily.

"OK, good," said Adam. "Me too. Well, I didn't go to UVM. I didn't even know you went to UVM." He glanced uphill. "Did you want to visit, see any old friends?"

"No, six years was enough, thanks. We've all moved on." We started walking again. "I wasn't done."

"With school?"

I shot him a grimace. "School was lovely. The town was a blast. I haven't kept in touch with anyone who lives here anymore. I meant, I wasn't done answering you."

Adam laughed. "Oh." He turned us onto a pier, striding

into the face of the stiffening breeze.

"That was why I wanted to come, and why I agreed to come," I continued. "But then my friend, Mangal, suggested I should definitely come with you, and wrangle a berth on your ark. Because maybe I wouldn't get into UNC's ark. And then I didn't want to come at all, because to date you for a berth on an ark, that's… I don't know what that is."

"I see… No, I don't."

"Yeah, right?" I kicked a piling on the pier. "So then I started wondering what would be repulsive. You know, not horrible, but something that would kinda take the wind out of any romance, because then it would be OK. Because then I wouldn't be trying to entrap you or something. I think that's when I started shopping."

Adam's eyes lit with amusement. "OK. So you don't really want to go shopping."

"Well, no, now I do. You know, once I got started. I already made these deals."

"Your beer was stronger than it looked."

My face was burning. "No, I'm really like this."

He laughed out loud and flung an arm around me. We headed back up the pier. "So where shall we shop, Dee?"

-o-

First stop was the textile mill on the Winooski falls. This was old New England industry, in its heyday from the mid-1800's to mid-1900's, and now rising from the dead. Some of the falls produced hydroelectric power. Other initiatives were reviving a saw mill and grain mill. But the old textile mill was the most ambitious renovation project.

Placards about the place explained all this. Vermonters knew how to play to the tourists. The cloth retail space was in a cavernous mall built in part of the old brick mill complex, with modern picture windows framing the view across the Winooski

River and the falls. Educational nooks featured old industrial machinery and photos. My guilt level evaporated as Adam happily worked his way around the hall, studying the displays. The mill building was busier than the nearly empty lakefront district, but not by much.

I ended up with two fine bolts of cloth, and they cost me a mint. One bolt was a light but sturdy cotton duck with blue ticking stripes. The other was a navy wool blend from local wool and southern cotton.

Cotton supplies in New England were running low already. As a mostly-GMO crop, raw cotton was quarantined, though the blight hadn't jumped species to cotton yet. None of it was allowed across the Mason-Dixon line border from the South. The nice saleslady's apologetic explanation added at least a hundred dollars to each bolt.

Adam meandered over to help carry when I finished paying. "I guess you sew."

I grinned. "I make all my steampunk."

He looked suitably impressed. "Shouldn't it be brown then?"

I considered the browns lovingly. "Yeah... What I really wear is blue, though. These blues are perfect."

Second stop was the swap meet. The cheese and battery sellers I'd corresponded with online had said they planned to be there for the day. They brought along thousands of their closest friends, it appeared. Burlington never had Black Friday shopping at Walmart. The city never allowed a Walmart. But the barter economy was booming.

We found the battery guy first, to get rid of my produce crate. He had other heavy wares, too, so his stall was set up close to the road. I'd forgotten just how heavy those batteries were when making this plan. But the seller's partner minded the table while he carted and trucked the 200-pound monster back to Adam's car for us.

"So, are you all shopped out?" I challenged Adam.

"I'm still game if you are," he offered.

We waded back into the enormous party. The lion's share of the goods were tag sale fodder, unloved old junk that people were thinning out of garages and attics. But a fair number of people had crafts on display, from herb teas to belt buckles, vegetable spreads and breads to fine furniture and original paintings, and a bazillion yarn crafts. From watching others bicker, it was clear that my cabbages and dried tomatoes and canned peppers had nearly as high trade value as the thousand dollars I'd also given the Tesla battery seller.

"Give unto Caesar what is Caesar's. I gotta eat," is how one weathered older vendor put it, as we walked by.

Adam got interested in finding a heavy woolen sweater for himself. "Good warmth when wet."

"Kinda bulky," I pointed out. This seemed at odds with the duffel-sized allotment of belongings he'd indicated before.

He winked. "Doesn't include what you're wearing on check-in day. What do you think of this one?" He held up a heavy pullover, knit in a Nordic pattern from four colors of natural yarn.

"That's a beauty," I agreed. I tweaked it across his shoulders and tugged it down to his hips. This careful attention to his well-toned anatomy was getting to me a bit. "Snug," I commented, feeling the blush.

"I don't think I need it larger?"

"Nope. No, that's perfect," I agreed.

"Well," he told the vendor. "The lady says it's perfect."

The woman, about my age, nodded appreciatively. "Oh, yeah." She'd been watching while I draped the sweater on Adam.

Her husband thwacked her butt playfully. "A sweater for the lady, too?" he suggested.

"Not for me, thanks."

I boggled as Adam dickered the price down to twelve hundred dollars.

"Guess money doesn't fit in those footlockers either, huh?" I quipped, as we wandered away.

"It really doesn't," Adam agreed. He wasn't joking. But then he smiled and gave my shoulders a brief hug. He left his arm there as we continued hunting for my cheesemaker. It felt great.

Footsore and forty pounds of cheddar richer, we finally collapsed in the parlor of the gracious Victorian B&B. The fifty-something landlady provided hot tea and a couple large oatmeal cookies with a smile, and retired to her office. A large fire danced in the hearth to leech away any remaining ambition.

"B&B's don't really offer dinner, do they," Adam pondered. He sunk into his winged chair, stocking feet gratefully elevated on a divan, reaching toward the warmth of the fireplace. He looked unequal to the task of supper even if it magically appeared before him.

I felt the same way. I shrugged lower into my overstuffed, over pillowed couch. "I'm amazed they offer car recharging."

"That's why I chose this place." He frowned. "I never had my filet mignon. I was looking forward to that filet mignon."

" 'Filet mignon' is French," I observed lazily. "I bet they could do miraculous things with filet mignon in Montreal."

"A good French restaurant can do miraculous things with an onion," opined Adam. "Seize the day."

At this rallying cry, we both fell asleep for a nap before the fireplace.

-o-

B&B's do provide breakfast, and this one did us proud. Which we enjoyed thoroughly, having eventually roused just enough for sandwiches and beer at a pub before crashing Friday night in our separate rooms. We were the only guests despite the holiday weekend. We'd come to accept this as the new normal.

Everyone in touristy Vermont seemed faintly surprised we were there. But they were as eager as ever to relieve us of money, of course.

Settled up and with the car fully charged, we hit the road by 11:00 for the 100 mile trip to Montreal, maybe an hour and a half the way Adam drove. Don't get me wrong, he drove very well. Carefully, courteously, and fast. We made good time running up I-89 through St. Albans. The day was remarkably clear for November, well above freezing with a deep blue sky, the warm sun winter-low in the sky behind us as we headed north.

We passed large orange signs, twice, advising that Route 2 and Route 78 were only open for Vermont local traffic through the islands on Lake Champlain. No through traffic was possible to New York state at Plattsburgh or Rouses Point. That was a surprise. With the Canadian border closing so soon, we would have expected traffic to divert into upstate New York. The border that was to close off the six states of New England from New York wasn't due for another month. They seemed to be closing the northern edge early.

Approaching the actual turnoff to Route 78, Adam slowed way down. An RV entered the interstate ahead of us, set itself across all lanes of traffic, and parked. Fortunately there was no one behind us. And Adam really was a good driver. From going 70 miles per hour, he managed to stop with several feet to spare before plowing into that RV.

He laid on the horn, as a matter of principle. The RV driver cheerfully flipped him off in return. She was a petite senior citizen with wiggy ash blond curls. Gigantic purple plastic earrings matched purple lipstick and glasses frames. She cranked up the music in her RV loud enough for us to hear. *Thunder Road,* by Bruce Springsteen.

Adam carefully engaged the emergency flashers, and backed the car up onto the left-hand shoulder a ways so we could see what was going on. RV after RV piled onto the road in front of the lane-blocking vehicle, and headed north.

"It's a gran caravan. They're real," Adam breathed in wonder. "I thought that was urban myth."

Chapter 7

Interesting fact: By this time, all recreational drugs had been legalized in the U.S. Opiates were available without a prescription. Meanwhile, Medicare was replaced with a voucher system, and the Affordable Care Act repealed. Congress decided we couldn't afford health care anymore due to the exploding costs of climate-related disasters.

I'd read about several incidents with gran caravans the other day. I studied the fey nonchalance of the purple-dangly ancient Baby Boomer for several minutes. She was rocking out to *Born in the U.S.A.* now. I got busy with the car's navigation system.

"It won't make any difference," Adam pointed out. "I-89 is the only border crossing." Orange signs had helpfully pointed that out, as well. "If we get off the highway, we'd just have to rejoin it farther up. Just relax and wait, I guess. How many of them can there be?"

"Hundreds," I suggested. "Maybe thousands." I considered, and decided to go further out on a limb. "Adam, I work at UNC. I hear more than most people. This could be dangerous."

"Dangerous? Ancient hippies reliving Woodstock?"

"Adam... they have nothing to lose."

He considered that sadly. "Well. That's probably true of most people these days. Oh, look, Lady Gaga up there is moving on, good riddance. That couldn't have been more than fifty RV's."

In the time we'd waited, a half dozen other cars and trucks, and maybe a dozen semis, had joined the group waiting for the caravan to release the road to traffic again. We waited on the meridian until Adam could safely merge into the fast lane behind them from a standing stop.

"Adam, I have a really bad feeling about this," I eventually resumed.

He took my hand and squeezed it reassuringly. "We're going to Montreal. We came here to visit Montreal."

It was only a few more miles until the left exit into the U.S. border compound. I looked at it longingly with pursed lips. I noted that most of the semis took that left exit. I caught a glimpse of parked U.S. troop carriers as we passed the compound itself.

Adam pressed my hand again. Within moments we were back to the rear view of fifty RV's, clogging the plaza where the highway splayed out for Canadian border inspection.

"Adam, see that marker? We're in the U.S. until there."

"Yes?"

"See those old guys getting out the back of the RV there? The ones with the semi-automatic weapons."

"Jesus."

"Turn left."

"There is no left! It's blocked." And there were posts there. I thought we could make it around the posts, though.

One of the semis that had tried to push on through the border in front of us, started reversing toward us.

"Dammit, *again* with this!" Adam swore some more, and backed onto the left shoulder to get out of the truck's way.

Having backed up far enough, the semi took the U-turn to the left in front of the Canadian line. He took out a couple posts along the way. A number of Canadian border police in bullet-proof jackets came out running. I had to respect them— I'd always been impressed with the Canadian border police. They skidded to a stop, somewhat into the U.S. side of the border, and started directing traffic. One pointed to Adam.

You! Turn left. Here. Get the hell back to the U.S.! The border guard had no trouble expressing this with arms and a little orange flag.

Adam hesitated.

Now, NOW! the border cop insisted.

I heard one lone gunshot. Followed by quite a lot of gunshots.

Hyperventilating, Adam made it around the U-turn back towards U.S. customs. I looked back. The border guards who'd tried to direct traffic gave that up and pelted back across the border toward the nearest building.

"Stay to the right!" I called out. There was little time to speed up before we were at the U.S. side border plaza. "We want to exit I-89."

"Why...?" But thankfully Adam headed to the right. Other cars backed up to the left to go through the standard toll-booth arrangement. We seemed to be in the truck inspection lane.

We slowly passed a building into the semi truck parking lot. There were a lot more troop carriers than I realized when we passed on the far side of the interstate. The troops they carried were loading up at a run, well armed. "Stop, Adam! Turn right here," I ordered.

"But, we haven't passed inspection," Adam quibbled.

"Turn right, or I'm getting out of the car," I explained. "Now, Adam!"

"*Dammit!*" he swore, but did as I asked.

"Jog left."

Here we found our first U.S. border patrol, cordoned across the street in orange. As one of the nice officers approached us, Adam rolled down his window, shooting me a dirty look.

I figured it was only fair that I did the talking, since I'd been doing the navigation. I leaned across Adam and smiled at the nice armed man. "Hello, sir. We were trying to go to Montreal today. But there was gunfire at the border. Now we're trying to exit to Route 7." I smiled winningly. "Here are our passports.

We never left the country today." I had the passports ready for Canadian inspection just a few minutes ago.

He saw the blue passports in my hand, glanced at the chaotic army staging area beyond us, pursed his lips, and waved us on. "Go," he said. He signalled to the other guards to let us through.

Adam navigated through the guards at a cautious and sober speed, and nodded to them respectfully. I leaned back into my seat, and blew out a long breath I hadn't realized I was holding.

"You want to tell me what all that was about?" Adam asked.

"Not just yet, thanks," I replied, as another pocket of Army vehicles appeared in the woods to the right. This group was more of the wide-body Jeep variety, with a superstructure for mounted artillery on top. They were starting up their engines. "Turn left at the intersection. Good, we're now on Route 7. Just follow it around. We'll cross over I-89 and head south."

A few hundred feet past the last entrance back onto I-89 North, I pointed. "Duty free store. Let's stop there."

With the car safely parked, we both sat back and simply breathed for a few minutes, to soothe jangling nerves. The duty free parking lot was unsurprisingly empty. Not even a house or gas station was visible in the Vermont winter woods surrounding us and Route 7.

I rolled down my window experimentally. The isolated rural tranquility of the setting had a deep bass soundtrack of large trucks moving up the interstate, with gunshot percussion still wafting down from the border.

"Why not I-89 south?" Adam prompted again.

"I don't really want to be associated with that border right now. Do you?"

He snorted. "No. Though we haven't done anything wrong."

"Yes, but the guys with the guns are kinda stressed right now. The border guards were OK, but I don't trust the soldiers to make fine distinctions. They're here to put down citizen terrorists. Not a good place to be an innocent bystander."

"Point taken. This duty-free is closed."

I chuckled. "Sorry."

"That's alright," Adam allowed. "I didn't really need any liquor or cigarettes. I wouldn't mind a stretch, though."

We got out of the car and stretched, and walked around the parking lot a bit to decompress. Then we got back on Route 7 heading south. A typical state 'highway', Route 7 was basically a two lane road linking hither to yon. Vermont standard frost heaves ridged across the road every 100 feet or so, making me appreciate the smooth suspension of Adam's car. Sometimes we paralleled quite close to I-89, giving us glimpses of the road not travelled. It still looked well worth not travelling. We spotted occasional Army vehicles and zero civilian traffic, before Route 7 wended away from the interstate again.

"This seems ridiculous," Adam said. "That RV driver who blocked the interstate, a terrorist? She must have been 80 years old."

"Exactly, Adam. She has nothing left to lose. Maybe she has breast cancer, maybe she needs a heart bypass or a hip replacement. She's not going to get treatment. The Medicare vouchers can't cover anything like that. Maybe she has kids and grandkids, a stake in the future of the world. They can't help her, they can barely help themselves. They need to toe the line and please bosses or doctors or whoever, hoping to pay for food, maybe an ark berth, and get a chance to live. Maybe she can do something they can't, about how screwed up the world is."

Adam considered that. "Baby Boomers? They gave up idealism and switched to materialism a long time ago."

I shrugged yes-and-no. "Some of that is age-related. In your middle decades, you work hard, amass money, launch kids or careers or businesses. But there comes a point when that's done, whether for good, bad, or indifferent. Then you look around and say, 'What's left? What else did I need to get around to?' "

"OK, I could see that," Adam allowed. "But why attack the Canadian border? You know if they'd wanted to, they could have simply driven through that border crossing today in peace."

I grinned. "They'd have to give up their weapons to do it."

Adam grinned wryly in return. "Well, yeah. And on second thought, I'm not so sure the Canadians would have let them in. If I were Canada, I wouldn't want to take refugees from the American health care fiasco."

"Agreed." I shrugged again. "Maybe the gran caravan just wants to make a big noise. Say 'I matter, and this is not OK,' as loudly as they can. Or maybe they want to keep the Quebec border open. Or, force it closed early, with certain people successfully caught on the wrong side. I don't know."

What I did know was a bit too specific to share. Deanna Jo's squelched research included an investigation into this social movement. When a gran caravan staged an assault like this, there were usually demands. The demands might involve freedom, opening the borders, health care, banning the arks, or something else.

But they generally weren't demands that the people attacked could grant. A demonstration like this was staged theater. Civil disobedience was the point.

As we entered the fine town of Swanton Vermont, population 6,000, I offered Adam three choices for our route back to Burlington. We could continue for more of Route 7, try rejoining I-89, or head out to the islands in Lake Champlain for some scenery.

"You don't sound too happy about I-89," he observed.

"I think all those men with the uniforms and guns are garrisoned closer to Burlington," I replied. "That's what interstates were originally for. Mobilizing troops quickly."

"Well, you went to school here. Does Route 7 ever get more interesting?"

So far Route 7 featured plenty of trees punctuated by winter fields of stubble, and a smattering of Vermont-standard black-spotted white cows. Scenic, but repetitive. That was pretty much the standard scenery all the way down to Massachusetts.

"I went to school here, and no one ever mentioned Route 7. There are some national parks out on the islands."

Adam considered this. "So, more trees, fewer cows. If you don't mind, I'd just as soon get back to Burlington faster. Let's try I-89 again. Unless you're going to threaten to jump out of the car again."

"Not right this moment," I said sweetly. I reserved the right to change my mind later.

But in the event, the I-89 entrance ramps were blocked off in Swanton, both north and south-bound. We pulled into a gas station at the intersection to use the facilities and buy snacks.

Adam was already interviewing the cashier in the store by the time I made it in.

"Army did that, about a half hour ago," the beefy teenager supplied at the checkout counter. "None of them came in. Don't know why they did it. Accident, maybe."

"Have you heard anything about Route 7 down to Burlington? Or Route 78 out to the islands?"

The teenager shrugged. He jerked his head to indicate the orange sawhorses across the nearest entrance ramp, visible out the store window. "That was the only excitement today. Been pretty slow. It's 8 dollars for the gallon water jug."

That last was directed at me. I nodded thanks and continued roaming the sparsely populated shelves. There was only one free-standing aisle left, plus the refrigerated wall. All the freezers were powered off, along with half the refrigerators. Even with the diminished capacity, there was still plenty of

Ginger Booth

empty between the neatly spaced cold items for sale, mostly from local dairies. I considered, and decided against, pre-packaged egg salad sandwiches on wheat, vegetable-free. No telling how old the mayonnaise might be in those. On the open shelves, the usual candy and chips sections were missing, along with almost everything else. Having reviewed all the options, I joined Adam with nothing but the water jug and a sliced round sourdough boule loaf that felt fairly fresh.

The teenager charged us 10 dollars for the bread, and added 2 dollars each for using the bathrooms.

Before we got underway again, I unpacked some dried strawberries I brought along for driving snacks, and our selection of three cheeses. Adam supplied refillable coffee cups from Starbucks and Dunkin Donuts, and a clever hand-held cheese slicing tool he'd picked up at the flea market. Compared to what we'd hoped for in Montreal, it was a bare little meal. Then again, it was Thanksgiving week. We were hardly starving. And the sourdough bread turned out to be surprisingly good.

"Navigator, I fancy islands," announced Adam, as he turned back toward downtown Swanton.

"A lovely choice. But fair warning, it's longer that way," I said.

Adam shrugged. "Doesn't look like we're going to Montreal. Might as well take the scenic route."

"Islands it is."

The ride was a little prettier, following the Mississquoi River, through a national wildlife refuge. The first 'island,' Alburg, was actually a headland that jutted down from Canada. As we turned south again on Route 2, signs reiterated what we'd already seen advertised on I-89—the border crossings here were already closed, both to Canada and to New York state. In fact, Route 2 thataway was barricaded off with the orange sawhorses I was suddenly growing very tired of.

"I think there's an ark up there," Adam murmured.

78

End Game

I looked back over my shoulder, trying to see what would make him think so. "Seems like a good place for one. I guess."

He gave me a quick glance and a smile. "It's the housing along the road. Every place we've passed seems to have new construction or renovations, fresh paint, new outbuildings. Have you seen new construction anywhere else on this trip?"

"No," I agreed, looking at the rare buildings with fresh eyes as we passed them. "I guess I always thought of an ark as being closed in from the atmosphere."

He nodded. "The main facilities would be sealed. But outside the ark they'd have a military and agricultural buffer zone. Sort of like farm villages scattered around a medieval castle. They can go out to tend the fields and fight off any attackers, and take refuge part-time inside the ark if the air is bad. Or if they're injured, or put their children inside the ark for safety, and so on."

"Serfs. Soldiers, volunteering to be peasants?"

Adam nodded slowly. "It's their way into an ark. Sort of."

I wasn't sure whether to be irate at the idea of ark-serfs, or annoyed that I'd never heard of this job opportunity. Not that I had any experience soldiering. I'd never even fired a gun. "Is that how it is with your ark?" My voice betrayed a touch of the irate.

"No. My ark is... different."

I didn't get to follow up this intriguing comment right away.

Adam stopped the car just before the Route 2 bridge across to the next island, North Hero. Four men in Army camouflage fatigues with helmets, goggles, and submachine guns stood blocking the road.

A sign to the right read Albert Dunes State Park. Behind it stretched a long line of RV's. We'd found the rest of the gran caravan.

-o-

We were taken to their immediate leader in Adam's own car. The distance was an easy walk, but the guard grabbed the chance to drive the Tesla. His sidekick enjoyed simply sitting in one, though he only got to sit backwards and point a gun at us in the back seat. The guys were still in a grand mood as they marched away after delivering us, thumping each other on the back and joking around. They looked to be maybe 30 years old, maybe less.

The leader had emerged from an RV when they knocked for him. He was maybe 45, pleasantly handsome, lean and square-faced, with a shaggy brown mane and large glasses, wearing a light blue hospital scrub top over thick unbleached thermal shirt, paired with blue jeans and hiking boots. He took our keys and put them in his pocket with a shrug.

"Come in, come in!" He invited cheerfully, in a heavy French accent. "We get so few visitors in Alburg! Because Alburg is evacuated." He waved apologetically about this inconvenient state of affairs. "Jean-Claude Alarie, of *Médecins Sans Frontières*. From France. And you are?"

"Adam Lacey, an engineer from Connecticut, and my friend Dee Baker, a programmer. We're here as tourists. We had hoped to visit Montreal today. Before the border closed."

"Ah!" Jean-Claude laughed out loud at this great joke. "Yes! Not a good day for that, may be?"

"May be," I agreed, with a smile and a bow. Adam smiled stiffly as well.

"And what are you an engineer of, Adam Lacey, may I ask?"

"Marine engineer," Adam replied.

If so, this was news to me. If not, I hoped he was a good liar.

"And Dee Baker? What do you program?"

"Just websites," I demurred. True enough.

"Well, welcome to my modest clinic and home," he said.

He waved expansively around the beat up old RV. Another wave bid us be seated in the tiny galley behind the front seats. The galley's small cabinets overflowed with bandages and medical paraphernalia, with extra storage crates stacked around the door as well. Behind this were triple decker bunk cots, lining the sides all the way to the back of the vehicle, plus a small privy at the rear, all empty at present. There were more crates and a collection of picnic tables outside, under a cheerful pink striped awning larger than the interior of the RV. I didn't spot any red cross logo.

"Would you like some wine? I hope you're not hungry. I'm sorry, our food stocks are low." Jean-Claude passed out fresh disposable plastic cups and grabbed a jug of wine.

"We had bread and cheese in the car," I assured him.

"How wonderful! I love some, thank you!"

Smiling crookedly, I went back to the car and retrieved some food.

When I got back, Jean-Claude filled me in on what I'd missed. "I was just telling Adam Lacey, I am not the 'leader.' The men at the bridge, they are jokers. No, I am just a doctor with the gran caravan. I am with them only a few weeks."

"You have no patients today," Adam observed.

"No," Jean-Claude agreed solemnly. "They go to demonstrate at the border. Where you saw them. Now I wait for them to come back. Maybe some."

"What is their goal?" asked Adam. "We'd heard of the gran caravans, but thought it was just a myth."

"No myth. Just old people, sick people, their families. You see we are not all old. We travel, enjoy freedom and companionship. Many wait to die. There is no medical care for them. If they go to the American doctor, he tells them they are old, and old people die. And he gives them this." He scrounged in a drawer and tossed a large white prescription bottle to Adam.

Adam passed it to me after he read it in silence. It was oxycontin, an opiate. The instructions said to take 1 every 6 hours for pain, 20 for painless death. The bottle held 50 pills.

"You may keep that," Jean-Claude invited. "We have many."

"Thank you," I said, and put it in my bag. Adam looked a bit scandalized at this. I shrugged in response. Oxy was a good hoardable. It might have trade value.

I got the feeling Jean-Claude missed nothing in that exchange.

"But what do they hope for by attacking the Canadian border?" asked Adam doggedly.

"Hope? Ah. Some will be injured, and taken to Canadian hospitals. Some will die, and say a glorious '*fuck you!*' on the way out, eh?"

'Eh', indeed. Jean-Claude claimed to be French, but I wondered if he was really French Canadian. If I were the Canadian government, I'd certainly want to keep an eye out south of the border. And gran caravans travelled. As we'd seen, nearly everyone else had already learned not to travel, and we were learning fast.

Adam resigned himself to not getting any better answer. I suspected it was actually the truth. Pointless as it seemed, there were few better points available.

I smiled. "And what have you seen, on the gran caravan's travels, Jean-Claude?"

"Ah, many trees," he returned with a smile.

"And are we free to go?"

"Where do you go?"

"We need to return to Burlington to recharge my car," Adam replied. "Then back home, to Connecticut."

"This should be no problem," Jean-Claude said. "After dark. At the moment, we like the roads empty. Mm, then we move. Maybe midnight when you go. So relax! Have more wine."

So we drank and made merry. Jean-Claude regaled us with some tales, and I believed none of them. Eventually an elderly patient came in who required Jean-Claude's attention. He suggested we take a walk down the island to admire the dunes of Albert Dunes State Park.

Before we made it far, I asked Adam to wait for me. I ran back to the Jean-Claude's RV to leave him my card. I scribbled a web address, login and password on the back, to the unadulterated satellite feeds, though I didn't explain what they were. It seemed low-risk. He could use the information. It was credible enough that he could have gotten such access through other connections, without it coming from me. And it might be interesting, to hear from him, and maybe where this caravan went.

It did feel peculiar, trusting a complete stranger I knew wasn't on the level, when I wouldn't have shared that access with Adam, or Zack. I'd trust them to sleep with them, but not to share a web address. I didn't know what these nomads really hoped to accomplish, but earnestly wished them luck at it. How screwy is that.

Back with Adam, we didn't find any dunes. I doubt anything I'd call a 'dune' exists on Lake Champlain. But I could be wrong. The lake shore was pretty, with endless evergreens marching up as close to the water as people allowed.

We saw plenty of new-made gypsies along the way, out enjoying the last of the sunny afternoon. Most of them seemed to be age 60 and up. They enjoyed robust good health for all I could tell. Perhaps they piled all the infirm into their strike forces.

But there were also younger families, and children out playing between the RV's. A very few middle-aged men and women had communal cook fires going. Some kids played a giant card game. I remembered that, in the seemingly endless days of childhood summer vacation. We'd get a bunch of kids together when it rained, under an awning or in a tent, and played card games. I'd even done it camping with my family, in sites like this.

I smiled and waved at each group. They nodded and turned away. Jean-Claude was the only one who wanted to talk to us.

We reached the southern beach near sunset. We'd left the gran caravan behind, and had the beach all to ourselves. The orange orb of sun slanted slowly into the mists of the Adirondacks in upstate New York across the lake, and a near-full moon was already rising in the southeast. We rolled our jeans up to our knees and waded. The water was chilly, but not bad. It held the summer warmth still. In the evening stillness, the smooth pewter lake reflected the sunset and moonlight like glass.

I gazed out at the view transfixed, cold water lapping quietly on my calves, and muddy sand squishing between my toes.

Adam came up behind me and wrapped his arms around my waist. He whispered tickling in my ear, "Sorry about the sorbet. Missing Montreal."

"Well," I murmured, "I think we found a romantic spot anyway." He kissed me long and deep there in the water, then drew me up onto the beach. Despite the abandoned beach and gathering dark, we played at being a bit discreet. The kids in the caravan were still in mind if not in view. He stood between me and the land as he unhooked my bra and shimmied my layered shirts up to my shoulders. It was warm for November, sure, but cold for bare nipples, providing powerful contrast to his hot mouth.

The front of his jeans faced the lake. I soon got revenge.

It didn't take long to trip each other down onto the sand and forget all about those kids in the caravan. It was dark enough that the stars were coming out, anyway.

Chapter 8

Interesting fact: The roots of the word 'disaster' are 'anti stars,' or an ill-starred event.

"I was right about you," Adam said in the dark.

We walked cautiously up the middle of the road, me folded in Adam's arm for warmth, back to Jean-Claude and the car. The Milky Way was a brilliant swath above us, and the moon fairly bright. This was good, since there were zero man-made lights visible. There's only so much a phone can do, used as a flashlight. I loved it. Of all the recent changes in the world, my favorite was giving the night back to nature and the stars.

In other words, my mind was out there in the woods and the galaxy instead of with Adam. "Hmm?"

"What I said before, why I wanted to take you to Montreal. Because you'd still see it fresh, and enjoy it, and laugh."

A slow smile took over my face invisibly in the dark. "That was about the nicest compliment I've ever received," I admitted softly. "You have a real gift. You could twist women around your pinkie with a gift like that."

"No, I don't," Adam chuckled. "I'm an engineer. I was just telling you straight, what I thought. Don't start expecting poetry out of me, alright?"

"Deal."

"But all this is exactly what I meant. Our romantic getaway to Montreal was waylaid by crazed and armed senior citizens. Gunfire erupted and we fled for our lives. Fleeing from the fire into the frying pan, we're taken captive by armed men—"

"It wasn't that bad, Adam. I kinda enjoyed Jean-Claude."

"Exactly! You never whined, never lost your head, smiled and made friends with a zealot French doctor. And as for our romantic evening, well. I think Montreal would have been a shallow cliché compared to the evening we've had."

"I don't believe you. You couldn't be this good at giving compliments without a lot of practice. You just topped your previous compliment. I have a new best compliment ever. Now I'm scrambling to come up with anything to match it, you know? The best I've got is, 'You sure know how to show a girl a good time.' "

Adam cracked up laughing. It had been a stressful afternoon. He laughed so hard tears came, glistening in the starlight. "You're good," he finally managed. "Did I mention your sense of humor?"

"Funny, people often mention my sense of humor. They call it 'dark.' Speaking of dark, are we lost?"

"We should have reached the caravan by now," Adam agreed. There were no looming black humps of RV's anywhere. "But there was only the one road, and we're still on it. How could we be lost?"

Eventually the park road we were on met Route 2 at the bridge, where the armed guards waylaid our car. They and the whole gran caravan were gone. So far as we could tell, we had the entire U.S. Alburg promontory to ourselves.

Adam was sure the 'jokers' had stolen the car and taken it with them. I insisted Jean-Claude wouldn't have let them. And at any rate, I wasn't willing to cross the bridge to the next island until we'd searched here by daylight. I won the debate. We backtracked and eventually found the Tesla, keys in the ignition.

Clouds stole over the gorgeous skies, houses were dark, and there was virtually no traffic on the roads. It wasn't all that far, but it took hours on the unfamiliar dark back roads to reach Burlington. We felt only slightly bad waking the landlady at the B&B, it being late winter dawn by the time we reached it.

End Game

She still had no other guests. But we took only the one room to crash in this time. She was kind enough to serve us a big Sunday brunch at 2 p.m. when we got up.

We asked what she'd heard on the news, from the armed conflict on the border. She answered slowly that there was nothing on the news about that. But a lot of reservists left the day before. She thought they were National Guard reserves, but she wasn't sure, now that she thought about it. They didn't have uniforms, just footlockers. She knew some of them were veterans. She'd turned on the news hoping to hear what was going on with that. But instead the news reported that the border closing to Canada was going exceptionally well. So well that they'd moved up the date and closed it Saturday.

She'd wondered what had become of us, but assumed they'd just turned us back at the border, and we'd gone home to Connecticut. Where had we spent the night, anyway?

I might have invented a fairy tale at this question. The B&B lady wasn't important enough to me to risk defying the Calm Act by spreading public unrest. But Adam earnestly told her the truth.

I'm not sure she believed him. She looked concerned and excused herself. I heard her making several tense phone calls from her office. Apparently that didn't help. Her gracious smile of Friday was replaced by a pinched and haunted ghost of a smile, as we checked out and said our good-byes.

We never did wear our steampunk outfits that weekend. We agreed jeans were more comfortable for an interstate drive. We were past each other's costumes by then anyway.

I'd love to say that it was an uneventful drive back to Connecticut. But we got detoured off I-89 twice on the way down to I-91. One of those times we got lost in the dark empty back roads. Neither detour came with any explanation. Then a hellish thunderstorm overtook us in Massachusetts. We sat out part of it under an overpass for shelter, with St. Elmo's Fire dancing all over the car and our hair standing up from the static. I still wasn't sure about our part of Connecticut, but Massachusetts did have tornado sirens. We heard some. The radio news out of Springfield didn't even admit there was a thunderstorm.

Between the Vermont detours and Massachusetts electrical effects, we needed another Connecticut detour to find a charging station for the car. And had to spend a couple hours napping in the car after midnight waiting for that to finish.

Adam proved himself a gentleman extraordinaire. He didn't wake me from that nap until we arrived at my house. We agreed to deal with my overweight battery some other time, gave each other a quick peck good-night, and continued to our respective beds to catch a couple more hours sleep before our respective Monday morning alarm clocks rang.

Despite the undeniably wonderful romantic weekend, rich with learning opportunities and Adam's delicious company, I never wanted to travel again in my life.

-o-

Monday sucked.

The section manager had decreed that work weeks should begin all bright-eyed and bushy-tailed with a 9 a.m. section meeting by video, especially after holiday weekends. This was to counteract that distinct programmer tendency toward clock drift. Programmers, over-endowed with the ability to concentrate on something that enthralls them, tend to let the clock slide an hour or two later every day unless something with authority intervenes.

Whose lame idea was this? Oh, yeah. Mine.

With about ten hours of sleep and four hair-raising adventures in the past two days, I was not at my best getting the gang back on task that morning. My material didn't help. They were unanimously outraged when I told them that Connor was fired. Well, except for our intern Shelley, who was red-eyed, morose, and silently self-absorbed. I made a note to call her later.

They didn't buy the idea that ark interviews would resume after the New Year. If I'd been a little more with it that morning, I would have realized those two bits of news shouldn't have been served up at the same meeting.

When I explained our new assignment to do understanding-the-crazy-weather interactives, our graphic designer flat-out asked me if we'd be telling the truth or lying. I assured them that we would do our best to give good actionable information. And I did have the facts available. And I'd be handling the censors for the team.

It's a bright group. And I have no poker face at all. They had no trouble unravelling that circumlocution.

"You'll *be* the fucking censor for the team, you mean," challenged Will, the graphics designer again.

That went a little too far. God, I hated it when they did that. "Will, I think you and I need to talk one on one after the meeting. Because I don't care to be spoken to that way." I waited him out several seconds, staring directly into the video camera. Fortunately he nodded and backed down. My to-call list of awkward conversations grew to three.

They nearly mutinied when I asked who wanted to volunteer to take over Connor's job and implement the weather API.

"Guys!" I interrupted, hand held up. They angrily muttered to a stop. "Just think about it. There are skills to gain. Good work to do. I'm not threatening your firstborn. We'll talk tomorrow in Stamford." I considered a cheerful, upbeat close to the meeting. I couldn't think of any. I gave up and just signed off.

Managing Will's ego took a half hour and another cup of coffee. Shelley's tale of woe made me really regret ever asking.

It sounded like her poor lonely mother was coming unhinged and taking it out on Shelley.

The third phone call was the worst. I called Connor's apartment to check up on him. His mother answered and accused me of killing her baby boy. She was there packing up his things. He committed suicide on Thanksgiving Day. He overdosed on oxycontin. His suicide note mentioned that he'd been fired.

There wasn't a damned thing I could do about it except let this poor woman hurl all her pain and invective and abuse on me.

The fourth phone call was to Mangal because I was too upset to work, and I didn't think I ought to tell Dan, because Dan would think it was all his fault that Connor killed himself.

The fifth phone call was from Dan, because Mangal thought he needed to know.

Not a hell of a lot of work got done that Monday in my section. Whose job was it to make sure we were productive? Oh, yeah. Mine.

-o-

Zack arrived on my doorstep just before 6:00.

"Ah! You should call first. I just got out of the shower," I said apologetically, waving him in. I was dressed in the next best thing to pajamas, a baggy sweatshirt and loose thin cargo pants.

"I like it," he said with a grin. He handed me a plate piled with Thanksgiving dinner. Once my hands were full he ducked in for a peck of a kiss.

If a kiss is light enough, it isn't entirely obvious that you don't return it.

"Thank you. This looks incredible." I stared at the plate. I hadn't thought what to do about Zack yet. I put the plate into the refrigerator while Zack settled into a recliner in the living room.

Ethically, I was on safe ground doing whatever I wanted with Adam or Zack. No commitments had been made. Emotionally, I was pretty sure that argument didn't hold water.

I returned to curl up on the couch next to his recliner.

"So how was Montreal?" he asked eagerly.

Zack was such a guarded guy, and his face was wide open tonight. I felt like a cad. But I launched into telling him about my adventures.

" 'Adam,' " he interrupted. "Another old friend?"

"Not exactly. Actually I met him about the same time I met you."

"Ah." Yes, that eager wide open face shut like a clamshell.

"Zack…" I tilted my head away from him. "Adam and I joked about Montreal when we met, how it would be great to see it before the borders closed." My head tilted toward Zack. "And then I went mushrooming with you." Head tilted away. "And then he said, let's do it." Head back toward Zack. "I almost said no, because I had such a great dinner with you."

Zack stopped my head bobbing with a firm hand on my crown. "Yeah, I get it." He sat back and crossed his legs. Elbows on chair arms, fingers interleaved, thumbs flicking at each other tensely. "So. How was Montreal?"

I guess he wanted to know about Montreal more than he wanted to storm out in a huff. So I told him about the gran caravan at the border, and then getting waylaid by it again near Albert Dunes State Park. His tense thumb-flicking slowed and stopped, as he became riveted by the adventure.

"Lucky guy," he murmured, when I reached the empty beach.

"What?" I accidentally caught his eye.

Zack deliberately held my eye in a strong cool blue challenge. "A lot more romantic than Montreal, for you. Wish I'd been there with you."

I stared back like a deer caught in headlights. I didn't know what to say. I dropped my eyes.

"So how long did the gran caravan keep you?" he prompted.

I resumed the story, quickly summarizing the long road back to Connecticut.

"Wow," Zack said at the end. He thought a few moments, then added, "A shame you didn't make any contacts in the gran caravan. I'd love to hear what they see going forward."

"Oh. Actually I did. I exchanged contact info with the 'French' doctor."

After work, when I unpacked from the weekend, I found a note from Dr. Jean-Claude Alarie in my luggage. "Let's keep in touch!" He included several websites, with logins and passwords, a cell phone number, and email addresses. One of them was Canadian.

"Yeah, it'll be interesting to see what comes of that."

"Really." Zack was staring at me again, thoughtfully.

I wished he'd stop that. It was unnerving. Was he angry? Jilted? Laying counterclaim? Calculating something else? What?

I sighed. "Zack, it's been a hell of a day." I don't know why he didn't just leave. Instead, he made gentle interrogative noises and drew the story of my day and Connor's suicide out of me, too. I lost it recounting how his mother had screamed at me and said I'd murdered her son.

Zack teleported to the couch and held me while I cried it all out. He didn't tell me it was all OK, or not my fault, or any of those other inane things people say to tell you there's nothing to cry about when you're bawling. Instead he told me to cry it out and let it go. He stroked my back slowly and steadily and just held me. Fortunately there were tissues on the end-table. I went through a wad of them.

"Thank you," I mumbled eventually. "Sorry. I needed that."

"You're tough," Zack replied softly. "We're rooted in Connecticut granite, you and I, Dee Baker."

In the wiped-out calm after a hard cry, that simply seemed true, to me. "Yeah."

I can't help wondering what that might have led to, if the house phone hadn't rung. I let it go to voicemail. But it was Adam. I lunged for the phone before he got any more explicit over the answering machine speaker.

"Yeah... yeah... Yeah, I need to call you back. Someone's over right now. Yeah. Bye."

"Adam," Zack echoed stonily.

Yeah, that being rooted in Connecticut granite thing was working real well, for Zack and me both right now.

"Zack... Look, I wouldn't blame you for storming out the door. But I'm wiped out and I haven't eaten dinner yet. I wanna try this wild turkey. You wanna split the wild turkey?"

"Well, thank you. No. I don't need to storm out. But I think I should go."

At the door, he enfolded me in a friendly hug and pecked a kiss on the top of my head. "You're alright, Dee Baker."

"Thank you," I mumbled into his shoulder. His strong hug felt good, no demands, just strength and comfort. It's a shame we ever had to talk. We understood each other so well when we didn't say anything.

And the doorbell rang. So I opened the door.

"Alex! Hi, how are you? Zack Harkonnen, this is my neighbor Alex. Montoya, isn't it?"

Alex hugged in on himself in his hoodie sweatshirt. "I'm hungry," he blurted out. "Can I come in?"

"Of course," I said. I looked at Zack blankly. Zack took one look out the door and closed it. He followed Alex into the dining end of the kitchen. I didn't have a separate dining room. And that's just who Zack was. Emotional context be damned, he wasn't going to leave in the face of a possible emergency. He made himself comfortable at the table and made sure Alex did the same.

"Alex, I was just about to have Thanksgiving leftovers that Zack brought me. Shall I split them three ways?" Zack shook his head to indicate none for him. "Alex, Zack caught this wild turkey as a baby and raised it for Thanksgiving."

That was the perfect ice-breaker. The guys entertained each other. I softened some butter and set the table, with bread and three settings of bread plates and water. Then I carefully microwaved the leftovers, to get the relative temperatures right and not spoil any of the textures. Zack watched this with interest.

Alex got wrapped up in his own misery when the conversation lapsed. So Zack kept it going, mostly on farm animals, since Alex seemed to brighten at animals.

"Here we go," I said, setting two full plates before us. Alex had already inhaled three slices of buttered bread. That allowed him to slow down and appreciate the Thanksgiving plate.

"This is fantastic, Zack," I said, and I meant it. "The turkey is really moist. I would have thought it would be tougher and drier than the supermarket birds."

"Thanks. Yeah, free-range is tougher, so I brined it."

"I need to get your recipe for that. And I think I recognize the mushrooms in this stuffing. Alex, Zack is a master mushroom hunter." That successfully got the guys talking again while I enjoyed the sumptuous bits of pure locally grown and made traditional Thanksgiving. Occasionally I interjected things like, "This succotash is divine." Zack's sister froze the corn, zucchini, peppers, and lima beans in summer, and seasoned them in a butter sauce after cooking. Tricky, and delicious.

I was delightedly full after half of what Zack brought. Alex wiped his plate clean and slathered another slice of bread with butter. "Oh! I forgot the pie." I'd separated that out to defrost but serve cold. I handed half the pie to Alex.

"Sure you don't want to split mine, Zack?"

"I'm good," he assured me with a smile.

End Game

Alex buttered yet another slice of bread after the sliver of pie. Teenaged boys sure can eat.

"So, Alex? I guess your Mom hasn't come back?"

He paused in his chewing, then shook his head no vigorously. He turtled down toward his plate.

"How long has she been gone now?"

He shrugged. I left the question hanging in the air to be answered. "Couple weeks."

"Did she say anything about where she was going?"

"Um, she said she was going to the doctor. I was at school. Before they closed the school."

I blinked. "They closed the schools?"

Zack nodded. "Three weeks ago. They couldn't pay the teachers."

"Some of the teachers tried to keep it going anyway," Alex offered. "But the police came and kicked us out."

So it had been at least three weeks, maybe four. "Wow, that leaves you with a lot of free time on your hands, doesn't it? Lot of video games?"

Alex grinned shyly and nodded.

"Lot of friends over?"

"Nah... I didn't... I was afraid they'd..." After a couple false starts he brought out in a rush, "You're not going to turn me in, are you?" He sat looking at me with huge terrified eyes.

I steepled my fingers judiciously. "Turn you into what, I wonder? A frog ? A newt?" I confided to Zack, as an aside, "I don't actually know what a newt looks like."

"Well," Zack replied reasonably, "you can't very well turn him into a newt, if you don't know what a newt looks like."

Alex giggled in spite of himself. "I like rabbits," he suggested shyly.

"And you'd make a fine rabbit," I assured him. Satisfied that the tone had lightened, I observed, "Alex, if the schools aren't even open, I'm not sure who I'd turn you in *to*. You're

95

safe and warm and fed now. We can make sure you stay that way. Let's play it by ear for a while. OK? See how it goes."

"Friends are important," Zack interjected. "I think you should see your friends again. If their parents give you any trouble, just tell them Dee and I are looking out for you while your Mom's away."

I nodded. "Just tell them to talk to one of us. Want to sleep over here tonight?"

"No, I got the pets and stuff." He rose to flee, then turned back. "Could I... come back for breakfast?"

I smiled at him. "See you then. No earlier than 8:30, OK?" I added to his receding back.

"Really?" said Zack. "You're not up until 8:30?"

"I start work at 9:00," I said quellingly. "It's a very short commute." I pointed to the room I used as my office. That's the one the architect intended as a dining room.

He snorted. At long last, I successfully saw him out the door.

After a bit, I called Adam. I lacked any desire to tell him how my day went. I gathered he wasn't free to discuss much of his day. We set a date for Wednesday evening for him to deliver my monster battery from Burlington, and help me install it.

The conversation was light and easy. We were both dead tired. So we encouraged each other to go to bed early and hung up soon.

I sat there staring at the phone afterwards. Comparing Zack and Adam seemed monstrously unfair. Also impossible, because events and our reactions to them seemed to dominate how I knew them. Though, if things kept up like this, maybe their reactions to life's little challenges were key.

But they were both awfully good in that respect. Adam had an edge in following my lead. Zack seemed more likely to present a lead I'd follow.

After the previous date I had with Zack, I thought Adam

didn't stand a chance. Then after the weekend I had with Adam, I thought Zack didn't stand a chance, due to sheer shared experience. Zack disabused me of that notion real quick tonight, though.

I liked them both. Which I already knew before this little bout of introspection. Introspection wasn't my strong suit. I gave it up and went to bed.

Chapter 9

Interesting fact: Not all boundaries were along previous state lines. The New York City northern boundary ran from halfway up Connecticut, west to the point where Pennsylvania, New Jersey, and New York states met. Its southern boundary nearly bisected New Jersey across its waist, running from Trenton to the Jersey shore south of Asbury Park. Those boundaries were built from interstate highways, I-84 in the north, and I-195 to the south. This was explained as extra epidemiology control for the most densely populated corner of America.

Adam and I were see-sawing my battery out of his car when Zack emerged from Alex's house. "Gah," I muttered.

Adam lifted an eyebrow. "Problem?"

"Um, kinda had first dates with you and him the same week," I said hurriedly, before Zack reached earshot. He headed straight for us.

Thankfully, Adam looked amused.

"Hey, Dee," called Zack. He strode up to Adam and held out his hand to shake. The guys introduced themselves, eye on each other instead of me. Then he offered, "Need a hand?"

"Sure!" decided Adam.

Zack grabbed my corner. "Motherf–! What's this made of, gold?"

"Real grateful for the help, Zack," I assured him. "It's too heavy for me."

Adam was less impish and more eager for the help. I mostly held my garden wagon steady while the engineer and the muscle

99

figured out how to get the battery onto it. Adam had already prepped the installation spot indoors with wiring.

They worked surprisingly well together. I was impressed at the firewood-and-towel roller system they devised to get the battery through the door from the garage without breaking wallboard or doorframe. And Adam was smart enough from the first not to try to mount the hefty battery on anything but the floor. It was only anchored to the wall; the floor took its weight.

They shook hands and slapped each other on the back once the battery was in place. Zack wiped sweat off his brow despite the freezing cold. The muscle differential between the guys didn't seem to bother them. Adam respected Zack's greater strength. Though Zack needled Adam a bit on strength, he also recognized Adam's planning would have allowed him to accomplish all this with only me for assistance, if Zack hadn't come along.

I wandered into the kitchen to rustle up a round of beer, while Adam verified the electrical connections, and that the new battery was charging properly in series with the old one. Zack watched with interest.

"Zack? Come here a minute?" I called from the kitchen. When he arrived, I thrust a beer into his hand, and asked, "What's up with Alex?"

"Had some chores I wanted to hire him for. Trying to get him out of the house. I know you're busy during the day, Dee. But it's not good for him to just hide in there playing video games."

"OK. Thank you. But the kid just lost his mother, Zack. He only came out of hiding two days ago. I've barely got him eating out of my hand yet."

Zack shrugged. "A guy's got to earn his keep, Dee. I just thought, maybe, you could be the warm and supportive backing. And I could kick his butt into action a bit. Boys that age respond well to a man ordering them around."

"Alright. Thank you. What's he doing for you?"

"Oh, kind of a neighborhood survey. You've got empty houses here, and so do I. So, who's left?"

My eyes narrowed. "You're canvassing for landscaping clients?"

"Call it a civic activity. I'm coordinating with the RTM."

The Representative Town Meeting—the RTM—was the local equivalent of a town council. Members represented their sections of town.

"The RTM that closed the schools?" I asked sourly.

"They closed the schools?" Adam asked in surprise, wandering in. I handed him a beer and he parked himself across the table from Zack.

"I guess neither of you follow local politics," Zack observed. "Anyway, Dee, I had something for you, too. You know this town better than I do. If you were setting up a food cache, where would you put it?"

"A food cache! Personal, or a big one?"

"Big one. You been in a supermarket lately?"

"Yeah..."

"I haven't," said Adam.

"It's getting rough," I told him. "And winter's coming. They're running out of the staples, and pretty soon fresh produce and meat."

I grabbed an old tablet I used to control the picture-window sized display in the living room. The guys wandered out to watch.

"I think," I said, "the middle of the marsh." I brought up a good satellite photo and centered it where I wanted it. "You are here," I dropped a marker. "And right here is an old World War II bunker."

"Why?" asked Zack.

"Well, there aren't any roads to there, and it's surrounded

by marsh. No one's going to find it by accident. Even if they know where it is, it's hard to reach, hard to attack, and easy to defend. Wasn't that what you wanted?"

"No, that's great, it looks defensible. I meant, why is there a bunker there?"

All three of us contemplated this hummock of hill, the water's end of the next ridge west of mine. It lay next to an abandoned railway track, in the middle of a vast marsh, a good half mile from the sea.

"Rampant paranoia?" suggested Adam. We considered the map a bit longer. "Zoom out a bit," he suggested. "Do you know of any other bunkers like this?"

I dropped a few more markers. "Maybe… here? And here. And there? Those are all the ones I know."

"You're right," said Zack. "Rampant paranoia. It's a line of bunkers running up the coast."

I shrugged. "Maybe, maybe not. There's old industrial… stuff… here. Trap rock quarry. Reservoir. One of these high points is called Beacon Hill and another Watch Hill, which probably meant something some other century. Those other bunkers connect up to New Haven harbor, and its fuel oil drums. One of the librarians might know, but I don't." I shrugged again. "Anyway, if I were hiding a cache, that might be good."

"What about this island? Or the headland?" Zack suggested. Zoomed out to see the other bunkers, the display now included the uneven shoreline, full of stony inlets, islands, headlands, rivers, and marshes.

"No. If you had to pick a headland it would be that one, not this one. You can't tell because of all the trees in the photo, but this one is densely populated. That one's mostly a wildlife sanctuary, with a marshy lagoon. But still, kids are always ripping off the islands and the points. Even when they're not crowded, they're rich. They're well worth ripping off. And they make great party pads."

Adam snorted rueful agreement. He owned just that sort of property, a break-in Mecca for partying teenagers.

"The islands are a little harder to reach and easier to defend, but then you need a boat to get food on and off the island. Over here in the marsh, there's actually a nice wide paved path starting here, with a little parking lot that's always empty." I marked it. "You're under tree cover the whole way to the bunker. There's a nice overlook about here to watch a great white heron's nest."

Zack laughed. "And that's why there's a path?"

"I have no idea why they paved the path," I replied. "It was dirt when I was a kid. I've never seen anyone else there. Though I know the guy who built the heron perch. He was a few years ahead of me in school."

"Raspberries all through there, I bet," said Zack, grinning.

"You know it," I agreed. "Blueberries, too. Deer. Heron. Great crabbing in the marsh."

Zack nodded, smiling appreciation. "I'll have to check it out. Thank you."

"You're welcome." I powered off the displays.

"So, Zack," Adam interjected. "We had dinner plans tonight we ought to get to. So… Thanks so much, man, for helping out with the battery. That would have taken us twice as long without you." He offered a manly handshake.

"Yeah, thanks, Zack. And thanks for helping with Alex," I chimed in. I relieved him of his empty beer bottle and steered him toward the front door. "And I'll think about the, um, cache thing. There might be some other spots. Of course, you want more than one."

Zack's head whipped around toward me. "Yes. Yes, you're right. More than one would be good." Maybe he hadn't considered that. Two egg baskets are better than one, after all.

"Maybe even a line of them running up the coast. In

rampant paranoia," Adam chimed in cheerily. Zack laughed pro forma.

We finally got him out the door.

Adam wandered back toward his handiwork on the battery, but then leaned up against the wall and looked at me. "So, I'm not sure how to ask this."

"Have I slept with him?"

He grinned crookedly. "That was the question, yeah."

"No." I pulled off my grubby sweatshirt and tossed it on the couch. This showed off the pink striped steampunk corset beneath. "I haven't."

Adam smiled and took a stroll around me to examine the corset. He drew a finger down a lace side insert to rest on the jeans waistband. "And you make these?"

"I do. There's a lot of piece work. Like here." I traced the seaming on the cup nearest his hand. "I try to match the stripes neatly."

He raised the cup to examine it more closely. "Yes, it's beautiful work. And these grommets are so tidy down the front." He twanged the strings tying the grommets together down the front.

We ate later.

-o-

I was just getting used to Alex when Mangal moved in next door, the following weekend.

"Dee!" Mangal launched in when I answered his video call. "You said Alex is finding plenty of vacant houses near you."

"Yes?"

"And is there violence?"

"Violence! No. Mangal, what's going on?"

"There's this survivalist group. They grabbed Shanti outside the supermarket today and flung her to the ground." Shanti was Mangal's wife. "They kicked her in the ribs, saying how all

Muslims should die. They stole all the food she bought. Right in front of the children in the shopping cart. A cop was just standing there. He turned his back on her. The supermarket guards did nothing. This was a crowded parking lot. No one helped her. They just looked away."

"Oh, my God. Is Shanti alright?"

"She's very upset. The bruises will heal. But we don't feel safe here. She wants to pack up the car and leave right this minute. She's putting food in the car right now."

"Wow. Yes, the house next door with the swimming pool is empty. Looks like they left all their furniture. I pay the utilities so the pipes don't freeze. I could get a group together and come help you pack?"

"No, I'll get the community here to help with that. If you could get the refrigerator running and the heat on and stuff like that?"

"Will do. Muslim, huh?"

"I don't know. We're brown, so it's OK to hurt us and steal from us. Maybe…"

For a Jain, that was a remarkably immoderate and judgmental statement. Picture Mahatma Gandhi dealing with thugs. Gandhi wasn't even a Jain. He was just inspired by them.

In the end, four households worth of Jains transplanted from Broomfield to my neighborhood. Alex selected houses for them. In retrospect, I imagine Zack helped him pick. Mangal and Shanti moved in next door that very day with their two preschoolers, and a very old man we just called 'Grandfather.' Grandfather wasn't too clear mentally, but Shanti insisted he was a great help with the children.

I called my state legislator to complain of hate crimes in Broomfield. At first she thought I was talking about our district and was shocked and eager to get right on it. But when I clarified it was Broomfield, she changed her tune. "Oh. Well, it's good that they got away from there. If they run into any trouble here, let me know."

No one was going to do anything about Broomfield. The local news, of course, said nothing. Who knows. Maybe in this case it was for the best. Stressed people latch onto weird ideas. I sure didn't want copy-cat hate crimes on defenseless women with small children.

The Jains soon hooked up with the local enclave of Nepalese Buddhists and assorted other minorities in the overwhelmingly white township. Alex, and probably Zack, placed them together for mutual support. Shanti's days were packed with community service. One day a week their home was packed with a community preschool, filled with an adorable rainbow of little kids. The eventual white kids looked as colorful as the rest, with their olive or white or speckled pink skins, red frizzy or brown wavy or pale yellow straight hair. It took a couple months for the school to expand beyond the first Jain and Nepalese kids, though.

But four days a week somebody else had Shanti's kids and she was free to pursue other projects. Her burning priority was that she wanted a community that had her back. So she was a whirlwind of helpfulness.

The best part of having Shanti next door was that procuring food was getting to be a time-consuming hassle. She processed her trauma in Broomfield by becoming a lead shopper for her family and friends. If there was bulk rice or flour or sugar or cabbage to be found anywhere in the New Haven area, Shanti found it. And she braved any crush of people to get it. She did get bruised a few more times. Grandfather came home once with a terrible gash to his forehead that needed stitches. She left him home after that. But she would not back down, or compromise her pacifist values. She charged back into the fray again and again with courtesy and respect for her fellow shoppers, no matter how they behaved.

It was a shame she wouldn't buy meat. But she was willing

to acquire dairy products and eggs for me, and that would do. She probably saved me a lot of money that way. Meat prices were skyrocketing.

Alex preferred the violent sorts of video games popular with boys his age. He kept the Jain camp and their Buddhist buddies at arm's length when they tried to share their values with him. He and Mangal especially became the most cautious of friends. Mangal was consistently courteous, even-tempered, and interested in Alex's activities. Alex kinda sidled around the edge of the room to avoid him when the topic of video games came up.

Alex longed to use my giant display for gaming. I made clear that wasn't going to happen.

But Alex and I cooperated with community cooking. Meaning, we cooked as Shanti directed us sometimes, and made extras as instructed. We rarely ate Shanti's cooking, though, because it was hotter than hell.

The net result was that Alex was no burden on me at all, just a young friend who was frequently around. Between Zack, Shanti, Mangal, and me, he was well looked after and encouraged. He came out of his shell regularly seeking food, and we put him to work. He tackled his work with a will. Pointed assignments led him to team up with other teens.

Alex was still sad about his Mom. He still insisted on living alone in his own house, with his guinea pigs and rabbits. But his self-esteem soared, and he seemed to be well-liked. I certainly liked him. He was good company.

I wasn't used to having so much company around. Aside from Mangal, the crowd respected my workday, though. Mangal often came over to beg a quieter place to work.

-o-

Our work assignments were aggravating as hell.

After a few days of paranoia, we realized there was no reason for Mangal and me to be shy about saying anything we wanted to each other in my office, about the classified materials we'd been given. Our story was that we shared staffing and workload and subbed in for each other, so we shared classified background files, and we stuck to that story. I don't know if anyone up the food chain would have agreed with us. Our boss Dan certainly wouldn't want to know. But no Secret Service types arrived to drag us away.

Mangal knew exactly where the borders were going. He had full satellite intel on how they were progressing. He had complete plans and schedules and even the military headcounts. He came up with suitably cheerful cartoony overlays showing the borders extending into place over time. His copywriter must have rewritten the explanatory blurbs a dozen times just for the northern section of the I-95 corridor, the Northeast. But every prototype got shot down by the censors.

With the weather interactives, I tried going for a strictly you-are-here approach, featuring only the strange weather events for the user's own local area. The prototypes and copywriting were approved when I submitted samples explaining familiar old weather patterns. What creates a thunderstorm. How hail forms. But new weather innovations like St. Elmo's Fire, ball lightning, the Dust Bowl dust storms, the hurricane and tornado seasons that were now twelve months long, the new and improved Alberta Clipper—all censored, redacted, or turned into lies by the censors.

"Our viewership asked for these things for a reason," I complained to Mangal one day. "If these interactives don't answer the user's questions, they're garbage."

"You're preaching to the choir again," Mangal replied with a sigh.

"But look, I tested these blurbs through Google Censor

yesterday. It passed," I said, loading it in again to demonstrate.

Calumet was a free plugin hosted by Google that virtually all social sites depended on these days to comply with the Calm Act. It conveniently encapsulated communications with the censorship web services provided by Homeland Security. Much to Google's annoyance, everyone called it Google Censor instead of Calumet. Google even ran an advertising campaign to explain and politely disown the utility. But that just cemented 'Google Censor' in everyone's minds.

"Hello. It's down," I said.

"What's down? Google Censor?" Mangal tried it himself.

Calumet is temporarily offline in your area.

Please try your post again tomorrow.

"Shit," said Mangal.

"You said a bad word," I observed mildly. He didn't like to do that.

"No, I've read about this on the hack sites. Google Censor goes down in an area when events are expected that they just don't want discussed. In any way."

We shared a look. We turned back to our keyboards and told our people to get home if they weren't home, and batten down the hatches. I couldn't reach Shelley, but figured she'd be alright. The interns didn't telecommute. I asked Dan to keep an eye out for her at the Stamford office, and have her check in by email.

"National Weather Service?" I asked.

Mangal checked. "It's partly cloudy today. With a 30% chance of showers later."

I snorted. It had been drizzling all day. "And the real National Weather Service?" As opposed to the censored one. Sometimes it was interesting to check both and see how they diverged.

"That was the real one. Checking real satellite… Nothing interesting."   •

"OK." I called Alex. He was at a friend's house helping with a carpentry project. I asked him to stay put for now, and promised to feed his furries for him.

Mangal called Shanti and told her something was wrong and he didn't know what. Shanti took the ball from there for everyone Mangal knew.

I checked on Zack. He was working on building the cache out in the marsh. I told him exactly what I knew—no clues so far except Google Censor down. "It could just be a network glitch," I said.

"No, thank you for telling me. I mean, yeah, it could be, but —I appreciate the head's up. We can wrap up here and head home."

"Any food stashed in there yet?"

"Not a crumb."

Last I called Adam. Not because he was less important, but because he was more likely to be somewhere safe. I was wrong.

"Hello, Dee! I am amazed. I haven't been able to get a single phone call out in the past hour. Everyone around me now is grabbing their phones, and yeah, failing to getting a signal. How did you get through?"

"Uh, magic pixie dust, you know," I replied randomly. "You're at the ark?"

"No. In fact. I was in Manhattan for a meeting. Now I'm walking along the railroad tracks just east of the New York line. The border closed very suddenly. I caught the last train out. Along with several thousand new friends. I have never seen a train that long on the New Haven line, not even the holiday trains. It was supposed to be an express to Greenwich. But they kicked us off at Port Chester and told us to walk to Greenwich station. Along the railroad tracks. They were quite specific on that point."

Port Chester was the last New York town on the train line, with Greenwich the first Connecticut stop. A river between them formed the state and town border.

"Is there an armed escort?"

"Yes, plenty of company. A lot less now, though. The railroad bridge across the river to Greenwich was interesting. I had ID proving Connecticut residency, a valid passport with proof of Ebola vaccination, and my security clearances. That got me expedited permission to cross the bridge. Most of the others—Wait, hang on."

Adam didn't muffle the phone, but I couldn't hear the other party to his side conversation well. Someone was yelling at him, but not from close by. "My girlfriend... I don't know, she called me... Absolutely, officer... Trooper, excuse me..."

"Dee, sorry about that. Me talking on the phone is causing unrest here. I'll call you when I make it home, OK?"

"Please. No matter how late, OK? Bye, Adam."

I turned to Mangal. "CDC and borders. Maybe Ebola."

"On it." I filled him in on what Adam said while his fingers flew on the keyboard.

Mangal was incensed. "If that was an emergency closure for quarantine, no one should have been allowed out."

"Adam had proof of Ebola immunization. It's not clear the rest of them are getting out," I said.

"Found it," said Mangal. "This can't be right. Looks like over 150 confirmed cases. All boroughs of New York, plus Hoboken, Newark, Hempstead on Long Island, all over. Why would they allow anyone into the city from Connecticut today?"

"When were the cases confirmed?"

Tap. Tap-tap. "Just last night, for the first one. A couple more before dawn, and then blam, most of these just since this morning. Another 50 or so cases added just since we've been looking." Mangal sat back. "Does that... make any sense?"

"Does seem odd." We contemplated that for a moment. "Do you doubt that it's really an Ebola outbreak?"

Mangal considered that. Unlike me, he'd been to the

pandemic areas in Africa, and was immunized. "Lifestyle makes it hard to catch here. Ebola is communicated through contact with an infected person's bodily fluids. That's hard to avoid in West Africa, but it's really unusual in New York. Well, for bystanders. First responders and hospital staff are more at risk. If they didn't realize quickly enough that's what they were dealing with, I suppose it could be Ebola."

I checked the borders status. All New York City borders were closed tight, over two weeks ahead of schedule. The remaining fragment of open border on the western edge of New England, between New York state and Massachusetts and the northern bit of Connecticut, appeared to be closing as fast as they could manage it. The Coast Guard was deployed in force along Long Island Sound. The Sound separated Connecticut and the 100-mile Long Island just south of us. Long Island hosted two of New York City's five boroughs, and perhaps six million other people. Other New York, Pennsylvania, and New Jersey borders seemed to be a mishmash of open and closed.

"Passing 500 confirmed cases," said Mangal. "A lot of these are at border checkpoints."

"How long does it take to verify Ebola?"

"Oh, it's pretty quick these days," he assured me. "They've had a lot of practice managing the situation in Africa. There's a 10-minute screening test with a low rate of false negatives. Once someone has a fever. Quite a few false positives." He sighed.

That was not a test you'd care to have a false positive on. In Africa, you'd immediately be thrown into an Ebola ward with active disease cases. If you didn't really have Ebola yet, you would soon.

I checked the incoming video news, stories UNC was submitting to the censors for approval. The first 'Breaking News' report was probably already self-censored. I pulled it up to watch. Rapidly developing story of Ebola outbreak in New York. Video of a crowded hospital ward in Brooklyn, caregivers in hazmat suits. Sudden border closings to prevent contagion. Rioting and trampling deaths in Grand Central Station and Penn Station. Commuters caught inside the city, while public transportation shut down. Video of a veritable army trudging down a pedestrian lane in the Holland Tunnel into New Jersey. A wide shot of a blocks-long line of commuters waiting to descend into the Tunnel. Authorities are urging citizens to—

The streaming video cut off and automatically loaded a revised story. Authorities closed all public transportation this afternoon in Greater New York due to a credible terrorist threat involving—

I don't know where they were going with that version. It cut off too quickly.

Next up, a very cheerful young woman, no backup video. Authorities have closed all public transportation in New York City. This is part of a dry run of the border closings planned on January first. Disaster preparedness drills will also be running throughout the metro area. Citizens are encouraged to stay home, and enjoy a day off. She smiled winningly. End of report.

"You've got to be kidding me."

Mangal pointed at the screen with thumb and forefinger, one of his less American gestures. "That doesn't accomplish anything."

"It explains hazmat suits, I guess," I said. "Keeps people calm. Maybe." I checked. "They broadcast that last version."

"It doesn't warn people what to do in response to an active disease threat," Mangal argued.

"You're preaching to the choir again," I sighed.

I called Alex and Zack back, and asked Alex to come home and stay home for the rest of the day. Zack I just told the official news report.

He snorted. "And you believe that?"

"No."

"That was a short answer," he observed.

"Yes."

"Alex?"

"Coming home. Now."

"...I see. Well, maybe I'll drop by."

I must have sighed too hard when we hung up.

"Problem?" inquired Mangal.

"I'm not very good at lying. And Zack is really good at reading me."

"Get better at it," Mangal advised. "Quickly."

In the end, I told Zack outdoors about my phone conversation with Adam at the Greenwich border, with a stress on the Ebola part. "But maybe I'm just overreacting," smile.

And I took a snapshot of the CDC confirmed cases map, added a more emphatic 'Ebola' label and circled the date and time. I compressed it, renamed the file ChristmasParty.png as though it were uncompressed, and sent it to Jean-Claude Alarie's Canadian email address, with a burbling note about how adorable my kids were at the caroling party last week. I'd mentioned to Jean-Claude that I didn't have children. I sent it to my friends in Asia as well, more securely by prearranged encodings.

"Give me a copy of that picture," Mangal asked.

Drat. I hadn't thought he was paying attention. We'd supposedly gotten back to work. I dropped the picture to him without it passing outside my local network. I know he encoded it far more thoroughly than I had, but I don't know who he sent it to.

Adam finally made it home six hours after I talked to him in Greenwich.

Chapter 10

Interesting fact: Alex's survey of homes in our end of Totoket turned up about 50% of homes abandoned. Many of the missing were middle-aged or elderly home-owners. In most cases, neighbors didn't know where they'd gone.

"I want to marry your view, Adam." I sighed happily, gazing out at Long Island Sound from the main floor of his house.

The house was raised on pylons, as were most of the neighboring beach houses. Hurricane Irene, back in 2011, caved in many of them. They were rebuilt on stilts to let future storms wash through underneath. At the moment, our cars were parked down below. The parking spaces were swept clean, but it looked like sand had washed into the back lawn again recently. Or perhaps he'd just given up on clearing it. Adam's immediate neighbors were gone, maybe for the winter, maybe forever, storm shutters secured across their extravagant Sound views.

"Telescope." Adam pointed to a corner. He was making tea in the open kitchen. The whole main floor was one room, seemingly half walled in glass. "I spotted some otters out on the reef this morning. Take a look."

"Really?" I eagerly peered into the telescope, a classy-looking brass affair with brass tripod, already trained on the reef. "Seals," I breathed, in rapture. Gulls wheeled in and out of the telescope view as well. They dive-bombed the seals on a low scrap of dark seaweedy rock that peeked out of the calm grey water.

"Oh, the seals are always there," Adam assured me. "I can

stare at that view for hours. There are binoculars too, on the bookcase, if you want them. The telescope is pretty high-powered. It's a little hard to find things with it."

I picked up the binoculars and checked the horizon, toward Long Island. But it was too misty to see anything, including Coast Guard vessels. That seemed fair enough. If they were out there, they'd be close to Long Island, 18 miles away. We were near the widest part of the Sound. I scanned the beach, but no one was out there. For once, we had a December day that felt like December ought to, clammy with temperatures hovering just above freezing. My ears froze going for a beach walk on a day like that. There was hardly a footprint in the sand below the high tide line. I'd walked this beach often, though it was supposedly private property. It was about half tide now, the water receding. I watched the wildlife a bit more, gulls here, a cormorant diving for fish there, the seals at ease. I set aside the binoculars, breathing deep the salt air and beauty.

"Sunday afternoon tea is served, my lady," Adam invited, from the dining table. He bowed in his steampunk finery.

His brown suit featured wide lapels on a frock coat whose pleats swished enchantingly in the back. A watch bob dangled between pockets on a lavender floral brocade vest. A high white collar framed his jawline, with a stock of the same fabric as the vest. I wore the same ensemble I'd worn the day we met, complete with striped rose sateen skirts, lace gaiters, pleated brown jacket, and silly little plumed hat.

"Well, welcome to my home. I'm sorry it's taken so long," said Adam. He admired my outfit as he sat back and sipped his tea. "Busy time." He smiled apologetically.

"I'm just glad to finally be here." We'd barely seen each other since Montreal, just a couple short visits at my house. "And finally share our steampunk."

"Oh, and finally have our filet mignon later," he promised. "I must admit, I liked the corset better. But your outfit today

116

brings back happy memories."

"Mm, of a time gone by, what, a month and a half ago?" We laughed. It was the Sunday before Christmas, and we'd met near Halloween. "Let's not," I said suddenly. "We're here and now, and it's lovely. That's all."

"You never fail, do you," he murmured, with a slow smile. "Alright. I was going to compare Christmas plans and ask whether you'd managed to reach your parents yet. But you're right. That's boring, and depressing."

"Yeah. No. Let's not. Your tea is delicious, sir. And the cookies." They were delicious, thin crisp cookies that tasted of caramel. The tea tasted British somehow. I knew my herb teas, not the imported real ones. We sipped, and crunched, and admired each other.

"I'm sorry. I blighted the conversation," I said eventually.

Adam smiled. "Don't think of the word 'wolf,' " he agreed. "I appreciated the sentiment deeply, though."

"So, you'll be seeing your family for Christmas in Greenwich?" I inquired brightly.

"Yes. One last time."

My smile hurt, but I insisted on keeping it up. "Last time?"

"They enter their ark the day after Christmas." He flashed me an attempt at a smile. "I don't expect I'll see them again."

"I guess I assumed you'd all be in the same ark."

"No. No, mine is… Well. Not open to the public, anyway. The rest of the family bought into a nice ark up in the northwest corner of the state. That's where I was last weekend. My father wanted me to look the place over, check for any obvious issues I felt ought to be addressed. I wasn't allowed to see much, though, aside from the public areas and the hydroponics. No visitors allowed in the power plant and water supplies and such, even as a professional courtesy. My stepmother cried a lot, about me not being with them."

"I'm sorry, Adam. That sounds thoroughly miserable. So

was it? A sound, well-designed ark?"

He shrugged. "It's about standard."

"Is yours? Standard?"

"No, as a matter of fact. It's not. Want to come see?" He managed a real smile again at my surprise. "I'd like you to see it."

"Yes! I'd love to. Thank you!"

"I would like you to see it. My life has revolved around it for a few years now. I guess I'd like to show it off. But... Heard anything more about the UNC ark?"

"They still say they'll resume interviews after New Year's." I took a sip of tea. "We're pretty sure I won't be in that ark, aren't we?"

"No," he agreed. "But if you wanted to believe that you would be... Some people need to believe that things will get better soon. A magic pill, who knows."

"I think I need to believe I'm living today. Really living, as though there is no tomorrow."

"There might not be."

"Yet a little hoarding is only prudent. There might be a tomorrow. Did you have any other downers you needed to get out of the way?"

He laughed. "No. You?"

"Nah."

"Good. Did you bring a bathing suit?"

"No. Why?"

"Good." He smiled crookedly. "I thought we might catch the sunset from the hot tub."

I examined the deck out the windows. It was a nice deck, complete with specially canted plexiglass railings so as not to obstruct the expensive view. It blocked the wind without catching it like a sail. Nice teak furniture. Empty planters, it being December. No hot tub.

Adam pointed up. "Three season porch off the master

bedroom."

"This is the fourth of three seasons," I pointed out.

"The water's nice and hot," he promised.

"We might have to imagine the sunset." Though the cloud cover did seem to be breaking, and the breeze freshening.

"I have every confidence in your imagination," said Adam. "Shall we?"

Getting undressed from our steampunk finery led to one thing and another. By the time we made it from Adam's bedroom out to the hot-tub, the cloud cover had broken. The last gasp of orange sun peeked between two remnant strands of grey and hot pink cloud, tipping the twilight view with soft golden highlights.

I couldn't help padding out to the hot-tub with arms hugging my chest for the cold, and bent over for modesty. The Sound side of the porch was all window, and I didn't have a bathing suit. Adam stood tall and laughed at me. There was no one outside those windows to see us but seagulls. He easily flipped off the hot-tub cover, unleashing a cloud of steam, and powered up the water jets to set the cauldron roiling.

I slipped into the broiling hot-tub down to my ears, and listened to the water burble and frolic. I only came up when I started getting overheated and dizzy. Adam leaned back, head on the edge of the tub, and watched the last drop of sun, scarlet now, vanish into a band of haze at the horizon. I scooted up to him, and he flung a lazy arm over my shoulders.

"Relaxed?" he inquired.

"Molten," I agreed. "You?"

"Absolutely. Don't let me fall asleep."

"First star," I pointed out. The bright white flare shone out of red-violet sky in the southwest.

"Venus," he disagreed.

"Close enough. Star light, star bright, first star I see tonight. I wish I may, I wish I might, get this wish I wish tonight."

Adam frowned slightly in concentration, then gave it up. "What do you wish for, Dee?"

"Earth to be alright. Healthy and vibrant and full of life."

He pulled me closer and rested his head on mine. "Good wish," he whispered.

We didn't turn any lights on. The sky darkened and the Milky Way appeared. It was like being suspended in the stars. Without a moon, there was only the barest flicker of reflection on the water below. I hadn't been to the beach at night since the streetlights were banned. It used to be that the horizon never lost a sickly glow. A Milky Way that vivid was only visible far from the city lights. But the cold winter air held little moisture or haze, and no man-made light pollution intruded. The stars were gorgeous, and I felt like I could reach out and touch them, as I used to feel only in the Rockies or mid-desert.

"If I had this tub and this view, I think I'd be here every night for hours," I said.

"You think that, when you buy it. But then you hardly use it," Adam replied. "This is what I intended when I bought the place. But this is the first time I've used the hot tub that really matched that vision."

"I think you've had women in this hot tub before, Adam Lacey."

"I have," he allowed. "But not the right ones. Too... I don't know. Brittle. Not real."

"You're talking to someone who showed up in costume."

He laughed. "I hate to break this to you, Dee Baker," he whispered in my ear. "But your costume doesn't hide you very well. You shine right through."

"Now, that's another one of those unmanageable extravagant compliments. It's like an arms race. And I was so relaxed." I sighed a put-upon sigh. "Let's see. I really love your bath tub, Adam. And the décor. First rate sparkly bits out there. The company's not too shabby, either."

End Game

He laughed and dunked me.

Eventually we wandered down to the kitchen, both dressed in his pajamas. Adam confessed he wasn't much of a cook, except for breakfast. But he'd acquired superb ingredients. Glass of red wine at hand, I fixed us herbed new potatoes, caramelized onions and mushrooms, fresh local greenhouse spinach with onions and dill, and meltingly delicious medium rare filet mignons, crusted with Montreal steak seasoning. It was grass-fed all natural beef. I drenched it in drawn butter to compensate for its low fat content. Forget $100 a pound—this was nearly $500 in meat. For dessert, he'd bought a ready-made fresh apple pie and a pint of deluxe vanilla bean ice cream. No Montreal palate-clearing sorbet between courses, alas, but we didn't really miss it.

After that we killed the lights and the rest of the red wine, stared out at the stars some more, and cuddled on the living room couch until bedtime. We slept deep in the winter silence, lulled by the gently lapping waves.

It was like a last gasp of the very finest, of a lifestyle that was already gone forever. I'm glad I got to use that home, that hot tub, that view with him, the right way.

-o-

Being cut off from the rest of the world certainly mattered. The New York and Canadian borders completed New England's isolation. We had no further imports. The natural gas pipelines still worked—for now. But gasoline and fuel oil were not produced in New England, and the power grid was severed at the borders. Gasoline was rationed, almost entirely reserved for government services. I certainly didn't rate any. At Christmas that year, we still had enough power and gas heat. There were usage caps, but we simply figured out how to stay beneath them.

We certainly didn't put up Christmas lights. The few people

121

who did, got fined.

And we still had Internet. From several different directions, in fact. Mangal noticed that our three adjacent houses had three different Internet providers using two different technologies. He laid some cables and switchboxes to extend the services to each house.

Although they still went through the motions, there was no credible national or international news. State and local news tended to focus on new government regulations and supply issues, and feel-good stories of neighbors working together in harmony. Grapevine news tended more to local bully outfits trying to steal other people's hoards. There were no trials for people caught doing this. Attempted looters were killed on sight.

There were a lot of wild rumors about what was happening in New York and Boston and Providence. Most of the interior state borders in New England were postponed while the Boston-Providence area was cordoned off ahead of schedule. New England no longer included its southeast corner. I learned reliably that Cape Cod organized its own border, cutting itself off from the mainland. I wished them luck with it, but doubted they had the means to hold back millions of people determined to overrun them, if it came to that. And Cape Cod on its own was woefully lacking in resources.

Work was kind of a joke, under the circumstances. The net outcome of hundreds of skilled man-hours thrown at the censors, was a few pretty static weather infographics on 20th century weather phenomena, and a single page national border map that was a flat-out lie. Mangal and I and our teams went back to doing little bits of national news broadcast support, mostly graphic overlays and charts of data that were half fiction.

Shelley's Mom vanished, like so many others. UNC closed down the headquarters in Stamford after the Christmas party in mid-December. I suggested Shelley move into New Haven, where there were plenty of college students and young people and a bit of residual night-life. But she was scared of the cities, even Connecticut's small ones. I sent Alex off with her to find her an abandoned place in the neighborhood. She ended up moving in with him and his rabbits and guinea pigs.

When I saw her crappy little furnished efficiency room in Stamford, I didn't blame her for wanting to leave. Alex and I went down with her to help carry stuff back by train and foot. It didn't really require three of us. Alex had better bedding and bath and kitchenware. There wasn't much to carry except her clothes and a box of mementos she'd taken from her Mom's. We respectfully left her alone with the place to say good-bye. It was her first home of her own, after all. Even if it smelled a bit rank and had discolored peeling paint and rust-stained plumbing. She didn't cry long. Tough young woman.

Of course, Mangal and I knew what was happening in New York and Boston, at least to some degree. Mangal looked grey with it, especially when the putrid smoke blew from the west from unimaginable pyres of burning bodies. After a while the confirmed Ebola case counts weren't updated anymore. CDC personnel were withdrawn, at least the ones who were willing to leave. Health care, public services, first responders, all the social systems broke down in the city itself. Without any credible care, the virus proved unusually deadly. The CDC records stopped at 75% fatality, but it had been climbing for days. Past experience with the hemorrhagic fever topped out at 90% fatal to the afflicted.

Fleeing refugees within the New York borders met scared locals trying, and mostly failing, to barricade them out of their towns. Phenomenal quantities of ammunition were expended. Tunnels and bridges into New Jersey and Long Island were blown up where possible, but it couldn't stem the tide of refugees. The disease crossed the waters before the border was closed.

Boston-Providence, at that point, was probably descending into anarchy without viral assist. Our secret sources could only tell us so much about what was happening there, as public order broke down. Before the cities were hemmed in, populations were assured that food and medicine and fuel and power would still cross the boundaries to support them in safety. It simply wasn't true. And those metro areas didn't have the agricultural capacity, or even enough fresh water in Boston's case, to support the number of people penned in. They didn't wait for shortages to develop. Riots broke out as soon as food shipments stopped.

The metro borders were simply planned slaughter to cull the population. At least, that's what it looked like.

Jean-Claude responded to my email. Under the guise of more Christmas greetings, he sent codes to reach him more carefully. He pressed for further details and regular updates. But I wasn't willing to play. Telling him something important now and then was different than researching and reporting to a foreign agent. If that's what he was.

Not that the U.S. government was exactly inspiring my loyalty these days.

Yet the damnedest part of it was, I prayed those borders would hold. With the agricultural output of half of America dead or dying to climate change and storms, I knew full well we couldn't all survive. For all the people who defended the borders and lived behind those borders, it was our chance to live that we were defending in deadly earnest.

To the best of my knowledge, the U.S. government never formally admitted that this was the plan all along. The President committed suicide on Christmas Day. The borders and other Calm Act policies marched on without him.

Chapter 11

Interesting fact: Atmospheric carbon dioxide levels began to fall at this time. The collapse of trans-Pacific trade, and local revolt against killing levels of air pollution, cut coal emissions in China. In North America, radical reductions in air traffic, trucked goods, automobile traffic, turning out the lights at night, industrial agriculture, and livestock, cut emissions sharply. However, these reductions were almost offset by melting tundra, burning forests, and vast grasslands turning to dust.

I was kneeling in my garden pulling up spuds for Christmas Eve when Zack dropped by. The potato plants were long dead, but the tubers kept pretty well in the ground until about Christmas time. They'd all have to be dug up before the deep arctic cold that froze the ground. If that came, it came about New Year's, so any day now. We were still working our way through the cabbages, kale, and late spinach, as well. Those were still alive, but not growing, in a plastic tunnel. The short hours of sunlight weren't enough for crops to grow, even if it were warmer. But merely staying alive kept the greens fresh.

"You've got quite the farm here," said Zack, plonking himself down on the cold muddy ground. I kneeled on a pad to save my wardrobe. "Can I help?"

"I'm just sorting now. This is enough potatoes for today. I don't think Alex is home."

"No, he's off doing some work for me," Zack clarified. "I was hoping to talk to you, if you have a few minutes."

"Sure. Let's move these into the garage to dry." I grabbed

the trays of small and medium potatoes, and Zack picked up a heavier tray of the large ones. We stowed them on shelves in the garage. I grabbed a harvest basket and knife, closed the garage again, and headed to the poly tunnel.

"Sorry, just need to grab some greens," I explained. "Almost done." I cut the heads off three cabbages and tossed them in my basket. Debris went into a second basket for Alex's many rodent pets. Then Zack helped me harvest spinach, all that remained in the tunnel.

I stood up and stretched the small of my back. "That'll do it. Or—would you like anything? Christmas present." I smiled at him.

"For me?" Still kneeling, Zack placed his hand on his own chest and grinned. He looked honestly touched by the offer. "I would love some cabbage and kale. I'd kill for some of those potatoes, too."

I pursed my lips. "Not a felicitous choice of words these days."

"No. Sorry."

"How about two cabbages," I knelt back down and started cutting, "one each of the three kale varieties, and we yank you up another potato plant."

"Thank you! That's generous. Sure you can spare it?"

"Oh, this all needs to come up within the next few days," I assured him. "I'm happy to have some more of it enjoyed fresh, you know? And I really appreciate all you've done for Alex, Zack. And the rest of us."

Eventually we landed in the kitchen, me washing vegetables, and him drying. He was good at pitching in and being quiet while I focused on doing something. Companionable silence is a wonderful thing. But, he had an agenda I was ignoring. I sighed.

"You wanted to talk to me about something, Zack? And here I've been dragging you around on my chores. I'm sure you have your own."

"Oh, don't apologize. I love my Christmas presents. Thank you."

"You're very welcome." I dumped another head of cabbage into detergent water to loosen any critters. "And?"

He looked up and across, as though sifting through topics. "What do you think of the new neighbors?"

"The ones you moved out from New Haven? Alex said you hand-picked them for gardening skill and recruited them to move here. That was interesting." I shot him a look of inquiry. "I helped a couple last weekend, down the block. They were trying to peel off the turf and turn lawn loam into vegetable beds. I talked them into raised beds instead. I explained how to get leaf compost from the town recycling complex. I liked them."

"Not too dark for you?"

I took a deep breath. "Had another talk with the neighbors down thataway," I nodded toward the opposite end of the block. "They were... concerned. But they allowed that they were concerned when Mangal and Shanti moved in, too. Shanti converted them to her love slaves real quick." We both laughed. Shanti's shopping, considerate ways, and electric car, had won her raving fans in the neighborhood, in mere weeks.

Zack was a Shanti fan himself. But he sighed and said, "I'm not sure we needed more pacifists. But the Jains make good leavening."

"It's a neighborhood. Not a loaf of bread." I wiped a strand of hair off my face. "Look, people in Totoket are mostly white. And racism is tricky. It sneaks up on you. It's hard to even see when you're being racist, or who's being racist to whom. But I think we're mostly good people. Some more than others. I don't think we have crazies here like the ones who attacked Shanti in Broomfield. People have concerns. We address the concerns. And everybody gets used to each other. I introduced them," I nodded left, "to them," nodded right, "and we got a start on that. Anybody gets too hot and bothered, we can always sick Shanti on 'em."

"And you personally?"

"Well, I'm grateful for new people who can shoot. I'm more grateful for people who can produce food."

"You're certainly good at it. What do you grow with those light rigs in the garage, by the way?"

"Seed starting, transplants. I'll rev them up soon for spring cabbages and such. You never quite know when spring will come anymore. And I have the poly tunnels for early crops."

"Hydroponics?"

"For greens indoors," I agreed. "My indoor cucumbers and tomatoes are starting to bear, too. I use soil for those."

"There's a lot of gardening expertise in the community co-op," he said thoughtfully. "But they're heavily into the... politics of organic gardening. They're pretty anti-technology."

"Technology is a girl's best friend," I quipped, finger to my chin coquettishly. "I noticed, with the co-op. That's why I don't have a plot there. I like tech. I like it a lot. It's my career. I think the co-op and I would get on each other's nerves."

Zack gave me a rueful look, probably agreeing. He picked up a potato. "Good seed potato?"

"Too small." I grabbed a bright green plastic bag out of a cupboard. "Take some of the bigger ones with good eyes. Keep them in this bag, maybe twice as many as you think you'll want for seed potatoes. Eat the ones that start shriveling. But this bag absorbs ethylene gas, which keeps them from rotting. Keep them in the fridge, and most of them will keep for planting in March. The bag will help keep the rest of your vegetables fresh, too."

He folded up the bag. "Technology. The girl's best friend," he echoed.

"I'm sure there's a difficult, chancy, and organically correct way to do it," I allowed. "And I'll be sure to learn it. After I run out of ethylene absorbing bags and a refrigerator."

I smiled pleasantly. The vegetable cleaning was done.

Zack tapped thoughtfully at a new potato. "What do you think of our local RTM member?"

"I should think your opinion was the one worth having. You've spent more time with her. She always seemed big on zoning and maintaining high property values, to me. She got on my case once for growing vegetables in front of the house. I told her to take a hike, and planted a few more flowers as neighbor repellent. How's she handling the conversion to... life within borders?"

"Not very well. She's trying the fire up the town to evict the 'squatters' here. She claims they depress our property values."

"Our property values are effectively zero. No buyers."

"Some of the RTM members are buying what she's selling."

"Well, you can't fix stupid."

He snorted a laugh. "What I'm trying to do, is to organize a West Totoket civic zone, with a more local government. To handle things like the food cache, neighborhood defense— neighborhood watch, I mean—and arbitrate between neighbors, manage resources. With a direct democracy, instead of the representative town meeting. All within walking distance. Are you interested?"

"Sounds smart," I allowed. "Interested, in what way? A democratic meeting is one person one vote."

"There's always leadership."

"I nominate Shanti for the junta. She likes community crap."

Zack's cheek twitched. "I think we need people who've been here a while."

"Paler."

"That too. But only to get it off the ground. Once we've got the town's blessing and a state charter, I'd back Shanti for president of the thing. I don't think she'd win. But she'd be on the leadership, for sure."

I considered this. "What does the town's blessing buy you?"

"Police, fire department, public works, trash collection, sewers..."

I shrugged. "We have all that now. We pay taxes, as much as anyone does. Which is probably fewer people all the time. What I meant was, what does an official charter buy you? If it includes any real authority, I don't think they'll give it to you. You just need to take it. After building up support, of course."

He stared at me. "That was Plan B," he allowed.

"OK, so you're talking to a middle-class homeowner. I'm afraid that the zombie apocalypse is heading up the road to rape and pillage any day now. Tattered rags a-flutter on Ebola-carrying, gun-toting inner city hoodlums, who'll kill me for my food because I've got more than they've got. What's your pitch, Mr. Harkonnen?" As role-playing, this was mighty thin. I was exactly the audience I pretended to be.

"We're organizing for the defense of West Totoket and to pool resources. We have an armed cache to defend bulk food supplies, so that anyone who gets through our lines can't steal all our food and seed."

Now I stared at him. "That's exactly what you're doing, isn't it."

"Yes."

"The West Totoket survivalist camp." I scowled.

"No camp. But I think organizing for survival is a good thing."

"And what do you want from me, an ordinary neighbor?"

"Contribute your bulk supplies to the cache—"

I tossed my dishtowel onto the counter. "No way in hell. Thanks for dropping by. Door slams."

"I'd ask you to contribute your guns to the cause, but do you know how to shoot?"

"No. I don't have any fighting skills. But your pitch needs work."

"Like what? No, Dee, I'm really asking. Like what?"

I considered, arms crossed, lips pursed at him. Then I sighed. "Beat back your first horde of Ebola-bearing zombies, I guess. You need a track record."

"Already have that. I don't know about Ebola, or zombies, but we've got Route 1 blocked at the reservoir, and the bridge over the estuary at the south end of the marsh. So far the gangs coming out of New Haven have turned back at verbal advice that they weren't welcome in. The gangs are getting larger, though. At some point, someone will open fire."

The side of our neighborhood facing the rest of Totoket was wide open. But the side facing East Haven, and beyond it New Haven, was pretty easy to block off, now that he mentioned it. There were only those two ways across a giant reservoir, a giant marsh, and a river, unless the intruders knew the land.

"There's an old railway bridge from East Haven into the marsh," I warned thoughtfully.

"We blew that bridge."

"And who's manning these barriers?"

"I'm coordinating," Zack said. I easily read that as 'I'm in command', but he continued. "I had the boys inventory all the fighting men in the area when they were doing the housing survey. Some women. Cops, National Guard, veterans, hunters, armed survivalists. We could train more."

I considered this, then shrugged. I said quietly, "I value your effort. I'm amazed at how quickly you've organized what you have. Nothing I can contribute to defense, though. Sorry."

He nodded slowly. "Are you sure about that?" he asked softly. "Alex seems to think that you and Mangal know more than, say, gets past the censors."

"Well... Just a couple things. The rumors about an Ebola

epidemic in New York? Believe those."

"Shit."

"Boston-Providence is just anarchy so far, turned inwards. New Haven... You know East Haven isn't your problem. Neither is the part of New Haven on this side of the harbor. These gangs don't have gas or vehicles, really. The interstate and the railroad are closed to them."

"Effectively?"

"I think so, for now at least. But there are two pedestrian-friendly bridges across the Quinnipiac River and the harbor. The gangs could try boats, if they can get boats. But there's the harbor patrol and quite a lot of firepower out there guarding the fuel oil tanks."

New Haven was a fuel oil depot for tankers coming into Connecticut. There were no more tankers arriving. But the giant storage drums in New Haven were still filling tanker trucks, so they still held precious fuel oil.

I continued, "My point is, blocking off the Forbes and Grand Avenue bridges would make for a really long and pointless walk to Totoket. Easier to head north than east. And it shouldn't be too hard to block two small bridges, right? Getting people from *Totoket* to do it might be more of a problem. Those bridges are inside New Haven."

He nodded thoughtfully. "Thank you. I'll see what I can do there. Any other... privileged information?"

I led him into the living room. Once there, I brought up a live satellite feed, uncensored, with map overlays, on the living room TV. This kind of live map hadn't been available even to the police for over a year. Zack's eyes widened. I put a finger to my lips for discretion. I showed him how to pan around with the tablet controller. I left him to study the bird's eye view of the current state of Connecticut while I chopped vegetables for supper.

"Seeing this on the big screen is really helpful, Dee," Zack called from the living room. "Could I borrow a pencil and paper?"

In my office, I printed street maps of New Haven, East Haven, and western Totoket for his annotating convenience. He also wanted overview maps of the state and county, so I printed those, too. I laid out graph paper, lined paper, and 11x17 sheets of Bristol board for pencil drawing on the desk, and pointed out my drawer of drafting and coloring tools. I left my huge work screens in the office showing the same illicit maps as on the big display in the living room.

"Have fun," I bade him. "You staying for supper?"

"I'd love to," he said wonderingly. "This—Thank you."

"No problem. Just a map." I looked him in the eye inquiringly, until he nodded. "Just a map."

Eventually I had food on the table, and killed all the electronics. I helpfully shoved all Zack's annotated papers into a large envelope for him. "No work while we eat," I explained, and waved him to the table.

Zack might have been expecting a rather awkward intimate dinner for two. I knew better. I served supper at 6:30 on the nose. Alex blew in with a gust of cold at 6:30 on the nose. He stomped off his winter boots and unraveled himself from scarves. He washed his hands in nothing flat, and parked himself at the table.

"Hi, Zack. Aw, cabbage again? What good is it to have a rich boyfriend if you don't bring home leftovers. Zack, Dee had *filet mignon* Sunday night. And she didn't bring me home any."

If you have any sensitive subjects lying around, don't bring a teenager into your life. "Cabbage is good," I informed Alex firmly.

"Not as good as filet mignon," he whined.

"I grow cabbage and potatoes. Not filet mignon."

"I think it's delicious, Dee. You're an excellent cook. Thank you for sharing." Zack eyed Alex reprovingly. "Not many people are willing to share food these days. You're lucky, Alex," he reminded the teen.

"Yeah, yeah…" Alex hunkered down and inhaled his plate of cabbage and tomatoes, and new potatoes with drawn butter and home-grown herbs. "This is pretty good," he allowed.

Just as Zack was trying to formulate a family-like dinner conversation for three, Shelley blew in, having crossed the side yard without benefit of coat.

"It's cold, cold, cold out there!" she complained. "And now it's sleeting!"

She grabbed her own plate of food from the kitchen. She was less predictable about dinner. She'd reliably eat the plate of food I prepared for her, but might come over later and reheat it, or take it next door with her. She hesitated, seeing Zack, nodded her head in greeting, and headed back home.

"How are you and Shelley getting along, Alex?" I asked.

"Good," reported Alex. "Any dessert?" His plate was wiped clean.

"Saving it up for Christmas tomorrow," I reported.

He shrugged and stashed his dinner things in the dishwasher. "Thanks, Dee. Later, Zack," he called on his way out. He didn't bother to wrap up again, just shoved feet into untied boots, hugged the rest of his outerwear to his chest, and exited.

"I'd sort of hoped for better dinner conversation from this arrangement," I complained to Zack.

He laughed. Neither of us was half-finished eating yet. He swallowed, and took a thoughtful drink of water. "I did have one other thing to talk to you about, Dee. Um," he paused for a long moment. "I was able to confirm what happened to Alex's mom."

"Oh?"

"She definitely went through the suicide doctor in the center of town."

End Game

"The *what?*"

"You know that general practice clinic across from the funeral home on Main Street? Low pink building, with the parking lot in front? They've teamed up to do suicide and cremation services. Quite the business. They hand out those oxycontin bottles. You know about those?"

"Yes."

"Well, apparently they offer a deluxe service, too, to minimize distress to the next of kin. A comfortable room to die in, with supervised suicide, and cremation, death certificate 'of natural causes,' all included at a low package price."

"My God."

"There are a lot worse places. In New Haven, there's one outfit where people sign the papers and get loaded onto a bus. They have to down a full bottle of oxycontin when they board the bus. Then—" He took a deep breath, and blew it out slowly. "Sorry. Too much information."

"Yeah. So that's where they go, the ones who vanish."

"Some of them. A lot of them. I got my hands on the register at the place in town. A whole lot of addresses from around here. One family went with three little kids."

"May they rest in peace," I whispered. "I guess... that makes sense."

"There's nothing that 'makes sense' about murdering your own children," Zack said vehemently.

"There but for the grace of God," I said vaguely, still shaken. "Zack, please. I'm not defending anyone to you. I just..." I swallowed. "I didn't kill the people of New York City. I'm not killing them in Boston. But because I live, at their expense, because my government penned them up to die, because I help someone I believe in—you—to protect me against my innocent neighbors across a river, who are just trying to live, just like I am—Zack, I'm not a murderer, but my hands aren't clean." I wiped one angry tear out of my eye. I'd probably said too much, but the wild rumors everyone was passing included some truth by then. "I can't judge them. I won't judge them. I could have done more to help them. Maybe. But I didn't."

Tears were standing in his eyes too at that. But none fell. He nodded slowly. "Your hands are clean. Your soul is clean, Dee. We're about building a new life here. Not just killing. I *have* to believe that."

I nodded slowly. I broke eye contact and played with my water goblet. There was still a little cabbage on my plate. And I would eat that. But I sure wasn't hungry. "Alex deserves to know. But not right now, OK? He's building a new life, and it's only been a couple months since his Mom left. Let him get stronger. His mom was his whole world. His world needs to fill in a bit more. This won't help him now." I gave a huge sigh. "But thank you. Now we know. I'd always wondered, where they all went."

Though I got the feeling Zack had known all along, or at least strongly suspected.

Zack shrugged. "A bunch of them might have gone into arks."

I shook my head. "Maybe a handful. More, on the richer side of town, but not around here."

Zack took a deep breath. "There's you and Mangal. The UNC ark."

"I don't know about that," I said.

He paused. "You know, I can't see you in an ark. Divorced from the sleet and soil and wild berries, cut off from the Earth. Whisked away from the land you know and love, and incarcerated in Tennessee. That's not you. That's not real, to you."

I stared back into his hard blue eyes, doubtfully. I swallowed. "I like tech. I'm good with hydroponics. I could do it." I listened. "I think that's Adam's car. Excuse me."

End Game

I opened the front door onto a full ice storm. Adam carefully walked toward me on the lawn where possible. The slick icy grass provided better traction than the smooth paved walkway to the front door. He wore the most gorgeous charcoal wool greatcoat, large lapels elegantly tied up around his ears with a classy dark green scarf, tied with a European slip-knot.

Adam came bearing gifts. "Ho, ho, ho!" he cried.

"Ho-ho and merry-merry, hello!" I kissed him with a quick peck. "I wasn't expecting you. Ah, Adam, you remember Zack?"

"I do! Merry Christmas, Zack!"

Adam showed no concern over catching me at dinner with another man. I wryly decided that left him in a much stronger position than either Zack or me. He was a class act, no doubt about that.

"You didn't have to have bring us presents," I said, taking them into my arms.

"Ah, so you didn't get me anything. Oh, well."

I grinned and pointed my head to a basket under the tree. I did have a fake Christmas tree up, with baubles and hand-made toys hanging from the branches. I just didn't put lights on it.

"I should go..." said Zack, collecting up his maps and gift bags of Christmas vegetables.

"Are you on foot, Zack?" Adam asked. "Hang on, and I'll give you a lift. The footing is pretty treacherous. Dee, I just wanted to drop off presents on the way to the train. I'd planned to drive down to Greenwich in the morning, but the weather isn't going to cooperate."

"You're driving to the train station?" I asked doubtfully.

"Totoket station, not New Haven. That car has pretty good traction. The batteries make it heavy." We all nodded ruefully. He poked in the basket and found dried tomatoes, a jar of roast peppers, and a cabbage, just like the box I'd brought to Vermont for barter. And a two-pound block of Vermont

137

cheddar. He grinned in memory.

"Hard to know what to get for the guy who has everything," I said defensively.

"It's perfect, Dee. Thank you." He kissed me again. "I ought to run. But open the big thing tonight. It needs to go in the fridge. Talk to you soon. Ready, Zack?"

With deep misgivings, I watched from the door and waved, as Adam backed out onto the street, fish-tailed on the ice, and drove away. I wondered what they would talk about in the car. I hated to think of them comparing notes on me. But neither man seemed the type to do that. Adam was too classy to do anything but assume possession and leave it at that. Zack was just too reserved to discuss it. Or so I hoped.

The ice-storm, at least, was nothing new. A classic Connecticut Christmas ice storm, it left half an inch of ice coating everything, and brought down trees onto power lines across the state. That was a bit heart-stopping, by then. Each time the power or Internet went out, you had to wonder if it was ever coming back.

The refrigerated gift was a spiral-sliced honey ham, to share with Alex and Shelley. Other boxes contained cotton flannel pajamas printed with Vermont black and white cows, and gorgeous matching steampunk earrings and necklace, in brass cogwork and amber. I loved them. And I felt really guilty.

I still really liked both guys.

Chapter 12

Interesting fact: Electric power generation in New England was dominated by natural gas and nuclear, followed by hydroelectric and burning refuse, with smaller contributions from oil, coal, wind, and solar power. Natural gas reached the region via pipelines from Texas, Tennessee, and Canada.

Christmas turned out a lot more fun than I expected. Shelley and Alex helped me bake a coffee cake for breakfast, and we exchanged good gifts. Shelley gave me all of her remaining Dee-clothes. We're about the same size. I gave her a basket of hard-to-find toiletries, including large bottles of her favorite shampoo and conditioner. Alex knitted me a hat, with skill I'd never suspected him of. I gave him a hundred dollars to spend on video gaming as he saw fit.

There was still no power from the ice storm, so video gaming and work and Internet surfing were off limits. The giant batteries were reserved for running the furnaces and fridges. We got out a board game and played for a while. By noon we were thoroughly bored.

About then, Mangal dropped by to invite us to a last-minute community party being thrown at the non-denominational Protestant church hall. We dispatched Alex to invite the neighbors and everyone he knew. Shelley and I carved up some of Adam's huge ham into bite-size pieces to share. Then we dressed up in our party finery for dancing and set out.

The church was only a half mile away. The roads were melted clear, easy walking in the bright sunshine. Icicle-covered trees shone brilliant in the light, with tinkling and dripping everywhere. We called out a few neighbors I knew along the way. Others came out to inquire as they saw a gathering throng of people dressed up and marching past with food. Many of them had nothing better to do, either, and grabbed some stuff and trailed along.

The church parking lot wasn't large—most people walked to this church—but it was empty. Kids already had a kickball game going out there when we arrived, and more kids joined in all the time. Inside the hall, we were among the first fifty, but eventually hundreds came and went. My ham wasn't the only extravagance shared on the potluck tables, either. Other plates offered roast beef, cheeses, and Christmas candy, among the more common rice and pasta dishes, pies, and mounds of Christmas cookies. Someone even donated a small beer keg.

Alex appeared out of nowhere to introduce me to Zack's sister Delilah, apparently on demand, then zipped away again with his teenage friends. She was as blond and blue-eyed as Zack, nearly six feet tall, and dressed in an Army camouflage uniform. This looked a lot better on Zack, but Delilah was an athletic and handsome woman. She stuck out a large, garden-worn hand to shake firmly. Unlike Zack, she had the ancestral Finnish scary manic grin down pat.

"I've been wanting to meet you, Dee!" she boomed. The crowd was getting a bit loud, but she was easily louder.

"Pleased to meet you, Delilah! Zack mentions you all the time. Are you on duty?" I asked, with a wave to encompass her Army green pullover sweater, down to ochre Army boots.

My own dress wasn't steampunk that day. I wore a deep Christmas red with low square-cut fitted bodice and wide flouncy knee-length skirts for dancing, topped with a deep green bolero short sweater for warmth. I'd added a tacky holly-and-berries broach, and the steampunk jewelry from Adam.

"We should all be on duty!" she replied with a fierce grin. "Zack says you garden, but aren't organic. This'll teach you."

I popped a bit of honey ham in my mouth and smiled pleasantly while I chewed, mouth closed.

Still grinning, she said, "You know that ham was probably raised in a gestational crate. Locked up for months—"

"Mm, it's delicious," I interrupted her. "I brought it. Try some." As it happens, it was organic free-range pork, but damned if I was going to tell her that.

She took a piece wryly, and chewed. "That is good," she allowed. "Zack says you never took a plot at the community gardens because we're too 'organically correct.' Is that supposed to be a joke on 'politically correct' or something?"

Yes, obviously. Sadly, the woman appeared to be humor impaired. "You seem very protective of your baby brother," I suggested.

Her grin lost some firmness. "Zack's my older brother."

"Ah. I didn't mean anything by it. You look about the same age."

She looked over my dress. "These are hard times. Zack needs a tough woman. Not a frill. Not a pacifist-lover." She jerked her head toward Mangal and Shanti's clique.

I grinned at her. "Good thing he has you to look out for him." This was actually sincere on my part. I thought it was kind of cool that his sister was looking me over, for Zack's sake if not for mine. "So did your grandmother teach you mushroom hunting and gardening too?"

"Well, Zack liked to work more than I did when we were young. I liked to fight more, but then he was the one who went into the Army."

I indicated her uniform. "Now you've got your chance too."

This mild sparring match was interrupted by a couple violins striking up. To my delight, the neighborhood supplied two fiddlers (formerly from different bands) and a dance caller for contra line dancing. The pastor, Reverend Connolly, went around herding people back to arrange a clear dance floor in the social hall. Overflow squeezed out the door into the church nave to sit on pews and socialize in the aisles.

On a lark, I seized Delilah's arm. "Dance with me!"

"Oh, no," she objected.

"The caller will start by teaching us the steps, you'll see," I encouraged, dragging her into the center of the hall, where couples were already converging. I saw Shelley looking around dejectedly, then a clump of three guys matching Delilah's uniform. "Maybe they'd like to dance?"

I dragged them onto the floor, too, along with Shelley, for three guys to match with three women. The one who teamed up with Delilah, I'd seen before. I suspected he was her husband or somesuch. Shanti laughingly dragged Mangal out to the floor. My own partner was a medium-height black man named Jamal, younger than me, one of the new imports from New Haven. From true enthusiasm and shyness, I suspected Shelley's partner was pleased and frightened to be thrust into the arms of a blonde his own age and more attractive than he was. I liked him.

As the beginner training dances progressed, I got to swing a few rounds with each on the men's side. You rarely spend much time with your own assigned partner in contra dancing. It is greatly less confusing, though, to keep men on one side and women on the other, to cue you in on whose hand to grasp next. I was glad I hadn't partnered with Delilah, as the beginners array kept hiccupping on the two successive lesbian couples in line, inexperienced at the dance. The male gay couple were no trouble, as they were old hands at contra, and moved confidently. After the first dance, the good-natured caller, looking rather Amish with a great flowing grey beard, laughingly asked the same-sex couples to show an emblem or trade partners for clarity. We muffed the steps a lot less after that.

After 20 minutes of training, we all fell out laughing for refreshments and a breather before the real dances. Grinning from ear to ear, I tapped Delilah on the arm, and asked, "You had fun? Oh, here." I unpinned my tacky holly brooch and pinned it on her fatigue sweater.

Delilah laughed, and leaned toward my ear. "I was wrong about you. You're fun."

I curtseyed. "Thank you, Ma'am."

A commotion at the outside door caught my eye. Zack and a few other guys appeared, in uniform and fully armed. Delilah and her trio of guys headed over to intercept. Weapons and ammo were exchanged at the door, rather than bring weapons into the church hall. At something Delilah said, Zack looked over and met my eye, looking a bit alarmed. Then he laughed and punched his sister lightly. Delilah's team departed, loaded for bear. Zack threaded his way through the crowd toward me.

"Merry Christmas, Dee," he said, and kissed me on the cheek. I returned the kiss with a smile. "My sister asked me to return this." He placed the holly pin in my hand and squeezed my hand closed over it. "Sorry about that. I mean, I hope that was alright. Delilah can be a bit, um, intense."

"A family trait," I twigged him. "It was fine. I enjoyed how she tried to protect you from the 'useless frill.' " Zack's eyes closed in a grimace. "But we've lost our contra dance partners. And we'd just trained up the lads not to step on our feet."

"Oh? I'm pretty good at stepping on feet." He waited for me to purse my lips, then added wryly, "I used to be a regular at the contra dances down at the Rec Center. Ah, I had a regular partner I broke up with last year."

"A useless frill, no doubt," I intoned solemnly. "I brought honey ham for the buffet, but it went fast. You should drop by for some before Alex devours it all. You know how teenage boys are."

"I remember it well," he agreed. He loaded up a plate from what was left on the buffet, mostly cookies and roast squash. We sat on a pew and chatted, missing muster for the first real set of dances. He'd just come off a six hour shift at the Route 1 barricade down by the reservoir, having walked there and back, and wanted to sit for a bit before dancing. I chose to keep him company rather than seek another partner.

"No Christmas truce, huh?"

"Nope," he sighed. "Nobody in charge on the other side to negotiate a truce with. It hasn't been bad today." He smelled like gunpowder, though. I think his barricades had been in operation barely over a week, at that point.

Alex popped by to say he was heading down to the Catholic church a couple blocks away. They had a party going too, but they were dancing to rock instead of old fogey music. I told him to have a blast, and let me know when he got in tonight. Shelley chose to leave with him and waved good-bye from the door.

Reverend Connolly made the rounds visiting with people. I introduced Zack to him. Connolly solemnly thanked Zack and his people for protecting the neighborhood, and extended an offer to help anyone on his team 'who experienced difficulties.' Apparently the church business was booming lately with people lost and frightened. Connolly had a soup kitchen going daily at noon, followed by services, then group counselling.

Zack thanked him for his services, as well, and assured the minister of his whole-hearted support. Zack asked if it might be possible to use the church hall for civic association organizational meetings. The Reverend was enthusiastic about organizing the community. But he offered to discuss the matter with Father Marks, the pastor at St. Mary's down the road. He felt it might be more inclusive if the two congregations took turns. The two men clasped hands on it warmly, and Reverend Connolly moved on.

"So Connolly is Protestant, and Marks is the Catholic?" Zack clarified quietly to me.

"Counter-intuitive, but yes," I assured him. "They're both great pastors, and good friends. We're lucky to have them. And we're lucky to have you."

He smiled gratefully and squeezed my hand. "You know, sometimes I think we just might be able to make this work."

I squeezed his hand back. In the short run, I had no doubt of it. In the long run, it seemed highly unlikely, but worthy of our best efforts, considering the alternative. "Are you religious?"

"No. Or rather, the spirit moves me out in nature, like in the woods at Sleeping Giant, or at harvest in the garden, or watching the livestock when the sun is just so. A church like this, it just feels comfortable."

We both gazed around the nave of the Union Church. Not a well-funded church, the congregation mostly chipped in their time and skills instead of money. It was a well-loved but rather splintery wooden affair. Time and paint were easy to donate. Sanding down and refinishing warped floorboards were less so. It felt warm and happy, though, safe and peaceful. St. Mary's down the street was posh and modern, but felt homey, too.

"You?" he asked.

"The same," I agreed softly.

I had no idea how Adam felt spiritually about anything. Or even politically. Or perhaps that wasn't true. We both felt at peace staring out at beautiful views. We'd just never spoken of it.

The lights came back on, after two days without power. The whole church erupted in whooping and applause, and we joined in. There was much rustling and movement as many in the crowd said their farewells and headed out to check their homes.

To a diminished house, the contra caller announced one last set. Zack offered his arm to lead me to the dance floor. His Army boots were a bit inhibiting, in a clompy sort of way. But he really was good at the line dance, and joy shone out on his face as we twirled towards and away from each other along the line of partners. He'd mastered smiling and saying a brief word to each person as he linked up with them, as well. I'd never seen him look so free and happy.

It looked good on him.

As Mangal switched in to swing me around, he murmured, "Zack's a keeper."

"They both are," I said helplessly.

"You need to choose," he admonished, and he twirled away.

After three wonderful dances, the caller and fiddlers called it quits. Reverend Connolly said the sun was going down, and suggested everyone get home before dark. Many split immediately after that. But we and the Jain community and others spent an extra 10 minutes helping the pastor clean up and put away. No one took food home. The leftovers were left for the Reverend's soup kitchen, which was long on customers and spiritual comfort, but short on food.

Mangal and Shanti left us to walk alone together, while they joined their Jain friends. The last drop of fiery orange sun slid behind the next ridge while we walked. The sunny afternoon had cleared the icicles from the trees, and left the road clear and dry. When we reached Zack's house, Venus shining brightly in a violet post-sunset sky, I invited him to come on over for Christmas supper at my house. I wasn't sure how many takers I'd have, if Shelley and Alex were still out partying. Mangal and Shanti wouldn't join us for ham on Christmas.

"Um, I need to tend the livestock, and be back at the barricade by eight," Zack demurred. That gave him less than three hours. "I'd like to, but."

"Man's got to eat," I countered. Though privately I was relieved to hear he couldn't stay long. "And woman's got to cook—dinner isn't ready yet. You're welcome to come by when your chores are done."

By this point, everyone else was well out of earshot. Zack looked around to check that point. "I'm a little confused, Dee.

End Game

You're with Adam, but we're dancing. You invite me over to a dinner that might be just the two of us, and... Look, I like Adam."

"I like Adam, too," I agreed, studying my boot toes. My fancy boots weren't going to stay fancy too long if I kept using them this hard. I looked up to meet Zack's eye. "And I like you, too. I haven't known either of you very long. Not long enough to make a commitment to either of you. But, you're right. It's awkward.

"The fact remains, Harkonnen. Dinner is on offer, spiral sliced honey ham, scalloped potatoes, and a cabbage salad. I'm not inviting you to spend the night. But I do care that you're on the barricade protecting me and mine. You could accept the meal as payment and a token of esteem for the work you do for us. I mean, even if my company for its own sake is dubious and all."

He flashed a tiny smile at that last, but mostly still gazed at me seriously. "Alright. Thank you. I'll be a half hour behind you or so."

Nearly three hours seemed like a long time until Zack had to leave, until I started scrubbing potatoes and onions. But he arrived before I'd gotten any further.

"How about I expedite the potatoes while you do the rest," he offered. I'd seen him cook before, and he was good at it. But anyone can make an omelet. Zack was just as comfortable making scalloped potatoes from scratch. All while he danced around me in a strange kitchen, while I prepared the ham and a cabbage salad.

It was a lot of fun. I was done with my part before he was done with his. I poured us some goblets of the excellent hard cider he contributed, and sat at the table to get out of his way.

"Damn, you're good," I said in admiration, after he slapped his final half-pre-cooked scalloped potatoes into the oven.

He shrugged. "I like cooking. It doesn't feel like Christmas

147

dinner if I haven't made any of it." He slid into a seat at the table with me.

"I know the feeling," I agreed. "Your cider is good. Thank you for bringing it."

He shrugged. "I just bought it fresh pressed, and let it sit there to harden."

"Zack, I'm going to give you a compliment now. And you're going to accept it. I know you're not any better at accepting compliments than I am, but exert yourself. Ready? You're a *good cook*."

He laughed out loud. "*Thank you.*"

"Well done!" I raised my cider in toast. "Merry Christmas, Zack!"

"Merry Christmas, Dee," he agreed, still smiling warmly.

"How's it going out there, really? On the barricades," I asked.

"I don't know if I should talk about that at Christmas dinner."

"Up to you, if you want to take a break from it. But if you're doing it on Christmas Day, I'm certainly up to hearing about it on Christmas night."

He nodded. "Thank you. Actually… If I could look at your map again? I could explain more easily."

"Absolutely," I said, and pulled up the latest satellite feed. It was dark, so I demonstrated silently how to turn back time to about 4 p.m., and back to present.

"You can do that?" he said, interested. He took the controller from me and nosed around the night view first. "So those fires. That's the Route 1 barricade, and the estuary bridge. And the Forbes avenue bridge in New Haven. That's barricaded now." He panned along I-95, and explained, "The National Guard controls the interstate." He studied the fires in East Haven carefully. "We had a few, um, customers this morning on Route 1. One group of forty we had to fire upon. I injured a couple. I don't think we've killed anyone. Yet."

"I'm sorry."

"Why are you sorry?"

I shrugged. "Not much of a present for Christmas morning."

"They didn't get through. That's present enough." He scrolled to the East Haven waterfront, where a number of larger fires were burning. Some orange flashes appeared, and Zack mimed gunshots with his hand as a pistol. Those flashes were considerably more than just pistol fire, but I got the gist. "Adam lives where?" he asked.

I pointed. That particular stretch of beach was dark and quiet. Zack nodded. "Good."

He panned back to the East Haven side of the Route 1 barricade at maximum resolution. He turned the display back to 4 p.m., 4:05, 4:10, and 4:15. Then he panned further into East Haven over a supermarket complex, and did it again. There was a gang ransacking the supermarket. My eyes widened. As Zack ran the time sequence through again, we both counted as well as we could. That group might have been over a hundred, heavily armed. There were fights over supermarket carts of stuff. There were bodies left lying in the parking lot.

I wondered if it was racist of me to immediately notice that the dead bodies were black. East Haven is a more affordable town than Totoket, except for the premium waterfront. But it was heavily Italian. The black and Neapolitan Italian cultures clashed badly, and often violently. Vanishingly few blacks chose to live in East Haven. The Italians had moved en masse to East Haven when the blacks were imported up north to New Haven to work the munitions factories during World War II. This oil and water did not mix.

Zack turned the TV off. "Thanks, good to know," he said. He actually looked grateful rather than grim. "I don't suppose we want to see the news."

"I turned it on last night. My team did the graphics for Santa's progress to a chimney near you. They were *good* graphics," I assured him.

"Is that the companion website for real-time satellite tracking of Santa?"

I gave an exaggerated childish nod. "We do good work." To his continued amused look, I replied, "Hey, I get paid to play for a living. It pays surprisingly well. And there are benefits." I nodded at the big display.

He nodded thoughtfully, and mouthed an exaggerated and heart-felt, "Thank you." What he actually said was, "When were we going to put that ham in the oven to warm? The potatoes should be almost ready to come out."

While I finished getting dinner onto to the table, he stepped outside to have a brief chat with Delilah down at the barricade. He used a hunter's long-range walkie-talkie instead of a cell phone, I was glad to see. As he returned and sat down to eat, he placed it on the table next to his dinner knife. I pursed my lips at the place setting and him until he wryly tucked the walkie-talkie away in a pocket.

"How many people are down at the barricade?" I asked, while serving out the potatoes.

"Eight."

My arm froze as I looked at him stricken.

"More on alert," he added. "We can call in reinforcements. Some. If and when there's some action. Delilah says it's quiet down there now."

"To peace on Earth," I toasted quietly.

Right then, the door slammed open with Alex and Shelley arriving for dinner. They both reeked of marijuana, stoned with a case of the munchies. I glared at Shelley, who shrugged and said, "He started it…"

Legal adult or not, Shelley was closer to Alex's age than ours. And if anything, losing her mother had made her regress.

The two of them bonded over their grief, and behaved like brother and sister.

"It's Christmas, Dee. Let it go," Zack suggested. Though he thwacked Alex, who sheepishly slid into a seat and tried to grab at the hard cider. "Go get a glass of water. You, too," he told Shelley. "The hard cider is for Dee and me."

The miscreants didn't bother looking repentant very long. The ham and Zack's potatoes absorbed everyone's attention and glee. We'd dug into the succulent sweet ham several times already, but the potatoes were new and wonderful. The smoky paprika and onion and ham sweetness were perfectly controlled with the sharp pepper and mustard notes, and brought out the rich savory cream and cheese and potatoes. His incremental speed-it-up cooking had brought out extra texture in the dish.

"Dee, you should make this more often," Alex requested.

"Every night would be awesome," agreed Shelley.

"Zack made the potatoes. I'm going to steal his ideas, though," I chimed in.

"Glad you like. Dee's cabbage is excellent, too," Zack attempted.

The black and blond heads of my young neighbors bobbed perfunctorily. They were sick of cabbage, no matter how well dressed.

When eating slowed, Shelley and Alex filled us in on the party at St. Mary's. Alex flat-out preferred the Catholic party, which had concentrated the teen crowd. Shelley tried to subtly grill Zack about the soldier, Jake, she'd danced with at the Protestant hall. Shelley wasn't subtle when she was sober, and being stoned didn't help. Zack supplied that the young man was an import from Niantic up the coast. His family had decided to suicide, except for him. He wanted to leave all that behind and find a place to fight. He'd inquired at the Totoket police department, and Zack snapped him up as soon as he was offered.

"So Jake's a soldier?" asked Alex.

"No, I think he went to some military academy high school. Irritated his stepfather by getting stoned or something," Zack supplied.

This clearly earned Jake extra brownie points in Shelley and Alex's esteem.

"I'll tell him you asked about him," Zack told Shelley with a smile.

"Oh, no, don't do that!" she cried.

Zack's walkie-talkie buzzed and he answered, without apology. His hostess, me, already knew why, after all. "Right... God. On my way." He was already up and at the door, pulling back on his fatigue sweater.

"Zack, take my car." I grabbed up and handed him the car keys. "There's not much gas, but it'll get you to the reservoir."

"You're sure? Thanks!" And he was gone.

Alex turned on the living room screen, still set to show the aerial view of the reservoir barricade and its approach. "That's a lot of muzzle flashes," he said. He was stoned and safe and well-fed. He said this as an observation, seemingly devoid of fear for us, or concern for Zack's safety.

I hadn't even realized he knew about those satellite maps. I dragged both Alex and Shelley outdoors by the figurative ears and gave them a stern lecture on the lawn about staying the hell away from my stuff.

My rant was derailed by Alex. He asked, "How would we know? If you were dragged away by Homeland Security, or went off to a doctor of death, or just left us?"

I wondered whether he was asking about me, or his mother. "That's a good question," I allowed. "Alex, if I ever leave of my own free will, I won't leave without saying good-bye. I'd make sure you're OK first, and have another adult to lean on."

"I've got Shelley and Zack," he said.

"You've got lots of good people," I agreed. "I still won't

leave you without saying good-bye. Not if I can help it. I care about you, Alex." I folded him into a hug.

"Sorry I screwed with your stuff," he mumbled into my shoulder. "I didn't think about it being dangerous. I won't talk to people about it anymore."

My heart sank. "How many people have you told about it?"

"Just Shelley... and a couple friends."

"OK. Thank you for telling me. Don't talk to them about it anymore, OK? Not even Shelley in your house. Only me or Mangal or Zack. Deal?"

"Deal," he agreed. I let him go, and he went back inside to finish eating. I started to follow him.

But Shelley stood her ground. "I want in. Whatever you're doing, I want in."

After a pause, I asked, "Why?"

"I don't want to be pushed around anymore. Go here, stay there, oops, you're dead. I want to know what's going on. I want to fight back."

I nodded my head slowly. Those were good reasons. "Alright. We'll think about what you can do. But you cannot, absolutely cannot, access my stuff without my permission again. Deal?"

"Deal. Dee? I don't really have a chance at the UNC ark, do I?"

"No. I don't think any of us do. Dan says I might, and Mangal might, but... I don't even think Dan will be in that ark, really. But Shelley, I don't really *know*."

"It's all a fucking lie. The arks."

"Pretty much. Or rather, they're real. Little castles for the rich, surrounded by soldier serfs. But we're not American royalty, and we're not soldiers."

"So what's Adam?"

"An engineer who makes the ark work. Royalty of a sort, I guess. His family bought their way into an ark. But not the ark

Adam is building."

"Can I eat the rest of this?" Alex called out from the door.

"No!" we replied in unison. We headed in to save our suppers.

"You should dump Adam for Zack," Shelley grumbled, on the way to the door.

I shrugged, and held the door as she stormed in. Her grief over her mother was gone, the stoned apathy gone. Her face was set in rage. That scared me more than anything, the rage. Faced with a climate gone haywire, family killed or suicided, friends getting murdered over a food fight, betrayed by their own politicians—just how many billions settled on rage as the only thing they had left?

Chapter 13

Interesting fact: The U.S. had more guns per capita than any other country, at about 0.9 guns per person. The runners-up were Serbia and Yemen, with less than 0.6 guns per person. These statistics were civilian guns, not including the military.

I had three invites to choose from for New Year's Eve. Zack's band of soldiers, political cronies, and community garden gang planned an outdoor bonfire party at the Route 1 barricade. Mangal and Shanti wouldn't go anywhere near that. They invited us to a quiet party at home with their Jain friends. I wasn't surprised to learn that Shelley and Alex chose Zack's. And Adam invited me to his house, for a reprise of our dinner and hot tub evening for two. Though this time he asked me to bring the food. All three options sounded fun.

I opted for Adam's house.

Early the day before, the rains began. The news simply reported heavy rain in the Northeast. The talking heads joked about driving extra-carefully to those New Year's Eve parties, wink-wink. Increasingly, tuning in to the news was like receiving video-grams from an alien planet. Our world was turned upside-down, but they cheerfully pretended that most of life was unchanged in middle-class America. There was truth reported there, but watered down to prevent alarm. For instance, the Ebola epidemic in New York City was a particularly bad flu season. And today there was heavy rain in the Northeast. Cut to heartwarming puppy segment.

I checked the satellite feeds and pre-censored National Weather Service. The 'heavy rain' was a tropical storm sporting large circular bands of heavy weather, named Nolan. This was our second 'N' of the year. Nadia was one of the hurricanes that hit Houston. They'd started the alphabet over with flipped genders. Nolan was off the outer banks of North Carolina when the hard rains reached us in Connecticut, still only a tropical storm. They expected the eye to track east off Cape Cod. That was the highest probability track, at least. There was the usual wide fan of other possibilities, including the entirety of the mid-Atlantic and southern New England seaboards.

I called Zack. "Hey, Zack, it's Dee. How's the car-shopping going?"

My car had not survived the Christmas night battle by the reservoir. Its burned hulk now formed part of the Route 1 barricade. Zack said he used it as a fire-bomb on the looter gang. I didn't press for details lest the conversation go further downhill. None of our guys died. Many on the other side did. Good enough. Zack promised to replace the car with an electric one.

"Just teasing. Say, Zack, I hope you have an alternate venue for your party tomorrow. This rain feels warm and tropical to me. Doesn't it feel tropical to you?"

"Now that you mention it. Yeah, it is a bit warm," said Zack. It was in fact over 60 degrees, at a time of year that often saw lows in the teens. "Could get worse before it gets better, huh?"

"It could. Yeah, I'd really rather not have Alex out in that kind of storm. You know me, I'm such a scaredy-cat with the weather. My head spins. Well, let him know if you plan to move the party indoors, OK?"

"Right. Thanks for the head's up, Dee. About the car—"

"Bye now." I hung up. OK, so maybe I was still a little peeved about him making a bomb out of my car. I didn't expect to stay mad at him, but it might take me a few more days to get past it. That and a replacement car.

End Game

By early New Year's Eve, Nolan had strengthened to Category 1. It was nearly unheard of for a tropical storm to develop into a hurricane as it headed into the Northeast. Generally they weakened as they headed north across colder water. They broke up fast, of course, once they hit land. But so far Nolan stayed offshore. Though the track had edged westward slightly. It was now predicted to clip the arm of Cape Cod, about 200 miles east of us. Not a good night for Nantucket, or anywhere else within the Boston-Providence borders. But 'heavy rain' and gusts up to gale force were all we should see near New Haven.

The censored news continued to report nothing more than 'heavy rain', don't drink too much, good night to cozy up at home, wink-wink. I suspect many screens around that time were bashed in with chairs and bottles, in reaction to the fake news reports. I was even more critical than most, being in the business. But I needed my screen, so I confined myself to rude gestures and cat-calls.

Adam picked me up at 8 p.m. as promised. He held on to my arm firmly as we walked into slashing sheets of warm rain. We still had to stop once for a few moments and just brace against the wind. The sustained winds felt like gale force to me, and that gust we braced through was a whole lot stronger than that. It was a battle closing the car doors after us.

"Adam, maybe we should stay here," I suggested.

"It's just a rainstorm," he said, and started the car.

I laid my hand on his. "It's not just a rainstorm. *That* was a hurricane-force wind."

He pulled out onto the street. "We'll be fine. But I would like to close my storm shutters, OK?"

I pondered when exactly the man closed his storm shutters, as I watched trees wave and bow nearly 90 degrees in the wind. This was especially impressive for trees with no leaves on them. I nearly slammed into the windshield as he skidded to miss a

157

bough and live power line dancing on the road. He just backed up and went around.

"Remember the Canadian border, Adam?"

"I'm not likely to forget it, Dee, but we're going to my house tonight." He swerved suddenly again, off the pavement, but made it back onto the road. He'd missed a large animal, but I wasn't sure what kind. Adam really was a skilled driver. If pigheaded. "Maybe you should let me concentrate on my driving."

Our guys at the southern bridge simply waved us through the single-lane break in the barrier, without trying to make us stop. "They know you?" I asked.

"I just drove through here 20 minutes ago, Dee. We're fine."

There were white-capped waves on the sheltered estuary, crashing onto the bridge, shooting spray into the air over the car. It was still a couple hours shy of high tide. I settled back in fatalistic enjoyment of the ride. I couldn't see much except in the path of the headlights.

Adam parked a couple blocks inland from his house. He claimed the salt water had never reached there, even in Hurricane Irene, when his stretch of houses was crushed in 2011. Not that he lived there then. He carried the box of supper I'd packed, and I held onto his arm as we trudged into the unbroken wind off Long Island Sound.

He'd been busy. All the deck furniture was tied down to a storage garage at the back of his property, farthest from the waves. The waves weren't breaking on the pylons yet, but they'd washed through the carport under the house. I could see fresh seaweed before the doorstep, as we entered via a utilitarian enclosed staircase. This staircase column was tacked onto the rear of the house, behind one of the 6 foot diameter concrete pylons, wrapped in winding burlap like fat stubby palm trees. The main entrance to Adam's place was exposed outdoor slat steps leading up to the glorious waterfront view from the front deck. I was grateful we weren't climbing up that in the buffeting wind.

When we emerged into the relative quiet of the kitchen, Adam left the house lights off, but brought up the deck floodlights onto his stretch of beach. He peeled off his foul weather jacket. I kept walking, rapt, to the front picture windows.

'Storm surge' is a wonderful term to describe it, the massive megatons of grey-brown water heaving, cresting, crashing forward on the beach, and then that irresistible undertow drawing back into the next vast wave. Next to a few of those waves, the gorgeous house I stood in, up on its brave tubby pylons, amounted to tinker toys. Between the slashing rain sheeting the windows, heaving hills of water, and the short range of the floodlights, I couldn't see very far. Yet the undertow scoured out the sand in front of the house, unearthing boulders I hadn't seen before, and drawing mere head-sized rocks back into the cauldron. Wind gusts slammed into the side of the house to my left, sometimes making the floor lift, just a little bit.

I usually loved storms, standing small and in awe before the exhilaration and power of nature unleashed. But I was uneasy then. My best friend, Earth, was going a little crazy lately. With a human friend, like my late coworker Connor, you made allowances, you tried to help, maybe added a little distance, let go if you had to. But Connor didn't frighten me, much. There's a power imbalance with a planet, with storms that can crush you in your trans-million dollar house to kindling with a single swat. More like a small child realizing their idolized God-like parent is going a bit bonkers. Only more so. This one storm, let alone Earth, was a lot more powerful than any parent was. This storm made me uneasy. Something was wrong.

Well, of course something was wrong. Hurricane season used to end months ago. Hurricanes couldn't feed on the vast and cold dark waters of the North Atlantic in winter. Three hurricanes devastated Houston in a week.

No. What's wrong with this picture?

My eyes narrowed. Another blast of wind pounded the wall to my left, and I looked out the picture windows that way. And back at the front window, where rain and ocean spray streamed almost horizontally left to right across it. The waves hit the beach on a diagonal, left to right, crests flying off the breakers to the right. The easterly wind was piling the storm surge into Long Island Sound. High tide would be extra-high.

I drew a circle with my finger on the glass, counter-clockwise, like a water drain, or a cyclone in the Northern Hemisphere. *Shit.*

"Adam, this is a hurricane. The wind is blowing from the east. That means we're north of the eye. This hurricane isn't going to miss us."

"The news said this isn't..." He considered my face. "You know for a fact that this is a hurricane?"

"Yes. It was Category 1, last I checked. They said it was tracking for Cape Cod, that it would pass east of us. But it isn't passing east of us."

He took me seriously, and pondered this. I was gratified that he drew a circle with his finger, too, and looked worriedly at the left and front windows. Left, to the east, rain pattern splat. Center, to the south, rain pattern horizontal, east to west.

"Category 1?" he asked for confirmation, and drew out his phone.

I nodded. "Can this house take a Category 1 storm?"

"Sure." He swallowed a little nervousness. "Even Category 2. With some damage. Excuse me, Dee. I need to make a phone call." Northwest seemed to be the best signal in the house, as he drifted thataway. Which made sense. The small New Haven airport was over that way.

"Hello. Lacey here. I need to talk to Niedermeyer... Yes,

it's urgent... I'll wait... Sir, I've just learned that this storm is a hurricane—"

"Hurricane Nolan," I supplied.

"Hurricane Nolan," Adam echoed to the unknown Niedermeyer. Unknown to me, anyway. "Category 1. It was expected to track east of us and hit Cape Cod. But where I'm standing the wind is easterly, which says it's due south of us... I'm home, in East Haven... Southeasterly in Groton?... Yes, please, I'll wait... Northeasterly in Stamford? Awesome... I don't think that's an option, Sir... It's probably alright. I wouldn't do anything to it in the storm. Ferreira can keep an eye on it. But if it starts to go, there's not much he can do about it... Yes, sir... No, sir... I can inquire and call you back... Yes, sir."

Adam looked at me strangely. "You caught that? You're right. The hurricane seems to be tracking toward right about here—the eye seems to be east of Stamford, west of Groton, south of us. So it's pretty much coming straight at us." He stopped to consider how to word the next. "Any chance you can get an update on whether it's still Category 1?"

"Any chance of protecting my anonymity?"

"Certainly, oh Oracle. We need to know what, not who. And somehow that news didn't make it where it needed to go."

"To your ark?"

Adam's eye flicked upward, as it often does when someone adjusts the truth. "Yeah. The ark." He met my eye this time, and tilted his head in reluctant apology. "Niedermeyer is actually Coast Guard, in Groton."

"And he didn't know? Christ. I'll check. Adam—maybe it's time to draw those shutters?"

We swapped corners as I called Mangal. He needed to get private and login, then I had to walk him through it over the phone, where I'd found the wind speed data.

"It says 105 mph sustained," Mangal reported, "but it was

100 an hour ago. Oh, here, yeah, the storm was upgraded to Category 2 a couple hours ago. I guess 110 and higher is Category 3. Landfall, let's see. Right about high tide. In an hour. That's… bad, right?"

"It's not good. You'll be alright, there. Don't try to leave the house or anything. Especially not during the eye of the hurricane. You'll lose power, of course." The power lines ran above ground, frolicking in the tree tops. We always lost power.

"We're getting the *eye* of the…? Ah. Yes, I see that. I'll, um, call Alex and Shelley and make sure they stay put. And remind them about that eye thing," Mangal offered.

I hung up with Mangal and realized that he wouldn't contact Zack. Zack was in charge of pursuing violence, and Mangal could not contribute to violence. I turned my back to Adam and called Zack. "Hey, it's Dee! An even *better* band! Category 2 is playing in downtown New Haven! Don't you just love Category 2? Oops, starts in one hour. Gotta go. Seeya!"

Adam was looking at me funny, but simply confirmed the facts he'd overheard. "Upgraded to Category 2 now, 105 mph sustained winds, landfall one hour at high tide?" As I nodded, we traded places again, him taking his phone to the northwest, and me taking over at the storm-shutter master control panel at the southwest corner by the windows.

I didn't eavesdrop on him this time, because I saw something out the window, a flash of light behind the beach houses to our left, eastward. As I finished closing the front shutters, Adam turned on low lights in the kitchen and killed the floodlights. I peered out an unshuttered window at the back trying to get a better angle on what I'd seen, not easy through the stormy dark and runnels of rain. But I spotted it again, a couple flashlights and a group of people, at least three.

"Adam, do you have trouble with looters here?"

He begged off his phone call abruptly and joined me at the window. "We have, um, protection," he said. "I suspect there's a ranking Mafia type up the beach a ways. The… 'security force' came by and asked me for a 'donation' to subscribe. Three grand."

My eyes widened. "What did you do?"

"Gave them four grand, and thanked them for their efforts on my behalf, to butter them up. I don't want to sit around here all day with a gun, protecting my property. But I didn't see any of them out there tonight. What did you see?"

I pointed. "Flashlights, a group of people, maybe armed. Can't see them very well."

Adam kept peering out the window, and made another call. After the call, he confirmed to me, "Security doesn't have anybody out there tonight. Too dangerous in the storm." He sighed and considered a moment.

"Think we should leave?" I asked. "Wouldn't they call a mandatory evacuation on this beach, if they knew a Category 2 was headed straight for us?"

"They would have, yes." He considered. "The waves are already washing under the house. If we want to evacuate, we ought to leave right now. I'm sorry. 'You were right' doesn't begin to cover it." He spotted something, and ducked down lower to see. "More of them."

"Well, if we can't walk away from the house safely because of the waves, they can't walk into it, either," I suggested, weighing the options.

"Until the eye of the storm, maybe," Adam countered. "And after. There are plenty of houses on this beach for them to break into and take shelter in." He sighed. "Including this one."

"I want to go," I declared in sudden decision.

"We'll try it," Adam agreed, with clear reservations.

He immediately pulled his raingear back on. I'd never taken mine off. He took my hand and drew me down the sheltered back steps in the dark. Fortunately there was no storm door on

163

the back door. There was some water on the floor already, though, despite the floor being several steps above the paving stones of the carport. Adam opened the door and let the rain and wind in, and made sure the door would lock after us. A wave rushed past us into the back yard. He studied the undertow as it pulled back out.

Without ceasing his focus on the few sample waves, Adam called, "Whatever happens, don't let go of me. You're too light by yourself. If we get pulled back toward the water, we've got to make it back to this door. Right?"

"Right!"

The waves washing in were maybe 9 inches deep, over the top of the first step below us. We watched three more waves come in and out to get the pattern. "Now?" I called against the wind.

Adam jerked me back. "Not this one." He was right. I'd gotten the timing right, but it was a higher wave than the others, coming over the second step. He waited until that one was mostly withdrawn and the carport was almost clear. "Now!"

We ran full out, holding hands, the pull of that last wave still sucking our shoes backwards a bit at first, but too shallow to grab us. We got past the back mini-wall of the carport when I heard the next wave crash behind us. Adam grabbed me around the waist and we ran as fast as we could. The wash from the crashing wave caught us. We fell and ran, fell and ran another 30 feet or so, the water pushing us forward. Then Adam dove forward, sliding us into a fence post just as the water turned and started rushing out around us. We both held on to the post for dear life as the water tried to suck us back into the sea and the next wave crested in front of the house.

"Phew!" yelled Adam, grinning from the adrenaline rush, and surprise that we'd made it this far. "When I say go. We need to make it across the street this time. And… Go!"

End Game

The water wasn't as powerful back here, but still we set off as the last shallow bit of the undertow finished washing back. We headed into the street. The waves were less powerful here, but I hadn't bargained on the street being lower than Adam's yard. It was already flooded a foot deep. That really slows down your running, and was none too soft on the falling and splashing part of the program either, as the next in-rush of water knocked us down. On the plus side, that foot of water had tons of inertia that weren't pulling back into the Sound, so the undertow wasn't as vicious. We continued running—or at least wading fast—across the street during the ebb of the wave, and kept going until Adam had a good hold on a small ornamental tree in the across-the-street neighbor's yard.

Delivered from the power of the waves, we were now in the wind's hands. Without Adam to hold onto, I was too light to withstand that, either. The sustained winds were now at Category 1 hurricane force, with gusts far stronger. One of those gusts hit us at the tree, and Adam crushed me between him and the trunk while he held on. As the gust subsided to merely unbearable wind again, he yelled into my ear, "You alright?"

"I'm good," I assured him. "Need a breather."

"Ten seconds for a breather," he agreed. "We need to reach more shelter. Ready... now!"

Oh, I hated him then. I had not gotten my breath back, and the wind ripped it away. My chest was burning, and one of my boots had sucked half-off my heel. I couldn't stop to ram my foot back in, and we were still running through standing water several inches deep, alternating with slick muddy lawns. I'm nobody's pansy, but I was sobbing. Being in the power of the storm was bad enough, but I was entirely at Adam's mercy as well. And the damned man wasn't about to consult me. I was far too afraid to be fair at this point.

Adam dragged me along down his street, and up a side

street leading uphill away from the beach. He finally yanked us to a stop several houses up the side street, dragging me down to crouch under a retaining wall between lawns.

"How are you holding up?" he yelled.

"I hate you!" I reported. I shoved my foot firmly back into my boot. The laces were too wet to tighten them. I was still gasping for air. He had picked us a good spot, though. We were just enough sheltered from the worst of the wind to get our own wind back without having it torn away from us.

"Good. Use that anger," he advised. He was too tanked up on adrenaline to take it personally. "I don't know if you noticed, but the looters painted us with a flashlight a couple times. We need to catch our breath and start running again."

"Maybe one of these nice houses?"

"Not with looters hunting us. It's only one more block to the car, Dee. You can do it. Ten more seconds for a breather… *Now*."

So we ran uphill, buffeted by the vicious wind. There were cars on the street, that wouldn't have been there if anyone expected a hurricane. But they provided some shelter to run past at a crouch. I saw the flashlights of the looters zip past us, and Adam checked behind his shoulder a number of times. But the way he held me and kept dragging me along, I couldn't get a good look. I never heard any shots fired, as the wind tore the sound away. I did see a windshield explode in front of us from a gunshot behind us, though. It provided an extra spurt of motivation.

We dove into the car. Adam starting it rolling before I even got my door closed. A looter leapt out into the street in front of us, aiming a rifle. Adam scowled and gunned the car straight at him. The looter jumped out of the way instead of firing. Adam turned one way, then the next, weaving us out of the tiny streets filled with fallen branches at hair-raising speed, until he got us out to the wide open north-south four lane main drag in that part of town. He headed straight up the middle, straddling the yellow lines, doing about 30, away from the beach.

There was no other traffic. I almost complained, but one look at Adam's face dissuaded me. He was entirely focused on his driving, struggling to counteract the wind buffeting the car and dodge debris in the road. We passed the southern turn toward Totoket and kept going for Route 1. I didn't second-guess him. Those roads had downed power lines when we were through there over an hour ago. They were narrow and windy, hemmed in with trees, and the route included some low places near the Sound. On our current road or Route 1, even if a tree fell, there'd still be room left to get around it.

Thankfully, there were no suicidal storm-happy looters up by Route 1. Adam pulled up to the barricade right behind Zack's landscaping truck. Headlights and repeated honking eventually got through to Zack, who was in fact sitting in the cab of his truck. Judging from the under-chin glow, he'd been reading a book to pass the time. Zack shook his head at us through his rear window.

Adam turned on the inside car lights to show us, flashed the head-lights, and honked at Zack.

Zack held hands up facing each other, one above the other, spaced as far apart as the rear window allowed. He shook his head emphatically.

"Adam, he's trying to tell us something," I attempted.

"I'm not parking here, Dee," Adam insisted. He honked and flashed headlights again.

Zack reluctantly moved his truck just barely out of the way to let us through, flipped Adam the bird as we passed, then reversed his truck back into the barricade.

"*Stop!*" I screeched, as Adam sped up to climb Route 1 to my house. It was mostly uphill, but there was that low point first. Adam stopped. We gazed at the reservoir, which now overflowed its bank into this low point, laying a sheet of water right across Route 1. I added, "That's what Zack was trying to tell us. The water's too deep. We can't get up the hill this way."

Adam nodded. He closed his eyes and laid his head back on the seat, and just breathed raggedly for a bit. I didn't interrupt him. The thudding of my heart was finally quieting down. Having time to chill out and breathe, be one with the storm outside the strong safe windows, was actually kind of nice. The wind bounced the car a bit, but didn't move it. Of course, the wind couldn't get underneath, since we were parked in about 6 inches of water.

After a few minutes, Adam's breathing smoothed out, and he roused. "Dee… I'm sorry. Are you OK?" he said quietly.

"Yeah. Apology accepted."

"We can't sit here. The worst of the storm isn't even here yet, and this lake is growing. We can go back and park near Zack. Do you have any better ideas?"

That plan was exactly what I'd been thinking. I was just biting my lip to give him time to calm down before broaching the subject. "Sorry, no. I think Zack is the best option."

So the three of us spent New Year's Eve together. The eye of the hurricane passed us around midnight. We reluctantly got out of our vehicles and shook hands and exchanged hugs. God, that was awkward. A couple other guys were camping out there, too, manning the barricade. But they stayed in their separate vehicles.

We were all asleep by the time the storm died out.

Chapter 14

Interesting fact: Global Jihad began as an alliance between Al-Qaeda, the Taliban, ISIL in Syria and Iraq, the Islamic Jihad Union, Caliphate State, and other terrorist groups. When the U.S. withdrew its troops and oil dollars from the Middle East, Saudi Arabia and Iran backed the movement. National borders became fluid between the Mediterranean and Red Sea to the west, and China and India to the east. Russian-backed Turkey and Kazakhstan held fast against them in the north. Large Muslim populations in Africa and Europe rallied to the cause. Global Jihad formed a chaotic pseudo-nation of over 400 million Muslims. Their goal was to unite the entire world under Islam and Sharia law. Sectarian and tribal differences were downplayed in favor of united recruitment. Jordan and Israel were simply overrun.

Zack was gone when we woke up in Adam's car at the Route 1 barricade. We were hungry and still sopping wet, and didn't know what we'd find at Adam's beach house. I insisted Adam take me to my house, and stay to get fed and clean and dry.

There were downed boughs in the neighborhood, already being cleared by neighbors, and minor damage here and there, like missing shutters and bits of roof flapping loose. But for the most part my neighborhood and my house seemed to have weathered the storm OK. Without leaves to catch the high winds, trees don't take as much hurricane damage in winter as they do in summer. The rain had stopped for the first time in days. There was still high cloud cover, rapidly breaking apart into scudding smaller clouds. The sun would be out soon.

Adam kept his ark locker in the trunk of the car, so he had his own dry clothes to change into. I dumped our salt-sodden New Year's Eve steampunk finery into the washing machine to wait for the power to come back. After taking showers in our separate bathrooms, we met over plain cereal and hot tea for a subdued breakfast.

There was no romance at all that morning. But simple kindness would do.

"After breakfast," I said, "let's check out your house."

"You don't need to do that," Adam murmured.

"How long have you had it?"

"Three years, four in May." He played with his tea mug a moment. "When my mother... died... She came from money. Dad invested it for us, my brother and me. Dad refused to touch it for college or anything—he wanted to pay for everything we needed. Every year, we'd have a talk about managing money, and how our portfolios were doing. The annual money management lecture." He laughed softly. "It's what Dad does. He manages investments for people. And he taught us. When I turned 30, he suggested it was time. I should buy a house or start a business or something. So I did." He swallowed.

"I'd wondered how much money an arkitect makes, to afford a house like that."

He snorted. "Not much more than a programmer, I imagine. But without a mortgage, so it's almost all disposable income—it's a lot."

"Yeah. Do you mind my asking, how did your mother die?"

"An overdose. She was a party girl... I don't remember her. I was only a year old when she died. My brother remembers her, but Dad and I don't talk about her. I was about ten when Dad was willing to open up again, and started seeing my stepmother. She's good for Dad. I like her. And my sister is

170

cute." He smiled bravely.

"Sounds pretty rough. I'm sorry."

"No. No way." He shook his head vehemently. "I'm not a poor little rich boy, Dee. I went to school with them for years. Yeah, sure, we had nannies. They were good ones, usually grad students. We still keep in touch with them. But Dad was home nearly every night. He checked our homework, made it to our sailing regattas and lacrosse games and wrestling matches and stupid school plays. The three of us worked together on our yacht most weekends, or robotics projects, or the cars. We sailed together, and took long vacations together every year. My brother and I went to off to boarding school at seventh grade. But Dad drove us there, drove us back, called twice a week, never missed an event that parents were invited to, never delegated parenting to my stepmom. I had a *great* family, Dee."

I smiled. "Sounds like it."

He gazed at me for a moment. "But yeah. The beach house is all I have of my Mom. And I've never known what to do with... that."

"Keep it light. Keep it fun. Avoid the drugs and alcohol and self-pity like the poor little rich girls, maybe."

"Yeah." He played with his tea mug a while more. "I've been kind of an ass, last night. I'm sorry. But, um, I need to move onto the ark."

"Now?" I didn't have any particular excuse for being surprised. But I was. And yes, he'd been kind of an ass. And that made perfect sense now.

"Yeah. Tonight. I spoke to my boss while you were in the shower. So. Anything you want at the house, it's yours. This may be the last time I go back there." He winced. "Are you sure you want to do this?"

"I don't think you should do it alone. So, yes. I want to be there for you." His father and brother couldn't be there for him, not this time. Given what he'd said, that must have been

171

horribly strange.

"Thank you," he said quietly.

As we drove back to his house, several blocks up from the beach, we reached a grizzly new display. Three young black men hung from a tree, and a mixed racial handful of bodies were thrown over a white picket fence. Several guys were still working on stringing them up with rope for show. A detached garage door was tacked up against the next tree, with red letters a foot tall, 'LOOTERS BEWARE.'

I'd never seen dead bodies before, except peacefully arrayed in a funeral home. But I didn't have any sympathy for these dead. Part of me was revolted, shocked. Another part thought, 'Good.'

Adam slowed in shock to take a look, and a guy with a gun flagged him to stop. Adam presented proof of residency in the neighborhood. We were waved on our way.

Adam weaved us through the same streets we'd used last night, and parked on the same uphill street we'd run up during the hurricane, a few feet above the sand and seaweed line. I didn't say much as we walked down to Adam's street.

The house at the base of the street, on the beach, was tilted 20 degrees off the vertical. Adam walked slowly through the sand on the road, staring, as other broken beach houses came into view. One to the left had a crushed front pylon. It looked as though once that corner of house sagged into the oncoming waves, the house had shattered across the street. He was staring at the debris field when his own house came into view in the other direction.

"Adam, yours is still standing," I murmured, touching his arm.

He looked, nodded, and blew out through his lips. The houses on either side looked bad. One was laid open across the front. The other had half its roof off, and storm shutters hanging and banging in the fresh fishy breeze. The sun came and went rapidly as clouds tore across the sky.

Adam's street was still half-flooded, and he wanted to see everything from the beach side, anyway. We walked through the deep sand on a neighbor's lawn out onto the beach. There were a couple of houses laid open across the front. Living rooms and kitchens and bedrooms sat open to the Sound, soggy furniture tossed about a little, looking like broken doll-houses. The beach had eroded several feet, leaving us to walk more on rock than sand. White-topped high waves continued to roll in. But the tide was out, so we had some room between sea and houses, even with the beach so eroded.

Adam studied the first couple structural failures with an engineer's eye, seemingly reluctant to continue on to his own house. I walked on ahead to see. The gorgeous wrap-around deck was broken and sagging down to the sand. There was no visible grass left on the lawn. Beach sand washed through under the house, to the storage garage and street in back. But the storm shutters appeared intact, and the thick stubby pylons. Their burlap wrappings had come unwound, and one pylon had a big concrete chunk bitten out of it, showing the rusty steel rods of its core. But they still looked sound. There was a lot of wreckage in the carport area under the house. The pretty wooden latticework that went around the carport was simply gone, probably washed away.

Adam finally joined me. I put my arm around him, and he hugged me back. There was no question of using the outdoor steps up to the broken deck, so we headed around back toward the enclosed utility staircase.

Adam yanked me to a halt and stared at the storm wrack in his carport. He swallowed and made a phone call. "Yeah, this is Adam Lacey. I, um, have another body for your looter display. Could you come pick it up, or should I just... leave it here? Thanks." I hadn't spotted the body, half-covered in sand. It was tangled in a broken stretch of steps from the deck. A hand still clutched a half-buried assault rifle. It didn't seem real.

I squeezed Adam's waist again. He skipped the stairs and headed directly to the storage garage. The wide roll-up car door was badly dented, and he couldn't get it open by just yanking at it. But the structure had a side door. He found a length of fence pipe inside and used that to pry open the big door.

"The spare Tesla battery is in here, and my generator. You'll want those?"

"Yes, thank you. But Adam, don't you want to look in the house first?"

"The gas and power turn-offs are back here. I think I'd rather shut those off before going inside."

"Aha. Yes. That." Now that he mentioned it, I did smell gas. "Though... it looks OK."

Adam shrugged. He pulled a couple suitcases with wheels out of the neat but tightly packed shelves of the garage, where they'd sat safely above the high water line. Then he went back in to grab a toolbox and add a few extra tools to it. Last out came a sodden four-wheel dolly, the kind you lay on to scoot under a car to work on it, plus a generously sized hand-truck, and a tidy bucket of bungee cords. "Want some camping gear?" he asked.

"Sure!"

Best quality tent kits, in two sizes, a gazebo, a couple cots and air mattresses, electric and manual air pumps, and sleeping bags piled onto the dolly. "I'll get more out later. But I've stalled enough. Let's go inside." He brought the toolbox with him, and a suitcase. I rolled the other suitcase along.

The lowest step, made of cinder blocks, was askew. Adam kicked the blocks back into place as best he could, but there were new rocks in the way. The door was broken off its hinge, and the indoor-outdoor carpeting of the stairwell was sopping wet. All this was to be expected—he must not have taken the time to properly shut the door last night when our lives were on the line. He paused halfway up the stairs, though. There was a rusty stain on the carpeting, above the water line.

"Hello?" Adam called out loudly. "Anyone here?" No response, no noises.

We reached the kitchen at the back of the main floor, and Adam blew out his breath. No water or wind had broken in. It looked fine. Except, the dinner we'd never touched was out of its box, and eaten, the containers lying empty on the table. Adam motioned me to stay put at the head of the stairs, while he walked out into the living room, looking around. But there was no one there. I poked into the liquor cabinet in the kitchen. Everything was still there, so far as I could tell. I packed the bottles into the suitcase, padded with potholders and dish towels to keep them from clinking together. Top-shelf booze had great barter value.

Adam grabbed a tool out of his toolbox, and used it to manually crank open a big storm shutter partway to let in some light. Still nobody. Adam left the toolbox with me, and started cautiously upstairs to the bedroom floor. I decided to follow behind him, with a rolling pin from the potholder drawer. The gourmet stepmom and sister must have equipped the man's kitchen. He had high quality gear, hardly used if ever.

"*Shit!*" Adam yelled. I trotted the rest of the way up to his bedroom door, and peered around him in the doorway. A young black man was in Adam's bed, naked above the blankets except for a bloody Ace bandage on his arm. He sat up, the covers rucked up around his waist, his arms up. He didn't reach for the assault rifle next to him. More ammo was dumped on the floor, with wet boots and clothing. The room didn't seem molested other than the bed being used. A drawer hung open in the master bathroom, probably the source of the Ace bandage.

"I didn't hurt your place, man," the intruder said, hands still up and open. "I just needed shelter from the storm. I'm alone. I didn't take nothing but a little food, and a bandage."

175

Adam walked over to take the gun, both of them making a few jerky movements along the way. But the intruder's hands kept returning to surrender position. Adam passed the gun and ammo to me. I hadn't realized how heavy ammo was before.

"Is this the," *bang*, "safety."

"*Shit*, woman!" our guest exclaimed. He hugged his blanketed knees to his chest. Adam's perfectly unmolested bathroom now had a shattered vanity mirror where I'd just shot it by accident.

Adam took the gun back and set the safety on. We looked at each other, and he started laughing, in a stressed-out, creaky sort of way. I tried a grin. "Well, it broke the ice, right?"

Adam looked back at his guest without favor. "I'm Adam Lacey. This is my bedroom. She's Dee. Who are you?"

"Trey Cowan."

"They shoot looters here, Trey Cowan."

"Man, I'm not one of them. I mean, yeah, I wanted to get out of New Haven. But then, I couldn't escape those guys. Guy tries to leave, they shoot him in the back. They're nuts. I just used the storm to get the fuck away from them. I don't want to hurt nobody."

I heard a truck arriving out back. I peered out the bathroom window. The flatbed already had another body on it. A guy stood at the front of the truck with a rifle, while two others headed under the house. They looked like Adam's paid 'security', not looters. Sadly, I reflected that I had no basis for that except the color of their skin. Two of them looked Italian, the other fair.

"What do you do in New Haven, Trey?" I asked.

"Christmas break with my family, but they were gone when I got home. I got no idea where they went. I'm a student at Eastern in Willimantic. Studying earth science. Was. They closed the school. It's hell on the Hill in New Haven. I just want to get out."

"You know how to use a gun," Adam prodded.

"Yeah, even *she* could make a gun go bang," Trey countered, with a sour glance at me. I returned his glower.

"Would you be willing to fight looters, instead of be one?" Adam asked.

"Man, I just want to get out of here alive. Whatever."

Adam sighed. "You think Zack would want him?" he asked me.

I shrugged. "Up to Zack. If we took Trey here to the barricade, worst that'd happen is that they put him out on the East Haven side and tell him to run away. Unless he does something stupid. He doesn't seem stupid."

Adam nodded thoughtfully, and frowned at Trey. "Alright, Trey, here's how this goes. You're going to do some work with us. Nothing illegal. Just help me move my stuff from my house. As long as you cooperate, you've got a shot at a job over in Totoket. You try to run, or try anything against us, local security *will* kill you. They're downstairs right now, picking up the body of one of your looter buddies. They do not like the color of your skin."

"Man... And Totoket?" Trey asked. Helpless fury blazed in his eyes. I couldn't blame him.

"Not a problem in Totoket. Much." I shrugged. "The guy who runs the barricades, Zack, he'll give you a fair hearing. If he thinks he can use you, you're in. How well you get along with people once you're there, is up to you."

Trey swallowed. "Yeah. OK. I can do that."

Adam toed the soggy pile of gangland attire with his toe. "You look about my size. Here, put these on." He pulled out underwear, socks, a blue on white tattersall button-down Oxford, snug Levi's jeans without holes, and a Coast Guard Academy sweatshirt, and threw them on the bed.

"Wow, that's preppy, man," commented Trey.

"I did attend prep school, yes," replied Adam coolly. "And

the Coast Guard Academy."

"Oh, that's cool, man," Trey assured him. "I don't want to take your alma mater sweatshirt. How about that Brown hoodie instead?"

"No hoodie." Adam threw a navy blue Yale sweatshirt at his head. "Just get dressed, alright? Make it march, or I'll have to ask security to stick around. And I don't control these guys."

At Adam's urging, I headed back downstairs with the gun and ammo. Adam stayed upstairs to supervise Trey and grab some more clothes and personal effects for himself.

I wrapped the gun in a towel and stowed it under the suitcase. A quick ray of sun caught on the beautiful bronze telescope, sitting in front of the shutters Adam had cranked open. Irresistibly drawn, I peered out through it. With the tide so low, plenty of the reef was visible, with the seals lying blotto. I bet their night was even more harrowing than mine. The sea still heaved around them in angry grey pyramids of surging water.

I broke off my reverie at the telescope to find Adam and Trey leaning on the walls by the staircase, staring at me. Trey bore a pile of clothes and overnight toiletry bag, piled high. Adam had a small fireproof safe, the kind you stash your passport, car title, and other key papers in. Trey did indeed look preppy, and so neatly put together that I wondered if he were gay.

"The seals are taking a break," I reported to Adam, smiling.

"I'd like you to have that telescope. If you want it," offered Adam, smiling too. "And the binoculars."

"I'd love them. Thank you! Trey, do you want a look, before I move it?"

"Yeah!" He eagerly peered at the heaving gray sea, and the prone seals. Hostility and fear seemed to melt from him. Nature can do that.

I took the bundle he'd been carrying, and stashed it in the

178

other suitcase over the paper safe Adam had placed there. I added the binoculars in with the booze bottles in 'my' suitcase, and added most of Adam's spices and baking staples. Adam wandered through the main floor. Occasionally he would pick up an item, consider it, and put it back. When his circuit brought him back to the kitchen, he placed a hand on the small of my back. I turned and gave him a hug, for as long as he wanted it. After a couple minutes he placed a kiss on my forehead and broke away.

"You're not taking anything else?" I asked quietly.

He fished some coral bits out of his jeans pocket to show me, then returned them to the pocket. "Got those diving in the Caribbean with my father and brother, just before I started boarding school. We rented a 33-foot boat and sailed around the Virgin Islands for a month." He smiled softly. "Best vacation ever. I have all my photos digitally, and my memories. I'm all set, whenever you're ready. But there's more stuff than we could possibly get into the Tesla. Especially if you want my boats."

I'd seen several kayaks and a Sunfish type sailboard stashed in the garage. "I'd love your boats. The security guys have a truck. Do you think they'd help?"

"I don't know that your Zack would appreciate that."

"He's not my Zack." Though, he did have a truck, and gas, and might really want the boats.

"Short-hand, for lack of a better term. Your border captain. In any event, I've got a trailer buried underneath all that crap. We can bring it all. Hey, Trey—time to work off your keep."

Trey and I headed down first, while Adam closed the shutter and took a minute to say good-bye to his home.

It was a lot of work getting all that stuff to the car.

-o-

"That's all well and good," Zack said to Trey. He'd agreed to meet us at the Route 1 barricade to deal with Trey and look over the boats. "But how do I know you're not a plant from the looter gang? It'd be a lot easier to break through here with someone on the inside."

"Look, man, those guys are crazy. Some of them are with Global Jihad. I had no idea what I was getting into with them," pleaded Trey. "And they already got a plant on you. Guy named Jamal, I think."

"Jamal!" Zack called. "Get over here!"

When Jamal arrived, Zack started to explain Trey's accusation. Jamal denied it vehemently, though Zack kept their voices low.

"That ain't him," Trey interrupted. "This other guy has some kind of African accent. I heard them talking over a walkie-talkie. He said—tonight? Maybe tonight. He'd be in charge of some smaller bridge, and he'd let the looters through."

Zack and innocent-Jamal raised eyebrows at each other. "Jermar!" Zack yelled. "Get over here!"

Jermar broke off a conversation on the other side of Route 1, picked up his weapon and took a few steps toward us. Then he broke to his right at a run, through the barricade into East Haven, angling down toward the reservoir for cover. Innocent-Jamal proved to be an excellent shot, and got Jermar in the leg. Jermar took up his rifle to aim back at the barricade. Several more bullets stopped him from getting a shot off.

I stared at the bloody body. I guess it's called shock, when you feel nothing. Or perhaps I just didn't know what to feel.

"If he's still alive, I want to question him," Zack told Jamal, who went off to organize that. "Alright, Trey, we'll give you a chance. Betray our trust, and you *will* die. Consider this your last and only warning."

Watching all this, seeing Zack's face set in calm but firm

lines around his mouth, for the first time I could picture him as an officer in Estonia or Turkey, Iran or Afghanistan. This was a man who knew how to make a car bomb, and what to do with it.

Zack turned back to us. "Adam, Dee, you're free to go. Dee, I might want to borrow the kayaks, if you don't mind."

"Any time," I agreed, and started for Adam's car.

But Adam said, "Have you got a minute to speak privately, Zack? Wait in the car, Dee. Please." They walked up Route 1 about a hundred feet towards the reservoir puddle. They spoke quietly, side by side, looking away toward the water.

I never did get either of them to tell me what they discussed. I asked as soon as Adam was back in the car, but he shook his head and started driving.

-o-

"You're sure you can't spend the night?" I asked. I tried to keep the tone light and playful. It came out sort of mournful instead. I sighed. It had taken several more hours to get the car unpacked, get rid of my helpful neighbors, and have a candle-lit dinner for two. It was nearly 9:00, and even darker than usual with the power still out.

"Sorry," said Adam. He leaned against the kitchen wall and pulled me onto him for a long kiss, then hugged my head onto his shoulder. "This isn't good-bye, Dee. I hope. I'm not in control of when my ark closes. But I meant it, about the shakedown cruise. Will you still come for that, if I can get you on board?"

"It's a ship! Your ark is a ship?"

He laughed in surprise. He pushed me away just enough to look me in the eye. "Yeah. I thought you knew that. Sorry, I didn't mean to be *that* secretive. It's moored in Groton. Well, it should be coming back into Groton by now, anyway. They headed out to sea last night to weather the hurricane, after I called them."

"Into a hurricane?"

"Yeah, you don't want to be in port during a storm like that. It was awfully late in the game to head out to deep water, by the time they knew it was a hurricane. But that's what they did." He sighed. "I need to work tonight to check for damage."

"You're in the Coast Guard?"

"Not any more. I retired to take this ark building job."

He rummaged in his pocket and brought out a diamond ring. "My mother's ring," he said. "Kind of ill-fated. Dee... We've never talked about this. And we should. The truth is, I could bring you aboard my ark. If we were married. The captain could marry us. Someone else would get bumped from the ark, but I have priority.

"But we've been together, what, five weeks?" He looked at me searchingly. "So I'm not really asking you to marry me now. Just... hold onto the ring and think about it, OK?"

He lay the ring on my palm. We stared at it as though at a smelly and dubious bit of fish bait.

"Wow. Um," I said.

"I could stay another half hour," Adam offered, with a wry grin.

"Oh, I'm sure you could work a little harder than that," I challenged.

"Slave-driver!' He pulled me into the bedroom for another marital test-drive.

Around 10:00, I waved him off from the front lawn, hugging a chunky cardigan around myself. The perverse weather had suddenly decided to go clear and cold. It might dip below freezing overnight. I didn't really expect to see Adam again, any more than I had the first time I handed him my business card. That was in another world, when we rode a magic pumpkin carriage to the glass towers of corporate power.

As Adam's tail-lights vanished around the bend, I heard a

buzzing, followed by a flash of white light towards the smaller bridge, and a huge *whump*. Orange fire continued, lighting a black column of smoke, the brightest light in the dark night.

I sighed. Global Jihad looters were almost as good as Ebola-bearing zombies for scaring the neighborhood into cooperation. Captain Zack had his proof of concept.

Chapter 15

Interesting fact: Winter Storm Nemo was an 'extra-tropical cyclone event', or non-tropical hurricane. It formed around a low pressure of 968 mbar, and struck the Northeast and Maritime Provinces with winds up to 100 mph. Its maximum snowfall was 40 inches in Hamden, Connecticut, just north of New Haven. It was the fourth '100 year storm' to hit Connecticut in only 2 years. Property insurance rates skyrocketed. That was back in 2013.

To call work 'light' during the holidays would be charitable. Santa tracking was a simple overlay on NORAD's Santa-tracking. We just freshened the graphics. We'd supplied more than enough heartwarming puppy templates to UNC over the years. My team and Mangal's hadn't even pretended to accomplish anything since the Christmas party in mid-December. And with power outages wide-spread from the hurricane, paid vacation would continue until the first Tuesday in January, a week after New Year's.

Dan sent an email inviting us all to a video-conference that Tuesday. He promised an update on the UNC ark. Mangal and I could hardly wait.

I had plenty of time to consider whether I wanted to marry Adam Lacey. And to wonder whether Adam Lacey had any more desire to be married than I did. We talked by phone or video chat nearly every night. Neither of us wanted to talk about that. So the only net effect in the short term was that I now figured our relationship had graduated to 'serious.' Sort of serious. The ring lived on my bed stand.

Anyway, we had a lot of time on our hands. Before Christmas, Mangal and I decided that what we really wanted was to publish some of this information, in a way that couldn't be tracked or shut down by the censors. This was beyond our own hacker skills. We cautiously put out feelers, looking to hire someone.

Or rather, we sought to enlist someone in the cause, since the kind of hackers we wanted didn't seek money. 'Give unto Caesar what is Caesar's, I gotta eat.' Fortunately, we had hacker food to offer—information that sought to be free. But hacker enlistment was slow and awkward.

The day after Christmas, I told Mangal that Shelley wanted in. He sighed heavily, but agreed we didn't have a lot of choice if she already knew about us. She had the skills and access by proximity to get at anything we had. So we could make an enemy of her and kick her out, or bring her in all the way. Keeping her in seemed safer. Mangal tried to argue that it was also more ethical. Neither of us ended the conversation convinced on that point.

So we invited her to join us for a 'workday' at my office. We started by watching the day's Al Jazeera news summary, which gave fairly good short coverage of the day's happenings in the Eastern Hemisphere. Global Jihad had such direct success via social media, that they didn't feel any particular need to lean on Al Jazeera, leaving them free to be the moderate voice of educated Islam.

Shelley was impressed. That Christmas was a bad day in Europe, with European Muslims in a fever to prove that Europe was now theirs. They left the Jews alone for a change and targeted massive air strikes on cathedrals. Al Jazeera noted that the death tolls in the hundreds of thousands included some Muslims. Interviews with Parisian Muslims in the street seemed to agree that the collateral damage was worth it. Non-Muslim Parisians said there was no point in cooperation if they were going to get bombed anyway. But a peace with non-Muslims was not Global Jihad's goal.

Al Jazeera also reported several wholesale slaughters of Muslims in the United States as order broke down in that country. And that a quarter of the population of the New York City area was now dead, mostly due to Ebola. Shelley was shocked. Mangal and I already knew that, and were confident both death tolls would climb. The contagion scenario in New York hadn't had time to play out yet. And the vast majority wanted to stamp out Global Jihad in North America.

After the broadcast, we had Shelley read the summaries we'd written for our respective contacts. Mangal and I reviewed each other's while we waited for her. We both already knew the raw material each other had drawn on, but wanted to get a feel for what our contacts knew. I kept Shelley with me as we broke for lunch.

After lunch, Shanti joined us for a goals discussion. She and Shelley thought it was paramount that we get the news out about what was going on in Europe and the Middle East. Mangal and I looked at each other.

I shrugged and started. "We've thought about that. The problem is, we don't care. Americans don't care, not much. I mean, it's sad. But I'm not willing to risk my freedom for that. I can't solve the Global Jihad problem, because it's driven by overpopulation. Look at Iraq. In 1950, they had about 5 million people. Now they have 10 times that, and they're suffering drought about 4 years out of 5. The climate is only getting worse. They can't feed all those people. They talk about the Koran, but in the end, they'd stay home in peace if they could make a living and feed their families. But they can't. Their young men have no prospects. Russia and China are willing to kill them. If Europe wants to survive, they need to kill more. And they're becoming willing to do that. It isn't nice, but I can't help them. Any of them."

Mangal nodded. " 'Secure your own oxygen mask before attempting to help others.' Americans are interested in their own survival first, and their own food supply. And many of them aren't going to get it here, either."

Shanti pursed her lips. "How much of this food shortage is real?"

I shrugged. "The GMO blight is real, but we can get past that, to a point. The Dust Bowl is devastating. On the other hand, we used to export a lot of food, and now we don't. It's hard to say. At the moment, we're probably growing less than a quarter of what we used to, which is less than enough. But the population is falling, really fast. Most of the shortages now amount to a structural disruption. The borders are forcing us into locally sustainable agriculture, instead of industrial agriculture and transportation. And we just haven't adjusted production to that yet. But we can."

"If the weather cooperates enough for us to adjust," Mangal cautioned.

"There's that," I agreed with a sigh. "But, there are things you can do as a small-scale farmer that you can't on one of those county-sized satellite-controlled robo-farms in the Midwest. For instance, growing a single crop—why would I do that, if my survival depends on the crop? If there's no government bailout for crop failure? I wouldn't. I grow assorted things. I stagger the plantings. I keep plants indoors until they're half grown. My plots are small enough that I can throw protection over them."

"If you know the weather is coming," Mangal quibbled.

We stared at each other.

Shelley piped up, "The weather reports aren't the truth, are they?"

"No," I agreed slowly. "And they need to be. If I want to grow food."

"Well, there's news you can use," Mangal concluded.

"Travel and trade news, too, maybe. Steer clear of Broomfield. Town Hall is still in business in Totoket. The orchards in Otherford offer apples, seek wheat flour and cows. Stuff like that."

"How to escape New York," Shelley suggested darkly. "Where the arks are."

Mangal and Shanti looked alarmed. I felt the same, but pursed my lips and said, "Let's hold off on that for now, Shelley. You may not have thought those through. For example, if the border broke down between New York City and Connecticut right now, we'd all die, probably. Unless we had Ebola vaccinations."

"I've been vaccinated," Shanti offered. "Mangal, too, but not the children. And that's the sort of trade news we could really use. Because, Shelley, I don't think there's an Ebola vaccine left to be found in Connecticut. But maybe they have a surplus in Maine." She was good, our Shanti.

Mangal backed me up, too. "And the arks are protection from something else. I mean, our air is safe enough to breathe now. We can live and pursue agriculture out in the open. But the arks can survive nuclear fallout, epidemics, agricultural epidemics. They're more resilient to catastrophic weather. If the arks are needed to survive, the rest of us are dead anyway. They're a last gasp chance for humanity. I think it's best to just leave them be."

We'd seeded doubt, but Shelley still looked hungry for revenge and destruction. "Why should they live and us die?"

I shrugged. "Is it better if we all die?"

She folded her arms and slumped in on herself. She still wanted mayhem. But she was still awfully desperate for my approval. The high road was to tell her I had faith and confidence in her own best judgment. The truth was that I didn't trust her judgment at all.

"Look, Shelley, just promise me you won't do anything, or

189

tell anyone, about New York or the arks right now," I said. "Mangal and I had a big head start on this. We've had time to think about it. And if Homeland Security or whoever catches us, it's us who get dragged away, not you. We're the ones with the access, and we're the ones at risk. So we get veto rights. OK? Otherwise…"

"Otherwise you're out," Mangal said quietly but firmly.

I was grateful he didn't elaborate on just how far out. I just nodded and didn't meet her eyes.

"I promise. It's your show," Shelley agreed in a tiny voice.

Shanti gave her a motherly hug and warm smile, bathing her in approval. Mangal and I didn't feel that way at all.

-o-

I don't know what I expected from our hacker connection, when he finally arrived for interview on January 2nd. He drove an electric Cadillac. From his expensive but casual business suit, and overcoat and grooming, he reminded me of a 50-something real estate agent. On TV, hackers all seem to be portrayed as grubby bums and Goths.

"Amen1," he said with a warm smile and an offered hand to shake. "But let's say Dave for now."

"Oh! Amen1—Dave—good to meet you at last! Please come in. I'm Dee. And that's Mangal." The men met in the living room with a handshake, and sat down.

I collected tea while Mangal covered the social niceties. As I overheard it, 'Dave' had studied up on our local situation and decided to make a move down to Totoket to coordinate. In fact, he'd already moved into a place near the police station in town. 'In town' was east of 'western Totoket', outside our civic association self-defense zone. But I was still taken aback.

"I thought we hadn't fully decided to work together yet?" I put in, as I handed tea mugs around.

"I couldn't resist your township's Gigabit Internet," Dave

said, with a broad smile. "I'm happy to stay whether we do this project together or not. Other members are moving down this way as well. Not all of them, but some." He really did remind me of a real estate agent. "You also have this Gigabit Internet?"

"We're tapped into the town line, yes, and two alternates."

"Marvelous. We were based in Cambridge, you know, then moved into western Mass before the borders could shut us in. We've found it... limiting." Dave sipped his tea.

I found him moving into my town a bit claustrophobic. We'd intentionally sought hackers farther afield, and thus harder to connect to us. But it's not as though I had any control over what this man and his team did.

Enough with the small talk. "Well, I think we've decided on our end what we'd like to—"

"A moment, please," Dave interrupted. He fished a tablet-sized device out of his elegant leather messenger bag, and consulted several screens worth of information. "Good. We're private. You were saying?"

"How reliable is that device?" Mangal broke in. He held out his hand, asking to see it.

Dave smiled blandly and tucked the device back into his bag. "Reliable enough. Of course, we do not talk in rooms with web cameras, and we turn our cell-capable phones off."

"Those devices are in another room," I said.

"Good enough, then. Of course, anyone can track your access."

"We have legitimate access to the information we're showing you. We just don't have the right to share it."

"We can work with that." Dave sat forward to deliver his pitch. "As we've conveyed before, Amen1 is a white-hat hacker confederation. The name is based on Amendment 1 of the Constitution, that the U.S. government is forbidden to curtail free speech or the free press, or freedom of religion. We believe the Calm Act violates those rights. We've invested substantial effort in finding ways around the Federal Internet censorship schemes. We have the platform. We are open to proposed publications." He opened his hand to us in invitation.

Mangal nodded to me. I pulled up the true weather satellite feed from New Year's Eve, and told him how not even the Coast Guard was given correct information about a developing Category 2 hurricane and where it was headed. I switched to the live map view I'd shown Zack of the approaches to the Route 1 barricade, and explained how our local defense forces used this information.

The bland self-satisfied real estate agent pose was gone. Dave leaned toward my giant display with a look of pure lust.

I handed off the controller to Mangal. He ran through CDC models on the progress of the Ebola epidemic in New York. He showed status reports on force levels on the nearest borders. He turned on Al Jazeera without the sound, and set the controller aside.

"Our concept," I explained, "is news you can use. Local weather and traffic—the truth. Sufficient detail for local meteorologists to make good predictions, and share them online safely. Sufficient detail to enable safe trade. But not full satellite access to just anybody. We prefer to pick and choose who gets that."

"In sheer self-defense," Dave acknowledged.

"That is the problem," I agreed. "But it's to everyone's advantage to be able to trade in safety. My limited goal is to empower successful and protected agriculture and trade."

Mangal sat back and added, "I believe the U.S. government is pursuing a policy of depopulation, to track decreased agricultural output. The power vacuum they've created, intentionally or not, favors bullies and thieves, armed men intimidating people and stealing. We want to raise the floor on that scenario. If people can produce food in peace, we can afford a lot more people to live. Otherwise, I don't know how low the population has to go, how devolved our civilization has to get, to reach a stable equilibrium again. We seek to arrest that freefall at a higher level of civility."

Dave nodded. We all sipped our tea in thought. "I love it," he eventually concluded. "Amen1 will back it. You have a deal."

-o-

"Toilet paper is a *great* idea," I said from the leadership table. I beamed at the woman who'd made the bitchy complaint. "In *fact,* that ties in with an initiative I'd like to bring up with the community. Bob is the landlord of that vacant building where the dollar store used to be up on Route 1—stand up, Bob, and take a bow!" Doughy old blue-collar Bob received a rather puzzled spate of polite applause. He was surprised and pleased at the attention.

Zack, sitting next to me, irritably stabbed a finger at agenda item 10, 'workshop.' We were currently supposed to be on item 3.

"Bob's willing to donate space for a community workshop," I pressed on sunnily. "There we can share tools, sewing machines, and—make toilet paper. I bet that would have real trade value. And provide gainful work outside of agriculture and defense. Of course, food production and defense take priority. And Cameron—is Cameron here?"

Chino and button-down shirt clad Cameron stood and waved, and got an ovation as well. Father Marks, on Zack's other side, favored Zack with a beaming smile and bracing hand on his shoulder to keep him quiet.

This first community organizational meeting was Saturday afternoon at St. Mary's church. Father Marks celebrated Mass at noon for those who wished to come early, and we stayed in the nave for the meeting. It was standing room only, maybe 500 people attending. The church was slick modern, hushed and lovely. It featured giant non-stained windows, a definite plus since the church was still without power. Father Marks held the gavel because it was his place. He would be seen as a neutral authority, devoted to God and community and charity, but not politics.

"Cameron is general manager of the big box hardware store next to Bob's. The leadership," I waved up and down the table at our team, "is negotiating with Bob for a line of credit at his store. We're not 'liberating' Cameron's inventory, mind you— that would be looting. But it is *great* that we have those construction materials and tools available to us. *Thank you* for bringing it up!"

"I want to know about all these *new people* I see moving in," another heckler belted out. "Who the hell brought them here!"

Zack did, and me. So I dug my fingernails into Zack's arm as police officer Darren, off to our left down the table, fielded the question, and smoothed ruffled feathers. It's just amazing how many euphemisms and circumlocutions there are for 'scary black dudes' and 'non-whites' in the American lexicon. Darren was master of them all. Fortunately, we didn't have any Muslims in the community to protect.

"But there haven't *been* any looters!" someone yelled. That finally roused enough popular interest that we turned to Zack on the dais. *Now that's your cue.*

Zack stood and told everyone how his cadre had secured the bridge and the reservoir barricade—they knew that. He introduced all the members of his team present at the meeting. They were about a third black, which went unmentioned. We at the leadership table modeled polite listening and enthusiastic applause, and the crowd practiced following our lead.

"Father Marks, I wanted to give a summary of our actions against looters," Zack said. "With your permission?"

"I would *very* much like to hear that, Captain Harkonnen. I think everyone would like to hear that, yes?" Father Marks drummed up a strong round of applause.

194

So Zack did. Even I was astonished at how many attacks they'd turned back. Even I was silent and rapt as anyone, as Zack told the story of the January 1st double-cross from Global Jihad. Trey Cowan had gone back into East Haven to spot for them, and very nearly got himself killed in the drone strike that took out the looter mob. Shelley wasn't the only girl in the audience who threw arms around Trey and kissed him. At the end of Zack's recitation, Father Marks instigated a standing ovation, followed by the rest of us at the table, and then the entire hall.

Inevitably, hecklers demanded to know how Zack had arranged for a drone strike, and other details, but he simply refused. "Look, I won't tell you operational details. Because they might get my people killed. So that's final. But I am looking for more volunteers. Please contact me, or any of my people that I introduced, after the meeting."

I squeezed his hand after he sat down. *You did great!*

I had to get up later to outline my grand agricultural plan. My proposed agricultural czar was Caruso Farms, down by the reservoir, the only commercial farm in West Totoket. They made most of their money growing flower and vegetable transplants, before. But they had huge greenhouses, and farm market vegetable fields as well. The Carusos coordinated the East Haven farm market, and fully intended to keep doing so. But they were willing to organize a new market in West Totoket as well.

This hadn't gone over well with Zack's community garden crowd. But the fact was that we only had experience with home-scale gardening. We needed the Carusos, with their staff of a dozen and their vast commercial-grade greenhouses, to lead us on the road to food self-sufficiency.

In the end, we'd chosen Reverend Connolly to present the toughest sell of the meeting, donating food and supplies to the caches. On both the agricultural initiative and the caches, we made plain that membership was voluntary. But there would be no food distribution to non-members, nor participation in the community workshop, nor help with planting, and so forth. And that a cut of the contributions would be used to support Zack's defenders.

We gave the community a lot to think about in a couple hours. And we asked them to sign up their intent to become members before they left.

Over 300 households signed up. That was nearly everyone there, considering households who brought more than one person to the meeting. I was impressed.

"Toilet paper?" Zack asked, when the church finally emptied down to just the organizers. "Have you ever made paper?"

"Yes. And I hope to God never to use toilet paper that rough," I replied. "I'd rather use a wet rag. I just worked with what they gave me, Zack."

"You said you sucked at politics."

"No, I said I hated them. Still do. A decade in corporate America will teach you a few tricks, though." I sighed. "You were fantastic, Zack."

"Thank you." Too quietly for the others to overhear, he added, "I hope this means you're staying to see it through."

He didn't give me a chance to reply. He just turned and left, to lead the night shift at the barricades.

I would have loved to leave myself. But I stayed for tea and cookies by candle-light in the gathering night, with the clergymen, the policeman, the farmers, the landlord, the hardware store manager, and the other key lights of the non-military community.

Chapter 16

Interesting fact: Though rising carbon dioxide (CO_2) levels in the atmosphere drove greenhouse warming, they never exceeded 500 ppm (parts per million), thanks to the sudden radical decrease in fossil fuel abuse. This was about double the pre-industrial level. But for most people, health and cognitive clarity were not adversely affected until the gas reached 1000 ppm. However, poor ventilation could concentrate the gas indoors, especially on lower floors, and people varied in their susceptibility.

Our boss Dan looked like hell on the video chat. I'd last seen him in Stamford at the Christmas party only a month ago. Then he looked his usual smooth self—well-dressed, well-adjusted middle management, with a sort of humming bland smile. On screen, when we reconvened work for the new year, he looked strung out. He'd lost 10 or 20 pounds, and had purple baggy circles under his eyes. The left side of his face twitched.

This was entirely at odds with what he was saying. Which reminded me of the old quote from Emerson, 'Who you are speaks so loudly I can't hear what you're saying.' But then, I didn't believe what he was saying.

"...Ark intake interviews will resume soon. The Stamford office is still closed, but the corporate psychologist will be travelling to a location near you..."

"Sure she will," commented Mangal, dripping with sarcasm. "Because it's so much easier for her to travel all over the state than for us to get to Stamford."

The three of us, including Shelley, shared a single video chat screen in my office. We had our feet up, and munched popcorn. Mangal and I had long since figured out how to record a video loop to run on automatic, to hide behind during dull video conferences. My box on the screen showed a loop of me looking up, smiling a private smile, looking down, looking straight at the camera, pursing my lips, and making a note. This automaton represented all three of us. If anyone asked one of us a question, we could freeze the video, experience technical difficulties, and come back on live.

"...I'm happy to report the UNC ark is well ahead of schedule, and coming online soon..."

"Asshole," commented Shelley, tossing popcorn at my screen. Yes, she'd come far under my tutelage.

"...present a virtual tour of the UNC ark..."

"Oh, cool," I said, and full-screened the presentation. We got a helicopter-eye view of the rolling wooded Tennessee landscape, approaching a geodesic complex shining like Camelot in the distance. Before we could see any detailed environs of the ark, the video cut inside to the 'welcome center.' This area reminded me of the Totoket high school cafeteria—a two-story big open space with tables and no side windows, but natural light overhead. I even caught a brief glimpse off to the side of a cafeteria serving line. By comparison to the familiar high school cafeteria, I guessed the space could serve food to about 300 people at a seating.

The view jumped to an 'efficient and comfortable' berth. The narrator didn't mention how many people shared this private space, about 12 x 16 feet. It looked like two bunks and two sleeper sofas, a small table, and a steel mesh storage loft, all crammed into a small windowless children's bedroom. They dressed it up with cheery fabrics and flowers on the table, and didn't clutter the ambiance with actual belongings up in the storage loft.

Neglecting to show the sanitary facilities, we zoomed on

along into the state of the art hydroponics facility.

"That footage is from Epcot," I commented, frowning. "And the hydroponics aren't state of the art." I'd loved the hydroponic gardens exhibit at Epcot Center in Orlando, and visited them several times. It wasn't that this looked like Epcot. It *was* Epcot, complete with the little river-running-through track that the guided tour boats ran on.

The video moved on to the 'oxygen forest.' "And *that* footage is from Moody Gardens, in Galveston, the rainforest pyramid," I said. I'd only been there once. It was part of an awesome theme park on the Texas Gulf coast, about an hour from Houston.

"Does this UNC ark even exist?" wondered Mangal.

The video went on to showcase world-class athletic facilities, footage they could have shot at a fancy athletic club anywhere. I loved the whirlpool bath and the compact swim-in-place lap pools. I'd always wanted to try one of those. But I doubted the video was taken at the UNC ark in Tennessee.

The camera panned over a cubicle maze, still empty of people or chairs or work screens, while the narrator uttered platitudes about arkinauts pursuing their life work in safety and comfort. Cut to the UNC logo and mission statement. And back to Dan.

"A beautiful facility, as you can see," Dan commented, looking deflated. "Well... welcome back to work. We'll, um, continue telecommuting for the foreseeable future. I'll be speaking with the supervisors today, and no doubt they'll speak with the rest of you in section meetings or one on one within the next day or so. Happy New Year." He attempted a smile, and logged off quickly.

"That son-of-a—" Shelley began.

"Shelley, Dan's a good man," I interrupted her. "Now Mangal and I have to do supervisor stuff. Go work at your own house, OK?"

"What work?"

I shrugged, with a smile. "Feel free to wander off and do something useful. But I'll shoot for a section meeting by phone before the end of the day. Four-ish, maybe."

Shelley left, disillusioned not only with the UNC ark, but seeing the man behind the curtain in her managerial chain as well. Mangal and I checked our assorted electronic communications for contacts from our staff, while waiting for the door to close on Shelley.

"Do you need privacy to talk to people?" Mangal offered.

I waggled a hand yes-and-no. Two of my people hadn't shown up for the video conference, nor responded to phone or email hails. The others appeared to be waiting for me to make the first move. Mangal had three missing. I scrubbed my face with my hands. "Yeah. Dan will probably talk to us together, but—"

The phone rang. I took one glance, and pressed a button to put the call on speaker. "Hey, Dan! Happy New Year! Shelley left. You're speaking to Dee and Mangal." I smiled pleasantly. They taught us about that in boss school, that people could hear your smile or frown on a phone call.

"Happy New Year, Dan," Mangal chimed in, smiling confidently back at me. "Good Christmas break?"

"Christ, no," Dan bit out. "What's the situation there?" He made it sound like a frontline sitrep request, from a combat unit about to be overrun.

"We're good," I replied. "Shelley's settling in next door. Lost power in the ice storm, and then in the hurricane, but nothing we couldn't handle. The neighborhood has armed barricades against looters. They're holding so far. How're things down in your area?"

"It's a nightmare," Dan gasped. "Laura and I have guns. The children sleep in the basement while we guard against looters. My tennis partner at the yacht club, his wife and kids were murdered by looters while he was out buying gas. He shot himself to death on New Year's Eve. Our families are in the city. I can't reach them." He gave a huge shuddering sigh. Dan was a true New Yorker. 'The city' could only mean New York.

"I'm sorry to hear that, Dan," Mangal said. We attended boss school together, of course. I could almost taste the donuts we ate during that fun workshop day on 'how to deal with emotional employees.' We'd taken turns role playing hysterical staff.

Mangal continued to 'mirror back the speaker's upset, to validate his feelings, but defuse the tone.' "It sounds like you've had an upsetting time, Dan. But you're safe now, right?"

"Laura's guarding the door. I can't talk long. She needs sleep."

"Sleep is good," I ventured. "Have you gotten any sleep, Dan?"

"Christ, no. Look, there aren't any assignments, just... make something up, OK? You'll need to do a RIF, lay off one person each, you pick. Tell them they'll get two weeks' severance pay and back sick days and vacation. They probably won't, but I don't know. There is no fucking ark, not for us, not for them. I don't know what I'm going to do."

In case of emergency, secure your own oxygen mask before attempting to help others.

"Alright, Dan," I said, pursing my lips at Mangal. "We've got it. Just make sure we've got all the passwords we need to cover for you, OK? Or did you want to leave someone else acting manager for you?"

"Acting manager—yes! That's what I need. Yeah, I can't deal with this." Dan muttered some things to himself we couldn't catch. "God bless," he concluded, and hung up.

To my surprise, Dan did send us the passwords, private files, everything we needed to take over his job indefinitely. We'd taken turns acting for him while he was away on vacation before. But that was nothing compared to the access he gave us now. And it wasn't just Dan's own access. Dan, in turn, was acting for his boss, Chet Marley. The day the Ebola epidemic went public, Marley was in Manhattan for a nooner with his mistress. He missed the last train out of the Big Apple, and hadn't been heard from since.

We sat contemplating the keys to the kingdom for a few minutes. I was the first to act.

"What did you do?" Mangal asked.

"Changed all of Dan's passwords. He's gone zombie. That's contagious. We need to protect UNC from him. Of course, we care about Dan and don't want to embarrass him. So we handled this quietly."

Mangal nodded thoughtfully. We both sat back to contemplate our new options, until Mangal acted.

"Amen1 Dave reminds me of Toby," he said. Toby was one of Mangal's three missing employees. "I think I'll just update Toby's address. We don't want to be short-handed. So Dave can replace him." It didn't take long to arrange for our hacker contact to take over Toby's UNC accounts, including his paycheck. Maybe Toby was dead, maybe he was alive. But he wasn't earning his paycheck, and we couldn't reach him. And Dave could make good use of his UNC logins.

We laid off our weakest two of the five employees we couldn't reach. For the remaining two missing staff, we also submitted change of address requests. Effective immediately, they lived with us. Salaries were redirected to pile up in a newly-created second checking account at my bank. We wanted to use that to fund the civic association 'credit line' with the hardware store.

Redirecting the salaries made me feel acutely queasy. We weren't stealing the money for ourselves, but to fund our community and Amenac project. But we were still stealing from our employer. Once upon a time, I couldn't have done this.

Mangal wouldn't have done this.

"Mangal... maybe we've gone too far. This is outright theft. If they catch us..."

"Do we regret it? Other than fear of getting caught? UNC will never know the difference. These salaries are nothing to UNC. There's no one left above us with a soul."

With a soul? "I don't think I've ever seen you this angry."

"That video, that bald-faced *lie*, was a betrayal of our entire careers! We were *good employees*, Dee. We were *trustworthy*." Mangal spat the terms out like swear words. "They stole our honor. They made us lie to the American people about the borders and the weather. Now they can damn well pay the tab while we take our honor back."

-o-

"Welcome back! And I've got great news, guys and gals!" I beamed with enthusiasm at my 4 o'clock section video meeting. We held it jointly with Mangal's section. "We've got an *awesome* assignment for the new year. You all know the trouble we had with the censors on that little weather website... debacle. Now we're going to take another approach!"

Mangal leaned in and swiveled the camera his way. "We're going to incorporate some of our up-to-the-minute map data, as well. Our new theme is 'news you can use.' On the mapping side, we're going to focus on safe travel routes and marketplaces. Accurate state of the borders, too. The truth and nothing but the truth."

I swiveled the camera back to me. "All truth on the weather side as well. We're going to supply raw weather data by location. We're going to empower local meteorologists to make best-of-class weather forecasts."

Several flags were raised by people who wanted to break in. "Let's hold off on the questions for a bit," Mangal put in. "I will add this, though—Dee and I are taking over for Dan temporarily, while he handles some personal matters. Our combined sections will focus on the presentation layer, as always. But we'll have support from the data analysis and site admin teams, as much as we need. Dee and I are their bosses, for the moment." He smiled confidently.

I swiveled the camera, beamed appreciation of Mangal's points, and resumed talking fast. "Because UNC has its own 'official' website voice, we're going to try something a bit different this time. We're going to host this new project off-site from UNC's servers, and focus on a particular demographic— farmers, fisherman, lumber, and other outdoor workers. Think 'New Farmer's Almanac', with a touch of the 'Prairie Home Companion.' We're going to call it 'Amenac.' "

Mangal swiveled the camera to show both of us. "This is going to be great, Dee!"

"It really is, Mangal!"

They bought it. We built a website carefully pitched to spread like wildfire among good people trying to make the best of a bad situation. Meteorologists yearning to tell the truth, based on true data. Fishermen who needed to know if it was safe to go out. Farmers who needed to know when a frost was expected. The website came together at lightning speed, using familiar software architectures we ported wholesale from UNC.

The Amen1 hacker team was good, no question of that. What we published would never have passed the censors. We had social features, people chatting up a storm, and crowd-sourced map overlays of hostilities and safety zones, with not a Google Censor plugin anywhere. Homeland Security went berserk trying to shut us down. But they couldn't. Amen1 saw to that.

Yet Amenac was almost unknown in the general population, because it was so thoroughly farmer-oriented. The average looter, hoodlum, and hostile survivalist never knew the Amenac existed. But I made sure that the good folk of

Minnesota, who burned out Montagro Corp. and took their own damned state back, were up and running with best of breed weather forecasts within a couple weeks. Though of course, Connecticut got there first.

The team was deeply into the project by the time anyone noticed that the UNC websites still didn't link to the Amenac. I just shrugged it off. I told them we were still going back and forth with the censors, and appealing some judgments through other federal agencies. But not to worry, Amenac was a go.

-o-

So I was pretty busy with Amenac development in January. Outside of work, I had the civic association farm planning, and started my own seedlings for spring, and as many extras as I could for neighbors. I was pleased with how the agriculture plans were coming together. Grain production would be limited. But there were some big fields available here and there, for rotation planting with alfalfa and other things. None of us had ever grown grain in earnest before, so that took a lot of study. But we hoped to get nearly everyone growing potatoes and kitchen vegetables. There were a lot of gardening novices, but they'd have lots of support.

The weather, of course, was a big wildcard. Crops planted out of season do not thrive. And the seasons had come unglued. The only thing we could do about that was to plant in waves, and hope that most plantings got close enough to the right conditions.

My main contribution was drawing up the maps to communicate the plan. I used Amenac to publish the plans and promote Amenac. Word began to spread, and we got great feedback from professional farmers elsewhere to improve our planting scheme. More Connecticut planting plans were published all the time, and technical discussion blossomed. Once we got the state agricultural extension and master gardeners hooked in—and overjoyed to finally get to tell the truth online—the whole thing took off.

Yes, it was dangerous for participants to bypass the censors like this. But the time had come that people just didn't care. The Federal government had enjoyed rock-bottom public approval rates for years.

-o-

"Dee," Zack greeted me when I answered the doorbell. "We've come to collect for the cache." Zack and the two men behind him were armed to the gills.

"Why, how nice to see you, Zack. Come in," I invited. Once he was through the door, I closed it on the other two. "They can wait outside. What the hell, Zack? And don't you have captaining business to do or something?"

Zack tilted his head to indicate his minions outside. "They need some help to finesse their approach."

"Here's a hint. Three armed thugs showing up at my doorstep to steal my food? That's not 'finesse.' That's not on the same planet as 'finesse.' They're going to get shot."

"Useful feedback," he allowed. "You see the problem. We wanted to start with friendly faces, to help us work this out," he explained with a wan smile.

My arms were still folded over my chest, as unfriendly as I could manage. "So you started with me. I should feel honored?"

"Actually, I started with Shanti and Mangal. At least they wouldn't shoot at us."

I snorted amusement. "Bet you didn't get any food from them, though."

Zack sighed. "They said to come back in an hour."

"Damn, Shanti's good. So hey, Zack, how 'bout you come back in an hour?"

"Cute. Look, Dee, we've already had three houses ripped off. It's not that looters are getting past the barricades. We caught one middle-aged hunter from the other side of Totoket. His crew attacked an elderly couple down on Pentecost Street. The old guy shot this one in the leg on the way out. The rest of them got away with all the food. Another condo, ripped off by a bunch of teenagers, probably local. Last night, the third attack, we have no idea. Homeowners knifed to death, all the food gone. And the neighbors say they had a lot of food."

"My God. Who?"

"Carruthers? Carmichaels? Something like that. On Shoreline. Did you know them?"

"No. I'm sorry to hear that." I sighed. "OK, yeah, it's time to fill the caches. But wouldn't it be better to have a central collection point? That way you wouldn't be invading people's homes with the Rambo routine."

Zack wobbled his head yes-and-no. "Food's heavy. Most people don't have transportation anymore. The idea was to send out teams that could carry for members, and protect the collections van. And to do the book-keeping. When you contribute, you're buying shares of the cache. You did agree to this, you know."

"I believe my actual words were, 'No way in hell.' But yeah, eventually... Sort of." The thing was, yes, rationally, I believed the caches were a good idea. Emotionally, the idea of letting them take my stash was well-nigh unbearable.

"...A collection center, huh?" Zack asked.

"I guess it is all pretty heavy," I allowed. "You have freezers in this cache?"

"No... We lose power all the time. How much of your food is frozen?"

"Well, I've got a generator, and batteries, and a minus-40 freezer. It can stay frozen for days if I leave it closed," I said defensively.

"Show me," said Zack. He raised his hands in surrender when I bridled. "I won't take anything. Promise. Just show me.

Dee, please, I'm here because we really need to work this out for the community."

It was agony, but I led him back to my stash. Not even Alex or Adam had seen my hoard before. This appears to be a two-bedroom house, with a linen closet and bathroom between the two bedrooms. In my experience, most people are spatially challenged. It's actually a three-bedroom house.

I opened the linen closet. Along with linens, it revealed a few 6-packs of toilet paper, and a sad little shallow pantry of canned goods, sauerkraut and beets and such. I groped behind a bit of wooden molding to release the two door bolts at the right which secured the bookcase to the doorframe. The discreetly wheeled linen shelves rotated back on hinges to the left, to enter the hidden bedroom.

Zack grinned broadly. "You're good. If you weren't here to give it away, they'd never find it."

Within, the eye was immediately drawn to some tomatoes and cucumbers growing under lights. Less obviously, I had what was left of a year's harvest of potatoes and onions. Winter squash and cabbages, apples and pears from the local orchards. Several hundred pounds of wheat flour and rice and oats. Bulk peanut butter. Gallons of oil. Hundreds of rolls of toilet paper. Giant brown cartons of boxed cereal and pasta. Batteries of assorted shapes. A bookcase of home canned goods. And the fridges and freezers.

I pointed to one fridge and three freezers. "Dried food. Meat and bread dough. Prepared dinners. I mostly cook the summer harvests, eat a meal, and freeze the rest to eat in winter."

An astonished Zack opened the meat-and-bread-dough freezer, and quickly closed it again. That one was a minus-40 freezer. "No wonder you're so generous, Dee. You must have more food than any three other houses combined."

I had a fairly good idea of what Shanti had socked away. "I

wouldn't bet on that."

"Is this all of it?"

No. "Yeah…"

"No," he said wryly. "Dee, you really can't lie worth a damn. This can't stay here. But…"

"But you don't have freezers in your caches. So maybe I could just deposit some of my non-frozen stuff…"

"Or maybe I could fix my plan," said Zack. He caught and held my eye. "I'm here to fine-tune the cache plan." He gazed back at my freezers, and sighed. "We don't even have book-keeping equivalents to account for this stuff. Help, Dee. Please?"

"Well," I said reluctantly, "what if you had a third cache, the collection facility. Strictly members only, needs guarding 24/7. Out on Route 1, where power is always restored first, easy enough to get to. You could probably use Bob's space, that we're setting up for a workshop. That space used to have fridges and freezers, and a stockroom out back. I think they already have a backup generator. People can go there and deposit their stashes. But they can also trade *up* for value-added stuff. Sort of like a barter supermarket concept."

"So I could come in with a 10-pound bag of rice, and trade it for a few loaves of your bread dough?"

I scowled at him. "Maybe *two* loaves of my bread dough. Maybe one. Well, this year anyway. By next year, rice could be pretty rare in New England. It won't grow here."

Zack rubbed his forehead, frustrated. "I don't like it, for security."

I sighed. "No, but I like it for a trading post. We're always going to have fresh food coming in, Zack. Eggs. Milk. Fresh vegetables and fruit. Meat. And as a member, I *feel better* going in to the general store, depositing to my account, and picking up a few things in trade. I think it's worth the risk. Or rather, you need to pay the piper and do this. Although 'pounds of rice' is a bad yardstick. Call them 'clams' or something. One 'clam' is roughly equivalent to a dollar's buying power last October, maybe. And adjust prices as time goes on. Rice keeps getting more expensive. Cabbage is cheap in July."

"And curbside pickup?"

"A premium service you offer. Curbside delivery, too. If you want me to keep no more than a couple weeks' supply of food on hand, I'll need to pick up more food all the time."

"Maybe we should have it down by the barricade, as a trading post."

"No. This is strictly internal, members only. Down by the barricade should be an open farm market, to trade with East Haven, New Haven, anybody who shows up. We don't want them seeing what we have for members only."

Zack nodded, but looked around the room sadly. "I need this done yesterday."

I opened the minus-forty and pulled out bread and meat for a week, and tossed them on a chair. "Start by carting the freezers to the workshop." I continued adding potatoes and frozen dinners, shelf-stable milk, fruit and vegetables, toilet paper, etc., to my pile. "I want these containers *back*, Zack." My set-aside pile grew to over two weeks' worth of supplies for the three of us. "And I want my minus-40 freezer back by spring, you hear? I *like* freezing dinners."

Carting all that stuff into the van took time, and the book-keeping even more so. Their first-pass system was inadequate for half of my haul. We needed to add a wide range of products that they hadn't considered, of radically unequal value. A pound of rice was not equivalent to a pound of ready-to-eat meatloaf or dried berries or chicken breasts. There were also some items I wanted back verbatim—no equivalents accepted.

"And I want to donate 5% to Reverend Connolly's food kitchen," I added. "So make sure to create and credit an account for Reverend Connolly. And you can have the clerks ask that, whenever someone deposits food at the trading post. 'Would you like to donate 5% to the food kitchen?' "

"On top of the 20% we already take to support the defenders?" Zack asked.

I shrugged. "Most people don't have it. But I do. Shanti does. Though she may want to donate it elsewhere. For me, this is a convenience. I'm willing to support the food kitchen, but I don't get around to it." I considered. "Do you really need 20%? Seems like a lot."

"It's for trade, too. We need ammo and guns. Favors like a drone strike."

"Ah. That."

After an hour, as Shanti promised, Mangal started carrying stuff to the van, too. Zack's minions weren't allowed into their house. Actually, they only entered my house because I couldn't carry the freezers without them.

It really was agony watching them cart my food security away. Shanti looked like she was biting her nails, too. And from the level of loot in the van, neither of us were confessing to our whole hoards, not just yet. The book-keeping was a helpful distraction. Being able to mark a few things we wanted back verbatim was a relief. My saved meatloaf and quiches and dried fruit were *mine*. Shanti felt the same way about her dried chilies. Oy, that woman's cooking was hot. A few more book-keeping tricks needed devising for her stash.

Zack needed some very sensitive, creative, and trustworthy book-keeping talent for this operation.

Eventually the van headed off. I gnawed my fingernail, hoping they plugged in the fridge soon.

"Thank you, ladies, Mangal, for your contributions. But especially thank you for your help working this out," said Zack. "I know that wasn't easy."

Shanti nodded jerkily, arms hugging herself, eyes still tracking the van. Mangal looked at his wife with clear misgivings. I think my eyes darted nervously to the garage. I had more hidden there.

"I also know you didn't give me everything," Zack continued wryly. He held up a hand to forestall objections. "And that's fine. You've contributed enough to support my defenders, the Reverend, and yourselves. This is voluntary, and that's still your food we're protecting. But please—don't get yourselves hurt defending what you've kept back. You're more important than whatever you've still got tucked away. OK?"

Shanti and Mangal's reaction didn't budge from their previous nervousness. Then Mangal put his arm around Shanti to draw her inside. "Thank you for your service, Zack," Mangal offered unconvincingly as he turned away.

"They really don't like me, do they?" Zack asked.

"They like you fine," I said, hugging myself miserably. This clawing, needy sensation from having my hoard taken was awful, like a drug addict craving in withdrawal. I'd worked so hard to amass that security. Any distraction was welcome. "They just can't support violence. You know that."

"Yeah. I know that." Zack sighed. He looked around at the weather, ready to stride off. The lowering clouds were getting dark, and starting to sprinkle.

He did know that about pacifists. And that was strange, in a military man, I thought.

"Carlson," I thought, and said out loud. "Cyndi and Ron Carlson? On Shoreline."

"Yeah, that was it," Zack agreed. "You knew them?"

I nodded. "Not well. Good people. Cyndi was a Master Gardener. She tried to talk me into getting certified, but I never took the time. Ron was a paramedic. Both really active in volunteer work. Cyndi had the most beautiful hollyhocks and hydrangeas."

Zack started. Maybe he'd stopped to admire the flowers and chat, too. "Oh. Them. Guess I never knew their names."

"We should hold a community service for the dead. I'll call the Reverend. You could speak at the service, remind the community why you built the caches, say the trading post is open for deposits. Come on in and check it out. That sort of thing."

Zack breathed a soft laugh. "Dee, if we make this work, you rate a huge share of the credit for it."

I shrugged off the compliment, and frowned slightly. "Haven't seen you much lately." It wasn't about the car, anymore. He'd found me an adorable little electric car to replace the one he'd used as a firebomb. He didn't pay for it—it was abandoned somewhere. "Are you avoiding me?"

"Busy," he said. He looked away when he said it.

"Uh-huh. Me, too. What did you and Adam talk about at the barricade that day?"

"Ask him," he said sourly. "Gotta go. I have a meeting in New Haven this afternoon."

"Is that... safe?"

He looked surprised. "Sure. Most of New Haven is a great town. DJ is making good progress on the rough side of town, too." He clarified, "DJ is Captain Zack of the Hill section of New Haven. He's damned good. Most of the new blacks here are people DJ sent me."

"Huh! I didn't realize you had a guild of neighborhood captains."

"Yeah, well, we'll need it."

"Soon?" I asked, eyes narrowing. "I thought things were getting better."

Zack's face set along harsh Captain lines. "Dee, we haven't been up against anyone organized yet. See ya."

Chapter 17

Interesting fact: The location of Ark 1 was a closely held secret. Ark 1 would take the President of the U.S. and his family, the Cabinet, and the Supreme Court, for continuity of government. Speculations included Mount Weather, in Virginia; the Greenbriar Resort in West Virginia; Raven Rock Mountain, Pennsylvania; and either Cheyenne Mountain or Peterson Air Force Base, both in Colorado Springs. These sites were also candidates for Arks 2 through 5. The Vice President, Congress, and Senate had ark berths, as well as the Joint Chiefs of Staff and other key teams, such as FEMA and the CDC. Federal funds also built several brain trust arks.

I finally had a date for Adam's ark shakedown cruise—Sunday January 26th. He even gave me five days' advance notice, a lot more than I expected.

I almost wished he'd given me only an hour before I had to run out the door. This outlook was ungrateful and perverse, but heart-felt. I didn't want to go. And thinking about it wouldn't help. I was going. I wanted to see Adam. I wanted to see his ark. I was curious.

We were also just starting to get real traction and attention with Amenac at work. Shelley was getting involved with Trey Cowan, who it turns out was not gay, just unusually opinionated about fashion for a straight guy. She'd made a play for Jake from Niantic, but he found her too brainy for him. Trey either liked brains or considered himself smarter than Shelley—probably both.

And Alex had a new litter of guinea piglets, and was breeding his lady rabbit. And my baby cabbages needed bigger pots. And I had steering committee meetings for the trading post and agriculture. And, and, and…

Someone else could cover for me, on all of it. I mattered—oh, I mattered!—but nothing would fall apart if I went away for a few days. If I took a little 'me time' to be an ambulatory stage prop in an ark rehearsal. If I spent a little time with my squeeze for the first time in a few weeks. We could talk about that… proposal thing.

I was pretty sure that proposals that end in, 'Yes! I do!' don't begin life as 'that proposal thing', discarded on the nightstand to gather dust.

What I wasn't so clear on was, why not Adam? He was fun to hang out with, a fantastic playmate in bed, gorgeous, smart, successful, appreciative. He made me feel great just being me. And he seemed to feel the same way.

-o-

"Zack?" I rang the doorbell again. I could see him through the window, or rather, his ragg socked feet up on the arm of the couch. Maybe he was asleep.

I'd already tried to 'run into him' at the Route 1 barricade during my lunch break. I had a good time there with Trey Cowan, being taught not to shoot. The man was convinced I was a menace to society and a waste of perfectly good ammunition. Since I was never going to hit anything anyway, he and Jamal persuaded me to trade in my semi-automatic rifle and ammo—once Trey's—for a little lady's purse pistol. They happily devoured the picnic lunch I brought along.

But Zack was taking the day off, and the evening, too. "Captain's got stuff on his mind," was all Jamal cared to share on the topic.

Maybe it was bad idea, coming to tell him I'd be away for a

few days. Maybe I should just call and not make such a big deal out of it. I turned away from the door to spot an enormous rubbery bovine nose off the end of the porch. I walked over to see the whole cow, one of the Vermont standard black and white type, a Holstein. She slowly turned enormous brown eyes on me. Finding me wholly uninteresting, she returned her attention to a bale of hay.

"Dee?" The front door had opened behind me, and Zack leaned out.

"You have a cow! How—cool." I stumbled to a stop when I turned to look at him.

Zack was dressed in unrelieved plain black, black mock turtleneck over black chinos.

"It's cold," Zack replied. "Come in."

It was cold, that clammy kind of just-above freezing that feels colder than snowfall. I followed him in.

"Another funeral?" I asked softly. It was Thursday. We'd just had the service for the Carlsons and the Kallinikos family on Sunday. The Kallinikos were robbed and murdered two days after I contributed to the cache. They'd lived two blocks from Zack. "Anyone I knew?"

"I don't think so. She left me the cow." He looked vaguely exasperated by this bequest. "I think I need to hire a dairy maid. Not Alex," he forestalled my suggestion. "I'm already keeping Alex busy enough. But he'll know someone."

"Was this the woman who made cheese from your goat's milk? The contra dancer?" That last was a guess.

Zack nodded. "Grace. My ex. An ex-girlfriend, that is." He rallied. "You needed something, Dee?"

I met his eye gently. "It can wait. How about a cup of tea?"

"I'm not very good company today," he said huskily, and swallowed.

"That's OK. I'm a foul weather friend. You've been there for me."

He acquiesced easily enough, and we settled into the cozy kitchen.

"You tried shaving the sassafras!" I smiled warmly, but kept my voice low.

"Yeah, I don't think November was the right time of year for that. The sapling's leaves were deep red. Not much flavor, so I just use a lot. Next summer, maybe I'll try this again."

"Tell me about Grace," I invited, when he joined me at the table. The orange wood-like shavings needed to boil for a while.

He shrugged. "We dated for a couple years, but we couldn't make it work. We broke it off over a year ago."

"You were still close, though," I observed. "She still made cheese for you. She left you a cow. What's the cow's name?"

"She just called it—her—'Cow'. Grace had a thing against anthropo... whatever. Projecting human qualities onto animals and plants." He sighed. "She had a lot of policies like that."

"All that political activism, and organic correctness—was that you, or her?" I hazarded. It had never seemed quite Zack, to me. Not incompatible, just not quite right.

"Her," he agreed. "Not that I object, exactly."

I nodded. "Was the funeral service nice?"

"Quaker funeral," he said flatly. "They meet at Yale. Her parents and brother made a point of telling me how grateful they were that she'd broken off with me. That it was better this way."

"I thought you were surprisingly patient with pacifists, for a soldier."

"Not a soldier anymore," he denied. "I accept pacifists fine. They don't accept me."

"It's a huge part of who you are. I don't know about this Grace and her family, but I know Mangal and Shanti. They like and respect you. They wouldn't judge." I was surprised at how irate I felt against this unknown dead woman and her family, if they rejected Zack for being who he was.

End Game

Zack gazed out the picture window unhappily. The goats were playing king of the hill on a couch-sized chunk of pink granite, laying decoratively in the back yard.

"How did she die?" I asked softly.

"Hard to say. Found dead in a chair in her home by a neighbor. The family declined any investigation. She was diabetic, very thin, never very robust. One Friend in the meeting was moved to say something about whether we should judge suicides these days—" Tears were standing in his eyes.

"Zack," I interrupted, and placed a hand over his. "She died peacefully in her own home. Yes?"

He squeezed his eyes shut, and nodded. "Yes. That's true."

"That's hard enough. And that's all it needs to be. I think this sassafras is about to boil away. I'll get it."

I rose and turned off the burner under the tea, but then turned to Zack's back and put an arm across his chest. I hugged him to me from behind. He accepted the hug wordlessly for a minute or so, then squeezed my hand to request release. I poured out half-empty mugs of sassafras tea, and sat down again with them.

"Do you want to tell me more about Grace? What was wonderful about her? She made good cheese."

He smiled softly. "She did that. Good gardener. Loved nature. Her cooking was a bit on the organically correct side."

I chuckled. I like food that tastes good.

"Grace loved to dance. She was so solemn most of the time. But she came alive when we danced." He smiled, just a little. "Career. She was working on a doctorate at Yale, in public health. She started it hoping to work for an NGO in the Middle East, to promote family planning." He sighed. There was no career like that in this year's world.

"Smart lady," I murmured. "Her skills were valuable for this new world, too. I hope she saw that."

"Yeah. Thanks."

He was so reserved. I wasn't sure what thread to tug on next. I settled on, "Can I help you, Zack?"

"You already have. I have work to do, but I kept… getting distracted. Wait—you came over here. What did you need?"

"Ah… that can wait."

He gave me a stern look.

I shrugged. "What are you working on at home?"

He blew out through his mouth. "There's an army procurement detail heading our way. I'm not sure what we're going to do about that."

"Oh, there was that, that I wanted to show you." I pulled out my phone and brought up the Amenac site. This was clearly not the reaction Zack expected. I pressed on. "Amenac. This is a new farmer-news website. I'm a beta tester. There's a snorricane coming. Here."

"…What?" Zack managed.

"When is this… 'procurement' detail… likely to arrive?"

"Tomorrow night. The Army. To steal our food."

"Yes, I caught that part. That'll work. The snorricane should start around 3 a.m. About 11 hours from now?" I stepped around behind him so I could poke at the screen and show him what I was talking about. "Yeah. This blizzard should dump 3 to 5 feet of snow on us. Were you around for the blizzard of 2013?"

He shook his head. "I was in the Baltics, I think. Really? That's a lot of snow."

I nodded. "Too deep to budge with a snowplow. You need front-loaders. So, maybe you could get together with Totoket public works and request where *not* to clear snow?"

Zack was still having trouble catching up. "That… yes. Hell, yes. You're… Deebe?" He was scrolling through a chat section. He paused at a Bible quote. It was from one of my favorite oddball stories in the Bible, where Jesus wins friends and influences people in the Galilee by driving a flock of pigs off a cliff to their deaths in the sea.

"Dee, what the hell is this?"

"You don't know that story? He drove demons into the pigs. I'm not sure how you'd tell the difference from normal pigs. Vicious creatures. Jews aren't supposed to keep pigs, anyway."

Zack's clawed hand reached toward my neck in an, 'I'm going to throttle you now' sort of exasperated gesture. He gave it up and dropped face to arms on the table, shoulders heaving, in sobs or laughter. I slipped back into my chair across from him. I think he was laughing, mostly. When he sat back up, he wiped a tear from his eye. He drummed a finger on the table next to the phone. "What is this website, Dee? What is your involvement, in this website?"

"I said. I'm just a beta user. I think it's great. News you can use, for farmers and other outdoor folk. Weather forecasts, safe markets, stuff like that. You should refer to it, for weather forecasts. They're very good."

"Like your hurricane forecast a couple weeks ago? The hurricane that no one else knew about?"

"Yeah. Like that."

He continued to stare at me, eyes narrowing in suspicion. I smiled back.

"Be careful, Dee," he warned.

I shrugged unrepentance. "Just a beta user. But if you have any suggestions for improvement, I'd be happy to relay them to the developers." They worked for me, after all. "I'll email you a link to the Totoket area news."

"It's a public website."

"Hidden in plain sight," I agreed. "Behind Bible quotes and everything. Good recipes for green tomatoes and over-sized zucchini, snails. Anyway, the snowstorm should help, shouldn't it?"

"Yes. Thank you." He sat back and blew out a long breath.

Then the cogs seemed to start turning on where he'd most like his strategic snowbanks.

"Well, maybe I should go," I offered.

"That was what you wanted to come see me about? And then said 'later'?"

Drat. The man was exceptionally hard to distract. "It can wait, Zack."

"If it could wait, why did you come over to tell me in person? Just tell me, Dee."

If a blizzard, Amenac, and demon pigs in the Galilee couldn't derail him, it was a lost cause. "I'm, um, going away for a few days. Starting Sunday. To see Adam's ark. I'll be back."

His breath stopped, while he stared at me. I could tell when it started again, with a deep heaving in-breath, that he blew out slowly through his mouth. Yeah, this was a bad time to bring it up.

"Dee, that's a betrayal of everything we're trying so damned hard to do here."

"No, it's not. I'm visiting a friend, who built an ark. I'll be back in a few days."

He nodded jerkily. "Get out of my house. *Leave.*"

I rose and stomped to the front door. I laid my hand resolutely on the doorknob, and… stood there. It's not just that I wanted Zack's good opinion, although I surely did. But we'd accomplished a lot together. West Totoket was better off, for us working together. In a world descending into savagery, we lived in a nice place. Good people stopped to mourn a fallen neighbor. We shot looters here, yeah. We also gave a man like Trey Cowan a second chance. I liked us. I was proud of us. And Zack and I were better together than apart, for West Totoket. And I liked him. If Adam hadn't come up with that crazy idea of visiting Montreal, Zack and I would be lovers now. Maybe even ex-lovers by now.

I lay my forehead briefly on the door, then wheeled to face

him. But he was standing across the living room, on the phone, and raised his hand in a 'wait' signal.

"Yes, Zack Harkonnen. Right, I have two pieces of news and a request. First, we expect a blizzard overnight... You follow the Amenac website, too?... Yeah, there's an Army battalion headed our way, to procure food from the citizens... Saturday... Yeah, I request you do not, repeat *not*, clear snow in West Totoket... Especially not Route 1... Sure, let them clear the railroad and I-95..."

While he spoke with Totoket public works, Zack walked slowly toward me. He needed to call them before they closed for the night, after all. He stopped about 6 inches from me, scowling down into my eyes, while arranging for another consultation after the snow stopped, for selected roads to be cleared. He hung up.

And he crushed me to the door with a violent, hard kiss. After half a minute of me pushing harder and harder against his chest, he let go and stepped back, glaring at me.

I glared right back. "You would go, too."

"Like hell I would!"

"Not to join the ark. I believe you. But Zack, I'm only *visiting* the ark. For years, UNC's been jerking me around, promising if I was a good and obedient employee, I'd be safe on an ark while the world went to hell all around me. Now I want to *see an ark*. My friend built this ark. I want to see it. That's all."

"Who's stopping you? *I* told you to *leave*."

"You don't get to do that. You're my friend—"

"You're not mine!"

"I am your friend. I was your goddamned friend right here, today! *And I still am.* You've done phenomenal things for Totoket, Zack. Nobody knows that better than I do. *And I helped.* You're not allowed to stop being friends with me. We're too good together for Totoket." Tears were standing in my eyes.

"Dee, you chose Adam. I get it, but—"

I grabbed his hair and kissed him, hard.

"I choose *me,* damn you," I hissed. "I choose *Earth. Totoket.* My *friends.* I'm right here, doing my damnedest for all of them. Including you! Don't you dare try to tell me that I've betrayed you, any of you!"

"What the *hell* do you want from me? If I say 'pretty please'? Dee, pretty please, could you please get out of my house, before I put my first through a wall? Because I don't have time to fix the wall."

I glowered at him. "And you'll check in on Alex while I'm gone? I may not be able to get through by phone."

Zack's face went through several more angry contortions. He settled for spitting out, "Sure."

"Right, then. I'll see you in a few days, maybe a week. When you'll still be my friend. Enjoy the blizzard." The tears were overflowing down my cheeks by then.

I let myself out. I jumped a little when I heard Zack put his fist through the wall anyway.

Yeah, that went well.

-o-

I walked home and veered into Alex's house, to play with his baby guinea pigs. He had an entire rodent room on the playroom floor of his split level house, presently hosting about a dozen guinea pigs and a half dozen rabbits, all running free except for the new mom and babies. This was supposed to keep the mama pig from getting stressed out protecting her young. But guinea pigs are born pretty advanced, for mammals, like giving birth to a three year old human child. The babies nurse a little, but they also eat adult food the day they're born. If anything, mama pig was happy for the break from the little ones pestering her for milk.

End Game

I cried myself out over a succession of piglets. Alex came in to hand me a box of tissues and play with the rabbits across the room.

When I quieted down, and blew my nose clear, he asked, "Everything alright?"

"Yeah. I had a fight with Zack, that's all. Listen, Alex, I'm going to go away for a few days starting Sunday. I *will* come back. I'm just going to see Adam's ark."

"That pissed off Zack?"

"It's complicated."

"It's not that complicated," Alex disagreed. "I think Zack likes you."

"I like him, too. I still promised Adam I'd go see his ark."

Alex nodded morosely and hugged a bunny. "When my mom broke up with a guy, I'd never see him again. He'd say we'd see each other again, but we wouldn't."

"Zack's not like that." I was pretty sure of that. "You can call him if you need him, while I'm away. He's pretty busy, though."

I told Alex about the snowstorm to cheer him up. He liked that.

By morning, we were in full white-out blizzard. Well, almost white. Dust Bowl dirt fell with some snow squalls, building snowdrifts swirled like chocolate and vanilla soft-serve ice cream.

The snow ended late Saturday afternoon. It averaged 38 inches in Totoket, deeper inland away from the Sound, and much deeper in the drifts. Which was deep enough. The legions of snowplows were helpless to clear the roads, which had to wait for the few available front-loaders.

Chapter 18

Interesting fact: Estimates range from 50,000 to several million, as to how many people Homeland Security 'disappeared' under the Calm Act. In other words, no one knows. It's fairly certain that most of these people were killed, as there were few reappearances.

"Why, bless you, young man, I would *love* a wheelchair," I assured the ice cream suited sailor at the head of the pier in Groton. I don't know military ranks, though I was confident the captain wasn't playing bell-hop. We couldn't see the pier or ship yet. We were in a reception building, which blocked the way.

"And I'll take that, sir." A second white-clad sailor took my overnight bag from Adam. "We appreciate your cooperation for the rehearsal. You'll be playing Dr. Anelise Møller and her grandson Hans Jensen today. We'll have several passengers who require wheelchairs, and they slow down the boarding process."

"Well, I'm sure you're all doing your very best," I assured him, and patted his arm.

"How old is Hans Jensen?" Adam asked mischievously.

The sailor grinned. "I believe he's 10, sir."

Adam took a piece of paper from the check-in desk and wrote a sign, '10 year old boy', to pin on his shirt. "Wish I had a propeller beanie. And a giant water gun."

I was grateful to be off my feet. The trip to Groton was exhausting. The original plan was for Adam to drive to Totoket to pick me up. The interstate highway was passable, being the top priority to clear of snow. But he wouldn't have gotten past the exit ramp on my end. The railroad was running, though. That was only 3 miles from my house, trudging through waist-deep snow. As an invasion deterrent, the thick white blanket with grubby brown stripes was first rate. The train was an hour late, and standing room only. The Navy or Coast Guard arranged a shuttle and clear streets from the train station to the harbor. That was another standing-room-only hour wait. Then someone paged Adam for me, and it took him a half hour to meet me.

Sitting was good.

Our guides—Ehrlich and Ames, said the nametags—navigated us through the line of 'passengers', and then to emerge onto the sunset-lit pier. Our fellow play-actors looked anything but Navy. There were families, plenty of middle-aged and older people, all in civilian clothes. Most dragged along ark-type footlockers on rolling caddies. The facility's industrial grey, concrete, pipe-protuberant décor was echoed throughout. Outdoors, the golden light failed to make it look much prettier, but I whole-heartedly approved of the staff's thoroughness in removing every last shred of snow from the pier.

"It's an aircraft carrier," I said dumbly.

"It was," Adam agreed. "There are other ships in the group, but the ark core is the aircraft carrier and a hospital ship." Adam made a playful dodge toward a pipe complex that would be called an 'attractive nuisance' with respect to 10-year-olds—great fun for climbing. Ames cordially reeled him back in.

"Is it easy to fit an aircraft carrier into New London harbor?" I asked. Groton was this side of the harbor, with New London across the water. Militarily, the harbor hosted a sub base for the Navy, and the Coast Guard Academy and regional operations.

"No," the three men chorused emphatically.

"But there is enough depth," Adam added. "Barely."

The other passengers headed for the normal type of ship

gangway, steep and replete with traction treads. Ehrlich steered us to a wide and flatter ramp instead, without the pesky speed bumps. We rolled into a vast cargo hold, and to a cargo elevator. Several elevators and a bewildering number of corridors and turns later, Ehrlich jacked me into Analise Møller's berth—the hatch had a high lip—and bid us farewell. Thankfully, he took the wheelchair with him.

I took a seat on the lowest of a stack of three narrow bunks, banging my head on the edge of the middle bunk. There were three other bunks across the 18-inch aisle, a bank of lockers at the far end from the hatch, and a fluorescent light strip above us. Definitely not an ocean-view stateroom.

I think my mouth was hanging open while I took all this in, back and neck hunched under the bunk above.

Adam grinned ever broader at me, then laughed out loud. "I knew you'd hate it!"

"Well…" I attempted.

"Oh, come on, Dee, please. Compliment the mattress or something. I'm just dying to hear what you come up with."

"It's kinda cool that you have these little privacy curtains on the bunks." The lack of width, or headroom, was a bit inhibiting as to what you could do with two people behind that little scrap of fabric, but still. There was a privacy curtain.

"That's to keep out the light, so you can sleep during watch change," Adam clarified. "Or keep the light in when you're reading and your berth mates are trying to sleep."

"Ah. Is your room…?"

"Cabin."

"Your cabin. Is it any…?"

"I'm in a nine-man cabin. The bunks are about the same. A bit more floor space."

The hatch opened for another sailor-led group, this time a family of four. The sailor came in first and snapped the family's ark-lockers into the locker area at the end of the room. He had to pop off the locker doors first. He exited with the retired hardware before the family could come in.

They hesitated in the doorway—hatch—for a moment, looking aghast. A boy and girl stepped in first.

"Can I have the top bunk?" asked the boy.

"I want the top bunk!" squealed the girl.

"There's two top bunks, stupid," said the boy.

"Don't call your sister stupid," the dad growled on automatic.

Adam, who'd ducked into the other bottom bunk to get out of the way, emerged to hold out a hand to shake with the man. "I'm Adam Lacey, and this is my friend Dee Baker. We're pretending to be Dr. Anelise Møller and her grandson, Hans. Hans is 10," he offered as an aside to the older boy, who looked to be not much younger. "Dr. Møller is wheelchair-bound, so she might need a lower bunk. Are you part of the rehearsal, or really joining us today?"

"Tom Aoyama of MIT. Good to meet you, Adam, Dee. My wife, Beth Agrawal of Harvard. Our kids, Dennis and Charity. We're… really embarking today. It's been a long wait. We've been in temporary housing in Norwich since the borders closed. The Boston borders, that is." Norwich was a couple towns north of Groton, maybe 15 miles away.

"Welcome aboard. I'm actually crew, sort of. Civilian contract engineer. We're only in your berth for the rehearsal. Speaking of which," Adam checked his watch, "I need to go join a staged riot on the pier now."

"Can I join you?" I begged.

"Don't you want to put on some dry clothes, Dee, and rest for a bit?" Adam added for the Aoyama-Agrawals' benefit, "Dee had to walk through a few miles of snowdrifts to get here today."

"Cool!" opined one of the kids, hidden above me. Tom and Beth had reluctantly selected the two stacked lower berths across from mine. Tom shushed the boy.

"Um, if you want me to stay put, I can stay put," I said, without enthusiasm.

"I'll find you at dinner. Promise." And with that, Adam left.

"Are you also crew, Dee?" Beth Agrawal inquired politely.

"No…" I explained my lack of status while fetching out dry clothes from my duffel bag, stuffed in a locker.

The privacy curtain was enough modesty for changing clothes. Where to put wet clothes and winter coat afterwards was a puzzle. Tom Aoyama eventually found a spring-loaded rope that extruded from a wall—bulkhead—and his daughter Charity located a matching wall latch to secure the other end of the rope.

Wet laundry hanging from a sagging rope above the miniscule aisle did nothing to improve the space. Periodic announcements from the loudspeaker—and the bunkroom was equipped with its own interior very loud speaker—reminded passengers to remain in their cabins until we were underway. At that time, dinner seatings would be announced.

"I have to go to the bathroom," Charity inevitably announced.

"Me, too!" I offered eagerly. "Wanna go find it together?"

"Me, three," said Beth, sighing. Though in the end, she waited for us to get back.

Finding the latrines was the highlight of our several hours together. After that, Tom declared quiet time so we could all take a nap until dinner.

"I hate this place," Charity said in a small voice, just before I drifted off to sleep. "I wanna go home."

-o-

"Found you," Adam whispered in my ear.

I jumped. I was in the middle of a computing skills exam, administered under the steely eye of seaman Mandy Nykes.

Adam grinned. "Sorry it took so long. Mandy, can I spring this passenger?" He gave her a wink.

Mandy clucked her tongue and shook her head dolefully. But she said, "Fine by me, Mr. Lacey. She's not going to pass that test anyway." That dig was for me.

Sadly, this was true. I had no security clearance. A bachelor's degree in computer science, and an entire career programming, were in disciplines entirely other than those employed by a nuclear aircraft carrier. So far the morning's aptitude tests gave me a thin hope of qualifying for kitchen patrol. I wanted hydroponics, but there was no test for that. "Everyone gets one watch a week in hydroponics," Mandy told me. "My turn tomorrow. I can't wait! You prefer cleaning, kitchen, or laundry?"

To be fair, Adam did find me during my dinner shift the night before, but only to tell me that he was on watch through midnight, and would have to find me the next day, today.

"How long do you have, before you're back on duty?" I asked Adam sadly, once we were out of Mandy Nykes' clutches.

"I'm a civilian. I don't stand a watch cycle. My systems passed their tests. I can take the rest of the day off," Adam explained. "Unless they page me with a problem."

"Nine-man berth, huh?"

"There usually aren't more than four sleeping in there at a time," Adam said. "But yeah. Not a lot of privacy. But! Just for today, just for us—there is an empty cabin. Let's get your gear."

Moving to my new bunk took about 45 minutes, 6 decks, and several miles of corridor, but it was a nicer room. One of the three stacks of bunks was perpendicular to the other two, making for a wider aisle down the middle. The cabin also featured a couple writing desks as well as lockers, and royal blue sheets. The bunks and desks were painted white, providing cheerful contrast to the sheets and grey bulkheads.

Adam sat at one of the desks, and waved me to a seat on

the bunk at his knee. "Better?"

I nodded. "Especially if you're staying here with me?"

"If I'm invited," he said with a smile.

"Invited," I echoed. "I came here to see you."

His smile grew wistful. "I think... I'd like to get this out of the way first. Dee—you don't belong here. Do you?"

I blew out a long breath. "God, no. I'm sorry, Adam, I—"

He held up a hand to stop me. "Nothing to apologize for. I never thought you did. But Dee—I do. This is my ship, my project, my life. Our world is crashing all around us, and we're lucky, you and me. We really are. We both have a place. We have something worth doing."

"Just, not together."

"No. I wanted to leave it open, offer you safety if you needed it, in case things went pear-shaped at home. Compared to New York, this is paradise. Your roomies last night were lucky to escape Boston. And they'll be happy here. But if you can make it work in Totoket..." Adam trailed off, then said, "I'm impressed as hell with what you're accomplishing in Totoket."

"But you're not tempted to leave the ark to join us."

"Tempted, sure. I enjoy your company. But Dee, there are other Totokets. This ark is a resource ship. A brain trust, labs, scientists, some naval force. We're not just about saving the five thousand people on this ship. We're about giving a power assist to places like Totoket. And serving the Navy and Coast Guard out here on the Atlantic blockade."

"Power assist?"

"Did that drone strike help, on New Year's?"

"*You* sent the drone strike!"

"Me? No. I put Zack in touch with someone who needed to carry out a drone test. Technically we're not in business yet, to intervene. But they have to run their tests somewhere." He shrugged. "The ark team was grateful for the head's up on the hurricane. The Navy, Coast Guard, and Marines were furious that we weren't on the 'need to know' list for real weather reports."

"And what do you do?"

"Plumbing, mostly." Adam laughed out loud at the look of consternation on my face. "Have you seen the flight deck and hydroponics yet?"

"I haven't even seen a porthole yet. For all I know we're still in New London harbor."

"We're just south of Martha's Vineyard or Nantucket, running dead slow while we finish systems checkout. Well, I was hoping for a little nookie first. But come on. Let me show you what I've been building the past few years."

As Adam drew me down another mile of pipe-lined corridor, and three more elevator rides, I sincerely hoped he'd be available to guide me back to that cabin. He pointed out assorted ship features along the way. That went in one ear and out the other. But if the man was in charge of the pipes, he sure had his work cut out for him.

"Here we are," Adam said at last. The elevator opened to a high-ceilinged cavern. Instead of human corridors decorated with pipes, we'd emerged at the pipe lair, with little walkways through the maze of pipes and giant thrumming machines.

"It's very nice," I hazarded. Actually, I felt like a tufty-haired kid lost in a Dr. Seuss book. We were nearly yelling over the sound of the machines.

Adam grinned. "We're right below the flight deck. This used to house the aircraft fueling system. And down that way, the systems to bring fixed wing aircraft up and down from the deck. We converted this area to water systems. Desalination, sewage reclamation, a lot of the air cleaning systems. This ship doesn't need to tank up on water in port. It's water self-sufficient now. And it can operate in closed-atmosphere mode. We sealed it up when we left New London. We're running in ark mode today."

"You did all that?"

"Our *company* did all that. It took years, and lots of engineers. I mostly worked on the desalination inputs and reclamation outputs of the hydroponics system upstairs."

"Wow. I don't know why I thought you were like, a chief engineer or something."

"I was, in the Coast Guard. Small boats. The Coast Guard doesn't have behemoths like this. This is Navy. But a few years ago, I was transferred down to the Gulf, and I just... It used to be more about Search and Rescue, helping people, in the Coast Guard. Maritime law enforcement, catching smugglers. Then in the Gulf and Caribbean, it got to be more about turning back desperate refugees, killing them outright sometimes. I just didn't want to do it any more. I put out feelers. This came up, and would bring me back home to Connecticut. I jumped at the chance."

I nodded understanding, then gazed around at the machines and pipes and gauges. "So this room is your life work from now on?"

"Nah. The Navy crew is taking over now. They'll probably transfer me around from ship to ship. I'm one of the civilian resource personnel, now that the ark conversion is complete. I go where I'm needed."

And as a civilian resource's wife, I'd be a dependent, like little Charity Aoyama. Maybe they'd let me follow Adam around, and maybe they wouldn't. At least it was a nice ark, dedicated to being useful to others instead of just saving some rich guy's skin. Well, that and military might. The U.S. didn't build a Navy for philanthropic good works.

"So my part serves the hydroponics above." Adam resumed the tour. We climbed a ladder to emerge blinking into the sunlight of paradise. Cucumber vines dangled down around my head level, from white pipes and tubs running above.

Greenhouse girders and glasslike panes stretched beyond that. I grinned from ear to ear.

"Watch your step. Be sure to stay on the grating," Adam warned. There was some kind of gurgling marsh system running under the grate, with all the food plants supported above grate level. Adam took my hand and gently pulled me, all eyes, through the plants.

I could well understand Mandy Nykes' comment, how the crew would look forward to working in hydroponics as a treat. Occasionally I spotted the eye-searing lighting systems above, that augmented the short days and thin slanting light of northern winter. It wasn't much past noon, but the lights were on full blast over the summer crops like cukes and tomatoes. It was toasty in there at the moment, maybe 80 degrees and 60% humidity.

"So the oxygen we're breathing in ark mode comes from these plants?"

"Not enough," said Adam. "There are other hydroponics inside the ship, too, but it's still not enough. We crack water into hydrogen and oxygen. It's a nuclear ship. We have enough power."

I plucked a ripe strawberry from a strawberry pillar and popped it into his mouth. "You made a very cool thing, Adam. This is awesome!"

"Thought you'd like it." He gave me a kiss full of strawberry juice. "You're going to get us both in trouble if you pick unauthorized fruit." He sighed. "This ship was a lot more fun before the crew joined us."

I could imagine. Having the run of this vast ship must have been a blast, like kids let loose in a school during summer break. Adam continued drawing me along until we reached the side of the greenhouse. At last I could see ocean, though the view was obstructed. The greenhouse angled down to end about 20 feet from the edge of the original giant flat-top flight deck. There were the usual assortment of Naval protuberances and contraptions I didn't understand. But beyond them gleamed the Atlantic, and a bit of island in the distance to the right, maybe a half dozen miles away.

"Martha's Vineyard, or Nantucket?" I asked.

Adam considered, squinting for some identifying feature. "Martha's Vineyard," he concluded. "We're starting to accelerate, though." Something caught his attention, and he leaned forward. "There!" He pulled me in front of him, hugging my back to his body, and pointed with an arm held above my shoulder, at eye level. "See it?"

"What am I... Oh!" A whale surfaced, and blowed a spume into the fresh sea wind. "Is it a pod?"

"Mm-hm, humpbacks. They're out of season. Used to be, April to October was whale season around the Cape. Now they're unpredictable."

I turned to look at him, gazing at whales. He glowed. The rich man, the clever engineer, the suits, the playacting and great sense of humor, were gone at this moment. He was in love, at one with the sea.

"What?" he said, not breaking his gaze on the stretch of water where the whales occasionally surfaced.

"Nice to meet you, Adam Lacey," I said.

He liked that. He hugged me closer and kissed my temple. "I could stand like this for hours," he murmured. He sighed, as a chopper took off from the deck and wandered past our view.

He rather promptly let go of me to answer his walkie-talkie type device when it buzzed him. Impenetrable engineer jargon ensued while I enjoyed the view.

"Sorry, Dee, I have to go," Adam said, as he tucked his walkie-talkie away. "The CO_2 levels are rising a bit fast down below."

"Are we in any danger?"

"No, not at all. The CO_2 levels are still lower in here than they are out there." He jutted his chin to indicate the great outdoors. "Maybe 300 ppm on the lowest decks. Earth's air hasn't been that low in CO_2 since before the Industrial Revolution. It's even lower here in the greenhouse. In fact..." He crooked a finger to beckon me, and I followed him through a wall of spinach to a pillar of gauges. "Yeah, the CO_2 is too low up here, too high below." He tugged out the walkie-talkie again to share this datum with a colleague.

I looked at the gauge, but it reported partial pressures, not atmospheric parts per million units. I didn't recall offhand how to convert one to the other, so had no idea what it meant. I studied the spinach instead. I've never been able to grow spinach hydroponically. I wondered what they did differently to get such lush plants.

Adam signed off again on the walkie-talkie, but he'd clearly switched into engineer mode. It's not so different from programmer mode. He had a theory of where the bug lay, and I was a distraction.

"Chief!" he called out, to one of several people we saw lurking in nearby vegetable banks. We walked toward this man, a Navy noncom around our age. Adam introduced us and asked if I could stay with him until the end of his watch in hydroponics. Then, if he could take me below and re-insert me into the new passenger orientation pageant.

Adam wrote down my cabin address for me as well, should I wish to play hooky instead. He said he'd find me there around bedtime if not before, but not to wait for him anywhere. And then he was off to help hunt down someone else's CO_2 cycling glitch.

The chief—Nez, according to his shirt—was amused by it all. He set me to pollinating a bank of tomatoes, peppers, and eggplant, back to back with him down the row. I pollinated my own every day at home, so the task was familiar and soothing, mobilizing pollen on flowers with the flick of a soft dry paintbrush. A hummingbird zoomed by to help for a moment. I didn't see any bees, sadly. From time to time we ran across a clutch of indicator tabs, and switched 'Sunday' to 'Monday' to record when the plants were last pollinated.

I tried asking Nez my questions about the greenhouse operation—what shape was the greenhouse to stand up to the ocean winds? what nutrient mix did they use?—but he said he was only here to play bee once a week. His usual duty station was on the nuclear pile.

Descending back into the grey belly of the carrier was very hard.

-o-

Aptitude testing was over for the day, so I was passed from hand to hand until I reached a new passenger dodgeball game and could resume following the herd. After the exercise period ended, I talked my way into working in the kitchen, where I prepped salad. Their cukes and lettuce and spinach were excellent, but the tomatoes were pretty vapid. In this floating city of 5,000, I wondered how long it would take me to run across the person who might appreciate hydroponic tomato tips, and let me in on their spinach secrets. Probably not by Wednesday when I was due to disembark, I suspected.

Supper proved that the ark had a large livestock operation somewhere. The veggie and potato and cheese omelets were very good, if a bit on the light side. Another passenger passed on news I'd missed, that our standard rations would be 1500 calories a day for women, 2000 for men. She was rather irate on that point, feeling that the rule should be by mass, not gender. She had some mass to spare, though she was also big of frame.

Before we could leave our assigned mess room—there were many scattered through the ship—there was an announcement horn. A video screen turned on, placed above our heads on the wall—bulkhead—I was facing.

An attractive woman reporter wearing Navy uniform announced that a magnitude 8.7 earthquake had hit Los Angeles. The dislocation on that fault had set off domino earthquakes in other faults near San Diego and San Francisco. Video showed collapsed highways, pancaked towers, and fires raging out of control. No rationed water would be used to put the fires out.

Of especial interest to the Navy, the quakes unleashed tsunamis up to 85 feet tall. Another amateur video clip showed a wave barreling over Hilo Hawaii, which had received no advance warning of the tsunami. Of the ships at sea on the Pacific blockade, one destroyer sank, but most of its crew were rescued. Personnel at the West Coast and Hawaiian naval bases were not so fortunate. Damage assessments were in progress.

The reporter looked directly at the camera, and deadpanned, "A spokesman from the Federal Emergency Management Agency gave a statement estimating 150 dead, with casualty lists incomplete." More lives than that had ceased in that few seconds of video footage of the drowning of Hilo.

The reporter referred back to her notes, and added, "The most comparable incident in recent history was the 2011 Tohoku tsunami in Japan, which killed 16,000. The 2004 Indian Ocean tsunami killed an estimated 230,000. A 2010 earthquake in Haiti measured only 7 on the Richter scale, with death toll estimates around 300,000."

She'd gone out on a limb there, calling out the U.S. government on a bald-faced lie. And the news report cut out abruptly. The screen went blank for maybe 30 seconds, and then a fit and attractive 50-something year old man came on.

"For those of you who haven't met me yet, this is Captain Amatrudo. In light of our mission on Ark 7, and the events on the West Coast, I'm sure you're wondering whether resource ships such as ours will be released to assist. I have received orders that the answer is no." Rage set in the lines around the man's mouth, with words unsaid. "We are to complete our shakedown cruise and return to New London harbor Wednesday morning. That is all."

I didn't hear the words in the angry clangor that rose all around me in the mess room. Many were sobbing in fear for loved ones on the West Coast.

But I was wondering if it was possible to intentionally generate those earthquakes, and decimate the huge population of California, with a well-placed bomb or three. And furthermore, what someone might do to obliterate Chicago or Philadelphia. Because culling Houston, New York, Los Angeles, and San Diego already accounted for four of the ten largest cities in the U.S.

Chapter 19

Interesting fact: UNC was the fourth ark to be liberated. The complex was built in central Tennessee, shared by UNC and two other media conglomerates, with berths for only 4,000, including executives, members of the boards of directors, star television news anchors and commentators, and their families. They were killed with a gas attack, which dissipated to leave the facility, equipment, and food stores safe for use. Most of the ark's defense staff survived, and likely conspired in the attack.

"Alex! I'm so glad to reach you!" I cried on the phone. It was no mean trick, getting a phone line out. Cell service doesn't work out in the Atlantic. I spent half the evening talking my way onto this phone, in a communications chamber under the conning tower of the ark. "Is everybody OK at home?"

"Sure, why not? Where are you, anyway?"

"I'll tell you when I get home. Should be Wednesday, maybe Thursday."

"Cool." There was a long pause. Alex wasn't much for conversation. "Oh. Mangal wanted to talk to you. I'll patch him in."

Unlike most people, including most of my UNC subordinates, Alex knew how to operate his phone to call other people and smoothly add them into a three-way call.

"Hey, Dee! How's the cruise?" Mangal greeted me.

"A bit cramped. The hydroponics are awesome. What's up?"

"Did you hear about the waves out west? Good. No one

else did. There seems to be a kink in the hose."

It took me a moment, but I got it. Somehow the information feed from the National Weather Service—the real one—to Amenac, hadn't included any tsunami warning. "That's interesting," I agreed. "How are the other hoses?"

"Hard to say all. Can definitely say several are kinked."

"Completely blocked, or just filtered? Like a trickle of extra clean water?"

"Blocked."

"OK. Well, I need to make another phone call. Mangal? You be sure and take care of yourself and the kids, right? Don't worry about me."

Silence from the other end.

"Mangal? Did you hear me?"

"I heard you," he agreed. "But let's wait to unkink the hoses after you get home."

No one had needed to die in Hilo, Hawaii. Tsunamis travel fast, but no faster than a jet plane. We'd had nearly 5 hours to warn Hawaii. A simple warning could have saved thousands, perhaps hundreds of thousands of lives. Their shades called to me from watery graves.

"I think it's more urgent than that," I replied reluctantly. "It'll be alright."

"Take care, Dee," Mangal said, and hung up.

Alex and I chatted a little longer about the latest guinea pig and rabbit happenings, and signed off too.

"Just one more call?" I begged the communications tech. "I'll keep it brief."

Unfortunately, Jean-Claude didn't answer his phone. I didn't leave a message. Probably just as well, I thought. A naval aircraft carrier wasn't the smartest place to commit treason.

-o-

"Hey! I was looking all over for you," Adam greeted me, back at our berthing. He rose to give me a kiss.

If a kiss is exploratory in nature, it's obvious when you don't really return it. Adam shrugged and sat at one of the desks.

"Do you want me to return to my own berth?" he asked.

"No. I just... You saw the news about the west coast earthquake and tsunami?"

"No, I was inside a pump at the time. I heard about it, though. I'd like to see the replay, but I don't have a screen in here."

"Will a phone do?" I pulled out my phone. "You have Internet in here?"

"Sure." He gave me a brief searching look, then told the phone to remember the wireless user name and password he entered. "This is the Navy news site," he said, and bookmarked it for my later use.

Adam's ordinary good cheer evaporated as he watched the news report, with me watching from the bunk beside him. His face went especially blank watching Captain Amatrudo's statement afterwards. He opened Amenac for Hawaii and looked at the weather feeds for today. No tsunami warning.

I was glad to see there was already an Amenac database up for people searching to report the missing and the known dead, and their locations, for Hawaii at least. That was quick work. I'd have to praise the database and server team. The known dead count, just from the database, was already over a thousand, with the missing count much higher. I was surprised Amenac had so much traction already in Hawaii.

My fingers itched to flip the Amenac display to California, but Adam turned off the screen. He flipped the phone around in his hands idly, thinking. Which left me more curious about him than about California.

"Are you going to be happy here?" I ventured.

He reached a hand over and traced the side of my face, tucking a lock of hair behind my ear. He smiled sadly. "I think… I'll miss you. But like Captain Amatrudo, I'm getting tired of sitting on the sidelines while the world goes to hell. Playing with you is a very good distraction." He let his hand drop back to his lap.

I reached over and kissed him, sincerely this time. "I'll miss you, too. Thank you for inviting me here, and offering me an ark berth. But I ought to return this." I fished his mother's ring out of my pocket, and folded it into his hand. "I can't sit on the sidelines. And I'm no good at obeying orders. I'd just get you into a pile of trouble here."

Adam laughed. "I bet you would," he agreed. "It's late. Maybe tomorrow we could—" This was interrupted by his buzzing walkie-talkie again. This was a text message instead of a voice call. "Maybe tomorrow I won't be here," Adam amended himself, after reading it. "Niedermeyer is requesting my transfer to a Coast Guard ship."

"Are you going to say yes?" I asked, surprised.

"Ah, that was a courtesy copy. The XO gets to say yes or no, not me." The device buzzed again with another text. "And there's my summons to see the XO." He thought a moment. "Come with me?"

"What, now? OK." Once we were off and threading the pipe-lined corridors again, I asked, "Are you friends with the XO?"

"I barely know the XO or the Captain. They were just installed, with the Navy running crew, a couple weeks ago. Niedermeyer I've known for years. He's a friend."

We found our way back to the conning tower, and a couple levels up, to some sort of situation room. Adam placed me by the hatch and asked me to wait there, while he waded into the center to meet the executive officer. Tall, grey-haired, and forty-something, this man was glowering at a number of displays, while minions alertly monitored other displays, all in a dark chamber lit mostly by the equipment.

There was one fairly simple display board high on a bulkhead labelled 'Countdown.' It showed two glowing red numbers, both rounded: 6.25 billion, and 296 million. The most obvious numbers I knew of, in those magnitudes, were the population of Earth at almost 8 billion, and of the U.S., at around 340 million. Or, they were. While I watched, a blue jumpsuited sailor walked over and updated the numbers, to 6.15 billion, and 294 million. She looked up at the numbers to verify her work, and crossed herself Catholic-fashion, before returning to her perch at a workstation.

I told myself firmly that those populations couldn't be what those numbers meant. That I didn't know what those numbers meant. And it wasn't possible anyway. Two billion people couldn't just... could they? And—countdown to *what?*

Adam spoke with the XO for nearly ten minutes, mostly both standing with arms crossed on their chests, but occasionally leaning into a display for details. I studied a matched pair of Marines standing near me, just outside the hatch. They didn't return my curiosity. Eventually Adam pointed at me. The XO took one glance in my direction, and said no. And apparently that was that.

Adam collected me at the door and pulled me along into an elevator back down. Once the doors closed, he explained. "They're sending a chopper. I'm transferring over to the Coast Guard tonight. The XO won't let me take you with me. Dee, I'm sorry. I need to grab my stuff from my berth, and be at the helipad in an hour. If you come with me, we could see the hydroponics garden at night for ten minutes, maybe. Or I could just drop you by your berth."

"I'll come with you."

I got only a brief peek into Adam's cabin as he slipped in to pack. Several guys were sleeping in there, with one working at a small glow on a desk. It had the same nine-bunk, two-desk layout as the bunk we'd commandeered. When Adam re-emerged in his greatcoat, rolling his footlocker, two of the men shook his hand warmly, quietly saying good-bye.

I was glad he had friends here. I encouraged him to talk about them for small talk, as we made our way up to the midnight hydroponics greenhouses on the deck. It was really all one greenhouse, but hatches and glass-like walls between sections limited the scope of accidents. Adam led me out from the pumping chamber below into a new area, far more open due to banks of baby plants interspersed with the older ones. There were Marines on guard here and there, but for the most part, the gardens were dark and gurgly and deserted.

Adam led me to a corner. A little area, maybe 6 feet square, was clear of plants here, around an airlock chambered door to the outer flight deck. To one side, we could see the conning tower and helipads, with several helicopters parked silent in the dark. The other side showed an open view onto the Atlantic, quietly heaving pewter below, glimmering softly with starlight.

Adam dumped his footlocker, and sighed, leaning onto a railing that kept people away from the greenhouse wall. "Not how I would have chosen to say good-bye. I was hoping to take you out for a meal in Groton before you left Wednesday."

He drew me into a long hug. We watched the Milky Way between ragged scudding clouds. I wasn't entirely sure in the dark, but the sky looked like it might be doing the green tinge with blue spots thing again, the pattern I'd come to think of as ball lightning weather. But no lightning appeared in the miles of oceanic empty.

"You'll be safe with your friends in the Coast Guard?" I asked.

He didn't answer immediately. "I think their main job around here at the moment is to keep Long Islanders and Rhode Islanders away from Connecticut. Enforcing the borders at water's edge."

"You mean they fire on refugee boats."

"Yeah." He kissed my forehead. He whispered, "I'll be safe enough. But I never wanted to do that again."

"Do you have to?"

"Fire on them? Not me personally, no. I'm a civilian now, so I just keep the boat in good repair. And the guns."

"I meant, did you have any choice about going."

"Not if the Navy says I don't. It doesn't matter. Better to stay on good terms with them. Their guns are a whole lot bigger than ours. And if I leave peaceably, they're more likely to invite me back when something needs work."

The chopper arrived, and hovered its way down to the deck. Adam drew me into his arms for a long, hard hug. "Good-bye, Dee. Get back to Totoket safely, you hear?"

"Will do," I said. "You really were a great time, Adam."

He muffled laughter and let me go. "You, too," he said, as he opened the first airlock door. There was no need for him to wait in the airlock, as the air was breathable out on the cold deck. He waved one more time from outside the door, then made his way head down toward the helicopter.

And I watched Adam fly away.

A couple months ago I'd cried because my employee's mother accused me of making her son commit suicide. A couple hours ago I'd stared dry-eyed at some numbers that suggested a seventh of the country, and a quarter of the human race, might be dead.

I didn't cry as Adam flew away. I just wished him luck finding his way off the sidelines. He was a good man, with important skills. He'd find things to do that mattered.

-o-

Back in my berth, with a 9-person cabin all to myself, I changed for bed, palmed my phone, and pulled my privacy curtain closed. I took a moment to satisfy my curiosity on the Amenac site about California. Over ten thousand confirmed dead, nearly a hundred thousand missing in the database. But that was just reports from Amenac users, and only ones who could still get online. How to scale up to the whole population, I wasn't sure. At least a factor of four. Maybe ten or twenty.

I set that aside, and rummaged weather data feeds at sample spots across the country. They'd all stopped updating at the same time, a few hours before the L.A. earthquake. Coincidence? Probably not.

I could try logging in to the unadulterated National Weather Service directly. But that could get Adam in trouble if I did it using his Navy Internet credentials. All Internet traffic was monitored to some extent, but it would be monitored thoroughly here. The computing aptitude exam I took earlier in the day gave me a good idea of just how pervasive their spying was on the crew. I didn't want to risk it, nor emailing Mangal, or Dave at Amen1.

I could try Jean-Claude again. I could get the phone to do a voice-over-Internet call. And for better or worse, I'd already used that number from the communications room, so they had it. But I hadn't gotten through. No, it was better to leave that one alone.

I'd just have to play good cooperative passenger until I got off the ship on Wednesday morning. And it was already the wee hours of Tuesday morning. It would have to do.

-o-

I set my alarm to wake me 30 minutes before the all-passenger wake-up call at 6:30, which I was afraid I wouldn't hear in this cabin. I hadn't heard any announcements out of its squawk box. And Adam said we only had the room for one night. I figured it would be easier to slip back into the good little passenger stream if I rejoined my original berth with the Aoyama-Agrawal family. So I packed up my stuff and got over there right before morning announcements.

Little Charity Aoyama, at least, was happy to see me again. Her parents Tom and Beth looked a little pinched. But they knew they'd eventually share the tiny chamber with two more people, one of them wheelchair-bound. They rose to the occasion with friendliness, and promptly excavated my lower bunk, which had already become that horizontal surface by the door that accumulates books, toys, walkie-talkies, jackets, and everything else you dump on the way in or out.

That limited-calorie diet had all of us eager for that 7:00 a.m. breakfast mess, but the orientation crew had impressed on us that we should not arrive early and slow the exit of the previous mess seating. Teeth fresh-brushed, Charity told me all about how she was already in school and loved her new teacher.

Dennis had the same new teacher and called her a dildo. I was fairly confident he didn't know the meaning of the term. Apparently Tom agreed, and ordered him to look it up in an online dictionary. Beth rolled her eyes at that suggestion. Charity mimicked the eye-roll. I bet Beth would regret that in a few years.

I liked this family.

"And how are you two fitting in, Tom? Beth?" I asked.

"I'm alright," said Beth. "My lab is already here, and I'm getting it all unpacked and running. It's cramped, but I'm eager to pick up my research again. I haven't been able to do anything since we left Cambridge." At my look of inquiry, she added, "Uh, biochemistry." A hand-wave stood in for further elaboration.

"I'm mopping corridors," Tom offered with false cheer. "Everyone should know how to clean a floor properly. Right, Dennis?"

"Uh, yeah, Dad." Dennis appeared deeply disturbed by the definition of 'dildo.' He was looking up secondary terms. He shot an occasional worried glance at me and his mother. Beth was doing her level best to ignore this. *Daddy broke it, Daddy can fix it.*

"I work with infectious disease," Tom explained to me. "I can't set up my lab until all my hazmat equipment is on board. Maybe next week."

I nodded understanding. "I'm on salad prep," I offered. "Apparently a dozen years of professional programming didn't prepare me to do anything useful with Navy computer systems."

Tom snorted appreciation. Beth, followed by Charity, rolled their eyes again.

"Did you see the news last night, Dee? About California and Hawaii?" Tom asked, suddenly dead serious. Beth pursed her lips and bent to making beds.

"I did," I agreed. "The Captain's announcement was very interesting, after."

"Christ," said Tom. "I didn't sign up to do nothing—"

This was interrupted as the hatch banged open. A large Marine squeezed himself in, sideways and head ducked down. He demanded, "Dee Baker?" After a brief survey of the room, his eyes landed right on mine.

"Yes, sir?"

"Grab your gear and come with us, Ma'am."

I stared at him a few seconds. "And what is this about?"

"Grab your gear," he repeated. It was hard to see around him, given his size and the room's lack of it, but there were at least two more Marines behind him.

Beth wordlessly retrieved my overnight bag up from the lockers at the back of the cabin and passed it toward me. The Marine intercepted the bag and handed it back to the guys in the corridor.

Tom glared at his wife. "See here," he cried to the Marine, "you can't just barge in and take a passenger without any explanation! What's this about?"

I still sat frozen on my lower bunk, Charity by my side. "I would like to know where you're taking me, and why—Mr. DePaul," I managed. All the military crew came conveniently labeled with their names. Their insignia probably provided their ranks as well, but I couldn't decipher those.

"You're to be detained for questioning by Homeland Security," the Marine answered reluctantly. "Come along now, Ma'am."

"Like hell she is!" Tom yelled. "Get out of my family's cabin! I demand to speak to the head of scientific staff, Dr. Wagner, right now!"

I was surprised and touched by Tom's efforts to protect me. The Marines were less than impressed, and the eventual net effect was that we were both dragged from the room in handcuffs. Beth grabbed the kids and buried their faces in her body, and looked away, tears in her eyes.

"Beth! Call Dr. Wagner!" Tom yelled as his parting shot.

Beth Agrawal didn't reply.

-o-

The aircraft carrier Ark 7 was staffed with an eclectic mix of Navy, Coast Guard, Marine, and probably some Air Force personnel as well. What it didn't have was Homeland Security. So there would be no questioning right away. At the brig, Tom and I were locked into a barred corner holding pen, devoid of seats, and too small in any direction for even one of us to lie down full-length. We both sat down on the triangular scrap of hard floor, backs to the wall, arms hugging our knees.

A 20-ish Marine, who looked like a high school football linebacker, sat at a desk across from us in the small chamber. He played video games on a handheld device. Tom harassed him until a breakfast of cornflakes and water was supplied.

"You didn't have to defend me," I suggested to Tom, once

we'd pushed the breakfast tray out under the bars of the pen. "I mean, thank you, Tom. But you hardly know me."

"I know you fine," returned Tom. "I've seen you for two days with my daughter Charity. You're no more threat to the U.S. than I am." This last was louder, and thrust toward 'Tibbs', our labelled and indifferent linebacker.

I suggested mildly, "Tom, I don't think the nice Mr. Tibbs over there is our problem. It's his job to make sure we're all comfortable and everything runs smoothly down here in the brig." I smiled at Tibbs.

Tibbs smirked, but declined to glance up from the video game.

Tom said, "If Adam hadn't been taken off the ship, he'd be here to help you. I'm standing in, since he can't be here." I'd told Tom about Adam's departure during the morning bathroom shuffle.

Tibbs cocked an eyebrow at that. I wondered if he was quite as dull and uninterested as he appeared.

"I was here as a guest," I explained in Tibbs' direction. "Of my fiancé, Adam Lacey. Adam's an engineer with the ark conversion team. He designed the closed water system we're depending on now. The Coast Guard requested his help last night, so he was transferred away by helicopter. Is there any way I could get word to my fiancé, Mr. Tibbs?"

Tibbs sighed. "No, Ma'am."

"Why are you buttering up the Cro-Magnon?" inquired Tom, not nearly *sotto voce* enough for my taste. Tibbs leveled a glare at him.

I began to see why Beth hadn't lifted a finger in the man's defense. Some men are just indefensible. I regretted, though, that I didn't get a chance to look up 'dildo' in a dictionary. The 8-or-9 year old Dennis' expression had been priceless.

"Tom, I think Mr. Tibbs may be smarter than you, in this context," I warned him gently. "I keep saying Mr. Tibbs, excuse me. Is it Sergeant, or…?"

"Corporal, Ma'am."

"Corporal Tibbs," I acknowledged, and smiled at him winningly. "Behave, Tom. And cheer up. You're only in here to cool your heels for mouthing off. I get to enjoy Corporal Tibbs and his buddies' company until tomorrow. When they hand me off to Homeland Security." I banged my head back on the wall.

"No one ever comes back from Homeland Security," Tom growled.

Gee, thanks for reminding me. Tibbs and I both scowled at him. "What did you do, anyway?" Tom asked.

Tibbs stared at him. *You call me a Cro-Magnon, when you're that stupid?* I felt I was making progress, if Tibbs was looking daggers at Tom instead of me. Not that Tibbs could do much for me. Probably. Actually, if I could get him to contact Adam for me, that might help as much as anything could.

"I think I'd like to hear what they accuse me of, rather than give them any ideas," I replied to Tom. "But my conscience is clear as a mountain stream."

Beguiling thought, that, the whitewater burbling beauty of a mountain stream, versus our tiny tonal grey-on-grey brig, in the bottom of an aircraft carrier. I wondered if we were below the water line of the ship. The only lower levels listed on the final elevator were down in the cargo holds. I'd never been much of one for claustrophobia before. But I thought I might take it up real soon now.

"Tell me about your work, Tom," I invited. Ask a scientist about his research—that ought to be good for hours of entertainment. I thought I heard Tibbs sigh in resignation. Well, he was welcome to provide us a deck of cards or something if he couldn't stand my choice of distraction. "What exactly do you do with infectious diseases?"

Fortunately, Tom Aoyama turned out to be one of those rare scientists who had an undergraduate teaching vocation to match his research standing. And with no discernible sense of self-preservation, he liberally sprinkled in examples from the ongoing Ebola epidemic in New York—still denied by the news and authorities—to illustrate his points. Once Tom got going, Tibbs participated too. Several times he looked up specialized terms before asking for Tom to expand on them. He was a smart one, Corporal Tibbs.

"So, just as a hypothetical," I broke in at one point, "if the ark were free to intervene in the New York situation right now, *could* the epidemic still be arrested? Or is the situation already so out of control that the disease just has to run its course?"

That earned me a sharp glance from Tibbs. But he wanted to hear the answer, too.

It was just getting good. We had a mental map of Long Island, just a few miles from our starting point in New London harbor, invisibly drawn on the floor. Tom was expounding on a plan for a quarantine cordon gradually moving west along the island. Then a very irritable-looking Dr. Wagner arrived, with a pair of Navy and Marine officers of some sort.

Corporal Tibbs was dragged around the corner by the Marine officer, for what looked like a firm rebuke, and instructions to forget everything he'd heard. The brig had a couple nice convex mirrors mounted in the ceiling corners for ease in watching the whole brig complex from Tibbs' desk. The cages back there featured bare-mattress bunks and open-air toilets.

"Tom," Dr. Wagner greeted him, shaking his head in dismay. "What the hell do you think you're doing?"

"Werner! Waiting for you to spring me out of here. It's been hours!" Tom accused.

"Tom, I don't think you quite appreciate our position here," Dr. Wagner attempted.

"We're here as a resource. To help people. Yeah, I get that the Captain said we're not free to do that yet. Damn

Washington to hell! But what's the harm in talking about it? Sooner or later, we *will* be released to help people. Right? I mean, that's what I signed up for. That's why I'm *here*."

Werner Wagner patted his hand downward on air to suggest Tom take it down a notch. He was a slightly-built and distinguished-looking silver-haired European, in a nice grey cashmere sweater and slacks over good deck-traction athletic shoes. I could picture him as the chairman of a fractious Ivy league biology department meeting, full of lofty credentials matched with planetary-scale egos. "We're here as guests of the U.S. Navy, Tom," he explained gently, in a faintly British-trained over Germanic accent.

"To hell with the U.S. Navy!" Tom continued to expand on this theme.

It astonished no one, except perhaps Tom Aoyama, when Dr. Wagner eventually left the brig without him.

Tom was still yelling to his back. "When are we going to relieve New York, Werner? When 20 million are dead? 30? 50? When the epidemic jumps the borders? *When?!*"

The brig hatch clanged shut. I patted his leg in compassion as Tom collapsed back onto the floor beside me. "I'm sure he'll tell Beth you're alright," I offered. "I wish someone would tell Adam."

I really, *really* wished someone would tell Adam, so he'd tell my people back in Totoket. And so that he'd know himself, that I hadn't just forgotten about him. So that Zack and Alex and Mangal and Shanti and Shelley would know, that I hadn't just run out on them. Especially Zack. I thought Mangal would know better, but I wasn't sure he'd even try to convince Zack. For Zack to think I'd just skated out on Totoket because Adam gave me a better offer, that hurt.

Not that it would do me or Amenac any good if they knew the truth, that HomeSec got me. Amenac was dead in the water unless I could connect Jean-Claude Alarie to Dave of Amen1. I would bet anything Jean-Claude had someone in Canada crack into those sites that powered Amenac by now. But no one in Totoket but me knew that about Jean-Claude, or how to contact him. As for me, I was already as good as disappeared.

A subdued Corporal Tibbs resumed his chair at the desk before us. "We're all going to enjoy quiet time now until lunch," he explained patiently.

I closed my eyes meekly and hugged knees to forehead. Tom continued to swear a blue streak—quietly.

Chapter 20

Interesting fact: It's hard to tease apart the effects of the earthquakes, versus the tsunamis, versus the drought and the fires, versus the famines and violence. No interior borders were ever established for population control within California, because California flat-out refused, and tied the matter up in federal court. Overall, the population of California was estimated at 9 million by the end of that year, from a high of 41 million.

We docked early on Wednesday, back in Groton, after a long and contemplative night in the brig bunkroom with the open-air toilet.

About the toilet, I decided the best thing to do was simply use it normally, with no attempt to hide. We were all grown-ups. It's not like anyone would rape me in that all-too-thoroughly-observed brig. A guy would just whip it out to pee in public. Thus to clutch at my modesty would be to paint myself a victim. Screw that.

Likewise, Tom and I shared the 6-bunk cell. We'd shared a berthing cabin outside the brig, after all. The brig version was actually more comfortable. More spacious, with a full-width hall outside the bars, convex mirrors to open up the space, and en suite plumbing. Linens were provided for the two mattresses we used.

Corporal Tibbs was back on duty in the morning to see us off. Yes, *us*. Tom demanded to be put ashore, and his wish was granted. "Beth knows what I'm doing," he told me quietly. Thoughts of his family still haunted his eyes, though.

I was glad someone knew what he was doing. It helped me to feel less responsible for getting the man crimed and separated from his family. Not that I'd suggested he do anything of the sort. Still, if I hadn't been 'detained' right in front of him, the man would have gone to breakfast with his wife and kids. He'd have been with his family that evening for Beth's revenge for making his son look up the word 'dildo.'

The thought made me smile. There are probably smarter things to hold tight to, to take your mind off the fear, as you're marched off a ship, hands chained, blinking in the harsh morning sun, to face the people who will disappear you to your probable death. But I had a 9-year-old's misadventures with the word 'dildo' for comfort. It was something.

We stopped in front of the Homeland Security suits. Corporal Tibbs handed over Tom's footlocker and my overnight bag.

"Wait a minute," said Tom. "*I'm* not being held for Homeland Security. Just Dee. I'm just leaving the ship."

Adam? I mouthed at Tibbs in entreaty, as he turned to go. He closed and reopened his eyes slowly. Maybe it meant yes.

"Tibbs! Tell them!" Tom yelled. "I'm just—I'm not—"

One of the suits grabbed him and started propelling him roughly toward the reception building at the foot of the pier. Another simply waved a hand thataway to invite me to walk under my own power. I had an easier walk.

"Aren't I entitled to a phone call?" I asked, once I'd established my cooperation.

"No," the suit replied. These suits didn't come equipped with name tags. My keeper was a woman of little expression, average shape, and unmemorable plain face under straight dirty-brown hair.

"They weren't able to tell me on the ship—what am I accused of?"

"Violating the Calm Act," she replied unhelpfully.

End Game

Though I supposed it was a good sign that she hadn't added 'and treason.' Not that it was clear that treason was any worse than insulting the Calm Act. They can only execute you once.

"Mr. Aoyama really was only thrown in the brig for mouthing off," I attempted. "When I was detained."

No response.

We were placed in the back seats of separate black electric SUVs. I didn't bother to look back as we headed onto I-95, and west, back toward New Haven. I doubted Adam was in Groton. Since they flew him off on a chopper, I was pretty sure he was still at sea somewhere. I wondered if the unknown Niedermeyer had yanked Adam off Ark 7 because he knew I was about to get arrested, and didn't want Adam going down with me. Or maybe he'd expected me to come with Adam, and be safe.

I was pleased to see out the window that deep snow still blanketed the landscape.

-o-

"Do you deny your involvement with the subversive website Amenac?" Ms. Humorless demanded for the Nth time. She never did me the courtesy of an introduction.

We were in an anonymous bland office building in Wallingford, Connecticut, a few towns inland of Totoket. The office floor was replete with anonymous cubicles reminiscent of the cubicle maze at UNC Stamford. Their corporate office art wasn't as good, though. Instead of wistful beach toys and the educational boat-tailed grackle, their walls were mostly dressed with motivational posters on black. Our bland conference room featured one with a kitten hanging from a twig, exhorting me to 'Hang in There!' I tried to see it as encouragement rather than a bad joke.

I replied, "I'm a beta tester on the Amenac website, as I've said. And I'm proud of my contributions. It's a great site for farmers and gardeners." That was my story, and I was sticking with it.

"You are undermining the security of the United States of America in time of crisis."

"Everyone's entitled to an opinion. Though of course I have never incited anyone to be rebellious, my purely *private* opinion is that the American people deserve access to accurate weather reports. And other bits of truth, like where it's safe to barter for what we need. Like food. As a gardener, who wants to grow enough food to *live*, I thank God for Amenac."

"There! You admit it!"

"Admit what," I said dully.

"Inciting to rebellion!"

"Actually, Ma'am," said the younger and better looking male suit who manned the assorted recording devices, "she said she *didn't* incite anyone to be rebellious."

"Well, you can edit it," Ms. Humorless suggested.

The young man looked appalled.

"Why do you care?" I inquired of him gently. "I mean, is there a quality control officer who reviews this? Do you need to make sure you've got it *just so* for your war crimes trial? There will be one, you know. Someday. If anyone survives this climate crisis, there *will be*. And they'll have a *special place* at that war crimes trial for Homeland Security."

I liked Mr. Secretary. He flinched each time I said 'war crimes.' There was a shred of decency left there—good to know.

Ms. Humorless didn't have that chink. "Are you threatening me? Are you *threatening* me?"

"Everyone's entitled to an opinion. Ma'am," I repeated.

"No, *Ms. Baker*. You are *not* entitled to an opinion, according to the Calm Act!"

She seemed to think I was going to flinch at my own name if she hissed it sinisterly enough. Perhaps she just struck me as too stupid to be sinister.

"I don't believe I'm familiar with that clause of the Calm Act. Ma'am," I replied. Again. "Of course, most of the Calm Act was never published. So I don't really know what's in there. Do I."

"Note for the record that the subject was *completely* uncooperative," she said, for the Nth time. Thankfully her phone buzzed her. "Uh-huh... Uh-huh... On my way. *You!*" She jabbed a finger at Mr. Secretary. "Keep an eye on her!" She slammed out.

Mr. Secretary took a deep breath of relief, and let it out. I mimicked him exactly. He sat back and crossed his ankles. I sat back and crossed my legs, then stretched the kinks out of my upper back. He stretched, too. We wordlessly relaxed together.

God, I'm grateful for that basics of supervision course. Best five days I ever invested in my career at UNC.

I'd spotted the e-cigarette in his jacket pocket, a real guy-rig with a miniature brass rocket of a battery on one end, and a generous e-liquid tank on the other. I hoped for his sake he wasn't over-compensating for something.

"Is that an e-cig?" I asked. "Any chance I could have a drag? I'd kill for some nicotine."

No, I'm not a smoker, or a vaper. But I knew plenty of people who were, and I bet he wanted to vape, right this instant, especially now that I'd brought it up. Ms. Humorless would have that effect on people. Sure enough, he looked guiltily around. Spotting no one watching us, he powered up his device. He surreptitiously inhaled a lungful and blew a thick cloud down under the conference table. He passed it to me.

I mimicked him, careful to keep the vapor out of my lungs so I didn't give myself a coughing fit. I blew it all out, then took another deep drag, and handed it back. "Thank you. God bless you."

"I know, right?" He took another drag.

We were complicit now, like teenagers smoking in the lav, partners in a little no-no. "What's your name?" I asked.

He looked guiltily over his shoulder again, and took another drag. "Mark. But we're not supposed to say."

Someone should have taught Mark why it was that he shouldn't say. Names have power.

"Mark," I repeated. "I love the design of your e-cig. I'm big on steampunk, myself. At home I have a big brass and silver cogwork one." My fingers described a chubby steampunk pen I owned, not an e-cig.

"Oh, yeah? Cool."

That earned me another turn at the e-cig. "Hey, Mark. I have a foster kid, Alex. I took him in after his mother, you know, suicided on that oxycontin they keep handing out. Just a couple months ago."

"Poor kid."

"Yeah. Could you let me make a phone call? Just to tell Alex. God, Mark, I don't want him to think I ran out on him like his mother did. I just want to say good-bye. My phone's right over there in my bag."

"I can't—"

"Mark, he's a fourteen year old boy. He'll never trust anybody again. Please, Mark." I was convincing, because it was all true, and all heart-felt.

And when Mark handed me the phone, I called Jean-Claude Alarie.

"Jean-Claude, hello Dee?" he answered.

"Alex! I'm so glad I caught you. Listen, sweetie, I only have 3 minutes." That was what your one phone call to a lawyer was limited to on cop shows, wasn't it?

"Oh, that's bad. Where are you?" As I'd hoped, Jean-Claude was quick on the uptake.

"Wallingford." Mark looked daggers at me. "Um, I meant Broomfield. Look, that doesn't matter. Honey, I'm not going to make it home. Something happened. They say I violated the Calm Act. They're not going to let me come home."

"Maybe my friends should visit this Wallingford," Jean-Claude suggested.

I wasn't sure what to make of that. "Ah, no, you don't need to do that, sweetie. But I do need you to call *Mangal*, OK? He'll get you in touch with *Dave* to fix the hoses. That's important. You've got to fix the hoses. I'll give you his number. Got a pen?"

"Of course."

I gave him Alex's number, twice.

"And I am to call *Mangal* to get *Dave* to fix the *hoses*," Jean-Claude confirmed.

"You're the best, sweetie. I love you, Alex. God bless." I touched the call end button.

But I pretended I hadn't hung up. "Alex?" I asked worriedly, as though the line had dropped out. I pretended to put the phone on speaker while I held it myopically close and brought up a particular app I'd installed, Fraggit. If it did what I paid for, I could click one button and it would write '010101...' over every shred of memory in my phone, including the GPS, then erase itself and power the phone off. The Fraggit app had wonderful reviews from people with excessive social photo habits and guilty consciences.

"Huh," I said. "I lost the signal. Well, I guess I told him everything I needed to say. He's just so fragile, you know?" And there, the phone screen went black again, though it was still cranking. "Thank you so much, Mark. This," I hugged the phone to my breast, "this means so much to me." And it really did.

Mark held out his hand for the phone. But it was still cranking out 0's and 1's, judging from its thrumming.

"Could I just make one more call? To my fiancé? Please, Mark? It's just, when Zack and I left off, we had a fight, and—"

Ginger Booth

I was pushing my luck, and Mark's narrowed eyes were getting suspicious. Thankfully, the phone stopped dead. "Oh!" I said. "That was why. The battery was going dead." I sighed melodrama, and meekly handed it over to him.

Not expecting anything from a phone with a dead battery, Mark dropped it back into my overnight bag. We shared a few more puffs on the e-cig, took a bathroom break, collected more coffee, and were quite comfortable when Ms. Humorless returned.

It was harder then. Not because Ms. Humorless got any more insightful—the woman was stupid, petty, vicious, and pretty much irrelevant. The thing was, I'd held tight to that one remaining ambition, that Amenac would survive me, still do some good. I'd now done all that could be done for that.

All that was left to do was save my own life. And I didn't see any way to do that. I'd never known, or even heard of, anyone who escaped Homeland Security after violating the Calm Act.

"Now we'll talk about your criminal accomplices," Ms. Humorless announced.

"Since I haven't committed a crime, there aren't any accomplices," I replied. Again.

It was a long afternoon.

-o-

Mr. Bad Cop was slightly more convincing than Ms. Humorless. So far as I could tell, she dragged him in simply because 4:30 was the end of her routine ho-hum harass-the-masses workday. The winter sun would set soon.

"Are you going to threaten to let me live?" I interrupted him.

"What?" He said it with a sneer. Maybe he didn't hear me correctly.

"From what I've heard, no one ever escapes you people

266

alive. It doesn't matter whether they're innocent or guilty, cooperative or not. So, if you're not going to let me live no matter what I do, what possible motive could I have to tell you anything? Not that I have anything to confess."

"We have ways!"

"No you don't. Sure, there's torture, but you know—or you *ought* to know—that any information you get by torture, is going to be a lie."

Mark unconsciously nodded agreement. That was heartening. These fools were taught some basic facts. I'd been worried about torture. But apparently they were just going to *imply* it at me.

"What if I threaten to kill *Alex?*" He leaned toward me to put his face inside my personal boundary.

I pushed my face closer to him, which made him reflexively back up a little. "I hope you try it. *You personally.* Because I'm pretty sure you'll be the one to die. Not Alex."

"Are you *threatening* me?"

The door banged open. "Well, hell, you were threatening her, and her kid." A medium-tall, wiry man, with bushy light brown hair, entered already speaking. He dressed in Army camouflage like Zack's crew, and spoke with a slow and twangy Southern accent. I wondered how much of the exaggerated hillbilly swagger was intentional. He continued, "Turnabout is fair play, huh? Fun time's over. She's mine now."

"Who the fuck are you?" demanded Mr. Bad Cop.

I had the same question.

"Major Emmett MacLaren, head community coordinator, Southern New Haven County. I claim this little lady as an official asset." He tossed some paperwork on the table. "Sorry, darlin'," he said to me, "took us a while. You wouldn't believe the red tape. You can call me Emmett."

"You can't—!" objected Mr. Bad Cop.

"I can, and I did. Called in a marker. She's mine. Check it."

Emmett pointed to Mark. "You can get those cuffs off her, and we'll just be on our way."

"We still need her sources—" objected Mr. Bad Cop.

"Ah, no," clarified Emmett, finger pointing stiffly at the paperwork. "I own her, and her sources, and the whole Amenac website. They're all claimed community assets of Southern New Haven County now, and you can't touch 'em. Sorry, Bubba." Emmett turned to me again. "Come on, darlin'."

Mr. Bad Cop made several further apoplectic objections, but Emmett just ignored him. He tossed my overnight bag over his shoulder, took me by the elbow in southern gentlemanly fashion, and escorted me out the building.

"Phew-ee," he commented as we reached his car just outside the boring glass entrance. "Every time I go into HomeSec, I wonder if I'm coming out again. Climb on in, darlin'. Let's get the hell away from here."

"Who *are* you?" I demanded. Anything beat Homeland Security, though. I climbed in and buckled my seatbelt with alacrity.

"Major Emmett MacLaren. Zack Harkonnen's boss."

Chapter 21

Interesting fact: Probably the single greatest factor leading to the breakup of NATO was Russia taking on the NATO allies in the Baltic—Estonia, Latvia, and Lithuania—plus Turkey and Romania. Russia was increasingly strident in its demands that U.S. forces stay out of any country bordering Russia. The U.S. was already at war in Afghanistan, Iran, and against Global Jihad in the roiling area that was once Israel, Jordan, Lebanon, Syria, and Iraq. The U.S. was stretched beyond the breaking point, with no hope of succeeding in all these conflicts. Hawks tried to call it World War III and frenzy the U.S. into World War II era total mobilization, without success. The public just wanted out.

"Zack was a plant?" I breathed. I remembered wondering that, during our first dinner together. Whether the secret services planted people in protest groups, to sow incompetence, indecision, and ineffectiveness. "He lied to me all along?"

"Get off your high horse, Dee," Emmett said cordially. "Zack Harkonnen's the most honest man I ever met. And you —shit." He barked a laugh. "I didn't even have to blow a marker on you. Some guy named Niedermeyer gave me another. On behalf of your *other* boyfriend. Adam, is it?" He shot me a look out the side of his eye. "Zack didn't lie to you. You lied to him."

"Zack and Adam already know about each other," I defended.

"Uh-huh. And the Amenac site came back up an hour ago. We didn't need to spring you to get that back."

"*Yes!* It worked!" I clenched a fist in victory and thumped my head back against the chair head-rest in relief.

"Yeah? What exactly was that, Dee Baker, that worked?" Emmett inquired drily.

"Mmm," I replied.

"Yeah, don't you go calling Zack Harkonnen a liar, darlin'. Cuz you're a piece of work."

I pursed my lips at him. "I still don't understand. Who are you people? What is a marker? How could you just walk out of Homeland Security with me?"

"Ah—there's Zack," said Emmett. And indeed, Zack was perched on my new electric car, in the twilight gloom by the wiggly snowy wooded road-side, not a mile from the Homeland Security offices. "I thought it'd be safer to leave someone on the outside, just in case. Besides, I thought the two of you might get to arguing, and complicate the extraction."

"Zack is not mad at me for anything," I denied. "Or, well..." We hadn't really talked since that last complex chat over his house when I told him I was going to visit the ark.

"Uh-huh," agreed Emmett laconically. OK, maybe Zack had vented to Emmett about me. Emmett parked the car behind Zack, and got out. "She's all yours, Harkonnen."

Zack ignored me climbing out of the car, instead going straight to Emmett for a heart-felt man-hug—shake hands, hug, bop fists. "I owe you, Emmett. I know it was a lot—"

"Wasn't so bad," Emmett denied.

"Wait—can you get someone else out?" I interrupted. I'd already pulled my overnight bag out of the car and stood awkwardly a few feet back from their man-bonding.

"She's a real nuisance, your girlfriend, Zack," Emmett observed mildly. "You might want to work on your taste in women." He made a move back toward his car door.

Zack scowled at me.

"Just listen to me, Emmett, three minutes," I insisted,

childishly holding up three fingers in the cold air. "There's a guy in there. Homeland Security wasn't after him. He just objected when I was taken, and... Well, he needs to learn when to shut up."

"Lotta that going around," Emmett observed.

I frowned at him and folded my arms over my chest. "His name's Tom Aoyama. He's an infectious disease specialist from MIT. He was supposed to be a resource on the Navy ark, an expert on how to make New York safe again after Ebola, find treatments for new diseases, stuff like that. But he didn't like them holding him in reserve in an ark, instead of letting him out to cure disease. Please. He's only in their clutches by accident, because he was trying to defend me."

"She really is high maintenance," Emmett commented to Zack. He looked dolefully back the way we'd come.

"Yeah," Zack agreed, followed by a martyred sigh. "But she has good ideas. When she gets this way and I take her advice, it usually turns out she was right. She dreams up solutions I'd never think of."

"You don't have to keep Tom, or anything," I pleaded. "You could just drop him off somewhere around Yale, and leave him to sink or swim. But no one else is going to give New York a chance. Doesn't New York deserve a chance? Somebody who'll fight for them?" Tears were standing in my eyes. I wiped them away angrily.

"Right. Zack, could you shut her up?"

"Probably not, but I could put her in the car and leave," Zack offered.

"Nah, just get in the car and wait. If I'm not back in an hour," Emmett snorted, "improvise."

"Can do," Zack agreed. "Good luck. Don't waste Niedermeyer's marker, alright? We got a drone strike out of him last time."

"Oh, is he the one you got that from? Yeah, that's too

valuable. I'll think of something," Emmett muttered, as he got into his car. He did a three-point turn on the empty state highway, and headed back toward the devil's playground.

Zack and I were alone in the dark and snow. I jumped when he popped the trunk.

"Would you like to put your luggage in the trunk?" he suggested, a glint of wry amusement in his eye.

"Oh. Yeah. Thanks." I stowed the bag, and closed the trunk with slow deliberateness.

"Did they hurt you?" he asked.

I shook my head vehemently. "No. They just scared me a little." I gulped.

"You're shocky," Zack murmured, and pulled me into his arms.

"No! No, I—I mean—I have questions, and—" I started to shiver, and shudder.

"Sure you do," Zack said, and folded my head onto his chest. "Just let go and cry it out. You're alright, Dee Baker."

I fought it a little longer, and then broke down completely, sobbing in his arms. "I didn't cry this whole time!" I yelled, irate. I even stomped my foot. "I didn't cry about L.A., or Hawaii, or—"

"Shhh," Zack whispered. "You're doing it right now. Just cry it out."

He really was good at that, letting me cry. Not just a little, but all the way, until I couldn't cry anymore, until I was entirely wrung out of tears and beyond all the scared. I mopped my nose and eyes, and dabbed at the big wet area on his jacket. I always keep tissues in my coat in winter. Cold ears make my nose run.

"It's getting too cold out here," said Zack. He offered me the keys—he'd given me the car after all—but I shuddered in revulsion and slid in through the passenger door.

After a few minutes' silence in the car, he took out his

phone, dialed it, and handed it to me without comment.

"Zack?" Adam cried in my ear. "Did you get her out?"

"It's Dee, Adam. Yeah, Zack got me out. I'm fine. We're still trying for Tom Aoyama. My bunkie on the ark? I don't know yet on Tom. Are you OK?"

"Yeah. I could kill Niedermeyer, but yeah, I'm OK. Dee, I am so sorry," he attempted.

"Not your fault. Hey, I don't want to talk much right now. Just—I'm out, I'm safe. Thank you." I end the call and handed the phone back to Zack. "Thanks. And thank you for getting me out of there, Zack."

He nodded. He checked his watch. "I'll call Emmett in another 30 minutes if we haven't heard from him."

"We should suck less at accepting thank you's and compliments," I grumbled.

"You're welcome," he said grudgingly.

I couldn't exactly apologize for visiting the ark, because I didn't mean it. But I felt I owed Zack something. "I shouldn't have gone to visit the ark, Zack. I didn't know it was loaded."

"Fair enough," he allowed. "I didn't know it was loaded, either. Of course, I didn't know what it was loaded *with*."

"I have a confession to make."

Zack growled, "Look, if it's about sleeping with Adam on that ark, I really don't want to hear it, Dee."

Actually I hadn't slept with Adam since he left Totoket a month ago. And I wasn't the slightest bit tempted to discuss that right now. That conversation could only go downhill. "Not that. But—well, never mind."

Zack growled louder.

"Oh, alright. You didn't need to get me out, is all. To get Amenac back. I managed that from inside there. Emmett said. It worked. So all you got, was my life. Thank you, for saving me."

"You were all we were trying for, Dee. You, not Amenac. If

273

Emmett got more, great."

"Thank you." That kind of choked me up, and invited tears to flow again. I squelched them, and swallowed. "Emmett got Amenac, whole hog. He claimed that me, the site, and all its sources are now 'community assets' of southern New Haven county. He said he's your boss."

Zack sighed. "You're not a beta tester on Amenac. You're one of its principals, aren't you."

"Well, yeah."

"Obviously you have a partner in crime, or you couldn't have gotten it back up while you were locked away. Mangal?"

"I'd need to confer with my associates before discussing them. Speaking of associates..." I softened my tone. "About that 'Emmett is your boss' thing? What are you, Zack?"

"I'm a community organizer. That's all. Emmett is still Army, technically, but I'm retired. 'Boss' is kind of stretching it. He's leader of the local organizers. He's good. Damned good. I served with him in Estonia. He's from Missouri, so he's better as a leader and interface, rather than trying to lead a local community directly, in Connecticut."

"But, you planned to do this? To become Captain Zack of Western Totoket? How did that happen?"

Zack fidgeted with the heater. "About a year ago, the Army started calling me, trying to recruit me back. First they asked if I was willing to suppress public protests, and I told them, 'Hell, no!' Then the borders. Then an ark. No, no, and no. I've compared notes with the other community organizers. It happened about the same with them. After all that screening, somebody else called, to ask if I wanted to stay right where I was, and protect my home area, and organize people to accomplish that. I told him that's what I intended to do, if it came to that. So he offered to put me in touch with like-minded people, and resources to be determined along the way. To that I said, 'Sure.' Then Emmett called to ask me about Connecticut.

A few weeks later we held our first meeting in New Haven."

"And this somebody who recruited you was in the Army?"

"Probably. Maybe National Guard." Zack shrugged. "Dee, there's this idea that the armed forces are this monolithic, obedient single-minded creature. They're anything but. They're millions of active citizens, with different strong opinions, in a bunch of different services. The whole Federal government is just a mob of citizens. A whole lot of them are as disgusted as everyone else, especially with the Calm Act. Some of the most disgusted were selected for other initiatives. Like mine."

"Wouldn't that kind of secret cabal be treason? But Emmett treated with Homeland as though he had some kind of inter-agency dibs."

"He does. We're actually authorized under one of the secret parts of the Calm Act."

"Huh? Wait, you've read the secret parts of the Calm Act?"

"No. Emmett summarized the parts related to us. We are 'resource centers.' Not just the community organizers, but outfits like Adam's brain trust ark, and this Niedermeyer. One of the secret targets of the Calm Act is to reduce the U.S. population to 'sustainable levels and geographic distribution.' Aside from the utter moral bankruptcy, one of the problems with that is the complete breakdown of civilization. The resource centers are supposed to find ways to limit the damage, and build civilization up again, each within our assigned areas."

"Good God, Zack, you're saying this really was *intentional?*"

"Yeah. The deaths of millions of our own people—yeah. They planned that."

"How many... I saw a 'countdown' on the ark. It said 294 million."

Zack swallowed. He stared out the window into the black. "Nearly 50 million down. The target is 200 million. Or next March. Whichever comes first. If we organize well enough, and make it through next winter with more people alive, it's still over. All the other initiatives to cull the population have to stop."

"After we saw the news about L.A., the ark captain said he hadn't been released to act. Is that…?"

"Yeah, that ark is forbidden to act until next March or 200 million. At that point, Emmett has a couple markers we can call in on it. There's talk of trying to pool our markers between districts, maybe even across state lines, to take on big things like the relief of New York and Boston-Providence. But who knows what we'll need 13 months down the road. If we wait that long."

"Zack, are you involved in 'culling' the—"

"*Fuck* no!"

"Who would do that?"

Zack sighed. "Who would put borders around New York City to contain epidemics? Who would hand out oxycontin to patients when there's no other treatment available? Who would shoot to defend their home and food and family? Dee, no one is being asked to murder people, not exactly, not directly. Or rather, if anyone is, we *will* find them and execute them when this is over. If this is ever over. I don't even know what 'over' means, here."

I contemplated that for a minute. The climate was destabilized. That wouldn't be 'over' in my lifetime. Cutting CO_2 emissions, or the population, or managing water better, wouldn't persuade the planet to restore some temporary state that humans happened to enjoy. It was hard to imagine the U.S. being at peace in my lifetime. It hadn't been so far. Trust in the government was broken beyond any hope of repair. I couldn't see anything likely to put the U.S. Humpty Dumpty back together again.

"What is a 'marker?' " I eventually asked.

"It's essentially an I.O.U. Somebody owes you a favor, or you owe somebody else a favor. We've all got markers to call in some help, not a lot, from outside. Or that was the Plan, anyway. In practice, we all like the markers, and helping each other, a hell of a lot more than we like the Plan. So we keep inventing new markers to offer. Like that drone strike. Nobody had a marker for that. It was just an idea Adam dreamed up. But it worked, and now there's a black market in drone attack markers. The C.I.A. operates the drones, and they're not supposed to do it. Niedermeyer is Coast Guard, so theoretically he shouldn't be able to authorize it. But we're all sickened by the progress of the Plan, and bypass it when we can."

"Why would anyone support this 'Plan'?"

"Because 200 million is all the people they believe the climate can support with water and food in the U.S. The whole Calm Act is about trying to collapse in a controlled fashion instead of into brutal anarchy. It was the best the think tanks could come up with. Without the Calm Act, the projection was a collapse to more like 50 million people, because the collapse went more slowly, more violently, and destroyed the environment along the way."

"And here I just thought you weren't a very cheerful man."

Zack chuckled, gradually building up to a full laugh. "Yeah. No. Well, to be fair, I probably wasn't very cheerful even before I knew all this."

"No doubt because of your deplorable taste in women. Or wait—did Grace know about this?"

"She dumped me because I agreed to join, yes."

I was getting remarkably irate with this dead Quaker ex-girlfriend. "But you only agreed to do what you intended to do all along!"

"I didn't 'intend' to have military resources to draw on. At least, not officially. I expected I'd have to beg, or subvert, or train some up. I didn't discuss that with her, though."

"Then she realized that you expected to fight for us all along."

"Yeah."

Zack tensed as headlights came up behind us. The other car slowed and pulled up alongside. It was Emmett. He and Zack rolled down windows to talk. The sudden rush of night air felt as though it had dropped another 10 degrees out there.

"Did you get Tom?" I blurted, while they were still on the 'Hello' stage.

"He's in the back, a little worse for wear," Emmett reported. "Hey, what are you doing?"

I jumped out of our car, and stepped quickly to open the back door of Emmett's car. "Tom? Are you OK?" Opening the door turned on the car's dome light, so I could see.

No one laid a hand on me, the whole time I was in the Navy brig or the HomeSec conference room. I even felt I'd bonded a little with my jailors, Marine Corporal Tibbs and HomeSec's Mark. But Tom Aoyama and his mouth—literally— were bloody and black and blue. His teeth were jagged, with several missing or broken. He was clutching his right wrist in agony. Several fingers on that hand were bent at wrong angles, that made me wince in sympathetic pain just to look at them.

"You've had a rough day," I murmured to Tom, and patted his shin. His head lay at the other end of the back seat. "But you're safe now, Tom. Right, Emmett? He's safe now." I held Emmett's eye.

"He is. Safe." Emmett's grudging tone showed his lack of pleasure at my challenge.

"Thank you, Emmett," I said. "I owe you. Come by for a good meal any time. You can even bring some friends."

"Well, well, darlin'. I think I'll take you up on that," promised Emmett. "We might want to do a little intelligence inventory while I'm there."

I bridled, but then recalled that thing where he now owned me as an asset. That would take some getting used to. "Of course," I acquiesced, with what grace I could muster. "I'm all in for whatever I can do for Zack's crew. I've told Zack that all along."

"She's a major asset," Zack allowed, backing me up.

I liked the term 'asset' even less when Zack used it. I turned back to Tom. "I'll try to get a message through to Beth, that you're OK. Is there anything I can tell her, so she knows it's really you?"

Tom thought about it. "Tell her when this is all over, we'll have a nice cottage again. I'll plant another pansy-ass planter for her in the garden."

I chose to smile. "Pansy-ass planter," I repeated.

"Yeah, I had this gnome with its pants down—"

"I get the picture." I patted his shin. "I'll tell her. You relax and get better, OK, Tom? You're safe now."

Zack's phone rang as I closed Emmett's rear door. Zack handed it out to me. "For you. Mangal." Emmett started making a move to leave but Zack signaled him to wait.

"Dee! Glad you're safe!" Apparently someone, maybe Adam or Zack, had already gotten through to Mangal with that news. Though he did have the satellite feed. Maybe he was just watching our progress from above. Before I could reply, he continued, "Hey, listen. There's a caravan barreling toward Wallingford. There's a gentleman here—I'm at Dave's—who came a couple hours ago to 'fix the hoses.' He wants you to stay put and meet with the caravan. I don't know if that's a good idea—"

I gather the phone was ripped from his hand. An unfamiliar man's voice cut in with, "Stay put. The caravan will rendezvous with you, after we take out Homeland Security. Movers will be fired upon." He hung up.

"Movers will be fired upon," I echoed, for Zack and Emmett's benefit. "Um, guys, we need to stay put for a bit. Apparently a gran caravan is on its way to meet us."

"What the—" Emmett and Zack both attempted.

279

"I'm not sure, but it's OK. They're, um, friends. You remember that gran caravan I met at the Canadian border, right, Zack?"

"Dee, what does a gran caravan have to do with any of this?" Zack asked slowly.

"Well, that's complicated. Hold on a moment while I make a call."

I dialed Adam again, and let him know that there would be a large explosion at Homeland Security in Wallingford, and that it would be really good if everybody just sort of turned a blind eye to that. Zack stared at me in disbelief through this. Emmett made a few quick calls.

"Oh, and Adam? We got Tom out safe. If you could get word to Beth Agrawal, his wife? Tell her there was something about a nice cottage with pansies for her, but it got garbled." I was back in the passenger seat next to Zack by then. Tom didn't need to hear that. And Beth sure didn't need a 'pansy-assed planter' if those were the last words she would ever receive from her husband.

Chapter 22

Interesting fact: Canada never accepted the U.S.'s right to withdraw from NATO or its free trade agreements. They claimed to retain co-ownership of North American NATO assets, satellites, natural gas pipelines, the Internet, and a host of other things.

There was something immensely satisfying about the massive fireball that erupted over the dark woods from the Homeland Security office building. I hoped my e-cig-sharing pal Mark had already left for the day. I hoped Ms. Humorless and Mr. Bad Cop were working late. But I've felt more guilty placing ant traps in the garden. I was still pretty shocky, I suppose, but my conscience hasn't twinged since, either.

"Dee," Zack asked patiently, "how did who do that?"

"I don't know much about military stuff, Zack. The guy said the caravan would meet us here. Maybe they'll have someone who's willing to answer questions." Maybe not.

" 'The guy.' What guy, Dee?"

"He didn't really identify himself. Mangal put him on the phone with me."

Zack didn't bother to frame another question. He just stared at me expectantly.

"That thing I was going to confess earlier," I hazarded. "I called someone I met in the gran caravan, to help get Amenac back online. Um, I think he's Canadian. He says he's French. Jean-Claude Alarie. He's a doctor."

Zack gave an exaggerated nod. "Could you please cut the bullshit, Dee?"

"I think I asked Canadian intelligence to hook Amenac back

up with real weather. It worked. While I was on the phone, I let Jean-Claude know I was being held in Wallingford. He suggested coming to get me, but I said no." I contemplated that for a moment. "I didn't really understand his suggestion." I glanced back at the lurid glow and black smoke above the trees. "I was afraid you might be mad at me for, um, sharing my little problems with a foreign government. Are you? Mad at me?"

Zack's face was in his hand, thumb and forefinger pinching the bridge of his nose. "Yes. No."

'Both' seemed a reasonable answer, under the circumstances, and I left it at that. "I didn't realize they were in Connecticut," I said. "Maybe they were coming to visit anyway."

Zack put his head back on his headrest. "A gran caravan attacked an ark earlier today in Litchfield. Not the one Adam's family is in—I already covered that with Adam. The security goons for this particular ark were stealing all the locals' food, raping and murdering as they went."

"Oh."

Another car arrived soon. Emmett's car, then the newcomer's, pulled ahead of us to park, to clear the road. The two drivers got out of their cars to chat. Zack told me the newcomer was Emmett's peer for Middlesex, the county just east of New Haven. Counties aren't used much in Connecticut, so I had only the haziest notion of how these fit together. Apparently Wallingford lay at a cusp between three Emmett-level coordinators' turf. The northern New Haven County guy, whose turf we were actually in, never joined us that night. He was probably busy with that Litchfield situation on the other end of his area.

Another vehicle drew up behind us and flashed its high-beams at us jauntily. Jean-Claude popped out. "Dee?" he called gaily. "I look for Dee Baker."

"Jean-Claude! How good to see you!" I cried, exiting my

End Game

car. The car that delivered Jean-Claude to us took off.

We hugged and did the French cheek-kissing. I continued, "I'm so glad you're here! I have a friend, Tom, who got a bit beat up by Homeland Security." I drew Jean-Claude along to Emmett's car and pointed to Tom in the back seat. "And this is my friend Emmett MacLaren, who got us out of Homeland. And his friend I haven't met yet?"

"Lieutenant Colonel Carlos Mora," the beefy greying man supplied, along with a handshake. Emmett shook hands with Jean-Claude as well, who in turn introduced himself with his familiar French Doctors Without Borders identity.

"Your friend, he is banged up," Jean-Claude observed. "And you, Dee, you are hungry, yes? Let's go to my place so I can treat your Tom, and we will eat!"

"You just blew up Homeland Security and invaded our turf," Emmett observed cordially. "Care to tell me about that?"

"Me? No! I am just a doctor," Jean-Claude laughed. "Maybe you come to my place, too, and someone can answer your questions." Jean-Claude helped himself into the passenger door of Emmett's car. "I show you the way. You follow us, Dee!"

"Dee?" Emmett inquired.

"Let's hear what they have to say," I said. "Jean-Claude can get Tom patched up. And I am hungry."

"Right," replied Emmett with sarcasm. But he drove off under Jean-Claude's direction. Zack and I, and Colonel Mora from Middlesex, followed behind.

"Lieutenant Colonels outrank Majors, don't they?" I asked Zack idly, while he drove.

"They do," Zack confirmed. "Mora grew up here, though."

"Is Emmett in trouble with his boss?"

Zack bobbed his head yes-and-no. "I'm not worried about Emmett."

-o-

"Aren't you guys coming with us?" Emmett asked. We were in Jean-Claude's camper, parked in a strip mall on a main drag shopping road in Wallingford. An elderly man who walked with a cane arrived to take the military types to speak with 'the General'. Emmett and Carlos Mora rose with alacrity.

Zack started to rise next to me, but I kept my seat in Jean-Claude's compact kitchenette. I pointed. "Is that brandy?"

"Help yourself to brandy, Dee!" Jean-Claude called merrily from the back. He was cleaning up Tom while he let a dose of oxycontin take effect, before he could straighten Tom's fingers. "Dee can stay with me!"

Zack sank back beside me. "I'll stay," he told Emmett.

Emmett rolled his eyes and set off to meet 'the General.'

"Good! More for us!" called Jean-Claude from the bunks in back. "Dee, there's steak and leftover *gratin* in the fridge!"

My knees wobbled as I stood. Zack gently pressed me back down and supplied a snifter of brandy. There wasn't room in the micro-kitchen for both of us to cook, anyway. So I put my feet up and sniffed my snifter. The elegant root vegetable and potato *au gratin*, beautifully cheesy and golden brown on top, could not possibly have been baked in the camper. The camper's compact two-burner propane stove and a grill pan worked fine for the succulent steak, though. While the steak rested, Zack heated the gratin on the stove, too. Jean-Claude called out cooking suggestions here and there.

Eventually the well-tended Tom was out like a light, and supper was served for three.

"*À la vôtre,*" Jean-Claude toasted us with a chunky wine goblet. I think that's 'to your health' in French.

"To freedom," Zack returned, with a plastic cup of water.

"To good friends," I offered, with my crystal brandy snifter.

After we applied ourselves to the meal for a while in near-religious earnestness, I said, "Jean-Claude, this steak is incredible—and perfectly cooked, Zack! Where did you get it?"

"Ah, payment during a medical clinic. My patients often pay me with food. A few towns northwest of here. The locals had some trouble with security thugs from an ark. The thugs felt the surrounding town should serve them with food and sex. The locals disagreed." Jean-Claude gave a jaunty Gallic shrug. "The caravan helped them with that."

"That was pretty impressive 'help,' " Zack commented.

Jean-Claude waved that away with a smile. "I am just a doctor."

"What brings you to Wallingford?" I asked.

"Ah, the caravan is always eager to clean out nests of Homeland Security. And we like your Amenac website very much, Dee! That must continue. Indeed, we've contracted for a more private site with your colleagues. The satellite spy data is *very* helpful! But it needs a more selective audience. Yes?"

"Yes," Zack and I both agreed.

"So we have business here. The caravan would like to stay, but that is for those other people to discuss. I think they talk all night. Feel free to go home after dinner. The last few days have been very tiring for Dee, yes?"

"Yes," I agreed. "I felt sure you'd gone into upstate New York after we met in Alburg?"

"Yes, the Adirondacks are lovely," Jean-Claude agreed.

"So you've crossed at least three closed borders since last we met."

"Oh, more than that."

I pondered how to ask what exactly Canada's intent was. But that might be as meaningless a question as what the U.S. government's intent was. Zack's comment came to mind, about the U.S. military and the alphabet soup of Federal agencies as just a mob of citizens with differing opinions. I eventually came up with, "How is Canada doing these days, have you heard?"

"Oh, very well, I hear," Jean-Claude replied. "Canada is not overpopulated. The weather, the blight, they are problems.

They deal with it. I hear they consider adding a southern tier of provinces. Minnesota, Wisconsin."

"Really," said Zack. "And northern New England?"

"I think that these states have not asked," replied Jean-Claude. "Too many states at once is too much, anyway. Like the snake eating an elephant! But, Vermont, New Hampshire, Maine—these states are smaller in population than Michigan, or northern New York, for example. Those are very big, compared to Canada. The snake would rupture, to eat such an elephant."

"I imagine Canada is concerned about what's going on down here," I prodded.

"Mm, Canada thinks there are war crimes," Jean-Claude allowed. "And Canada had a safe border to the south always before. Now not so much. We must adjust to the weather, yes?"

"We try," breathed Zack.

"But the gran caravan is not Canada," Jean-Claude stressed. "The caravan, it has other goals. Sometimes these goals align. Friends work together, yes? To friendship!"

"To friendship!" we all agreed.

-o-

True to plan, only the most circuitous route was cleared of snowbanks for car traffic from the I-95 exit into Totoket. The route wove through strategic armed bottlenecks at bridges and railroad overpasses. After driving about four miles for every one a crow flies from the interstate, Zack parked my car back where it began, in the cache trading post parking lot on Route 1.

Zack gentlemanly shouldered my bags, and pointed to the raggedly trodden path into the neighborhood, behind the trading post building. He let me clamber my way through about 25 feet of this non-path first, pretty much trying to step into the deep holes left by other people's steps. The snow had melted slightly during the days and re-frozen at night, for a wickedly sharp ice crust. In the dark, I mostly found my next toe holds by patting around with my mittens. I was exhausted and I'd drunk one too many fingers of brandy at Jean-Claude's, though that was wearing off.

Then Zack commented, "It's 1 a.m. It's two blocks to my house, ten blocks to yours. You're welcome to sleep over my house." He waited a moment, then added, "Was that suave?"

"Irresistible," I assured him. "Thank you, I'd love to sleep at your house. You've been planning this all the way from Wallingford, haven't you?"

"Emmett tells me I need to be more suave, to catch a better class of woman."

"Emmett doesn't think I'm a better class of woman."

"Emmett likes you," he assured me. "He was trying to drive a wedge between us, so he could make a play."

I laughed. About 20 feet further along, the boot-hole path spewed me out into a clear, wide plowed walkway down a block of front lawns—across the grass, not the sidewalk or pavement. "Does this go all the way to my house?" I accused.

"No. I cleared this for my cow and goats to exercise. Watch out for manure." I turned to glare at him. He laughed. "I'll go first." He turned on his phone as a flashlight, which at least kept us out of the cow patties. Mostly. We had to clamber through a ragged snow path again to reach his perfectly-cleared front porch. Apparently Zack wanted to discourage the livestock from lazing around on the porch.

And once again I stood dripping in Zack's tidy entry-way. I pulled off my grubby coat and snowy boots, as he did. I contemplated my jeans, crusted to the thigh in ice and snow.

"Uh, normally I just…" Zack attempted.

I peeled off my snow-stiff jeans and soggy socks, and held out an arm matter-of-factly to collect his. Anyone with sense would strip all that here instead of traipsing snow into the house. "Where's your laundry?"

He pointed. "I'll bring you a robe." We both padded off bare-legged, him to his bedroom and me to the laundry. It wasn't that risqué. We both wore layered shirts, and the lights were dim. The house was cool, but my legs were splotched red and itchy from the cold outside.

As I got the washing machine running, Zack joined me in the laundry. He'd changed into ragg socks and a black-and-grey striped robe that looked vaguely Scandinavian. He held a basket of laundry, with a cotton robe and more ragg socks on top for me.

"I got this kimono on Okinawa for Delilah," he explained. "They assured me it was the right size for a big woman. 'Big' is relative, I guess."

I laughed as I shook out the folds. It was a perfect fit for me, and far too small for Zack's sister Delilah. "*Yukata wa kirei desu,*" I assured him in Japanese. "It's called a yukata, not a kimono. It's gorgeous." Orange hibiscus, white cranes, and stylized wisps of golden cloud, with metallic highlights, cavorted across a field of hot pink. I couldn't imagine Delilah wearing anything so exuberantly cheerful. On Okinawa, this was a summer party dress for a teenager, not a house robe for a grown woman.

Zack set to feeding the rest of his laundry into the machine. I turned away, pulled off my shirts and bra, slid into the yukata, and slipped my panties to the pile at my feet. Holding the yukata closed with one hand, I pulled apart the rest of my clothes, plucked them up, and added them into the washing machine.

Zack was staring at me. He appeared to have forgotten what he was doing.

"There should be a belt, that goes with the yukata," I suggested, to reboot his mental processes. I dug into his laundry basket, hanging at his hip, and pulled the rest of his laundry into the already-gurgling sudsy machine, and closed the lid.

End Game

"Ah," he said. He thoughtfully ran his hand up the underside of my arm, and drew a belt out of the yukata sleeve. His hand left gooseflesh along its path. "This one?"

"How clever. I missed that. Thank you."

"Do you, um, want some tea? Or something? You must be exhausted." He reached out a finger to tuck my hair behind an ear.

"I may be getting a second wind." The humor and sensuality of the situation were getting to me, actually. "What I could really use is a quick shower before bed, if you don't mind. It's been four days."

"Sure." He pointed in the direction of the bathroom. "So, how was the ark?" he finally asked.

"Amazing. They made it out of an aircraft carrier. They turned the flight deck into the most gorgeous hydroponic greenhouse. The brig was surprisingly cordial and spacious. The normal berths were sardine cans. On the whole, I'm glad I don't live there."

Zack laughed, then his gaze turned smoky. "Dee, I'm not sure how to ask this..."

"I didn't sleep with Adam. We broke it off. He belongs at sea. I belong here. Is that what you wanted to ask?"

"Yes. Partly." He drew me to him hard and kissed me deeply. "I wasn't asking about *Adam*," he clarified, nose to nose, after he broke off the kiss.

"Hmm," I said, and rubbed noses side to side. "You meant to ask about *Zack*."

"Zack and Dee," he clarified. He held me more firmly waist to waist. The other hand pulled my head hard to his collarbone. He whispered in my ear, "Are we having sex tonight? Or going to sleep?" As an after-comment, he licked the lobe of my ear. "Because I'd really love to make love to you tonight."

Good idea, said my ear, and the whole body attached to it, in a delicious shiver. But needs must. "I'm not having sex tonight, without a shower first," I clarified, pushing back from him. "You're careful. I like that. Wanna come scrub my back?"

"Sure…"

I was home safe in his arms. As safe as I could be anywhere anymore, for a little while.

Chapter 23

Interesting fact: Earth's climate has never been stable. Human civilization emerged during an interglacial period only about 12,000 years old. Since then, there have been significant climate shifts, little ice ages, warm periods, civilization-destroying droughts, and shifting coastlines.

Emmett called in his marker on dinner a couple weeks later. By then, late February, the deep snow had all melted away under heavy rains. Then we'd had a few 60-degree sunny spring-like days. I hoped it was just the February fake-spring thaw—a little bit of warm weather, when everyone went out to play in shorts and tank tops and caught colds, then winter resumed. But it was not to be. That winter was truly over already, traded in for a long unpredictable spring with several hard freezes, that played havoc with the fruit tree orchards. Anyway, the roads were clear again.

Emmett invited all his community coordinators to the dinner, to make a regular meeting of the event. This was a smaller group than I'd imagined. Given that Zack's turf was only part of Totoket, and there were 16 towns, including the city of New Haven, under Emmett's purview, I would have expected more like 40 coordinators. In fact, they'd started with 10, plus Emmett, and only added one more so far. Like Zack, most had selected small strategic areas to build out from. Most neighborhoods had only what their townships could organize to deal with the new circumstances.

A dozen people is still an awful lot of guests for dinner. My little house was packed. The dining table served as a buffet, with chairs pushed against the walls to seat everybody. Once I'd carted out all the food, I took a plate and sat by Vito, the new guy. After New Year's, Zack and Emmett recruited him, the leader of Adam's beachfront security in East Haven, and encouraged him to expand his turf. To their discomfort, Vito rapidly expanded his operation all the way north to I-95, including Route 1 across East Haven and the whole downtown area, with the enthusiastic support of the town.

"Seems like you and me are the odd ones out here," I said to Vito with a smile, as he scooted over on a storage bench to make room for me. Emmett and Zack looked over with interest.

Vito nodded uncomfortably, and glanced around the ex-military types surrounding us. He was a powerfully built man in his mid-40's, with craggy features, his hair and 6 o'clock stubble still black with just a few strands of steel grey. "It's been good, though," he said. "We wouldn't have bothered organizing East Haven without these guys' encouragement. So you're with Zack? I thought there was a Dee Baker with Adam Lacey, over in my area?"

I was impressed. Vito paid attention to people. "I dated Adam and Zack both, yeah. But Adam's gone to sea now. You're married?" He had a fat gold ring on the appropriate finger.

"Yeah, 26 years. Brenda was my high school sweetheart." He grinned broadly, still clearly infatuated with Brenda after all these years. "She got pregnant. So I dropped out and went to work for the Boss, because I needed the money. It's been good. You?"

I shrugged. "I'm a web developer. Probably turn into a farmer this year, though."

Emmett rose and rang his glass with a fork to get everyone's attention, and call the meeting to order. "Our thanks to Dee Baker, Zack's pretty lady, for this most excellent feed!"

Round of applause. "I've got some announcements and news to start the meeting.

"First off, the gran caravan is staying indefinitely. The good news is that they'll help defend us against the procurement details from the borders. They've already driven off one raid. They're heavily armed, and good at it. The bad news, of course, is that they need to be fed, too. Colonel Mora over in Middlesex has been negotiating with the border commanders, and with the Coast Guard down in Groton, over how much food we need to deliver to support the border forces and stop their raids. And we need a deal to pay for electricity somehow, and town services. Looks like 15%, more if we have a bad year. The city of New Haven needs food, too, so that'll be like 25% in the townships."

Ouch. From my work with the agricultural planning committee, I knew that was more than the margin we hoped for, and probably weren't going to get. The meeting broke into a number of discussions, talking about how they might extract that much food from people who didn't have enough. Vito applied himself to his dinner beside me.

"Does East Haven have an agricultural production plan?" I asked him. I didn't recall having seen a single farm in his half of East Haven.

"Nope," confirmed Vito. "I'm not so good at math, but I think 25% of nothing, is nothing. Lots of gardens, and we'll get food in trade, though. Business is good. If people have anything, they're willing to spend it on what the Boss offers. And we've got some legit industries. Cheese factory. We're trying to get more cows, to supply the cheese factory. Graze them on the baseball fields."

"You've got a cheese factory! Can they make cheddar? Can they do small batches? Zack has a cow and some goats."

"They make mozzarella, ricotta. Oh, and provolone. Yeah, if they can make provolone, maybe they could make cheddar, I

293

dunno. They wouldn't do small batches. He'd just add his milk to the big batch, and get a share of the cheese back. I think there's another mozzarella maker up in North Haven, maybe some others."

Dishes were starting to perch precariously on corners. I hurriedly swallowed a couple last bites and got up to clear. "When you get a line on cows, Vito, please let Zack know, or Caruso Farms. We'd love more cows over here, too."

He nodded, with a smile. "Great way to turn lawns we can't eat, into food," he agreed, and handed me his finished plate.

Zack added another half dozen dishes to the kitchen counter for me as I loaded the first round I'd collected into the dishwasher. He nuzzled my ear from behind and squeezed an arm around my waist. "Great job, Baker. Everybody envies me now."

"Thank you, thank you. They'd better have liked it, this cleared out my larder for the week."

Emmett butted in, eye on Zack's arm around me. "Made friends with Vito, did you, Dee?"

I nodded. "He's nice."

"He's a Mafia enforcer," Emmett said, eyes narrowed. "They're into drugs, gambling, and prostitution, darlin'. Wouldn't have thought that was your kind of thing."

"He's running half a town, now," I countered. "Zack, they've got a cheese factory, and they're getting more cows." Emmett was still looking at me, so I added, "It takes all kinds, Emmett. You guys, the gran caravan, the Navy, who knows what's out there. It's not up to us to say who's got the right solution. We make friends with people who share common interests, people going our way. I think it's great you added Vito."

"Huh," he said, and wandered back out into the discussions. Zack gave me a quick peck and waded back in, too.

I mostly stuck to the kitchen while they handled business,

and tackled the pans and dishes that wouldn't fit in the machine. Several other coordinators wandered in to talk to me briefly, or just to grab some more water. Most of tonight's guests assured me of how much happier Zack looked with me around. I smiled gratefully at them, and silently vowed not to repeat the Zack's-little-woman act anytime soon.

After another hour of this, Emmett and Zack showed them the door. "Is it safe to come out yet?" I called.

Emmett, not Zack, popped into the kitchen doorway. "Sure, darlin'. No need to play Mrs. Zack anymore. It's high time I got my inventory. Show me what you've got. All of it."

No, Emmett wasn't likely to forget about that part. I sighed, wiped my hands dry, and sat them in the living room for the big screen treatment. The raw weather data. The satellite feeds. FEMA. CDC. Border action reports. Censored news stories and video footage. Current population estimates—I'd easily found that on FEMA, once I knew there was an official target. Canadian agricultural forecasts, the latest on Russia's southern front—

"What was that?" Emmett had me back up.

"Russia nuked the Middle East?" I asked for confirmation, and backed up, to show him a few clips of the Al Jazeera coverage. "Yeah, Russia got tired of waiting for Europe to bottle up Global Jihad from the west. They nuked Damascus, Teheran, and Kabul. It's like something out of the Inquisition now in Europe. Muslims either have to convert to Christianity and swear off Allah, or hit the road toward Mecca. It's illegal to speak Arabic or own a Koran in the E.U. now." I flipped to a clip of dusky women in Paris, wearing head scarves, being stoned in the street. "Russia said the E.U. either got rid of the Muslims, or Russia would come in and do it for them."

"It's not our war anymore, Emmett," Zack reminded him softly. I remembered he'd served with Emmett in Estonia, holding back the Russians. They'd both had tours in the Muslim battlefields as well.

"Shit," said Emmett, and rubbed his face hard. "Yeah. Guess not."

I changed the subject. "At our sponsor's request, Amenac now has a few limited access subsites, like the real satellite feeds." I showed him that. "I've already given you and Zack access to that one. You should probably give it to all your captains, but no one below that level. Niedermeyer has it, too, of course. The Feds weren't feeding the Coast Guard and Navy true weather data, and they need that."

"Who is 'our sponsor'?" Emmett demanded.

He wasn't happy when I told him the Canadian government owned us now.

And so on. It was a long evening, but eventually Emmett achieved information glut.

At the door, he said, "We just scratched the surface of what you've got tonight, didn't we? I'll be back, Dee."

And he was, often.

-o-

"Dee, could we talk?" Shelley asked. She'd come up behind me while I plugged the final wave of cabbage transplants into the ground in April. "Brought you some iced tea."

"Sure, I could use a break." I gulped the unsweetened rose-hip decoction she held out, before I took in her clothes. She wore Army fatigues, like Zack's crew, a pistol on her hip. I pointed to a pink granite boulder on the shady side of the house. To build anything in Connecticut requires relocating some granite. This particular chunk had been dynamite-sculpted with a nice flat shelf, for use as a bench. I waved Shelley to take a seat. "What's up?"

"I—I want to join the barricades, and work for Zack," she managed to blurt out. "Trey taught me how to shoot and stuff."

Shelley and Trey had become a steady item. Trey Cowan,

the once-looter we'd found in Adam's bed, seemed to sleep at Alex's house nearly as often as I slept at Zack's. Zack and I didn't move in together, because I had my gardens and computer office, and Zack had his livestock. But we cooked dinner and slept together as often as his work allowed.

I nodded. Shelley needed an outlet for her rage. "So you don't want to work on Amenac anymore?"

She nodded, worried.

"That's fine, Shelley. I'm hardly working on Amenac anymore, either," I assured her. "If this is what you want to do."

"You won't hold it against me? If I quit UNC?"

"Why would I do that? Shelley, UNC is a farce these days. I spend most of my time farming." After the corporate C-level died in Tennessee, I expected the servers to go dark and the paychecks to stop coming any time now. It didn't matter. The money wasn't worth anything. Our data access was now courtesy of the Canadian government, not UNC. Mangal kept his hand in on Amenac and its spin-off sites, working with the few of our people who stayed with it. That didn't need all of us.

"OK." Shelley breathed out. "Trey and I will leave as soon as we find a place."

"Why, is Alex tired of you? He hasn't said anything to me."

We exchanged puzzled looks.

"Shelley, you live at Alex's house because Alex invited you. Not because you work for me. If he's OK with Trey moving in full-time, that's great. I'd appreciate it if you chip in some food, though. Otherwise I'm paying taxes to feed you twice." I grinned to take the sting out of that.

"We will! I'll ask Alex," she said happily. "And Dee? Thank you, for everything. It's not that I'm not grateful, for the internship."

"I know. You're welcome, Shelley. The best part of being a supervisor is watching people grow. You've grown a lot. And it's a different world. I hope you're happy with Trey, here or wherever you land up."

She smiled warmly. "I am. You look happy with Zack, too. *He* looks happy."

I nodded judiciously, then broke into a grin. "We fit. We belong here, and believe in what we're doing."

Yeah, that new normal was pretty nice while it lasted. There were more raids to fight off, more people died, we worked hard with little security, and the psycho weather just wouldn't quit.

But we were happy then.

-o-

"Hey, Emmett!" I called, on my way into the kitchen to grab a drink. He was sitting in my living room when I came home, dressed in olive drab shorts and a gaudy Hawaiian shirt he must have borrowed from Zack. "Want something to drink?"

I'd played hooky that morning. It was a glorious sunny June day, the dry air so clear that the shadows were crisp and dark, making the early summer deep greens and riotous bright flowers glow. We'd been living under a brown cloud of Dust Bowl dirt, that unpredictably erupted in dry lightning, for days. The ozone and static in the air left me edgy and nervous all the time. When it cleared at last into such a beautiful day, I couldn't resist. I headed down to the beach and paddled a kayak out around the islands for a few hours.

"I helped myself, thanks, Dee," Emmett replied. His voice sounded raspy, his eyes red and puffy, and he had a roll of toilet paper on the end table at his elbow next to his water glass. I didn't have tissues anymore.

"You have a cold?" I inquired, plonking down across from him with my iced tea.

"No," he replied. He fidgeted with his glass. "Dee, I've, um…" A tear fell down his cheek.

I leapt over beside him on the couch. I took his hand to

comfort him. "Emmett? What's wrong? How can I help?"

He shook his head, and moved his other hand to hold my shoulder. "It's Zack, Dee. He went out with me last night—"

"No," I said.

"We were spotting for an artillery strike, on that pack of vipers in Broomfield—"

"No."

"The mission was a success. Our artillery took out the survivalist camp. We were on our way out. It was a lucky shot, from one of the stragglers. Unlucky for Zack. He was the only one of us hit. We carried him out, but—"

"No." I said "No" a lot of times, nearly every time Emmett took a breath. He folded me into his arms. I kept saying "No" into his chest, huddled there shaking.

"I sat with him while he died," Emmett told me. His voice broke on it. "Tanked him up on oxycontin, and talked. Took an hour or two. He told me a lot of things. I'll tell you, later, if you want. But he loved you. That's the main thing. Girl, he really, *really* loved you." Emmett was crying, too. He brushed his fingers through my hair as I sobbed on his chest. "I promised him I'd watch out for you and Alex. And I will do that."

Emmett stopped talking and just held me and let me cry. He didn't pat me quite the same way Zack would, but it was similar. His slighter, wiry build and twangy accent weren't the same at all.

For the first time, I couldn't cry my way out to the other side.

-o-

People lash out in different ways, when they're broken. I painstakingly dressed the morning of Zack's funeral in my best little black dress, black fishnet stockings, and spike heels. I had a tacky pin my sister gave me as a comment on losing my virginity long ago, a big red enameled 'A' on fake gold. I fixed that above my heart. Even for corporate-Tuesday-in-Stamford, I rarely bothered with makeup beyond lipstick and eyeliner, but I did up my face to go with the nightclubbing dress. I drew a tear on one cheek with black eye pencil.

Poor Alex took one look at this clown getup and ran off to fetch Mangal. Mangal took it all in, and kissed my forehead gently. "I think pearls would go better," he suggested mildly, and tapped the scarlet A with a finger. I refused. He shrugged acquiescence. He and Shanti flanked me loyally all the way to the church.

Adam came to the funeral, along with seemingly everyone in west Totoket, plus Zack's fellow community coordinators. Adam wore bright Coast Guard uniform, having accepted a permanent place as a Niedermeyer satellite.

I didn't know what Niedermeyer's official role was, but it was irrelevant. Niedermeyer was a power, like Jean-Claude Alarie and Emmett. Their titles revealed little.

Adam tapped my pin. "Is this for me?" he said with a sad smile. He detached my scarlet A and stuffed it into his pocket. "I'll treasure it. Always." He gave me a long, warm hug. I was grateful he came. But he wasn't Zack, and I wanted Zack, and I could never have him again. I went on to accept hugs and condolences from Vito and his wife Brenda next, then others.

Zack's sister Delilah assured me that she considered everything Zack had, to be mine, except some family keepsakes she wanted. She left me a few photos of Zack as a child, though.

It was all mechanical. I was miserable, just going through the motions. My inappropriate outfit kept most of the civic association acquaintances at bay. Only people who really knew me came up to share a hug.

Emmett gave Zack's eulogy. He told a story about when he and Zack served in Estonia, and survived an ambush, and the guilt of being a survivor, the loneliness of going on. That we were all survivors now, all struggling with survivor guilt. That the greatest anodyne to that kind of pain was to celebrate the life of the fallen, and to recommit to doing something meaningful in the world. That Zack had died a happy man, in love with a good woman, seeking to protect those he loved. His last mission was a success, and removed bad guys who preyed on good people. And that was a good death.

-o-

Then, of course, the hard part came. I had to take up my life again.

But I'd gone zombie, like so many before me. I had plenty of helping hands to keep my gardens alive, to help make me get it done. The neighbors all pitched in. They insisted they couldn't do anything without me telling them what to do. Maybe it was even partly true.

Once they got me moving in the garden, I didn't stop. The plants were beautiful, and I loved them. I didn't have to think, I could just be with them. The land, the sky, the sea, the natural beauty of Connecticut, even weird weather, have always given me that gift.

Emmett moved into Zack's house to supervise Jamal and Delilah taking over Zack's work. Emmett grew up on a farm in the Ozarks, and easily took over Zack's livestock. He came by nearly every evening for me to cook dinner for him. He wasn't much of a cook himself. But he was a good conversationalist while I cooked, and he did all the clean-up.

I told him to go away fairly regularly. He affably assured me that he'd promised Zack he'd look out for me, and he wasn't going anywhere.

-o-

Alex found a girl in the woods in August, maybe 6 weeks later. Zack had been teaching Alex mushrooming, though the

301

hunting wasn't nearly as good by the marsh as it was up on Sleeping Giant. Alex brought the waif home to me.

She never spoke. She was maybe 8 years old, with a stomach that looked bloated next to her stick-thin limbs. She went barefoot and her clothes were torn to grubby ribbons. She carried nothing.

I fed her carefully, very slowly at first. I cut away her filthy matted hair, got her clean and clothed, and took her to the doctor. He gave me some antibiotics and de-worming meds for her. Her expression was changeless, huge eyes not expressing interest or pleasure or dislike. She did what I asked her to do, and then stopped, staring off into space.

She slept in my food storage spare bedroom, and was starving when she came to me. But she didn't eat anything unless I explicitly gave it to her to eat.

Emmett found a giant picture-book of children's fairy tales for her. Not the Disney-cute versions, but the original horrible stories, that expressed children's fears in a darker age. He'd read it to her at bed-time. The girl showed no more interest in the stories than in anything else, but would sometimes trace a beautiful illustration with her finger.

Emmett called her 'Angel,' and perhaps she was.

She stayed with me a couple weeks. Then one day she was gone when I woke in the morning. No one knew where she'd gone in the night.

After searching for her all day without a trace, I cried on Emmett when he showed up for dinner. Then I got up to cook supper. But instead I started smashing plates and glasses on the floor, caught up in a sudden rage.

Emmett grabbed me. He pinned my arms and carried me and my bare feet out of the kitchen, and sat me on his lap on the couch. He let me give him a few weak punches to the chest, then shut me up with a deep hard kiss.

We made love, hard and urgent, there on the couch. Then,

both naked, he tucked me into my bed sheets. When he made to leave, I tugged his arm and pulled him into bed beside me. He settled in, and I snuggled onto his shoulder.

"Angel was a good name," I told him. "You were good with her." I accepted, then, that she too was gone for good, beyond my reach.

Emmett sighed, and replied, "My momma used to say that God sends us nothing but angels."

"Maybe your momma's an angel. The survivalist who killed Zack was not an angel. I'm not an angel." I almost added, *You're not*, but hesitated. I wasn't sure I believed that. I was waking up from zombie-dom, and it kinda hurt.

"You find angels better than most," Emmett contradicted me, "like Vito, or your pal at HomeSec." He'd wheedled the details of my stay at HomeSec out of me one night. One night out of many. By late August, Emmett had been an evening fixture in my life for nearly half a year. Almost as long I'd known Zack. "You're angel enough, darlin'."

"Like your momma?" I said sourly.

Emmett snorted. "My momma's a county sheriff," he said. "She's tough as nails, and knows a lot more survivalists than we do. Makes a point of making friends with them. You remind me of her that way. I came to Connecticut because she didn't need me back home. My old pal Zack had a tougher spot here. Momma and I talked it over. Her advice was to come here, give myself some scope, make a bigger difference."

"What did your Dad say?"

"My step-dad and I shared a farewell joint. He told me, 'Good luck.' "

I laughed softly.

"Good to hear you laugh again, Dee," he whispered. He kissed my forehead. "Don't stop."

"Did Zack really make you promise to keep me safe? I feel... I don't know what I feel. Disloyal, I guess."

"Not exactly. I told Zack I'd watch out for you, and asked if he'd mind if I courted you for myself. He said he wished you had that kinda sense. So sorta, on the whole, I'd take that as his blessing."

At that, I really laughed. "You know, the night we met, when you sprang me from Homeland? I told Zack you hated me. He said you just wanted me yourself."

"Oh, I was just ribbing him at first. You're definitely more my type than his. I love a tough, cheerful, ballsy woman. He used to go for the most tedious, most tiresome, politically correct shrews. I'd been on him about that for years. Delilah is a delight compared to Zack's women before you. But then, after I saw what they'd done to your pal Tom, and here you came out of HomeSec fresh as a daisy. Had the whole situation under control, arranged your own alternate rescue, and came out handing me demands." He laughed out loud. "I fell in love with you right then."

It's amazing how the word 'love' can throw a pall over a conversation. It's supposed to mean something nice.

Eventually Emmett added, "I think you missed part of that. I didn't promise Zack to 'keep you safe.' I said I'd watch your back."

"That's not the same thing?"

"No. You watch another fighter's back. You cover her blind side, pitch in when she's overextended. You don't keep her from the fight. You've been grieving a while. But I need you back in the game."

"I just wanted to be safe."

Did I really? I had a chance at safety in an ark. I turned it down to grow my own food, risk looters and armed procurement forces, to try and build a Totoket for a new world, to build Amenac to help farmers everywhere.

"You sure don't act like it," Emmett replied, confirming my second thoughts. "Death's safe, darlin'. We'll all get there, by and by. Life is risky."

"Yet you're here to keep people safe."

"No, Dee, I'm not. I'm here to build a new world order. I'd like a kind world, but mostly it just has to work. The old one didn't. People like you and me, we have the skills and resilience to keep going. Others don't. God bless 'em, but I can't save 'em. Everybody's got to save themselves."

I nodded slowly, and traced my hand across his chest. Emmett was a harsher man than Adam or Zack, and a stronger one. As we turned to lovemaking again, slow and gentle this time, I finally let go of feeling guilty over Zack. In truth, I never had anything to feel guilty about. I just loved him, and missed him. But he was gone, and I chose to live. No one could live in this time, this world, without losing people. And sex with Emmett was good, very good.

Eventually Emmett said quietly, "Dee, tonight, having sex, was about choosing life. I've wanted to do this a long time. But for it to happen again, you'd need to choose Emmett. I'm not like Zack. I won't share you with other men."

"I choose Emmett," I agreed.

-o-

"I got some interesting news today, darlin'," Emmett told me, as I cleaned out a winter squash for supper in October.

It was dark and weird outside that night. Dry lightning played scattered peek-a-boo through a towering overcast of cloud and dust, to a running grumble of distant thunder. The electric air left me energized and keyed up. I wanted a better physical outlet than a battle with squash guts. Once I got it into the oven, perhaps.

I cocked an eyebrow in inquiry, and Emmett continued. "The death rate seems to be flattening out, coasting in to about 230 million for the U.S."

"If they haven't stockpiled enough food, more will die over

the winter," I replied. "I thought that was the logic of waiting until March."

"That was the logic," Emmett agreed. "Screw logic."

"Oh?"

"Remember your loud-mouth pal, Tom Aoyama? He recruited a team, and set out to try his post-Ebola thing, walking a quarantine line west across Long Island. Looks like he's proved out his concept. But there's always been a catch to that. People hear about it inside New York, and flock to Long Island trying to get through. Too many millions to stay in Long Island. It was way depopulated, and the survivors didn't grow enough food to survive the onslaught. But at least, everyone's healthy east of the quarantine line."

"Need more exits," I said.

"What?"

"You can't have the survivors all running to Long Island. You need more exits." It seemed obvious to me. "So, what about screwing March?"

Emmett knew what I meant. "Niedermeyer wants to declare the depopulation phase over. He thinks we can rally people behind the relief of New York. Get people working together to build a new Northeast. He's made a call for proposals, what to do next. We're invited to present them at a meeting, a couple weeks from now at the Coast Guard Academy in New London."

I abandoned my squash and sat down beside Emmett at the table. Possibilities shot through my head like firecrackers, like the lightning outside. Disbanding the borders. Or establishing trade portals through the borders. Relieving Boston-Providence. Or inviting people from Boston-Providence to staff quarantine zones for exits from New York. Opening debate boards on Amenac. Or a new planning forum separate from Amenac. Getting the survivors in New York involved in planning the exits. What help Canada and the gran caravans would be willing to bring.

"We?" I asked. "So, southern New Haven County gets to offer a proposal?"

"Nope." Emmett grinned. "Emmett MacLaren, and Dee Baker, by name, are invited to present. Each of us. The scope of our proposals is up to us."

Emmett watched in enjoyment, as my grin spread from ear to ear. "Yeah, I thought you'd like that, darlin'." He poured cider into my glass on the table, and lifted his glass in a toast. "To new dreams."

"And good friends," I replied, clinking my glass to his.

Dedication

This book is dedicated to the natural beauty of Short Beach Bay, the Farm River marshes, the East Haven beaches, the orchards and raspberry brambles and wildlife of shoreline Connecticut, and the people who love them.

Acknowledgments

My father, Galt Booth, fell in love with a beautiful bay on the Connecticut shoreline when he was fresh out of Caltech. He grew up in Depression-era Los Angeles, surrounded by Dust Bowl refugee Okies. But he followed his dreams, and I grew up on that bay, and now live a few miles from it.

When we were little, Dad would make up stories for us on demand, with us in any starring role we picked. I wanted to make up stories like Dad, like magic out of thin air. And I've wanted to write this book for years. When Dad died this year, I decided, "Why the hell not."

The seed for *End Game* came when I heard a speaker (Dain Heer) suggest that if something didn't change, the world could end within 30 years. I've read and watched plenty of apocalyptic fiction. The plot usually centers on a larger-than-life hero. But – what if the end can't be stopped? What if you just have to face it? What do you do with that?

I'm deeply grateful to my test readers. Reading a book-length manuscript is a lot to ask of anyone. Julia Novak and Nathaniel Fuller, as first readers, helped keep me enthused about the project, and let me know where the book got dull. Brett and Georgie and the rest of our mastermind group on Facebook helped me believe in myself and stay on task. My friend Beth Grem kindly checked that my engineering and Navy details didn't go too far wrong. Of course, any mistakes are my own.

And thank you, for reading my book. Especially if you're so kind as to post a review on Amazon, or to tell someone else about it, or drop me a line. Books take a long time to write. Feedback is the fuel that powers the next story.

About The Author

Ginger Booth is a writer and programmer. She's worked in the seismic industry, semiconductor electronics, academic research in biology and environmental science, and online teaching simulators. She lives in shoreline Connecticut, with crops spilling out the balconies and down the driveway.

Her previous nonfiction includes:

Indoor Salad: How to Grow Vegetables Indoors

E-Cigarettes 101: How to Start Vaping

E-Cigarettes 102: DIY E-Liquid

You can contact her online at books.gingerbooth.com, and sign up for a mailing list to be notified of future books.

Made in the USA
San Bernardino, CA
28 January 2016